I0663246

The Bronze Eagle

A Story of the Hundred Days

The Bronze Eagle: A Story of the Hundred Days
Copyright © 2018 Reldaine Press
All rights reserved

This book is a reproduction of an important historical work. Forgotten Books uses state-of-the-art technology to digitally reconstruct the work, preserving the original format whilst repairing imperfections present in the aged copy. In rare cases, an imperfection in the original, such as a blemish or missing page, may be replicated in our edition. We do, however, repair the vast majority of imperfections successfully; any imperfections that remain are intentionally left to preserve the state of such historical works.

Baroness Emmuska Orczy

The Bronze Eagle: A Story of the Hundred Days

Copyright © 2020 Bibliotech Press
All rights reserved

The present edition is a reproduction of previous publication of this classic work. Minor typographical errors may have been corrected without note, however, for an authentic reading experience the spelling, punctuation, and capitalization have been retained from the original text.

ISBN: 978-1-64799-121-0

CONTENTS

THE LANDING AT JOUAN

The perfect calm of an early spring dawn lies over headland and sea—hardly a ripple stirs the blue cheek of the bay. The softness of departing night lies upon the bosom of the Mediterranean like the dew upon the heart of a flower.

A silent dawn.

Veils of transparent greys and purples and mauves still conceal the distant horizon. Breathless calm rests upon the water and that awed hush which at times descends upon Nature herself when the finger of Destiny marks an eventful hour.

But now the grey and the purple veils beyond the headland are lifted one by one; the midst of dawn rises upwards like the smoke of incense from some giant censers swung by unseen, mighty hands.

The sky above is of a translucent green, studded with stars that blink and now are slowly extinguished one by one: the green has turned to silver, and the silver to lemon-gold: the veils beyond the upland are flying in the wake of departing Night.

The lemon-gold turns to glowing amber, anon to orange and crimson, and far inland the mountain peaks, peeping shyly through the mist, blush a vivid rose to find themselves so fair.

And to the south, there where fiery sea blends and merges with fiery sky, a tiny black speck has just come into view. Larger and larger it grows as it draws nearer to the land, now it seems like a bird with wings outspread—an eagle flying swiftly to the shores of France.

In the bay the fisher folk, who are making ready for their day's work, pause a moment as they haul up their nets: with rough brown hands held above their eyes they look out upon that black speck—curious, interested, for the ship is not one they have seen in these waters before.

"'Tis the Emperor come back from Elba!" says someone.

The men laugh and shrug their shoulders: that tale has been told so often in these parts during the past year: the good folk have ceased to believe in it. It has almost become a legend now, that story that the Emperor was coming back—their Emperor—the man with the battered hat and the grey redingote: the people's Emperor, he who led them from victory to victory, whose eagles soared above every capital and every tower in Europe, he who made France glorious and respected: her citizens, men, her soldiers, heroes.

And with stately majesty the dawn yields to day, the last tones of orange have faded from the sky: it is once more of a translucent green merging into sapphire overhead. And the great orb in the east rises from out the trammels of the mist, and from awakening Earth and Sea comes the great love-call, the triumphant call of Day. And far away

1

upon the horizon to the south, the black speck becomes more distinct and more clear; it takes shape, substance, life.

It divides and multiplies, for now there are three or four specks silhouetted against the sky—not three or four, but five—no! six—no! seven! Seven black specks which detach themselves one by one, one from another and from the vagueness beyond—experienced eyes scan the horizon with enthusiasm and excitement which threaten to blur the clearness of their vision. Anyone with an eye for sea-going craft can distinguish that topsail-schooner there, well ahead of the rest of the tiny fleet, skimming the water with swift grace, and immediately behind her the three-masted polacca—hm! have we not seen her in these waters before?—and the two graceful feluccas whose lateen sails look so like the outspread wings of a bird!

But it is on the schooner that all eyes are riveted now: she skips along so fast that within an hour her pennant is easily distinguishable— red and white! the flag of Elba, of that diminutive toy-kingdom which for the past twelve months has been ruled over by the mightiest conqueror this modern world has ever known.

The flag of Elba! then it is the Emperor coming back!

A crowd had gathered on the headland now—a crowd made up of bare-footed fisher-folk, men, women, children, and of the labourers from the neighbouring fields and vineyards: they have all come to greet the Emperor—the man with the battered hat and the grey redingote, the curious, flashing eyes and mouth that always spoke genial words to the people of France!

Traitors turned against him—Ney! de Marmont! Bernadotte! those on whom he had showered the full measure of his friendship, whom he had loaded with honours, with glory and with wealth. Foreign armies joined in coalition against France and forced the people's Emperor to leave his country which he loved so well, had sent him to humiliation and to exile. But he had come back, as all his people had always said that he would! He had come back, there was the topsail-schooner that was bringing him home so swiftly now.

Another hour and the schooner's name can be deciphered quite easily—L'Inconstant, and that of the polacca Le Saint-Esprit ... and beyond these L'Etoile and Saint Joseph, Caroline. And the entire little fleet flies the flag of Elba.

The Emperor has come back! Bare-footed fisherfolk whisper it among themselves, the labourers in the valley call the news to those upon the hills.

Why! after another hour or so, there are those among the small knot who stand congregated on the highest point of the headland, who swear that they can see the Emperor—standing on the deck of the L'Inconstant.

He wears a black bicorne hat, and his grey redingote: he is pacing up and down the deck of the schooner, his hands held behind his back in the manner so familiar to the people of France. And on his hat is pinned the tricolour of France. Everyone on shore who is on the look-out for the schooner now can see the tricolour quite plainly. A mighty shout escapes the lusty throats of the men on the beach, the women are on the verge of tears from sheer excitement, and that shout is repeated again and again and sends its ringing echo from cliff to cliff, and from fort to fort as the red and white pennant of the kingdom of Elba is hauled down from the ship's stern and the tricolour flag—the flag of Liberty and of regenerate France—is hoisted in its stead.

The soft breeze from the south unfurls its folds and these respond to his caress. The red, white and blue make a trenchant note of colour now against the tender hues of the sea: flaunting its triumphant message in the face of awakening nature.

The eagle has left the bounds of its narrow cage of Elba: it has taken wing over the blue Mediterranean! within an hour, perhaps, or two, it will rest on the square church tower of Antibes—but not for long. Soon it will take to its adventurous flight again, and soar over valley and mountain peak, from church belfry to church belfry until it finds its resting-place upon the towers of Notre Dame.

One hour after noon the curtain has risen upon the first act of the most adventurous tragedy the world has ever known.

Napoleon Bonaparte has landed in the bay of Jouan with eleven hundred men and four guns to reconquer France and the sovereignty of the world. Six hundred of his old guard, six score of his Polish light cavalry, three or four hundred Corsican chasseurs: thus did that sublime adventurer embark upon an expedition the most mad, the most daring, the most heroic, the most egotistical, the most tragic and the most glorious which recording Destiny has ever written in the book of this world.

The boats were lowered at one hour after noon, and the landing was slowly and methodically begun: too slowly for the patience of the old guard—the old "growlers" with grizzled moustache and furrowed cheeks, down which tears of joy and enthusiasm were trickling at sight of the shores of France. They were not going to wait for the return of those boats which had conveyed the Polish troopers on shore: they took to the water and waded across the bay, tossing the salt spray all around them as they trod the shingle, like so many shaggy dogs enjoying a bath; and when six hundred fur bonnets darkened the sands of the bay at the foot of the Tower of la Gabelle, such a shout of "Vive l'Empereur" went forth from six hundred lusty throats that the midday spring air vibrated with kindred enthusiasm for miles and miles around.

CHAPTER I

THE GLORIOUS NEWS

I

Where the broad highway between Grenoble and Gap parts company from the turbulent Drac, and after crossing the ravine of Vaulx skirts the plateau of La Motte with its magnificent panorama of forests and mountain peaks, a narrow bridle path strikes off at a sharp angle on the left and in wayward curves continues its length through the woods upwards to the hamlet of Vaulx and the shrine of Notre Dame.

Far away to the west the valley of the Drac lies encircled by the pine-covered slopes of the Lans range, whilst towering some seven thousand and more feet up the snow-clad crest of Grande Moucherolle glistens like a sea of myriads of rose-coloured diamonds under the kiss of the morning sun.

There was more than a hint of snow in the sharp, stinging air this afternoon, even down in the valley, and now the keen wind from the northeast whipped up the faces of the two riders as they turned their horses at a sharp trot up the bridle path.

Though it was not long since the sun had first peeped out above the forests of Pelvoux, the riders looked as if they had already a long journey to their credit; their horses were covered with sweat and sprinkled with lather, and they themselves were plentifully bespattered with mud, for the road in the valley was soft after the thaw. But despite probable fatigue, both sat their horse with that ease and unconscious grace which marks the man accustomed to hard and constant riding, though—to the experienced eye—there would appear a vast difference in the style and manner in which each horseman handled his mount.

One of them had the rigid precision of bearing which denotes military training: he was young and slight of build, with unruly dark hair fluttering round the temples from beneath his white sugar-loaf hat, and escaping the trammels of the neatly-tied black silk bow at the nape of the neck; he held himself very erect and rode his horse on the curb, the reins gathered tightly in one gloved hand, and that hand held closely and almost immovably against his chest.

The other sat more carelessly—though in no way more loosely—in his saddle: he gave his horse more freedom, with a chain-snaffle and reins hanging lightly between his fingers. He was obviously taller and probably older than his companion, broader of shoulder and fairer of skin; you might imagine him riding this same powerful mount across a

4

sweep of open country, but his friend you would naturally picture to yourself in uniform on the parade ground.

The riders soon left the valley of the Drac behind them; on ahead the path became very rocky, winding its way beside a riotous little mountain stream, whilst higher up still, peeping through the intervening trees, the white-washed cottages of the tiny hamlet glimmered with dazzling clearness in the frosty atmosphere. At a sharp bend of the road, which effectually revealed the foremost of these cottages, distant less than two kilometres now, the younger of the two men drew rein suddenly, and lifting his hat with outstretched arm high above his head, he gave a long sigh which ended in a kind of exultant call of joy.

"There is Notre Dame de Vaulx," he cried at the top of his voice, and hat still in hand he pointed to the distant hamlet. "There's the spot where—before the sun darts its midday rays upon us—I shall hear great and glorious and authentic news of him from a man who has seen him as lately as forty-eight hours ago, who has touched his hand, heard the sound of his voice, seen the look of confidence and of hope in his eyes. Oh!" he went on speaking with extraordinary volubility, "it is all too good to be true! Since yesterday I have felt like a man in a dream!—I haven't lived, I have scarcely breathed, I ..."

The other man broke in upon his ravings with a good-humoured growl.

"You have certainly behaved like an escaped lunatic since early this morning, my good de Marmont," he said drily. "Don't you think that—as we shall have to mix again with our fellow-men presently—you might try to behave with some semblance of reasonableness."

But de Marmont only laughed. He was so excited that his lips trembled all the time, his hand shook and his eyes glowed just as if some inward fire was burning deep down in his soul.

"No! I can't," he retorted. "I want to shout and to sing and to cry 'Vive l'Empereur' till those frowning mountains over there echo with my shouts—and I'll have none of your English stiffness and reserve and curbing of enthusiasm to-day. I am a lunatic if you will—an escaped lunatic—if to be mad with joy be a proof of insanity. Clyffurde, my dear friend," he added more soberly, "I am honestly sorry for you to-day."

"Thank you," commented his companion drily. "May I ask how I have deserved this genuine sympathy?"

"Well! because you are an Englishman, and not a Frenchman," said the younger man earnestly; "because you—as an Englishman—must desire Napoleon's downfall, his humiliation, perhaps his death, instead of exulting in his glory, trusting in his star, believing in him, following him. If I were not a Frenchman on a day like this, if my nationality or my patriotism demanded that I should fight against Napoleon, that I should hate him, or vilify him, I firmly believe that I

5

would turn my sword against myself, so shamed should I feel in my own eyes."

It was the Englishman's turn to laugh, and he did it very heartily. His laugh was quite different to his friend's: it had more enjoyment in it, more good temper, more appreciation of everything that tends to gaiety in life and more direct defiance of what is gloomy.

He too had reined in his horse, presumably in order to listen to his friend's enthusiastic tirades, and as he did so there crept into his merry, pleasant eyes a quaint look of half contemptuous tolerance tempered by kindly humour.

"Well, you see, my good de Marmont," he said, still laughing, "you happen to be a Frenchman, a visionary and weaver of dreams. Believe me," he added more seriously, "if you had the misfortune to be a prosy, shop-keeping Englishman, you would certainly not commit suicide just because you could not enthuse over your favourite hero, but you would realise soberly and calmly that while Napoleon Bonaparte is allowed to rule over France—or over any country for the matter of that—there will never be peace in the world or prosperity in any land."

The younger man made no reply. A shadow seemed to gather over his face—a look almost of foreboding, as if Fate that already lay in wait for the great adventurer, had touched the young enthusiast with a warning finger.

Whereupon Clyffurde resumed gaily once more:

"Shall we," he said, "go slowly on now as far as the village? It is not yet ten o'clock. Emery cannot possibly be here before noon."

He put his horse to a walk, de Marmont keeping close behind him, and in silence the two men rode up the incline toward Notre Dame de Vaulx. On ahead the pines and beech and birch became more sparse, disclosing the great patches of moss-covered rock upon the slopes of Pelvoux. On Taillefer the eternal snows appeared wonderfully near in the brilliance of this early spring atmosphere, and here and there on the roadside bunches of wild crocus and of snowdrops were already visible rearing their delicate corollas up against a background of moss.

The tiny village still far away lay in the peaceful hush of a Sunday morning, only from the little chapel which holds the shrine of Notre Dame came the sweet, insistent sound of the bell calling the dwellers of these mountain fastnesses to prayer.

The northeasterly wind was still keen, but the sun was gaining power as it rose well above Pelvoux, and the sky over the dark forests and snow-crowned heights was of a glorious and vivid blue.

6

The words "Auberge du Grand Dauphin" looked remarkably inviting, written in bold, shiny black characters on the white-washed wall of one of the foremost houses in the village. The riders drew rein once more, this time in front of the little inn, and as a young ostler in blue blouse and sabots came hurriedly and officiously forward whilst mine host in the same attire appeared in the doorway, the two men dismounted, unstrapped their mantles from their saddle-bows and loudly called for mulled wine.

Mine host, typical of his calling and of his race, rubicund of cheek, portly of figure and genial in manner, was over-anxious to please his guests. It was not often that gentlemen of such distinguished appearance called at the "Auberge du Grand Dauphin," seeing that Notre Dame de Vaulx lies perdu on the outskirts of the forests of Pelvoux, that the bridle path having reached the village leads nowhere save into the mountains and that La Motte is close by with its medicinal springs and its fine hostels.

But these two highly-distinguished gentlemen evidently meant to make a stay of it. They even spoke of a friend who would come and join them later, when they would expect a substantial déjeuner to be served with the best wine mine host could put before them. Annette—mine host's dark-eyed daughter—was all a-flutter at sight of these gallant strangers, one of them with such fiery eyes and vivacious ways, and the other so tall and so dignified, with fair skin well-bronzed by the sun and large firm mouth that had such a pleasant smile on it; her eyes sparkled at sight of them both and her glib tongue rattled away at truly astonishing speed.

Would a well-baked omelette and a bit of fricandeau suit the gentlemen?—Admirably? Ah, well then, that could easily be done!—and now? in the meanwhile?—Only good mulled wine? That would present no difficulty either. Five minutes for it to get really hot, as Annette had made some the previous day for her father who had been on a tiring errand up to La Mure and had come home cold and starved—and it was specially good—all the better for having been hotted up once or twice and the cloves and nutmeg having soaked in for nearly four and twenty hours.

Where would the gentlemen have it—Outside in the sunshine? ... Well! it was very cold, and the wind biting ... but the gentlemen had mantles, and she, Annette, would see that the wine was piping hot.... Five minutes and everything would be ready....

What? ... the tall, fair-skinned gentleman wanted to wash? ... what a funny idea! ... hadn't he washed this morning when he got up? ... He had? Well, then, why should he want to wash again? ... She, Annette, managed to keep herself quite clean all day, and didn't need to

7

wash more than once a day.... But there! strangers had funny ways with them ... she had guessed at once that Monsieur was a stranger, he had such a fair skin and light brown hair. Well! so long as Monsieur wasn't English—for the English, she detested!

Why did she detest the English? ... Because they made war against France. Well! against the Emperor anyhow, and she, Annette, firmly believed that if the English could get hold of the Emperor they would kill him—oh, yes! they would put him on an island peopled by cannibals and let him be eaten, bones, marrow and all.

And Annette's dark eyes grew very round and very big as she gave forth her opinion upon the barbarous hatred of the English for "l'Empereur!" She prattled on very gaily and very volubly, while she dragged a couple of chairs out into the open, and placed them well in the lee of the wind and brought a couple of pewter mugs which she set on the table.

She was very much interested in the tall gentleman who had availed himself of her suggestion to use the pump at the back of the house, since he was so bent on washing himself; and she asked many questions about him from his friend.

Ten minutes later the steaming wine was on the table in a huge china bowl and the Englishman was ladling it out with a long-handled spoon and filling the two mugs with the deliciously scented cordial. Annette had disappeared into the house in response to a peremptory call from her father. The chapel bell had ceased to ring long ago, and she would miss hearing Mass altogether to-day; and M. le curé, who came on alternate Sundays all the way from La Motte to celebrate divine service, would be very angry indeed with her.

Well! that couldn't be helped! Annette would have loved to go to Mass, but the two distinguished gentlemen expected their friend to arrive at noon, and the déjeuner to be ready quite by then; so she comforted her conscience with a few prayers said on her knees before the picture of the Holy Virgin which hung above her bed, after which she went back to her housewifely duty with a light heart; but not before she had decided an important point in her mind—namely, which of those two handsome gentlemen she liked the best: the dark one with the fiery eyes that expressed such bold admiration of her young charms, or the tall one with the earnest grey eyes who looked as if he could pick her up like a feather and carry her running all the way to the summit of Taillefer.

Annette had indeed made up her mind that the giant with the soft brown hair and winning smile was, on the whole, the more attractive of the two.

III

The two friends, with mantles wrapped closely round them, sat outside the "Grand Dauphin" all unconscious of the problem which had been disturbing Annette's busy little brain.

The steaming wine had put plenty of warmth into their bones, and though both had been silent while they sipped their first mug-full, it was obvious that each was busy with his own thoughts.

Then suddenly the young Frenchman put his mug down and leaned with both elbows upon the rough deal table, because he wanted to talk confidentially with his friend, and there was never any knowing what prying ears might be about.

"I suppose," he said, even as a deep frown told of puzzling thoughts within the mind, "I suppose that when England hears the news, she will up and at him again, attacking him, snarling at him even before he has had time to settle down upon his reconquered throne."

"That throne is not reconquered yet, my friend," retorted the Englishman drily, "nor has the news of this mad adventure reached England so far, but ..."

"But when it does," broke in de Marmont sombrely, "your Castlereagh will rave and your Wellington will gather up his armies to try and crush the hero whom France loves and acclaims."

"Will France acclaim the hero, there's the question?"

"The army will—the people will——"

Clyffurde shrugged his shoulders.

"The army, yes," he said slowly, "but the people ... what people?— the peasantry of Provence and the Dauphiné, perhaps—what about the town folk?—your mayors and préfets?—your tradespeople? your shopkeepers who have been ruined by the wars which your hero has made to further his own ambition...."

"Don't say that, Clyffurde," once more broke in de Marmont, and this time more vehemently than before. "When you speak like that I could almost forget our friendship."

"Whether I say it or not, my good de Marmont," rejoined Clyffurde with his good-humoured smile, "you will anyhow—within the next few months—days, perhaps—bury our friendship beneath the ashes of your patriotism. No one, believe me," he added more earnestly, "has a greater admiration for the genius of Napoleon than I have; his love of France is sublime, his desire for her glory superb. But underlying his love of country, there is the love of self, the mad desire to rule, to conquer, to humiliate. It led him to Moscow and thence to Elba, it has brought him back to France. It will lead him once again to the Capitol, no doubt, but as surely too it will lead him on to the Tarpeian Rock whence he will be hurled down this time, not only

9

bruised, but shattered, a fallen hero—and you will—a broken idol, for posterity to deal with in after time as it lists."

"And England would like to be the one to give the hero the final push," said de Marmont, not without a sneer.

"The people of England, my friend, hate and fear Bonaparte as they have never hated and feared any one before in the whole course of their history—and tell me, have we not cause enough to hate him? For fifteen years has he not tried to ruin us, to bring us to our knees? tried to throttle our commerce? break our might upon the sea? He wanted to make a slave of Britain, and Britain proved unconquerable. Believe me, we hate your hero less than he hates us."

He had spoken with a good deal of earnestness, but now he added more lightly, as if in answer to de Marmont's glowering look:

"At the same time," he said, "I doubt if there is a single English gentleman living at the present moment—let alone the army—who would refuse ungrudging admiration to Napoleon himself and to his genius. But as a nation England has her interests to safeguard. She has suffered enough—and through him—in her commerce and her prosperity in the past twenty years—she must have peace now at any cost."

"Ah! I know," sighed the other, "a nation of shopkeepers...."

"Yes. We are that, I suppose. We are shopkeepers ... most of us...."

"I didn't mean to use the word in any derogatory sense," protested Victor de Marmont with the ready politeness peculiar to his race. "Why, even you ..."

"I don't see why you should say 'even you,'" broke in Clyffurde quietly. "I am a shopkeeper—nothing more.... I buy goods and sell them again.... I buy the gloves which our friend M. Dumoulin manufactures at Grenoble and sell them to any London draper who chooses to buy them ... a very mean and ungentlemanly occupation, is it not?"

He spoke French with perfect fluency, and only with the merest suspicion of a drawl in the intonation of the vowels, which suggested rather than proclaimed his nationality; and just now there was not the slightest tone of bitterness apparent in his deep-toned and mellow voice. Once more his friend would have protested, but he put up a restraining hand.

"Oh!" he said with a smile, "I don't imagine for a moment that you have the same prejudices as our mutual friend M. le Comte de Cambray, who must have made a very violent sacrifice to his feelings when he admitted me as a guest to his own table. I am sure he must often think that the servants' hall is the proper place for me."

"The Comte de Cambray," retorted de Marmont with a sneer, "is full up to his eyes with the prejudices and arrogance of his caste. It is men of his type—and not Marat or Robespierre—who made the revolution, who goaded the people of France into becoming something worse than man-devouring beasts. And, mind you, twenty years of exile did not sober them, nor did contact with democratic thought in England and America teach them the most elementary lessons of commonsense. If the Emperor had not come back to-day, we should be once more working up for revolution—more terrible this time, more bloody and vengeful, if possible, than the last."

Then as Clyffurde made no comment on this peroration, the younger man resumed more lightly:

"And—knowing the Comte de Cambray's prejudices as I do, imagine my surprise—after I had met you in his house as an honoured guest and on what appeared to be intimate terms of friendship—to learn that you ... in fact ..."

"That I was nothing more than a shopkeeper," broke in Clyffurde with a short laugh, "nothing better than our mutual friend M. Dumoulin, glovemaker, of Grenoble—a highly worthy man whom M. le Comte de Cambray esteems somewhat lower than his butler. It certainly must have surprised you very much."

"Well, you know, old de Cambray has a horror of anything that pertains to trade, and an avowed contempt for everything that he calls 'bourgeois.'"

"There's no doubt about that," assented Clyffurde fervently.

"Perhaps he does not know of your connection with ..."

"Gloves?"

"With business people in Grenoble generally."

"Oh, yes, he does!" replied the Englishman quietly.

"Well, then?" queried de Marmont.

Then as his friend sat there silent with that quiet, good-humoured smile lingering round his lips, he added apologetically:

"Perhaps I am indiscreet ... but I never could understand it ... and you English are so reserved ..."

"That I never told you how M. le Comte de Cambray, Commander of the Order of the Holy Ghost, Grand Cross of the Order du Lys, Hereditary Grand Chamberlain of France, etc., etc., came to sit at the same table as a vendor and buyer of gloves," said Clyffurde gaily. "There's no secret about it. I owe the Comte's exalted condescension to certain letters of recommendation which he could not very well disregard."

"Oh! as to that ..." quoth de Marmont with a shrug of the shoulders, "people like the de Cambrays have their own codes of courtesy and of friendship."

"In this case, my good de Marmont, it was the code of ordinary gratitude that imposed its dictum even upon the autocratic and aristocratic Comte de Cambray."

"Gratitude?" sneered de Marmont, "in a de Cambray?"

"M. le Comte de Cambray," said Clyffurde with slow emphasis, "his mother, his sister, his brother-in-law and two of their faithful

11

servants, were rescued from the very foot of the guillotine by a band of heroes—known in those days as the League of the Scarlet Pimpernel."

"I knew that!" said de Marmont quietly.

"Then perhaps you also knew that their leader was Sir Percy Blakeney—a prince among gallant English gentlemen and my dead father's friend. When my business affairs sent me to Grenoble, Sir Percy warmly recommended me to the man whose life he had saved. What could M. le Comte de Cambray do but receive me as a friend? You see, my credentials were exceptional and unimpeachable."

"Of course," assented de Marmont, "now I understand. But you will admit that I have had grounds for surprise. You—who were the friend of Dumoulin, a tradesman, and avowed Bonapartist—two unpardonable crimes in the eyes of M. le Comte de Cambray," he added with a return to his former bitterness, "you to be seated at his table and to shake him by the hand. Why, man! if he knew that I have remained faithful to the Emperor ..."

He paused abruptly, and his somewhat full, sensitive lips were pressed tightly together as if to suppress an insistent outburst of passion.

But Clyffurde frowned, and when he turned away from de Marmont it was in order to hide a harsh look of contempt.

"Surely," he said, "you have never led the Comte to suppose that you are a royalist!"

"I have never led him to suppose anything. But he has taken my political convictions for granted," rejoined de Marmont.

Then suddenly a look of bitter resentment darkened his face, making it appear hard and lined and considerably older.

"My uncle, Marshal de Marmont, Duc de Raguse, was an abominable traitor," he went on with ill-repressed vehemence. "He betrayed his Emperor, his benefactor and his friend. It was the vilest treachery that has ever disgraced an honourable name. Paris could have held out easily for another four and twenty hours, and by that time the Emperor would have been back. But de Marmont gave her over wilfully, scurvily to the allies. But for his abominable act of cowardice the Emperor never would have had to endure the shame of his temporary exile at Elba, and Louis de Bourbon would never have had the chance of wallowing for twelve months upon the throne of France. But that which is a source of irreparable shame to me is a virtue in the eyes of all these royalists. De Marmont's treachery against the Emperor has placed all his kindred in the forefront of those who now lick the boots of that infamous Bourbon dynasty, and it did not suit the plans of the Bonapartist party that we—in the provinces— should proclaim our faith too openly until such time as the Emperor returned."

"And if the Comte de Cambray had known that you are just an ardent Bonapartist? ..." suggested Clyffurde calmly.

"He would long before now have had me kicked out by his lacqueys," broke in de Marmont with ever-increasing bitterness as he brought his clenched fist crashing down upon the table, while his dark eyes glowed with a fierce and passionate resentment. "For men like de Cambray there is only one caste—the noblesse, one religion—the Catholic, one creed—adherence to the Bourbons. All else is scum, trash, beneath contempt, hardly human! Oh! if you knew how I loathe these people!" he continued, speaking volubly and in a voice shaking with suppressed excitement. "They have learnt nothing, these aristocrats, nothing, I tell you! the terrible reprisals of the revolution which culminated in that appalling Reign of Terror have taught them absolutely nothing! They have not learnt the great lesson of the revolution, that the people will no longer endure their arrogance and their pretensions, that the old regime is dead—dead! the regime of oppression and pride and intolerance! They have learnt nothing!" he reiterated with ever-growing excitement, "nothing! 'humanity begins with the noblesse' is still their watchword to-day as it was before the irate people sent hundreds of them to perish miserably on the guillotine—the rest of mankind, to them, is only cattle made to toil for the well-being of their class. Oh! I loathe them, I tell you! I loathe them from the bottom of my soul!"

"And yet you and your kind are rapidly becoming at one with them," said Clyffurde, his quiet voice in strange contrast to the other man's violent agitation.

"No, we are not," protested de Marmont emphatically. "The men whom Napoleon created marshals and peers of France have been openly snubbed at the Court of Louis XVIII. Ney, who is prince of Moskowa and next to Napoleon himself the greatest soldier of France, has seen his wife treated little better than a chambermaid by the Duchesse d'Angoulême and the ladies of the old noblesse. My uncle is marshal of France, and Duc de Raguse and I am the heir to his millions, but the Comte de Cambray will always consider it a mesalliance for his daughter to marry me."

The note of bitter resentment, of wounded pride and smouldering hatred became more and more marked while he spoke: his voice now sounded hoarse and his throat seemed dry. Presently he raised his mug to his lips and drank eagerly, but his hand was shaking visibly as he did this, and some of the wine was spilled on the table.

There was silence for a while outside the little inn, silence which seemed full of portent, for through the pure mountain air there was wafted the hot breath of men's passions—fierce, dominating, challenging. Love, hatred, prejudices and contempt—all were portrayed on de Marmont's mobile face: they glowed in his dark eyes and breathed through his quivering nostrils. Now he rested his elbow on the table and his chin in his hand, his nervy fingers played a tattoo

13

against his teeth, clenched together like those of some young feline creature which sees its prey coming along and is snarling at the sight.

Clyffurde, with those deep-set, earnest grey eyes of his, was silently watching his friend. His hand did not shake, nor did the breath come any quicker from his broad chest. Yet deep down behind the wide brow, behind those same overshadowed eyes, a keen observer would of a surety have detected the signs of a latent volcano of passions, all the more strong and virile as they were kept in perfect control. It was he who presently broke the silence, and his voice was quite steady when he spoke, though perhaps a trifle more toneless, more dead, than usual.

"And," he said, "what of Mlle. Crystal in all this?"

"Crystal?" queried the other curtly, "what about her?"

"She is an ardent royalist, more strong in her convictions and her enthusiasms than women usually are."

"And what of that?" rejoined de Marmont fiercely. "I love Crystal."

"But when she learns that you ..."

"She shall not learn it," rejoined the other cynically. "We sign our marriage contract to-night: the wedding is fixed for Tuesday. Until then I can hold my peace."

An exclamation of hot protest almost escaped the Englishman's lips: his hand which rested on the table became so tightly clenched that the hard knuckles looked as if they would burst through their fetters of sinew and skin, and he made no pretence at concealing the look of burning indignation which flashed from his eyes.

"But man!" he exclaimed, "a deception such as you propose is cruel and monstrous.... In view, too, of what has occurred in the past few days ... in view of what may happen if the news which we have heard is true ..."

"In view of all that, my friend," retorted de Marmont firmly, "the old regime has had its nine days of wonder and of splendour. The Emperor has come back! we, who believe in him, who have remained true to him in his humiliation and in his misfortunes may once more raise our heads and loudly proclaim our loyalty. The return of the Emperor will once more put his dukes and his marshals in their rightful place on a level with the highest nobility of France. The Comte de Cambray will realise that all his hopes of regaining his fortune through the favours of the Bourbons have by force of circumstances come to naught. Like most of the old noblesse who emigrated he is without a sou. He may choose to look on me with contempt, but he will no longer desire to kick me out of his house, for he will be glad enough to see the Cambray 'scutcheon regilt with de Marmont gold."

"But Mademoiselle Crystal?" insisted Clyffurde, almost appealingly, for his whole soul had revolted at the cynicism of the other man.

"Crystal has listened to that ape, St. Genis," replied de Marmont

14

drily, "one of her own caste ... a marquis with sixteen quarterings to his family escutcheon and not a sou in his pockets. She is very young, and very inexperienced. She has seen nothing of the world as yet—nothing. She was born and brought up in exile—in England, in the midst of that narrow society formed by impecunious émigrés...."

"And shopkeeping Englishmen," murmured Clyffurde, under his breath.

"She could never have married St. Genis," reiterated Victor de Marmont with deliberate emphasis. "The man hasn't a sou. Even Crystal realised from the first that nothing ever could have come of that boy and girl dallying. The Comte never would have consented...."

"Perhaps not. But she—Mademoiselle Crystal—would she ever have consented to marry you, if she had known what your convictions are?"

"Crystal is only a child," said de Marmont with a light shrug of the shoulders. "She will learn to love me presently when St. Genis has disappeared out of her little world, and she will accept my convictions as she has accepted me, submissive to my will as she was to that of her father."

Once more a hot protest of indignation rose to Clyffurde's lips, but this too he smothered resolutely. What was the use of protesting? Could he hope to change with a few arguments the whole cynical nature of a man? And what right had he even to interfere? The Comte de Cambray and Mademoiselle Crystal were nothing to him: in their minds they would never look upon him even as an equal—let alone as a friend. So the bitter words died upon his lips.

"And you have been content to win a wife on such terms!" was all that he said.

"I have had to be content," was de Marmont's retort. "Crystal is the only woman I have ever cared for. She will love me in time, I doubt not, and her sense of duty will make her forget St. Genis quickly enough."

Then as Clyffurde made no further comment silence fell once more between the two men. Perhaps even de Marmont felt that somehow, during the past few moments, the slender bond of friendship which similarity of tastes and a certain similarity of political ideals had forged between him and the stranger had been strained to snapping point, and this for a reason which he could not very well understand. He drank another draught of wine and gave a quick sigh of satisfaction with the world in general, and also with himself, for he did not feel that he had done or said anything which could offend the keenest susceptibilities of his friend.

He looked with a sudden sense of astonishment at Clyffurde, as if he were only seeing him now for the first time. His keen dark eyes took in with a rapid glance the Englishman's powerful personality, the square shoulders, the head well erect, the strong Anglo-Saxon chin firmly set, the slender hands always in repose. In the whole attitude of the man there was an air of will-power which had never struck de Marmont quite so forcibly as it did now, and a virility which looked as ready to challenge Fate as it was able to conquer her if she proved adverse.

And just now there was a curious look in those deep-set eyes—a look of contempt or of pity—de Marmont was not sure which, but somehow the look worried him and he would have given much to read the thoughts which were hidden behind the high, square brow.

However, he asked no questions, and thus the silence remained unbroken for some time save for the soughing of the northeast wind as it whistled through the pines, whilst from the tiny chapel which held the shrine of Notre Dame de Vaulx came the sound of a soft-toned bell, ringing the midday Angelus.

Just then round that same curve in the road, where the two riders had paused an hour ago in sight of the little hamlet, a man on horseback appeared, riding at a brisk trot up the rugged, stony path.

Victor de Marmont woke from his rêverie:

"There's Emery," he cried.

He jumped to his feet, then he picked up his hat from the table where he had laid it down, tossed it up into the air as high as it would go, and shouted with all his might:

"Vive l'Empereur!"

IV

The man who now drew rein with abrupt clumsiness in front of the auberge looked hot, tired and travel-stained. His face was covered with sweat and his horse with lather, the lapel of his coat was torn, his breeches and boots were covered with half-frozen mud.

But having brought his horse to a halt, he swung himself out of the saddle with the brisk air of a boy who has enjoyed his first ride across country. Surgeon-Captain Emery was a man well over forty, but to-day his eyes glowed with that concentrated fire which burns in the heart at twenty, and he shook de Marmont by the hand with a vigour which made the younger man wince with the pain of that iron grip.

"My friend, Mr. Clyffurde, an English gentleman," said Victor de Marmont hastily in response to a quick look of suspicious enquiry which flashed out from under Emery's bushy eyebrows. "You can talk quite freely, Emery; and for God's sake tell us your news!"

But Emery could hardly speak. He had been riding hard for the past three hours, his throat was parched, and through it his voice came

16

up hoarse and raucous: nevertheless he at once began talking in short, jerky sentences.

"He landed on Wednesday," he said. "I parted from him on Friday ... at Castellane ... you had my message?"

"This morning early—we came at once."

"I thought we could talk better here—first—but I was spent last night—I had to sleep at Corps ... so I sent to you.... But now, in Heaven's name, give me something to drink...."

While he drank eagerly and greedily of the cold spiced wine which Clyffurde had served out to him, he still scrutinised the Englishman closely from under his frowning and bushy eyebrows.

Clyffurde's winning glance, however, seemed to have conquered his mistrust, for presently, after he had put his mug down again, he stretched out a cordial hand to him.

"Now that our Emperor is back with us," he said as if in apology for his former suspicions, "we, his friends, are bound to look askance at every Englishman we meet."

"Of course you are," said Clyffurde with his habitual good-humoured smile as he grasped Surgeon-Captain Emery's extended hand.

"It is the hand of a friend I am grasping?" insisted Emery.

"Of a personal friend, if you will call him so," replied Clyffurde. "Politically, I hardly count, you see. I am just a looker-on at the game."

The surgeon-captain's keen eyes under their bushy brows shot a rapid glance at the tall, well-knit figure of the Englishman.

"You are not a fighting man?" he queried, much amazed.

"No," replied Clyffurde drily. "I am only a tradesman."

"Your news, Emery, your news!" here broke in Victor de Marmont, who during the brief colloquy between his two friends had been hardly able to keep his excitement in check.

Emery turned away from the other man in silence. Clearly there was something about that fine, noble-looking fellow—who proclaimed himself a tradesman while that splendid physique of his should be at his country's service—which still puzzled the worthy army surgeon.

But he was primarily very thirsty and secondly as eager to impart his news as de Marmont was to hear it, so now without wasting any further words on less important matter he sat down close to the table and stretched his short, thick legs out before him.

"My news is of the best," he said with lusty fervour. "We left Porto Ferrajo on Sunday last but only landed on Wednesday, as I told you, for we were severely becalmed in the Mediterranean. We came on shore at Antibes at midday of March 1st and bivouacked in an olive grove on the way to Cannes. That was a sight good for sore eyes, my friends, to see him sitting there by the camp fire, his feet firmly planted upon the soil of France. What a man, Sir, what a man!" he continued, turning directly to Clyffurde, "on board the Inconstant he had

17

composed and dictated his proclamation to the army, to the soldiers of France! the finest piece of prose, Sir, I have ever read in all my life. But you shall judge of it, Sir, you shall judge...."

And with hands shaking with excitement he fumbled in the bulging pocket of his coat and extracted therefrom a roll of loose papers roughly tied together with a piece of tape.

"You shall read it, Sir," he went on mumbling, while his trembling fingers vainly tried to undo the knot in the tape, "you shall read it. And then mayhap you'll tell me if your Pitt was ever half so eloquent. Curse these knots!" he exclaimed angrily.

"Will you allow me, Sir?" said Clyffurde quietly, and with steady hand and firm fingers he undid the refractory knots and spread the papers out upon the table.

Already de Marmont had given a cry of loyalty and of triumph.

"His proclamation!" he exclaimed, and a sigh of infinite satisfaction born of enthusiasm and of hero-worship escaped his quivering lips.

The papers bore the signature of that name which had once been all-powerful in its magical charm, at sound of which Europe had trembled and crowns had felt insecure, the name which men had breathed—nay! still breathed—either with passionate loyalty or with bitter hatred:—"Napoleon."

They were copies of the proclamation wherewith the heroic adventurer—confident in the power of his diction—meant to reconquer the hearts of that army whom he had once led to such glorious victories.

De Marmont read the long document through from end to end in a half-audible voice. Now and again he gave a little cry—a cry of loyalty at mention of those victories of Austerlitz and Jena, of Wagram and of Eckmühl, at mention of those imperial eagles which had led the armies of France conquering and glorious throughout the length and breadth of Europe—or a cry of shame and horror at mention of the traitor whose name he bore and who had delivered France into the hands of strangers and his Emperor into those of his enemies.

And when the young enthusiast had read the proclamation through to the end he raised the paper to his lips and fervently kissed the imprint of the revered name: "Napoleon."

"Now tell me more about him," he said finally, as he leaned both elbows on the table and fastened his glowing eyes upon the equally heated face of Surgeon-Captain Emery.

"Well!" resumed the latter, "as I told you we bivouacked among the olive trees on the way to Cannes. The Emperor had already sent Cambronne on ahead with forty of his grenadiers to commandeer what horses and mules he could, as we were not able to bring many across from Porto Ferrajo. 'Cambronne,' he said, 'you shall be in command of the vanguard in this the finest campaign which I have ever undertaken.

My orders are to you, that you do not fire a single unnecessary shot. Remember that I mean to reconquer my imperial crown without shedding one drop of French blood.' Oh! he is in excellent health and in excellent spirits! Such a man! such fire in his eyes! such determination in his actions! Younger, bolder than ever! I tell you, friends," continued the worthy surgeon-captain as he brought the palm of his hand flat down upon the table with an emphatic bang, "that it is going to be a triumphal march from end to end of France. The people are mad about him. At Roccavignon, just outside Cannes, where we bivouacked on Thursday, men, women and children were flocking round to see him, pressing close to his knees, bringing him wine and flowers; and the people were crying 'Vive l'Empereur!' even in the streets of Grasse."

"But the army, man? the army?" cried de Marmont, "the garrisons of Antibes and Cannes and Grasse? did the men go over to him at once?—and the officers?"

"We hadn't encountered the army yet when I parted from him on Friday," retorted Emery with equal impatience, "we didn't go into Antibes and we avoided Cannes. You must give him time. The people in the towns wouldn't at first believe that he had come back. General Masséna, who is in command at Marseilles, thought fit to spread the news that a band of Corsican pirates had landed on the littoral and were marching inland—devastating villages as they marched. The peasants from the mountains were the first to believe that the Emperor had really come, and they wandered down in their hundreds to see him first and to spread the news of his arrival ahead of him. By the time we reached Castellane the mayor was not only ready to receive him but also to furnish him with 5,000 rations of meat and bread, with horses and with mules. Since then he has been at Digue and at Sisteron. Be sure that the garrisons of those cities have rallied round his eagles by now."

Then whilst Emery paused for breath de Marmont queried eagerly:

"And so ... there has been no contretemps?"

"Nothing serious so far," replied the other. "We had to abandon our guns at Grasse, the Emperor felt that they would impede the rapidity of his progress; and our second day's march was rather trying, the mountain passes were covered in snow, the lancers had to lead their horses sometimes along the edge of sheer precipices, they were hampered too by their accoutrements, their long swords and their lances; others—who had no mounts—had to carry their heavy saddles and bridles on those slippery paths. But he was walking too, stick in hand, losing his footing now and then, just as they did, and once he nearly rolled down one of those cursed precipices: but always smiling, always cheerful, always full of hope. At Antibes young Casabianca got himself arrested with twenty grenadiers—they had gone into the town to requisition a few provisions. When the news reached us some of the

19

younger men tried to persuade the Emperor to march on the city and carry the place by force of arms before Casabianca's misfortune got bruited abroad: 'No!' he said, 'every minute is precious. All we can do is to get along faster than the evil news can travel. If half my small army were captive at Antibes, I would still move on. If every man were a prisoner in the citadel, I would march on alone.' That's the man, my friends," cried Emery with ever-growing enthusiasm, "that's our Emperor!"

And he cast a defiant look on Clyffurde, as much as to say: "Bring on your Wellington and your armies now! the Emperor has come back! the whole of France will know how to guard him!" Then he turned to de Marmont.

"And now tell me about Grenoble," he said.

"Grenoble had an inkling of the news already last night," said de Marmont, whose enthusiasm was no whit cooler than that of Emery. "Marchand has been secretly assembling his troops, he has sent to Chambéry for the 7th and 11th regiment of the line and to Vienne for the 4th Hussars. Inside Grenoble he has the 5th infantry regiment, the 4th of artillery and 3rd of engineers, with a train squadron. This morning he is holding a council of war, and I know that he has been in constant communication with Masséna. The news is gradually filtering through into the town: people stand at the street corners and whisper among themselves; the word 'l'Empereur' seemed wafted upon this morning's breeze...."

"And by to-night we'll have the Emperor's proclamation to his people pinned up on the walls of the Hôtel de Ville!" exclaimed Emery, and with hands still trembling with excitement he gathered the precious papers once more together and slipped them back into his coat pocket. Then he made a visible effort to speak more quietly: "And now," he said, "for one very important matter which, by the way, was the chief reason for my asking you, my good de Marmont, to meet me here before my getting to Grenoble."

"Yes? What is it?" queried de Marmont eagerly.

Surgeon-Captain Emery leaned across the table; instinctively he dropped his voice, and though his excitement had not abated one jot, though his eyes still glowed and his hands still fidgeted nervously, he had forced himself at last to a semblance of calm.

"The matter is one of money," he said slowly. "The Emperor has some funds at his disposal, but as you know, that scurvy government of the Restoration never handed him over one single sou of the yearly revenue which it had solemnly agreed and sworn to pay to him with regularity. Now, of course," he continued still more emphatically, "we who believe in our Emperor as we believe in God, we are absolutely convinced that the army will rally round him to a man. The army loves him and has never ceased to love him, the army will follow him to victory and to death. But the most loyal army in the world cannot

20

subsist without money, and the Emperor has little or none. The news of his triumphant march across France will reach Paris long before he does, it will enable His Most Excellent and Most Corpulent Majesty King Louis to skip over to England or to Ghent with everything in the treasury on which he can lay his august hands. Now, de Marmont, do you perceive what the serious matter is which caused me to meet you here—twenty-five kilomètres from Grenoble, where I ought to be at the present moment."

"Yes! I do perceive very grave trouble there," said de Marmont with characteristic insouciance, "but one which need not greatly worry the Emperor. I am rich, thank God! and ..."

"And may God bless you, my dear de Marmont, for the thought," broke in Emery earnestly, "but what may be called a large private fortune is as nothing before the needs of an army. Soon, of course, the Emperor will be in peaceful possession of his throne and will have all the resources of France at his command, but before that happy time arrives there will be much fighting, and many days—weeks perhaps—of anxiety to go through. During those weeks the army must be paid and fed; and your private fortune, my dear de Marmont, would—even if the Emperor were to accept your sacrifice, which is not likely—be but as a drop in the mighty ocean of the cost of a campaign. What are two or even three millions, my poor, dear friend? It is forty, fifty millions that the Emperor wants."

De Marmont this time had nothing to say. He was staring moodily and silently before him.

"Now, that is what I have come to talk to you about," continued Emery after a few seconds' pause, during which he had once more thrown a quick, half-suspicious glance on the impassive, though obviously interested face of the Englishman, "always supposing that Monsieur here is on our side."

"Neither on your side nor on the other, Captain," said Bobby Clyffurde with a slight tone of impatience. "I am a mere tradesman, as I have had the honour to tell you: a spectator at this game of political conflicts. M. de Marmont knows this well, else he had not asked me to accompany him to-day nor offered me a mount to enable me to do so. But if you prefer it," he added lightly, "I can go for a stroll while you discuss these graver matters."

He would have risen from the table only that Emery immediately detained him.

"No offence, Sir," said the surgeon-captain bluntly.

"None, I give you my word," assented the Englishman. "It is only natural that you should wish to discuss such grave matters in private. Let me go and see to our déjeuner in the meanwhile. I feel sure that the fricandeau is done to a turn by now. I'll have it dished up in ten minutes. I pray you take no heed of me," he added in response to murmured protestations from both de Marmont and Emery. "I would

21

much prefer to know nothing of these grave matters which you are about to discuss."

This time Emery did not detain him as he rose and turned to go within in order to find mine host or Annette. The two Frenchmen took no further heed of him: wrapped up in the all engrossing subject-matter they remained seated at the table, leaning across it, their faces close to one another, their eyes dancing with excitement, questions and answers—as soon as the stranger's back was turned—already tumbling out in confusion from their lips.

Clyffurde turned to have a last look at them before he went into the house, and while he did so his habitual, pleasant, gently-ironical smile still hovered round his lips. But anon a quickly-suppressed sigh chased the smile away, and over his face there crept a strange shadow—a look of longing and of bitter regret.

It was only for a moment, however, the next he had passed his hand slowly across his forehead, as if to wipe away that shadow and smooth out those lines of unspoken pain.

Soon his cheerful voice was heard, echoing along the low rafters of the little inn, loudly calling for Annette and for news of the baked omelette and the fricandeau.

V

"You really could have talked quite freely before Mr. Clyffurde, my good Emery," said de Marmont as soon as Bobby had disappeared inside the inn. "He really takes no part in politics. He is a friend alike of the Comte de Cambray and of glovemaker Dumoulin. He has visited our Bonapartist Club. Dumoulin has vouched for him. You see, he is not a fighting man."

"I suppose that you are equally sure that he is not an English spy," remarked Emery drily.

"Of course I am sure," asserted de Marmont emphatically. "Dumoulin has known him for years in business, though this is the first time that Clyffurde has visited Grenoble. He is in the glove trade in England: his interests are purely commercial. He came here with introductions to the Comte de Cambray from a mutual friend in England who seems to be a personage of vast importance in his own country and greatly esteemed by the Comte—else you may be sure that that stiff-necked aristocrat would never have received a tradesman as a guest in his house. But it was in Dumoulin's house that I first met Bobby Clyffurde. We took a liking to one another, and since then have ridden a great deal together. He is a splendid horseman, and I was very glad to be able to offer him a mount at different times. But our political conversations have never been very heated or very serious. Clyffurde maintains a detached impersonal attitude both to the Bonapartist and the royalist cause. I asked him to accompany me this morning and he gladly consented, for he dearly loves a horse. I assure you, you might have said anything before him."

"Eh bien! I'm sorry if I've been obstinate and ungracious," said the surgeon-captain, but in a tone that obviously belied his words, "though, frankly, I am very glad that we are alone for the moment."

He paused, and with a wave of his thick, short-fingered hand he dismissed this less important subject-matter and once more spoke with his wonted eagerness on that which lay nearest his heart.

"Now listen, my good de Marmont," he said, "do you recollect last April when the Empress—poor wretched, misguided woman—fled so precipitately from Paris, abandoning the capital, France and her crown at one and the same time, and taking away with her all the Crown diamonds and money and treasure belonging to the Emperor? She was terribly ill-advised, of course, but ..."

"Yes, I remember all that perfectly well," broke in de Marmont impatiently.

"Well, then, you know that that abominable Talleyrand sent one of his emissaries after the Empress and her suite ... that this emissary—Dudon was his name—reached Orleans just before Marie Louise herself got there...."

"And that he ordered, in Talleyrand's name, the seizure of the Empress' convoy as soon as it arrived in the city," broke in de Marmont again. "Yes. I recollect that abominable outrage perfectly. Dudon, backed by the officers of the gendarmerie, managed to rob the Empress of everything she had, even to the last knife and fork, even to the last pocket handkerchief belonging to the Emperor and marked with his initials. Oh! it was monstrous! hellish! devilish! It makes my blood boil whenever I think of it ... whenever I think of those fatuous, treacherous Bourbons gloating over those treasures at the Tuileries, while our Empress went her way as effectually despoiled as if she had been waylaid by so many brigands on a public highway."

"Just so," resumed Emery quietly after de Marmont's violent storm of wrath had subsided. "But I don't know if you also recollect that when the various cases containing the Emperor's belongings were opened at the Tuileries, there was just as much disappointment as gloating. Some of those fatuous Bourbons—as you so rightly call them—expected to find some forty or fifty millions of the Emperor's personal savings there—bank-notes and drafts on the banks of France, of England and of Amsterdam, which they were looking forward to distributing among themselves and their friends. Your friend the Comte de Cambray would no doubt have come in too for his share in this distribution. But M. de Talleyrand is a very wise man! always far-seeing, he knows the improvidence, the prodigality, the ostentation of these new masters whom he is so ready to serve. Ere Dudon reached Paris with his booty, M. de Talleyrand had very carefully eliminated therefrom some five and twenty million francs in bank-notes and bankers' drafts, which he felt would come in very usefully once for a rainy day."

"But M. de Talleyrand is immensely rich himself," protested de Marmont.

"Ah! he did not eliminate those five and twenty millions for his own benefit," said Emery. "I would not so boldly accuse him of theft. The money has been carefully put away by M. de Talleyrand for the use of His Corpulent Majesty Louis de Bourbon, XVIIIth of that name."

Then as Emery here made a dramatic pause and looked triumphantly across at his companion, de Marmont rejoined somewhat bewildered:

"But ... I don't understand ..."

"Why I am telling you this?" retorted Emery, still with that triumphant air. "You shall understand in a moment, my friend, when I tell you that those five and twenty millions were never taken north to Paris, they were conveyed in strict secrecy south to Grenoble!"

"To Grenoble?" exclaimed de Marmont.

"To Grenoble," reasserted Emery.

"But why? ... why such a long way?—why Grenoble?" queried the young man in obvious puzzlement.

"For several reasons," replied Emery. "Firstly both the préfet of the department and the military commandant are hot royalists, whilst the province of Dauphiné is not. In case of any army corps being sent down there to quell possible and probable revolt, the money would have been there to hand: also, if you remember, there was talk at the time of the King of Naples proving troublesome. There, too, in case of a campaign on the frontier, the money lying ready to hand at Grenoble could prove very useful. But of course I cannot possibly pretend to give you all the reasons which actuated M. de Talleyrand when he caused five and twenty millions of stolen money to be conveyed secretly to Grenoble rather than to Paris. His ways are more tortuous than any mere army-surgeon can possibly hope to gauge. Enough that he did it and that at this very moment there are five and twenty millions which are the rightful property of the Emperor locked up in the cellars of the Hôtel de Ville at Grenoble."

"But ..." murmured de Marmont, who still seemed very bewildered at all that he had heard, "are you sure?"

"Quite sure," affirmed Emery emphatically. "Dumoulin brought news of it to the Emperor at Elba several months ago, and you know that he and his Bonapartist Club always have plenty of spies in and around the préfecture. The money is there," he reiterated with still greater emphasis, "now the question is how are we going to get hold of it."

24

"Easily," rejoined de Marmont with his habitual enthusiasm, "when the Emperor marches into Grenoble and the whole of the garrison rallies around him, he can go straight to the Hôtel de Ville and take everything that he wants."

"Always supposing that M. le préfet does not anticipate the Emperor's coming by conveying the money to Paris or elsewhere before we can get hold of it," quoth Emery drily.

"Oh! Fourier is not sufficiently astute for that."

"Perhaps not. But we must not neglect possibilities. That money would be a perfect godsend to the Emperor. It was originally his too, par Dieu! Anyhow, my good de Marmont, that is what I wanted to talk over quietly with you before I get into Grenoble. Can you think of any means of getting hold of that money in case Fourier has the notion of conveying it to some other place of safety?"

"I would like to think that over, Emery," said de Marmont thoughtfully. "As you say, we of the Bonapartist Club at Grenoble have spies inside the Hôtel de Ville. We must try and find out what Fourier means to do as soon as he realises that the Emperor is marching on Grenoble: and then we must act accordingly and trust to luck and good fortune."

"And to the Emperor's star," rejoined Emery earnestly; "it is once more in the ascendant. But the matter of the money is a serious one, de Marmont. You will deal with it seriously?"

"Seriously!" ejaculated de Marmont.

Once more the unquenchable fire of undying devotion to his hero glowed in the young man's eyes.

"Everything pertaining to the Emperor," he said fervently, "is serious to me. For a whim of his I would lay down my life. I will think of all you have told me, Emery, and here, beneath the blue dome of God's sky, I swear that I will get the Emperor the money that he wants or lose mine honour and my life in the attempt.

"Amen to that," rejoined Emery with a deep sigh of satisfaction. "You are a brave man, de Marmont, would to heaven every Frenchman was like you. And now," he added with sudden transition to a lighter mood, "let Annette dish up the fricandeau. Here's our friend the tradesman, who was born to be a soldier. M. Clyffurde," he added loudly, calling to the Englishman who had just appeared in the doorway of the inn, "my grateful thanks to you—not only for your courtesy, but for expediting that delicious déjeuner which tickles my appetite so pleasantly. I pray you sit down without delay. I shall have to make an early start after the meal, as I must be inside Grenoble before dark."

Clyffurde, good-humoured, genial, quiet as usual, quickly responded to the surgeon-captain's desire. He took his seat once more at the table and spoke of the weather and the sunshine, the Alps and the snows the while Annette spread a cloth and laid plates and knives and forks before the distinguished gentlemen.

"We all want to make an early start, eh, my dear Clyffurde?" ejaculated de Marmont gaily. "We have serious business to transact this night with M. le Comte de Cambray, and partake too of his gracious hospitality, what?"

Emery laughed.

"Not I forsooth," he said. "M. le Comte would as soon have Satan or Beelzebub inside his doors. And I marvel, my good de Marmont, that you have succeeded in keeping on such friendly terms with that royalist ogre."

"I?" said de Marmont, whose inward exultation radiated from his entire personality, "I, my dear Emery? Did you not know that I am that royalist ogre's future son-in-law? Par Dieu! but this is a glorious day for me as well as a glorious day for France! Emery, dear friend, wish me joy and happiness. On Tuesday I wed Mademoiselle Crystal de Cambray—to-night we sign our marriage contract! Wish me joy, I say! she's a bride well worth the winning! Napoleon sets forth to conquer a throne—I to conquer love. And you, old sober-face, do not look so glum!" he added, turning to Clyffurde.

And his ringing laugh seemed to echo from end to end of the narrow valley.

After which a lighter atmosphere hung around the table outside the "Auberge du Grand Dauphin." There was but little talk of the political situation, still less of party hatred and caste prejudices. The hero's name was still on the lips of the two men who worshipped him, and Clyffurde, faithful to his attitude of detachment from political conflicts, listened quite unmoved to the impassioned dithyrambs of his friends.

But so absorbed were these two in their conversation and their joy that they failed to notice that Clyffurde hardly touched the excellent déjeuner set before him and left mine host's fine Burgundy almost untasted.

CHAPTER II
THE OLD REGIME

I

On that same day and at about the same time when Victor de Marmont and his English friend first turned their horses up the bridle path and sighted Notre Dame de Vaulx (when, if you remember, the young Frenchman drew rein and fell to apostrophising the hamlet, the day, the hour and the glorious news which he was expecting to hear) at about that self-same hour, I say, in the Château de Brestalou, situate on the right bank of the Isère at a couple of kilomètres from Grenoble, the big folding doors of solid mahogany which lead from the suite of vast reception rooms to the small boudoir beyond were thrown open and Hector appeared to announce that M. le Comte de Cambray would be ready to receive Mme. la Duchesse in the library in a quarter of an hour.

Mme. la Duchesse douairière d'Agen thereupon closed the gilt-edged, much-bethumbed Missal which she was reading—since this was Sunday and she had been unable to attend Mass owing to that severe twinge of rheumatism in her right knee—and placed it upon the table close to her elbow; then with delicate, bemittened hand she smoothed out one unruly crease in her puce silk gown and finally looked up through her round, bone-rimmed spectacles at the sober-visaged, majestic personage who stood at attention in the doorway.

"Tell M. le Comte, my good Hector," she said with slow deliberation, "that I will be with him at the time which he has so graciously appointed."

Hector bowed himself out of the room with that perfect decorum which proclaims the well-trained domestic of an aristocratic house. As soon as the tall mahogany doors were closed behind him, Mme. la Duchesse took her spectacles off from her high-bred nose and gave a little sniff, which caused Mademoiselle Crystal to look up from her book and mutely to question Madame with those wonderful blue eyes of hers.

"Ah ça, my little Crystal," was Madame's tart response to that eloquent enquiry, "does Monsieur my brother imagine himself to be a second Bourbon king, throning it in the Tuileries and granting audiences to the ladies of his court? or is it only for my edification that he plays this magnificent game of etiquette and ceremonial and other stupid paraphernalia which have set me wondering since last night? M. le Comte will receive Mme. la Duchesse in a quarter of an hour

27

forsooth," she added, mimicking Hector's pompous manner; "par Dieu! I should think indeed that he would receive his own sister when and where it suited her convenience—not his."

Crystal was silent for a moment or two: and in those same expressive eyes which she kept fixed on Madame's face, the look of mute enquiry had become more insistent. It almost seemed as if she were trying to penetrate the underlying thoughts of the older woman, as if she tried to read all that there was in that kindly glance of hidden sarcasm, of humour or tolerance, or of gentle contempt. Evidently what she read in the wrinkled face and the twinkling eyes pleased and reassured her, for now the suspicion of a smile found its way round the corners of her sensitive mouth.

There are some very old people living in Grenoble at the present day whose mothers or fathers have told them that they remembered Mademoiselle Crystal de Cambray quite well in the year that M. le Comte returned from England and once more took possession of his ancestral home on the bank of the Isère, which those awful Terrorists of '92 had taken away from him. Louis XVIII., the Benevolent king, had promptly restored the old château to its rightful owner, when he himself, after years of exile, mounted the throne of his fathers, and the usurper Bonaparte was driven out of France by the armies of Europe allied against him, and sent to cool his ambitions in the island fastnesses of Elba.

Mademoiselle de Cambray was just nineteen in that year 1814 which was so full of grace for the Bourbon dynasty and all its faithful adherents, and in February of the following year she attained her twentieth birthday. Of course you know that she was born in England, and that her mother was English, for had not M. le Comte been obliged to fly before the fury of the Terrorists, whose dreaded Committee of Public Safety had already arrested him as a "suspect" and condemned him to the guillotine. He had contrived to escape death by what was nothing short of a miracle, and he had lived for twenty years in England, and there had married a beautiful English girl from whom Mademoiselle Crystal had inherited the deep blue eyes and brilliant skin which were the greatest charm of her effulgent beauty.

I like to think of her just as she was on that memorable day early in March of the year 1815—just as she sat that morning on a low stool close to Mme. la Duchesse's high-backed chair, and with her eyes fixed so enquiringly upon Madame's kind old face. Her fair hair was done up in the quaint loops and curls which characterised the mode of the moment: she had on a white dress cut low at the neck and had wrapped a soft cashmere shawl round her shoulders, for the weather was cold and there was no fire in the stately open hearth.

Having presumably arrived at the happy conclusion that Madame's wrath was only on the surface, Crystal now said gently:

"Father loves all this etiquette, ma tante; it brings back memories of a very happy past. It is the only thing he has left now," she added with a little sigh, "the only bit out of the past which that awful revolution could not take away from him. You will try to be indulgent to him, aunt darling, won't you?"

"Indulgent?" retorted the old lady with a shrug of her shoulders, "of course I'll be indulgent. It's no affair of mine and he does as he pleases. But I should have thought that twenty years spent in England would have taught him commonsense, and twenty years' experience in earning a precarious livelihood as a teacher of languages in ..."

"Hush, aunt, for pity's sake," broke in Crystal hurriedly, and she put up her hands almost as if she wished to stop the words in the old lady's mouth.

"All right! all right! I won't mention it again," said Mme. la Duchesse good-humouredly. "I have only been in this house four and twenty hours, my dear child, but I have already learned my lesson. I know that the memory of the past twenty years must be blotted right out of our minds—out of the minds of every one of us...."

"Not of mine, aunt, altogether," murmured Crystal softly.

"No, my dear—not altogether," rejoined Mme. la Duchesse as she placed one of her fine white hands on the fair head of her niece; "your beautiful mother belongs to the unforgettable memories, of those twenty years...."

"And not only my beautiful mother, aunt dear. There are men living in England to-day whose names must remain for ever engraved upon my father's heart, as well as on mine—if we should ever forget those names and neglect for one single day our prayers of gratitude for their welfare and their reward, we should be the meanest and blackest of ingrates."

"Ah!" said Madame, "I am glad that Monsieur my brother remembers all that in the midst of his restored grandeur."

"Have you been wronging him in your heart all this while, ma tante?" asked Crystal, and there was a slight tone of reproach in her voices "you used not to be so cynical once upon a time."

"Cynical!" exclaimed the Duchesse, "bless the child's heart! Of course I am cynical—at my age what can you expect?—and what can I expect? But there, don't distress yourself, I am not wronging your father—far from it—only this grandeur—the state dinner last night—his gracious manner—all that upset me. I am not used to it, my dear, you see. Twenty years in that diminutive house in Worcester have altered my tastes, I see, more than they did your father's ... and these last ten months which he seems to have spent in reviving the old grandeur of his ancestral home, I spent, remember, with the dear little Sisters of Mercy at Boulogne, praying amidst very humble surroundings that the future may not become more unendurable than the past."

"But you are glad to be back at Brestalou again? and you will

29

remain here with us—always?" queried Crystal, and with tender eagerness she clasped the older woman's hands closely in her own.

"Yes, dear," replied Madame gently. "I am glad to be back in the old château—my dear old home—where I was very happy and very young once—oh, so very long ago! And I will remain with your father and look after him all the time that his young bird is absent from the nest."

Again she stroked her niece's soft, wavy hair with a gesture which apparently was habitual with her, and it seemed as if a note of sadness had crept into her brisk, sharp voice. Over Crystal's cheeks a wave of crimson had quickly swept at her aunt's last words: and the eyes which she now raised to Madame's kindly face were full of tears.

"It seems so terribly soon now, ma tante," she said wistfully.

"Hm, yes!" quoth Mme. la Duchesse drily, "time has a knack now and then of flying faster than we wish. Well, my dear, so long as this day brings you happiness, the old folk who stay at home have no right to grumble."

Then as Crystal made no reply and held her little head resolutely away, Madame said more insistently:

"You are happy, Crystal, are you not?"

"Of course I am happy, ma tante," replied Crystal quickly, "why should you ask?"

But still she would not look straight into Madame's eyes, and the tone of Madame's voice sounded anything but satisfied.

"Well!" she said, "I ask, I suppose, because I want an answer ... a satisfactory answer."

"You have had it, ma tante, have you not?"

"Yes, my dear. If you are happy, I am satisfied. But last night it seemed to me as if your ideas of your own happiness and those of your father on the same subject were somewhat at variance, eh?"

"Oh no, ma tante," rejoined Crystal quietly, "father and I are quite of one mind on that subject."

"But your heart is pulling a different way, is that it?"

Then as Crystal once more relapsed into silence and two hot tears dropped on the Duchesse's wrinkled hands, the old woman added softly:

"St. Genis, who hasn't a sou, was out of the question, I suppose."

Crystal shook her head in silence.

"And that young de Marmont is very rich?"

"He is his uncle's heir," murmured Crystal.

"And you, child, are marrying a kinsman of that abominable Duc de Raguse in order to regild our family escutcheon."

"My father wished it so very earnestly," rejoined Crystal, who was bravely swallowing her tears, "and I could not bear to run counter to his desire. The Duc de Raguse has promised father that when I am a de Marmont he will buy back all the forfeited Cambray estates and restore them to us: Victor will be allowed to take up the name of Cambray and ... and ... Oh!" she exclaimed passionately, "father has had such a hard life, so much sorrow, so many disappointments, and now this poverty is so horribly grinding.... I couldn't have the heart to disappoint him in this!"

"You are a good child, Crystal," said Madame gently, "and no doubt Victor de Marmont will prove a good husband to you. But I wish he wasn't a Marmont, that's all."

But this remark, delivered in the old lady's most uncompromising manner, brought forth a hot protest from Crystal:

"Why, aunt," she said, "the Duc de Raguse is the most faithful servant the king could possibly wish to have. It was he and no one else who delivered Paris to the allies and thus brought about the downfall of Bonaparte, and the restoration of our dear King Louis to the throne of France."

"Tush, child, I know that," said Madame with her habitual tartness of speech, "I know it just as well as history will know it presently, and methinks that history will pass on the Duc de Raguse just about the same judgment as I passed on him in my heart last year. God knows I hate that Bonaparte as much as anyone, and our Bourbon kings are almost as much a part of my religion as is the hierarchy of saints, but a traitor like de Marmont I cannot stomach. What was he before Bonaparte made him a marshal of France and created him Duc de Raguse?—An out-at-elbows ragamuffin in the ranks of the republican army. To Bonaparte he owed everything, title, money, consideration, even the military talents which gave him the power to turn on the hand that had fed him. Delivered Paris to the allies indeed!" continued the Duchesse with ever-increasing indignation and volubility, "betrayed Bonaparte, then licked the boots of the Czar of Russia, of the Emperor, of King Louis, of all the deadly enemies of the man to whom he owed his very existence. Pouah! I hate Bonaparte, but men like Ney and Berthier and de Marmont sicken me! Thank God that even in his life-time, de Marmont, Duc de Raguse, has already an inkling of what posterity will say of him. Has not the French language been enriched since the capitulation of Paris with a new word that henceforth and for all times will always spell disloyalty: and to-day when we wish to describe a particularly loathsome type of treachery, do we not already speak of a 'ragusade'?"

Crystal had listened in silence to her aunt's impassioned tirade. Now when Madame paused—presumably for want of breath—she said gently:

"That is all quite true, ma tante, but I am afraid that father would not altogether see eye to eye with you in this. After all," she added naively, "a pagan may become converted to Christianity without being called a traitor to his false gods, and the Duc de Raguse may have

31

learnt to hate the idol whom he once worshipped, and for this profession of faith we should honour him, I think."

"Yes," grunted Madame, unconvinced, "but we need not marry into his family."

"But in any case," retorted Crystal, "poor Victor cannot help what his uncle did."

"No, he cannot," assented the Duchesse decisively, "and he is very rich and he loves you, and as your husband he will own all the old Cambray estates which his uncle of ragusade fame will buy up for him, and presently your son, my darling, will be Comte de Cambray, just as if that awful revolution and all that robbing and spoliation had never been. And of course everything will be for the best in the best possible world, if only," concluded the old lady with a sigh, "if only I thought that you would be happy."

Crystal took care not to meet Madame's kindly glance just then, for of a surety the tears would have rushed in a stream to her eyes. But she would not give way to any access of self-pity: she had chosen her part in life and this she meant to play loyally, without regret and without murmur.

"But of course, ma tante, I shall be happy," she said after a while; "as you say, M. de Marmont is very kind and good and I know that father will be happy when Brestalou and Cambray and all the old lands are once more united in his name. Then he will be able to do something really great and good for the King and for France ... and I too, perhaps...."

"You, my poor darling!" exclaimed Madame, "what can you do, I should like to know."

A curious, dreamy look came into the girl's eyes, just as if a foreknowledge of the drama in which she was so soon destined to play the chief rôle had suddenly appeared to her through the cloudy and distant veils of futurity.

"I don't know, ma tante," she said slowly, "but somehow I have always felt that one day I might be called upon to do something for France. There are times when that feeling becomes so strong that all thoughts of myself and of my own happiness fade from my knowledge, and it seems as if my duty to France and to the King were more insistent than my duty to God."

"Poor France!" sighed Madame.

"Yes! that is just what I feel, ma tante. Poor France! She has suffered so much more than we have, and she has regained so much less! Enemies still lurk around her; the prowling wolf is still at her gate: even the throne of her king is still insecure! Poor, poor France! our country, ma tante! she should be our pride, our glory, and she is weak and torn and beset by treachery! Oh, if only I could do something for France and for the King I would count myself the happiest woman on God's earth."

Now she was a woman transformed. She seemed taller and stronger. Her girlishness, too, had vanished. Her cheeks burned, her eyes glowed, her breath came and went rapidly through her quivering nostrils. Mme. la Duchesse d'Agen looked down on her niece with naive admiration.

"Hé my little Joan of Arc!" she said merrily, "par Dieu, your eloquence, ma mignonne, has warmed up my old heart too. But, please God, our dear old country will not have need of heroism again."

"I am not so sure of that, ma tante."

"You are thinking of that ugly rumour which was current in Grenoble yesterday."

"Yes!"

"If that Corsican brigand dares to set his foot again upon this land ..." began the old lady vehemently.

"Let him come, ma tante," broke in Crystal exultantly, "we are ready for him. Let him come, and this time when God has punished him again, it won't be to Elba that he will be sent to expiate his villainies!"

"Amen to that, my child," concluded Madame fervently. "And now, my dear, don't let me forget the hour of my audience. Hector will be back in a moment or two, and I must not lose any more time gossiping. But before I go, little one, will you tell me one thing?"

"Of course I will, ma tante."

"Quite frankly?"

"Absolutely."

"Well then, I want to know ... about that English friend of yours...."

"Mr. Clyffurde, you mean?" asked Crystal. "What about him?"

"I want to know, my dear, what I ought to make of this Mr. Clyffurde."

Crystal laughed lightly, and looked up with astonished, inquiring, wide-open eyes to her aunt.

"What should you want to make of him, ma tante?" she asked, wholly unperturbed under the scrutinising gaze of Madame.

"Nothing," said the Duchesse abruptly. "I have had my answer, thank you, dear."

Evidently she had no intention of satisfying the girl's obvious curiosity, for she suddenly rose from her chair, gathered her lace shawl round her shoulders, and said with abrupt transition:

"The hour for my audience is at hand. Not one minute must I keep my august brother waiting. I can hear Hector's footsteps in the corridor, and I will not have him see me in a fluster."

Crystal looked as if she would have liked to question Madame a little more closely about her former cryptic utterance, but there was something in the sarcastic twinkle of those sharp eyes which caused the young girl to refrain from too many questions, and—very wisely—she decided to hold her peace.

Madame la Duchesse threw a quick glance into the gilt-framed mirror close by. She smoothed a stray wisp of hair which had escaped from under her lace cap: she gave a tug to her fichu and a pat to her skirts. Then, as the folding doors were once more thrown open, and Hector—stiff, solemn and pompous—appeared under the lintel, Madame threw back her head in the grand manner pertaining to the old days at Versailles.

"Precede me, Hector," she said with consummate dignity, "to M. le Comte's audience chamber."

And with hands folded before her, her aristocratic head very erect, her mouth and eyes composed to reposeful majesty, she sailed out through the mahogany doors in a style which no one who had never curtsied to the Bien-aimé Monarque could possibly hope to imitate.

II

For some little while after her aunt had sailed out of the room Crystal remained where she was sitting on the low stool beside the high-backed chair just vacated by the Duchess.

Her eyes were still glowing with the enthusiasm which had excited the admiration of the older woman a while ago, and the high colour in her cheeks, the tremor of her nostrils showed that that same enthusiasm still kept her nerves on the quiver and caused the young, hot blood to course swiftly through her veins.

But something of the lightness of her mood had vanished, something of the exultant joy of the heroine had given place to the calmer resignation of the potential martyr. Gradually the colour faded from her cheeks, the light died slowly out of her eyes, and the young fair head so lately tossed triumphantly in the ardour of patriotism sunk gradually upon the still heaving breast.

Crystal was alone, and she was not ashamed to let the tears well up to her eyes. Despite her proud profession of faith the insistent longing for happiness, which is the inalienable share of youth, knocked at the portals of her heart.

Not even to the devoted aunt who had brought her up, who had known her every childish sorrow and gleaned her every childish tear, not even to her would she show what it cost her to sink her individuality, her longings, her hopes of happiness into that overwhelming sense of duty to her father's wishes and to the demands of her name, her country and her caste.

She had repeated it to herself often and often that her father had suffered so much for the sake of his convictions, had endured poverty and exile where opportunism would have dictated submission to the usurper Bonaparte and the acceptance of riches and honours at his hands, he had remained loyal in his beliefs, steadfast to his King through twenty years of misery, akin to squalor, the remembrance of which would for ever darken the rest of his life, but he had endured all that without bitterness, scarcely without a murmur. And now that twenty years of self-abnegation were at last finding their reward, now that the King had come into his own, and the King's faithful friends were being compensated in accordance with the length of the King's purse, would it not be arrant cowardice and disloyalty for her—an only child—to oppose her father's will in the ordering of her own future, to refuse the rich marriage which would help to restore dignity and grandeur to the ancient name and to the old home?

Crystal de Cambray was born in England: she had lived the whole of her life in a small provincial town in this country. But she had been brought up by her aunt, the Duchesse douairière d'Agen, and through that upbringing she had been made to imbibe from her earliest childhood all the principles of the old regime. These principles consisted chiefly of implicit obedience by the children to the parents' decrees anent marriage, of blind worship of the dignity of station, and of duty to name and caste, to king and country.

The thought would never have entered Crystal's head that she could have the right to order her own future, or to demand from life her own special brand of happiness.

Now her fate had been finally decided on by her father, and she was on the point of taking—at his wish—the irrevocable step which would bind her for ever to a man whom she could never love. But she did not think of rebellion, she had no thought of grumbling at Fate or at her father: Crystal de Cambray had English blood in her veins, the blood that makes men and women accept the inevitable with set teeth and a determination to do the right thing even if it hurts. Crystal, therefore, had no thought of rebellion; she only felt an infinity of regret for something sweet and intangible which she had hardly realised, hardly expected, which had been too elusive to be called hope, too remote to be termed happiness. She gave herself the luxury of this short outburst of tears—since nobody was near and nobody could see: there was a fearful pain in her heart while she rested her head against the cushion of the stiff high-backed chair and cried till it seemed that she never could cry again whatever sorrow life might still have in store for her.

But when that outburst of grief had subsided she dried her eyes resolutely, rose to her feet, arranged her hair in front of the mirror, and feeling that her eyes were hot and her head heavy, she turned to the tall French window, opened it and stepped out into the garden.

It had suffered from years of neglect, the shrubs grew rank and stalky, the paths were covered with weeds, but there was a slight feeling of spring in the air, the bare branches of the trees seemed swollen with the rising sap, and upon the edge of the terrace balustrade a red-breasted robin cocked its mischievous little eye upon her.

At the bottom of the garden there was a fine row of ilex, with here and there a stone seat, and in the centre an old stone fountain moss-covered and overshadowed by the hanging boughs of the huge, melancholy trees. Crystal was very fond of this avenue; she liked to sit and watch the play of sunshine upon the stone of the fountain: the melancholy quietude of the place suited her present mood. It was so strange to look on these big evergreen trees and on the havoc caused by weeds and weather on the fine carving of the fountain, and to think of their going on here year after year for the past twenty years, while that hideous revolution had devastated the whole country, while men had murdered each other, slaughtered women and children and committed every crime and every infamy which lust of hate and revenge can engender in the hearts of men. The old trees and the stone fountain had remained peaceful and still the while, unscathed and undefiled, grand, dignified and majestic, while the owner of the fine château of the gardens and the fountain and of half the province around earned a precarious livelihood in a foreign land, half-starved in wretchedness and exile.

She, Crystal, had never seen them until some ten months ago, when her father came back into his own, and leading his daughter by the hand, had taken her on a tour of inspection to show her the magnificence of her ancestral home. She had loved at once the fine old château with its lichen-covered walls, its fine portcullis and crenelated towers, she had wept over the torn tapestries, the broken furniture, the family portraits which a rough and impious rabble had wilfully damaged, she had loved the wide sweep of the terrace walls, the views over the Isère and across the mountain range to the peaks of the Grande Chartreuse, but above all she had loved this sombre row of ilex trees, the broken fountain, the hush and peace which always lay over this secluded portion of the neglected garden.

The earth was moist and soft under her feet, the cheeky robin, curious after the manner of his kind, had followed her and was flying from seat to seat ahead of her watching her every movement.

"Crystal!"

At first she thought that it was the wind sighing through the trees, so softly had her name been spoken, so like a sigh did it seem as it reached her ears.

"Crystal!"

This time she could not be mistaken, someone had called her name, someone was walking up the avenue rapidly, behind her. She would not turn round, for she knew who it was that had called and she

36

would not allow surprise to resuscitate the outward signs of regret. But she stood quite still while those hasty footsteps drew nearer, and she made a great and successful effort to keep back the tears which once more threatened to fill her eyes.

A minute later she felt herself gently drawn to the nearest stone seat, and she sank down upon it, still trying very hard to remain calm and above all not to cry.

"Oh! why, why did you come, Maurice?" she said at last, when she felt that she could look with some semblance of composure on the half-sitting, half-kneeling figure of the young man beside her. Despite her obstinate resistance he had taken her hand in his and was covering it with kisses.

"Why did you come," she reiterated pleadingly, "you must know that it is no use...."

"I can't believe it. I won't believe it," he protested passionately. "Crystal, if you really cared you would not send me away from you."

"If I really cared?" she said dully. "Maurice, sometimes I think that if you really cared you would not make it so difficult for me. Can't you see," she added more vehemently, "that every time you come you make me more wretched, and my duty seem more hard? till sometimes I feel as if I could not bear it any longer—as if in the struggle my poor heart would suddenly break."

"And because your father is so heartless ..." he began vehemently.

"My father is not heartless, Maurice," she broke in firmly, "but you must try and see for yourself how impossible it was for him to give his consent to our marriage even if he knew that my happiness was bounded by your love.... Just think it over quietly—if you had a sister who was all the world to you, would you consent to such a marriage?..."

"With a penniless, out-at-elbows, good-for-nothing, you mean?" he said, with a kind of resentful bitterness. "No! I dare say I should not. Money!" he cried impetuously as he jumped to his feet, and burying his hands in the pockets of his breeches he began pacing the path up and down in front of her. "Money! always money! Always talk of duty and of obedience ... always your father and his sorrows and his desires ... do I count for nothing, then? Have I not suffered as he has suffered? did I not live in exile as he did? Have I not made sacrifices for my king and for my ideals? Why should I suffer in the future as well as in the past? Why, because my king is powerless or supine in giving me back what was filched from my father, should that be taken from me which alone gives me incentive to live ... you, Crystal," he added as once again he knelt beside her. He encircled her shoulders with his arms, then he seized her two hands and covered them with kisses. "You are all that I want in this world. After all, we can live in poverty ... we have been brought up in poverty, you and I ... and even then it is only a question of a few years ... months, perhaps ... the King must give us back what that abominable Revolution took from us—from us who remained loyal to him and because we were loyal. My father owned rich lands in Burgundy ... the King must give those back to me ... he must ... he shall ... he will ... if only you will be patient, Crystal ... if only you will wait...."

The fiery blood of his race had rushed into Maurice de St. Genis' head. He was talking volubly and at random, but he believed for the moment everything that he said. Tears of passion and of fervour came to his eyes and he buried his head in the folds of Crystal's white gown and heavy sobs shook his bent shoulders. She, moved by that motherly tenderness which is seldom absent from a good woman's love, stroked with soothing fingers the matted hair from his hot forehead. For a while she remained silent while the paroxysm of his passionate revolt spent itself in tears, then she said quite softly:

"I think, Maurice, that in your heart you do us all an injustice—to me, to father, to yourself, even to the King. The King cannot give you that which is not his; your property—like ours—was confiscated by that awful revolutionary government because your father and mine followed their king into exile. The rich lands were sold for the benefit of the nation: the nation presumably has spent the money, but the people who bought the lands in good faith cannot be dispossessed by our King without creating bitter ill-feeling against himself, as you well know, and once more endangering his throne. Those are the facts, Maurice, against which no hot-blooded argument, no passionate outbursts can prevail. The King gave my father back this dear old castle, because it happened to have proved unsaleable, and was still on the nation's hands. Our rich lands—like yours—can never be restored to us: that hard fact has been driven into poor father's head for the past ten months, and now it has gone home at last. These grey walls, this neglected garden, a few sticks of broken furniture, a handful of money from an over-generous king's treasury is all that Fate has rescued for him from out the ashes of the past. My father is every whit as penniless as you are yourself, Maurice, as penniless as ever he was in England, when he gave French and drawing lessons to a lot of young ragamuffins in a middle-class school. But Victor de Marmont is rich, and his money—once I am his wife—will purchase back all the estates which have been in our family for hundreds of years. For my father's sake, for the sake of the name which I bear, I must give my hand to Victor de Marmont, and pray to God that some semblance of peace, the sense of duty accomplished, will compensate me for the happiness to which I shall bid good-bye to-day."

"And you are willing to be sold to young de Marmont for the price of a few acres of land!" retorted Maurice de St. Genis hotly. "Oh! it's monstrous, Crystal, monstrous! All the more monstrous as you seem quite unconscious of the iniquity of such a bargain."

"Women of our caste, Maurice," she said in her turn with a touch of bitterness, "have often before now been sacrificed for the honour of their name. Men have been accustomed to look to them for help when their own means of gilding their escutcheons have failed."

"And you are willing, Crystal, to be sold like this?" he insisted.

"My father wishes me to marry Victor de Marmont," she replied with calm dignity, "and after all that he has suffered for the honour and dignity of our name, I should deem myself craven and treacherous if I refused to obey him in this."

Maurice de St. Genis once more rose to his feet. All his vehemence, his riotous outbreak of rebellion seemed to have been smothered beneath a pall of dreary despair. His young, good-looking face appeared sombre and sullen, his restless, dark eyes wandered obstinately from Crystal's fair bent head to her stooping shoulders, to her hands, to her feet. It seemed as if he was trying to engrave an image of her upon his turbulent brain, or that he wished to force her to look on him again before she spoke the last words of farewell.

But she wouldn't look at him. She kept her head resolutely averted, looking far out over the undulating lands of Dauphiné and Savoie to where in the far distant sky the stately Alps reared their snow-crowned heads. At last, unable to bear her silence any longer, he said dully:

"Then it is your last word, Crystal?"

"You know that it must be, Maurice," she murmured in reply. "My marriage contract will be signed to-night, and on Tuesday I go to the altar with Victor de Marmont."

"And you mean to tear your love for me out of your heart?"

"Yes!"

"Were its roots a little deeper, a little stronger, you could not do it, Crystal. But they are not so deep as those of your love for your father."

She made no reply ... perhaps something in her heart told her that after all he might be right, that, unbeknown to herself even, there were tendrils of affection in her that bound her, ivylike, and so closely— to her father that even her girlish love for Maurice de St. Genis—the first hint of passion that had stirred the smooth depths of her young heart—could not tear her from that bulwark to which she clung.

"This is the last time that I shall see you, Crystal," said Maurice with a sigh, seeing that obviously she meant to allow his taunt to pass unchallenged.

"You are going away?" she asked.

"How can I stay—here, under this roof, where anon—in a few hours—Victor de Marmont will have claims upon you which, if he exercised them before me would make me wish to kill him or myself. I shall leave to-morrow—early ..." he added more quietly.

"Where will you go?"

"To Paris—or abroad—or the devil, I don't know which," he replied moodily.

39

"Father will be sorry if you go?" she murmured under her breath, for once again the tears were very insistent, and she felt an awful pain in her heart, because of the misery which she had to inflict upon him.

"Your father has been passing kind to me. He gave me a home when I was homeless, but it is not fitting that I should trespass any longer upon his hospitality."

"Have you made any plans?"

"Not yet. But the King will give me a commission. There will be some fighting now ... there was a rumour in Grenoble last night that Bonaparte had landed at Antibes, and was marching on Paris."

"A false rumour as usual, I suppose," she said indifferently.

"Perhaps," he replied.

There was silence between them for awhile after that, silence only broken by the twitter of birds wakening to the call of spring. The word "good-bye" remained unspoken: neither of them dared to say it lest it broke the barrier of their resolve.

"Will you not go now, Maurice?" said Crystal at last in pitiable pleading, "we only make each other hopelessly wretched, by lingering near one another after this."

"Yes, I will go, Crystal," he replied, and this time he really forced his voice to tones of gentleness, although his inward resentment still bubbled out with every word he spoke, "I wish I could have left this house altogether—now—at once—but your father would resent it—and he has been so kind ... I wish I could go to-day," he reiterated obstinately, "I dread seeing Victor de Marmont in this house, where the laws of chivalry forbid my striking him in the face."

"Maurice!" she exclaimed reproachfully.

"Nay! I'll not say it again: I have sufficient reason left in me, I think, to show these parvenus how we, of the old regime, bear every blow which fate chooses to deal to us. They have taken everything from us, these new men—our lives, our lands, our very means of subsistence—now they have taken to filching our sweethearts—curse them! but at least let us keep our dignity!"

But again she was silent. What was there to say that had not been said?—save that unspoken word "good-bye." And he asked very softly:

"May I kiss you for the last time, Crystal?"

"No, Maurice," she replied, "never again."

"You are still free," he urged. "You are not plighted to de Marmont yet."

"No—not actually—not till to-night...."

"Then ... mayn't I?"

"No, Maurice," she said decisively.

"Your hand then?"

"If you like." He knelt down close to her; she yielded her hand to him and he with his usual impulsiveness covered it with kisses into which he tried to infuse the fervour of a last farewell.

40

Then without another word he rose to his feet and walked away with a long and firm stride down the avenue. Crystal watched his retreating figure until the overhanging branches of the ilex hid him from her view.

She made no attempt now to restrain her tears, they flowed uninterruptedly down her cheeks and dropped hot and searing upon her hands. With Maurice's figure disappearing down the dark avenue, with the echo of his footsteps dying away in the distance, the last chapter of her first book of romance seemed to be closing with relentless finality.

The afternoon sun was hidden behind a bank of grey clouds, the northeast wind came whistling insistently through the trees:—even that feeling of spring in the air had vanished. It was just a bleak grey winter's day now. Crystal felt herself shivering with cold. She drew her shawl more closely round her shoulders, then with eyes still wet with tears, but small head held well erect, she rose to her feet and walked rapidly back to the house.

III

Madame la Duchesse had in the meanwhile followed Hector along the corridor and down the finely carved marble staircase. At a monumental door on the ground floor the man paused, his hand upon the massive ormolu handle, waiting for Madame la Duchesse to come up.

He felt a little uncomfortable at her approach for here in the big square hall the light was very clear, and he could see Madame's keen, searching eyes looking him up and down and through and through. She even put up her lorgnon and though she was not very tall, she contrived to look Hector through them straight between the eyes.

"Is M. le Comte in there?" Madame la Duchesse deigned to ask as she pointed with her lorgnon to the door.

"In the small library beyond, Madame la Duchesse," replied Hector stiffly.

"And ..." she queried with sharp sarcasm, "is the antechamber very full of courtiers and ladies just now?"

A quick, almost imperceptible blush spread over Hector's impassive countenance, and as quickly vanished again.

"M. le Comte," he said imperturbably, "is disengaged at the present moment. He seldom receives visitors at this hour."

On Madame's mobile lips the sarcastic curl became more marked. "And I suppose, my good Hector," she said, "that since M. le Comte has only granted an audience to his sister to-day, you thought it

41

was a good opportunity for putting yourself at your ease and wearing your patched and mended clothes, eh?"

Once more that sudden wave of colour swept over Hector's solemn old face. He was evidently at a loss how to take Mme. la Duchesse's remark—whether as a rebuke or merely as one of those mild jokes of which every one knew that Madame was inordinately fond.

Something of his dignity of attitude seemed to fall away from him as he vainly tried to solve this portentous problem. His mouth felt dry and his head hot, and he did not know on which foot he could stand with the least possible discomfort, and how he could contrive to hide from Madame la Duchesse's piercing eyes that very obvious patch in the right knee of his breeches.

"Madame la Duchesse will forgive me, I hope," he stammered painfully.

But already Madame's kind old face had shed its mask of raillery.

"Never mind, Hector," she said gently, "you are a good fellow, and there's no occasion to tell me lies about the rich liveries which are put away somewhere, nor about the numerous retinue and countless number of flunkeys, all of whom are having unaccountably long holidays just now. It's no use trying to throw dust in my eyes, my poor friend, or put on that pompous manner with me. I know that the carpets are not all temporarily rolled up or the best of the furniture at a repairer's in Grenoble—what's the use of pretending with me, old Hector? Those days at Worcester are not so distant yet, are they? when all the family had to make a meal off a pound of sausages, or your wife Jeanne, God bless her! had to pawn her wedding-ring to buy M. le Comte de Cambray a second-hand overcoat."

"Madame la Duchesse, I humbly pray your Grace ..." entreated Hector whose wrinkled, parchment-like face had become the colour of a peony, and who, torn between the respect which he had for the great lady and his horror at what she said was ready to sink through the floor in his confusion.

"Eh what, man?" retorted the Duchesse lightly, "there is no one but these bare walls to hear me; and my words, you'll find, will clear the atmosphere round you—it was very stifling, my good Hector, when I arrived. There now!" she added, "announce me to M. le Comte and then go down to Jeanne and tell her that I for one have no intention of forgetting Worcester, or the pawned ring, or the sausages, and that the array of Grenoble louts dressed up for the occasion in moth-eaten liveries dragged up out of some old chests do not please me half as much round a dinner table as did her dear old, streaming face when she used to bring us the omelette straight out of the kitchen."

She dropped her lorgnon, and folding her aristocratic hands upon her bosom, she once more assumed the grand manner pertaining to Versailles, and Hector having swallowed an uncomfortable lump in his throat, threw open the huge, folding doors and announced in a stentorian voice:

"Madame la Duchesse douairière d'Agen!"

IV

M. le Comte de Cambray was at this time close on sixty years of age, and the hardships which he had endured for close upon a quarter of a century had left their indelible impress upon his wrinkled, careworn face.

But no one—least of all a younger man—could possibly rival him in dignity of bearing and gracious condescension of manner. He wore his clothes after the old-time fashion, and clung to the powdered peruque which had been the mode at the Tuileries and Versailles before these vulgar young republicans took to wearing their own hair in its natural colour.

Now as he advanced from the inner room to meet Mme. la Duchesse, he seemed a perfect presentation or rather resuscitation of the courtly and vanished epoch of the Roi Soleil. He held himself very erect and walked with measured step, and a stereotyped smile upon his lips. He paused just in front of Mme. la Duchesse, then stopped and lightly touched with his lips the hand which she held out to him.

"Tell me, Monsieur my brother," said Madame in her loudly-pitched voice, "do you expect me to make before you my best Versailles curtsey, for—with my rheumatic knee—I warn you that once I get down, you might find it very difficult to get me up on my feet again."

"Hush, Sophie," admonished M. le Comte impatiently, "you must try and subdue your voice a little, we are no longer in Worcester remember—"

But Madame only shrugged her thin shoulders.

"Bah!" she retorted, "there's only good old Hector on the other side of the door, and you don't imagine you are really throwing dust in his eyes do you? ... good old Hector with his threadbare livery and his ill-fed belly...."

"Sophie!" exclaimed M. le Comte who was really vexed this time, "I must insist...."

"All right, all right my dear André.... I won't say anything more. Take me to your audience chamber and I'll try to behave like a lady."

A smile that was distinctly mischievous still hovered round Madame's lips, but she forced her eyes to look grave: she held out the tips of her fingers to her brother and allowed him to lead her in the correct manner into the next room.

Here M. le Comte invited her to sit in an upright chair which was placed at a convenient angle close to his bureau while he himself sat upon a stately throne-like armchair, one shapely knee bent, the other slightly stretched forward, displaying the fine silk stocking and the set of his well-cut, satin breeches. Mme. la Duchesse kept her hands folded in front of her, and waited in silence for her brother to speak, but he seemed at a loss how to begin, for her piercing gaze was making him feel very uncomfortable: he could not help but detect in it the twinkle of good-humoured sarcasm.

Madame of course would not help him out. She enjoyed his obvious embarrassment, which took him down somewhat from that high altitude of dignity wherein he delighted to soar.

"My dear Sophie," he began at last, speaking very deliberately and carefully choosing his words, "before the step which Crystal is about to take to-day becomes absolutely irrevocable, I desired to talk the matter over with you, since it concerns the happiness of my only child."

"Isn't it a little late, my good André," remarked Madame drily, "to talk over a question which has been decided a month ago? The contract is to be signed to-night. Our present conversation might have been held to some purpose soon after the New Year. It is distinctly useless to-day."

At Madame's sharp and uncompromising words a quick blush had spread over the Comte's sunken cheeks.

"I could not consult you before, Sophie," he said coldly, "you chose to immure yourself in a convent, rather than come back straightaway to your old home as we all did when our King was restored to his throne. The post has been very disorganised and Boulogne is a far cry from Brestalou, but I did write to you as soon as Victor de Marmont made his formal request for Crystal's hand. To this letter I had no reply, and I could not keep him waiting in indefinite uncertainty."

"Your letter did not reach me until a month after it was written, as I had the honour to tell you in my reply."

"And that same reply only reached me a fortnight ago," retorted the Comte, "when Crystal had been formally engaged to Victor de Marmont for over a month and the date for the signature of the contract and the wedding-day had both been fixed. I then sent a courier at great expense and in great haste immediately to you," he added with a tone of dignified reproach, "I could do no more."

"Or less," she assented tartly. "And here I am, my dear brother, and I am not blaming you for delays in the post. I merely remarked that it was too late now to consult me upon a marriage which is to all intents and purposes, an accomplished fact already."

"That is so of course. But it would be a great personal satisfaction to me, my good Sophie, to hear your views upon the matter. You have brought Crystal up from babyhood: in a measure, you know her better than even I—her father—do and therefore you are better able than I am to judge whether Crystal's marriage with de Marmont will be conducive to her permanent happiness."

"As to that, my good André," quoth Madame, "you must remember that when our father and mother decided that a marriage between me and M. le Duc d'Agen was desirable, my personal feelings and character were never consulted for a moment ... and I suppose that—taking life as it is—I was never particularly unhappy as his wife."

"And what do you adduce from those reminiscences, my dear Sophie?" queried the Comte de Cambray suavely.

"That Victor de Marmont is not a bad fellow," replied Madame, "that he is no worse than was M. le Duc d'Agen and that therefore there is no reason to suppose that Crystal will be any more unhappy than I was in my time."

"But ..."

"There is no 'but' about it, my good André. Crystal is a sweet girl and a devoted daughter. She will make the best, never you fear! of the circumstances into which your blind worship of your own dignity and of your rank have placed her."

"My good Sophie," broke in the Count hotly, "you talk par Dieu, as if I was forcing my only child into a distasteful marriage."

"No, I do not talk as if you were forcing Crystal into a distasteful marriage, but you know quite well that she only accepted Victor de Marmont because it was your wish, and because his millions are going to buy back the old Cambray estates, and she is so imbued with the sense of her duty to you and to the family escutcheon, that she was willing to sacrifice every personal feeling in the fulfilment of that duty."

"By 'personal feeling' I suppose that you mean St. Genis."

"Well, yes ... I do," said Madame laconically.

"Crystal was very much in love with him at one time."

"She still is."

"But even you, my dear sister, must admit that a marriage with St. Genis was out of the question," retorted the Count in his turn with some acerbity. "I am very fond of Maurice and his name is as old and great as ours, but he hasn't a sou, and you know as well as I do by now that the restoration of confiscated lands is out of the question ... parliament will never allow it and the King will never dare...."

"I know all that, my poor André," sighed Madame in a more conciliatory spirit, "I know moreover that you yourself haven't a sou either, in spite of your grandeur and your prejudices.... Money must be got somehow, and our ancient family 'scutcheon must be regilt at any cost. I know that we must keep up this state pertaining to the old regime, we must have our lacqueys and our liveries, sycophants around us and gaping yokels on our way when we sally out into the open.... We must blot out from our lives those twenty years spent in a democratic and enlightened country where no one is ashamed either of poverty or of honest work—and above all things we must forget that there has ever been a revolution which sent M. le Comte de Cambray, Commander of the Order of the Holy Ghost, Grand Cross of the Ordre du Lys, Seigneur of Montfleury and St. Eynard, hereditary Grand Chamberlain of France, to teach French and drawing in an English Grammar School...."

"You wrong me there, Sophie, I wish to forget nothing of the past twenty years."

"I thought that you had given your memory a holiday."

"I forget nothing," he reiterated with dignified emphasis, "neither the squalid poverty which I endured, nor the bitter experiences which I gleaned in exile."

"Nor the devotion of those who saved your life."

"And yours ..." he interposed.

"And mine, at risk of their own."

"Perhaps you will believe me when I tell you that not a day goes by but Crystal and I speak of Sir Percy Blakeney, and of his gallant League of the Scarlet Pimpernel."

"Well! we owe our lives to them," said Madame with deep-drawn sigh. "I wonder if we shall ever see any of those fine fellows again!"

"God only knows," sighed M. le Comte in response. "But," he continued more lightly, "as you know the League itself has ceased to be. We saw very little of Sir Percy and Lady Blakeney latterly for we were too poor ever to travel up to London. Crystal and I saw them, before we left England, and I then had the opportunity of thanking Sir Percy Blakeney for the last time, for the many valuable French lives which his plucky little League had saved."

"He is indeed a gallant gentleman," said Mme. la Duchesse gently, even whilst her bright, shrewd eyes gazed straight out before her as if on the great bare walls of her own ancestral home, the ghostly hand of memory had conjured up pictures of long ago:—her own, her husband's and her brother's arrest here in this very room, the weeping servants, the rough, half-naked soldiery—then the agony of a nine days' imprisonment in a dark, dank prison-cell filled to overflowing with poor wretches in the same pitiable plight as herself—the hasty trial, the insults, the mockery:—her husband's death in prison and her own thoughts of approaching death!

Then the gallant deed!—after all these years she could still see herself, her brother and Jeanne, her faithful maid, and poor devoted Hector all huddled up in a rickety tumbril, being dragged through the streets of Paris on the road to death. On ahead she had seen the weird outline of the guillotine silhouetted against the evening sky, whilst all around her a howling, jeering mob sang that awful refrain: "Cà ira! Cà ira! les aristos à la lanterne!"

Then it was that she had felt unseen hands snatching her out of the tumbril, she had felt herself being dragged through that yelling

46

crowd to a place where there was silence and darkness and where she knew that she was safe: thence she was conveyed—she hardly realised how—to England, where she and her brother and Jeanne and Hector, their faithful servants, had found refuge for over twenty years.

"It was a gallant deed!" whispered Mme. la Duchesse once again, "and one which will always make me love every Englishman I meet, for the sake of one who was called The Scarlet Pimpernel."

"Then why should you attribute vulgar ingratitude to me?" retorted the Comte reproachfully. "My feelings I imagine are as sensitive as your own. Am I not trying my best to be kind to that Mr. Clyffurde, who is an honoured guest in my house—just because it was Sir Percy Blakeney who recommended him to me?"

"It can't be very difficult to be kind to such an attractive young man," was Mme. la Duchesse's dry comment. "Recommendation or no recommendation I liked your Mr. Clyffurde and if it were not so late in the day and there was still time to give my opinion, I should suggest that Mr. Clyffurde's money could quite well regild our family 'scutcheon. He is very rich too, I understand."

"My good Sophie!" exclaimed the Comte in horror, "what can you be thinking of?"

"Crystal principally," replied the Duchesse. "I thought Clyffurde a far nicer fellow than de Marmont."

"My dear sister," said the Comte stiffly, "I really must ask you to think sometimes before you speak. Of a truth you make suggestions and comments at times which literally stagger one."

"I don't see anything so very staggering in the idea of a penniless aristocrat marrying a wealthy English gentleman...."

"A gentleman! my dear!" exclaimed the Comte.

"Well! Mr. Clyffurde is a gentleman, isn't he?"

"His family is irreproachable, I believe."

"Well then?"

"But ... Mr. Clyffurde ... you know, my dear...."

"No! I don't know," said Madame decisively. "What is the matter with Mr. Clyffurde?"

"Well! I didn't like to tell you, Sophie, immediately on your arrival yesterday," said the Comte, who was making visible efforts to mitigate the horror of what he was about to say: "but ... as a matter of fact ... this Mr. Clyffurde whom you met in my house last night ... who sat next to you at my table ... with whom you had that long and animated conversation afterwards ... is nothing better than a shopkeeper!"

No doubt M. le Comte de Cambray expected that at this awful announcement, Mme. la Duchesse's indignation and anger would know no bounds. He was quite ready even now with a string of apologies which he would formulate directly she allowed him to speak. He certainly felt very guilty towards her for the undesirable acquaintance

47

which she had made in her brother's own house. Great was his surprise therefore when Madame's wrinkled face wreathed itself into a huge smile, which presently broadened into a merry laugh, as she threw back her head, and said still laughing:

"A shopkeeper, my dear Comte? A shopkeeper at your aristocratic table? and your meal did not choke you? Why! God forgive you, but I do believe you are actually becoming human."

"I ought to have told you sooner, of course," began the Comte stiffly.

"Why bless your heart, I knew it soon enough."

"You knew it?"

"Of course I did. Mr. Clyffurde told me that interesting fact before he had finished eating his soup."

"Did he tell you that ... that he traded in ... in gloves?"

"Well! and why not gloves?" she retorted. "Gloves are very nice things and better manufactured at Grenoble than anywhere else in the world. The English coquettes are very wise in getting their gloves from Grenoble through the good offices of Mr. Clyffurde."

"But, my dear Sophie ... Mr. Clyffurde buys gloves here from Dumoulin and sells them again to a shop in London ... he buys and sells other things too and he does it for profit...."

"Of course he does.... You don't suppose that any one would do that sort of thing for pleasure, do you? Mr. Clyffurde," continued Madame with sudden seriousness, "lost his father when he was six years old. His mother and four sisters had next to nothing to live on after the bulk of what they had went for the education of the boy. At eighteen he made up his mind that he would provide his mother and sisters with all the luxuries which they had lacked for so long and instead of going into the army—which had been the burning ambition of his boyhood—he went into business ... and in less than ten years has made a fortune."

"You seem to have learnt a great deal of the man's family history in so short a time."

"I liked him: and I made him talk to me about himself. It was not easy, for these English men are stupidly reticent, but I dragged his story out of him bit by bit—or at least as much of it as I could—and I can tell you, my good André, that never have I admired a man so much as I do this Mr. Clyffurde ... for never have I met so unselfish a one. I declare that if I were only a few years younger," she continued whimsically, "and even so ... heigh! but I am not so old after all...."

"My dear Sophie!" ejaculated the Comte.

"Eh, what?" she retorted tartly, "you would object to a tradesman as a brother-in-law, would you? What about a de Marmont for a son? Eh?"

"Victor de Marmont is a soldier in the army of our legitimate King. His uncle the Duc de Raguse...."

48

"That's just it," broke in Madame again, "I don't like de Marmont because he is a de Marmont."

"Is that the only reason for your not liking him?"

"The only one," she replied. "But I must say that this Mr. Clyffurde ..."

"You must not harp on that string, Sophie," said the Comte sternly. "It is too ridiculous. To begin with Clyffurde never cared for Crystal, and, secondly, Crystal was already engaged to de Marmont when Clyffurde arrived here, and, thirdly, let me tell you that my daughter has far too much pride in her ever to think of a shopkeeper in the light of a husband even if he had ten times this Mr. Clyffurde's fortune."

"Then everything is comfortably settled, André. And now that we have returned to our sheep, and have both arrived at the conclusion that nothing stands in the way of Crystal's marriage with Victor de Marmont, I suppose that I may presume that my audience is at an end."

"I only wished to hear your opinion, my good Sophie," rejoined M. le Comte. And he rose stiffly from his chair.

"Well! and you have heard it, André," concluded Madame as she too rose and gathered her lace shawl round her shoulders. "You may thank God, my dear brother, that you have in Crystal such an unselfish and obedient child, and in me such a submissive sister. Frankly—since you have chosen to ask my opinion at this eleventh hour—I don't like this de Marmont marriage, though I have admitted that I see nothing against the young man himself. If Crystal is not unhappy with him, I shall be content: if she is, I will make myself exceedingly disagreeable, both to him and to you, and that being my last word, I have the honour to wish you a polite 'good-day.'"

She swept her brother an imperceptibly ironical curtsey, but he detained her once again, as she turned to go.

"One word more, Sophie," he said solemnly. "You will be amiable with Victor de Marmont this evening?"

"Of course I will," she replied tartly. "Ah, ça, Monsieur my brother, do you take me for a washerwoman?"

"I am entertaining the préfet for the souper du contrat," continued the Comte, quietly ignoring the old lady's irascibility of temper, "and the general in command of the garrison. They are both converted Bonapartists, remember."

"Hm!" grunted Madame crossly, "whom else are you going to entertain?"

"Mme. Fourier, the préfet's wife, and Mlle. Marchand, the general's daughter, and of course the d'Embruns and the Genevois."

"Is that all?"

"Some half dozen or so notabilities of Grenoble. We shall sit down twenty to supper, and afterwards I hold a reception in honour of the coming marriage of Mlle. de Cambray de Brestalou with M. Victor de Marmont. One must do one's duty...."

"And pander to one's love of playing at being a little king in a limited way.... All right! I won't say anything more. I promise that I won't disgrace you, and that I'll put on a grand manner that will fill those worthy notabilities and their wives with awe and reverence. And now, I'd best go," she added whimsically, "ere my good resolutions break down before your pomposity ... I suppose the louts from the village will be again braced up in those moth-eaten liveries, and the bottles of thin Médoc purchased surreptitiously at a local grocer's will be duly smothered in the dust of ages.... All right! all right! I'm going. For gracious' sake don't conduct me to the door, or I'll really disgrace you under Hector's uplifted nose.... Oh! shades of cold beef and treacle pies of Worcester ... and washing-day ... do you remember? ... all right! all right, Monsieur my brother, I am dumb as a carp at last."

And with a final outburst of sarcastic laughter, Madame finally sailed across the room, while Monsieur fell back into his throne-like chair with a deep sigh of relief.

CHAPTER III

THE RETURN OF THE EMPEROR

I

But even as Madame la Duchesse douairière d'Agen placed her aristocratic hand upon the handle of the door, it was opened from without with what might almost be called undue haste, and Hector appeared in the doorway.

Hector in truth! but not the sober-faced, pompous, dignified Hector of the household of M. le Comte de Cambray, but a red-visaged, excited, fussy Hector, who for the moment seemed to have forgotten where he was, as well as the etiquette which surrounded the august personality of his master. He certainly contrived to murmur a humble if somewhat hasty apology, when he found himself confronted at the door by Mme. la Duchesse herself, but he did not stand aside to let her pass.

She had stepped back into the room at sight of him, for obviously something very much amiss must have occurred thus to ruffle Hector's

50

ingrained dignity, and even M. le Comte was involuntarily dragged out of his aristocratic aloofness and almost—though not quite—jumped up from his chair.

"What is it, Hector?" he exclaimed, peremptorily.

"M. le Comte," gasped Hector, who seemed to be out of breath from sheer excitement, "the Corsican ... he has come back ... he is marching on Grenoble ... M. le préfet is here! ..."

But already M. le Comte had—with a wave of the hand as it were—swept the unwelcome news aside.

"What rubbish is this?" he said wrathfully. "You have been dreaming in broad daylight, Hector ... and this excitement is most unseemly. Show Mme. la Duchesse to her apartments," he added with a great show of calm.

Hector—thus reproved, coloured a yet more violent crimson to the very roots of his hair. He made a great effort to recover his pomposity and actually took up the correct attitude which a well-trained servant assumes when he shows a great lady out of a room. But even then—despite the well-merited reproof—he took it upon himself to insist:

"M. le préfet is here, M. le Comte," he said, "and begs to be received at once."

"Well, then, you may show him up when Mme. la Duchesse has retired," said the Comte with quiet dignity.

"By your leave, my brother," quoth the Duchesse decisively, "I'll wait and hear what M. le préfet has to say. The news—if news there be—is too interesting to be kept waiting for me."

And accustomed as she was to get her own way in everything, Mme. la Duchesse calmly sailed back into the room, and once more sat down in the chair beside her brother's bureau, whilst Hector with as much grandeur of mien as he could assume under the circumstances was still waiting for orders.

M. le Comte would undoubtedly have preferred that his sister should leave the room before the préfet was shown in: he did not approve of women taking part in political conversations, and his manner now plainly showed to Mme. la Duchesse that he would like to receive M. le préfet alone. But he said nothing—probably because he knew that words would be useless if Madame had made up her mind to remain, which she evidently had, so, after a brief pause, he said curtly to Hector:

"Show M. le préfet in."

He took up his favourite position, in his throne-shaped chair—one leg bent, the other stretched out, displaying to advantage the shapely calf and well-shod foot. M. le préfet Fourier, mathematician of great renown, and member of the Institut was one of those converted Bonapartists to whom it behoved at all times to teach a lesson of decorum and dignity.

51

And certainly when, presently Hector showed M. Fourier in, the two men—the aristocrat of the old regime and the bureaucrat of the new—presented a marked and curious contrast. M. le Comte de Cambray calm, unperturbed, slightly supercilious, in a studied attitude and moving with pompous deliberation to greet his guest, and Jacques Fourier, man of science and préfet of the Isère department, short of stature, scant of breath, flurried and florid!

Both men were conscious of the contrast, and M. Fourier did his very best to approach Mme. la Duchesse with a semblance of dignity, and to kiss her hand in something of the approved courtly manner. When he had finally sat down, and mopped his streaming forehead, M. le Comte said with kindly condescension:

"You are perturbed, my good M. Fourier!"

"Alas, M. le Comte," replied the worthy préfet, still somewhat out of breath, "how can I help being agitated ... this awful news! ..."

"What news?" queried the Comte with a lifting of the brows, which was meant to convey complete detachment and indifference to the subject matter.

"What news?" exclaimed the préfet who, on the other hand, was unable to contain his agitation and had obviously given up the attempt, "haven't you heard? ..."

"No," replied the Comte.

And Madame also shook her head.

"Town-gossip does not travel as far as the Castle of Brestalou," added M. le Comte gravely.

"Town gossip!" reiterated M. Fourier, who seemed to be calling Heaven to witness this extraordinary levity, "town gossip, M. le Comte! ... But God in Heaven help us all. Bonaparte landed at Antibes five days ago. He was at Sisteron this morning, and unless the earth opens and swallows him up, he will be on us by Tuesday!"

"Bah! you have had a nightmare, M. le préfet," rejoined the Comte drily. "We have had news of the landing of Bonaparte at least once a month this half-year past."

"But it is authentic news this time, M. le Comte," retorted Fourier, who, gradually, under the influence of de Cambray's calm demeanour, had succeeded in keeping his agitation in check. "The préfet of the Var department, M. le Comte de Bouthillier, sent an express courier on Thursday last to the préfet of the Basses-Alpes, who sent that courier straight on to me, telling me that he and General Loverdo, who is in command of the troops in that district, promptly evacuated Digue because they were not certain of the loyalty of the garrison. The Corsican it seems only landed with about a thousand of his old guard, but since then, the troops in every district which he has traversed, have deserted in a body, and rallied round his standard. It has been, so I hear, a triumphal march for him from the Littoral to Digne, and altogether the news which the courier brought me this morning was of such alarming nature, that I thought it my duty, M. le Comte, to apprise you of it immediately."

"That," said M. le Comte condescendingly, "was exceedingly thoughtful and considerate, my good M. Fourier. And what is the alarming news?"

"Firstly, that Bonaparte made something like a state entry into Digne yesterday. The city was beflagged and decorated. The national guard turned out and presented arms, drums were beating, the population acclaimed him with cries of 'Vive l'Empereur!' The préfet and the general in command had intended to resist his entry into the city, but all the notabilities of the town forced them into submission. Duval, the préfet, fled to a neighbouring village, taking the public funds with him, while General Loverdo with a mere handful of loyal troops has retreated on Sisteron."

Though M. le Comte de Cambray had listened to the préfet's narrative with all his habitual grandeur of mien, it soon became obvious that some of his aristocratic sangfroid had already abandoned him. His furrowed cheeks had become a shade paler than usual, and the slender hand which toyed with an ivory paper-knife on his desk had not its wonted steadiness. Mme. la Duchesse perceived this, no doubt, for her keen eyes were fixed scrutinisingly upon her brother; she saw too that his thin lips were quivering and that the reason why he made no comment on what he had just heard was because he could not quite trust himself to speak. It was she, therefore, who now remarked quietly:

"And in your department, M. le préfet, in Grenoble itself, is the garrison equally likely to go over to the Corsican brigand?"

M. Fourier shrugged his shoulders. He was not at all sure.

"After what has happened at Digne, Mme. la Duchesse," he said, "I would not care to prophesy. Général Marchand does not intend to trust entirely to the garrison. He has sent to Vienne and to Chambéry for reinforcements ... but ..."

The préfet was hesitating, evidently he had not a great deal of faith in the loyalty of those reinforcements either.

M. le Comte made a vigorous protest. "Surely, M. Fourier," he said, "you don't mean to suggest that Grenoble is going to turn traitor to the King?"

But M. le préfet apparently had meant to suggest it.

"Alas, M. le Comte!" he said, "we must always bear in mind that the whole of the Dauphiné has remained throughout a bed of Bonapartism."

"But in that case ..." ejaculated the Comte.

"Général Marchand is doing all he can to ensure effectual resistance, M. le Comte. But we are in the hands of the army, and the army has never been truly loyal to the King. At the bottom of every soldier's haversack there is an old and worn tricolour cockade, which is there ready to be fetched out at a moment's notice, and will be fetched out at the mere sound of the Corsican's voice. We are in the hands of the army, M. le Comte, and in the Dauphiné; alas! the army is only too ready to cry: 'Vive l'Empereur!'"

There was silence in the stately room now, silence only broken by the tap-tap of the ivory paper-knife with which M. le Comte was still nervously fidgeting. M. Fourier was wiping the perspiration from his overheated brow.

"For God's sake, André, stop that irritating noise," said Mme. Duchesse after awhile, "that tapping has got on my nerves."

"I beg your pardon, Sophie," said the Comte loftily.

He was offended with her for drawing M. Fourier's attention to his own nervous restlessness, yet grateful to be thus forcibly made aware of it himself. His attitude was on the verge of incorrectness. Where was the aristocratic sangfroid which should have made him proof even against so much perturbing news? What had become of the lesson in decorum which should have been taught to this vulgar little bureaucrat?

M. le Comte pulled himself together with a jerk: he straightened out his spare figure, put on that air of detachment which became him so well, and finally turned once more to the préfet a perfectly calm and unruffled countenance.

Then he said with his accustomed urbanity:

"And now, my good M. Fourier, since you have so admirably put the situation before me, will you also tell me in what way I may be of service to you in this—or to Général Marchand?"

"I am coming to that, M. le Comte," replied the préfet. "It will explain the reason of my disturbing you at this hour, when I was coming anyhow to partake of your gracious hospitality later on. But I do want your assistance, M. le Comte, as the matter of which I wish to speak with you concerns the King himself."

"Everything that you have told me hitherto, my good M. Fourier, concerns His Majesty and the security of his throne. I cannot help wondering how much of this news has reached him by now."

"All of it at this hour, I should say. For already on Friday the Prince d'Essling sent a despatch to His Majesty—by courier as far as Lyons and thence by aërial telegraph to Paris. The King—may God preserve him!" added the ex-Bonapartist fervently, "knows as much of the Corsican's movements at the present moment as we do; and God alone knows what he will decide to do."

"Whatever happens," interjected the Comte de Cambray solemnly, "Louis de Bourbon, XVIIIth of his name, by the Grace of God, will act like a king and a gentleman."

"Amen to that," retorted the préfet. "And now let me come to my point, M. le Comte, and the chief object of my visit to you."

"I am at your service, my dear M. Fourier."

54

"You will remember, M. le Comte, that directly you were installed at Brestalou and I was confirmed in my position as préfet of this department, I thought it was my duty to tell you of the secret funds which are kept in the cellars of our Hôtel de Ville by order of M. de Talleyrand."

"Yes, of course I remember that perfectly. French money, which the unfortunate wife of that brigand Bonaparte was taking out of the country."

"Quite so," assented Fourier. "The funds are in a convenient and portable form, being chiefly notes and bankers' drafts to bearer, but the amount is considerable, namely, twenty-five millions of francs."

"A comfortable sum," interposed Mme. la Duchesse drily. "I did not know that Grenoble sheltered so vast a treasure."

"The money was seized," said the Comte, "from Marie Louise when she was fleeing the country. Talleyrand did it all, and it was his idea to keep the money in this part of the country against likely emergencies."

"But the emergency has arisen," exclaimed M. Fourier excitedly, "and the money at Grenoble is useless to His Majesty in Paris. Nay! it is worse than useless, it is in danger of spoliation," he added with unconscious naiveté. "If the Corsican marches into Grenoble, if the garrison and the townspeople rally to him, he will of a truth occupy the Hôtel de Ville and the brigand will seize the King's treasure which lies now in one of its cellars."

"True," mused the Comte, "I hadn't thought of that."

"Well!" exclaimed Madame with light sarcasm, "seeing that the money was originally taken from his wife, the brigand will not be committing an altogether unlikely act, I imagine, by taking what was originally his."

"His, my good Sophie?" exclaimed the Comte, highly shocked. "Money robbed by that usurper from France—his?"

"We won't argue, André," said Madame sharply, "let us hear what M. le préfet proposes."

"Propose, Mme. la Duchesse," ejaculated the unfortunate préfet, "I have nothing to propose! I am at my wits' end what to do! I came to M. le Comte for advice."

"And you were quite right, my dear M. Fourier," said the Comte affably.

He paused for a few seconds in order to collect his thoughts, then continued: "Now let us consider this question from every side, and then see to what conclusion we can arrive that will be for the best. Firstly, of course, there is the possibility of your following the example of the préfet of the Basses-Alpes and taking yourself and the money to a convenient place outside Grenoble."

But at this suggestion M. Fourier was ready to burst into tears.

"Impossible, M. le Comte," he cried pitiably, "I could not do it....

Where could I go? ... The existence of the money is known ... known to the Bonapartists, I am convinced.... There's Dumoulin, the glovemaker, he knows everything that goes on in Grenoble ... and his friend Emery, who is an army surgeon in the pay of Bonaparte ... both these men have been to and from Elba incessantly these past few months ... then there's the Bonapartist club in Grenoble ... with a membership of over two thousand ... the members have friends and spies everywhere ... even inside the Hôtel de Ville ... why! the other day I had to dismiss a servant who ..."

"Easy, easy, M. le préfet," broke in M. le Comte impatiently, "the long and the short of it is that you would not feel safe with the money anywhere outside Grenoble."

"Or inside it, M. le Comte."

"Very well, then, the money must be deposited there, where it will be safe. Now what do you think of Dupont's Bank?"

"Oh, M. le Comte! an avowed Bonapartist! ... M. de Talleyrand would not trust him with the money last year."

"That is so ... but ..."

"It seems to me," here interposed Mme. la Duchesse abruptly, "that by far the best plan—since this district seems to be a hot-bed of disloyalty—would be to convey the money straightway to Paris, and then the King or M. de Talleyrand can dispose of it as best they like."

"Ah, Mme. la Duchesse," sighed M. Fourier ecstatically as he clasped his podgy little hands together and looked on Madame with eyes full of admiration for her wisdom, "how cleverly that was spoken! If only I could be relieved from that awful responsibility ... five and twenty millions under my charge and that Corsican ogre at our gates!..."

"That is all very well!" quoth the Comte with marked impatience, "but how is it going to be done? 'Convey the money to Paris' is easily said. But who is going to do it? M. le préfet here says that the Bonapartists have spies everywhere round Grenoble, and ..."

"Ah, M. le Comte!" exclaimed the préfet eagerly. "I have already thought of such a beautiful plan! If only you would consent ..."

M. le Comte's thin lips curled in a sarcastic smile.

"Oh! you have thought it all out already, M. le préfet?" he said. "Well! let me hear your plan, but I warn you that I will not have the money brought here. I don't half trust the peasantry of the neighbourhood, and I won't have a fight or an outrage committed in my house!"

M. le préfet was ready with a protest:

"No, no, M. le Comte!" he said, "I wouldn't suggest such a thing for the world. If the Corsican brigand is successful in capturing Grenoble, no place would be sacred to him. No! My idea was if you, M. le Comte—who have oft before journeyed to Paris and back—would do it now ... before Bonaparte gets any nearer to Grenoble ... and take the money with you ..."

"I?" exclaimed the Comte. "But, man, if—as you say—Grenoble is full of Bonapartist spies, my movements are no doubt just as closely watched as your own."

"No, no, M. le Comte, not quite so closely, I am sure."

The insinuating manner of the worthy man, however, was apparently getting on M. le Comte's nerves.

"Ah, ça, M. le préfet," he ejaculated abruptly, "but meseems that the splendid plan you thought on merely consists in transferring responsibility from your shoulders to mine own."

And M. le Comte cast such a wrathful look on poor M. Fourier that the unfortunate man was stricken dumb with confusion.

"Moreover," concluded the Comte, "I don't know that you, M. le préfet, have the right to dispose of this money which was entrusted to you by M. de Talleyrand in the King's behalf without consulting His Majesty's wishes in the matter."

"Bah, André," broke in the Duchesse in her incisive way, "you are talking nonsense, and you know it. There is no time for red-tapeism now with that ogre at our gates. How are you going to consult His Majesty's wishes—who is in Paris—between now and Tuesday, I would like to know?" she added with a shrug of the shoulders.

Whereupon M. le Comte waxed politely sarcastic.

"Perhaps," he said, "you would prefer us to consult yours."

"You might do worse," she retorted imperturbably. "The question is one which is very easily solved. Ought His Majesty the King to have that money, or should M. le préfet here take the risk of its falling in Bonaparte's hands? Answer me that," she said decisively, "and then I will tell you how best to succeed in carrying out your own wishes."

"What a question, my good Sophie!" said the Comte stiffly. "Of course we desire His Majesty to have what is rightfully his."

"You mean he ought to have the twenty-five millions which the Prince de Bénévant stole from Marie Louise. Very well then, obviously that money ought to be taken to Paris before Bonaparte gets much nearer to Grenoble—but it should not be taken by you, my good André, nor yet by M. le préfet."

"By whom then?" queried the Comte irritably.

"By me," replied Mme. la Duchesse.

"By you, Sophie! Impossible!"

"And God alive, why impossible, I pray you?" she retorted. "The money, I understand, is in a very portable form, notes and bankers' drafts, which can be stowed away quite easily. Why shouldn't I be journeying back to Paris after Crystal's wedding? Who would suspect me, I should like to know, of carrying twenty-five millions under my petticoats? All I should want would be a couple of sturdy fellows on the box to protect me against footpads. Impossible?" she continued tartly.

"Men are always so ready with that word. Get a sensible woman, I say, and she will solve your difficulties before you have finished exclaiming: 'Impossible!'"

And she looked triumphantly from one man to the other. There was obvious relief on the ruddy face of little M. Fourier, and even M. le Comte was visibly taken with the idea.

"Well!" he at last condescended to say, "it does sound feasible after all."

"Feasible? Of course it's feasible," said Madame with a shrug of contempt. "Either the King is in want of the money, or he is not. Either Bonaparte is likely to get it or he is not. If the King wants it, he must have it at any cost and any risk. Twenty-five millions in Bonaparte's hands at this juncture would help him to reconstitute his army and make it very unpleasant for the King and for us all. M. le préfet, who has been in charge of the money all along, and M. le Comte de Cambray, who is the only true royalist in the district, are both marked down by spies: ergo Mme. la Duchesse d'Agen is the only possible agent for the business, and an inoffensive old woman without any political standing is the least likely to be molested in her task. If I fail, I fail," concluded Madame decisively, "if I am stopped on the way and the money taken from me, well! I am stopped, that's all! and M. le préfet or M. le Comte de Cambray or any male agent they may have sent would have been stopped likewise. But I maintain that a woman travelling alone is far safer at this business and more likely to succeed than a man. So now, for God's sake, don't let's argue any more about it. Crystal is to be married on Tuesday and I could start that same afternoon. Can you bring the money over with you to-night?"

She put her query directly to the préfet, who was obviously overjoyed, and intensely relieved at the suggestion.

M. le Comte too seemed to be won over by his sister's persuasive rhetoric: her strength of mind and firmness of purpose always imposed themselves on those over whom she chose to exert her will: and men of somewhat weak character like the Comte de Cambray came very easily under the sway of her dominating personality.

But he thought it incumbent upon his dignity to make one more protest before he finally yielded to his sister's arguments.

"I don't like," he said, "the idea of your travelling alone through the country without sufficient escort. The roads are none too safe and..."

"Bah!" broke in Madame impatiently. "I pray you, Monsieur my brother, to strengthen your arguments, if you are really determined to oppose this sensible scheme of mine. Travelling alone, forsooth! Did I not arrive only yesterday, having travelled all the way from Boulogne and with no escort save two louts on the box of a hired coach?"

"You chose to travel alone, my dear sister, for reasons best known to yourself," retorted the Comte, greatly angered that M. le préfet should hear the fact that Mme. la Duchesse douairière had travelled at any time without an escort.

"And who shall say me nay, if I choose to travel back alone again, I should like to know? So now if you have exhausted your string of objections, my dear brother, perhaps you will allow M. le préfet to answer my question."

Whereupon M. le préfet promptly satisfied Mme. la Duchesse on the point: he certainly could and would bring the money over with him this evening. And M. le Comte had no further objections to offer.

In the archives of the Ministry of War in Paris, any one who looks may read that in the subsequent trial of Général Marchand for high treason—after the Hundred Days and Napoleon's second abdication—préfet Fourier during the course of his evidence gave a detailed account of this same interview which he had with M. le Comte de Cambray and Mme. la Duchesse douairière d'Agen on Sunday, March the 5th. In his deposition he naturally laid great stress upon his own zeal in the matter, declaring that he it was who finally overcame by his eloquence M. le Comte's objections to the scheme and decided him to give his acquiescence thereto.[1]

Certain it is that there was but little argument after this between Mme. la Duchesse and the two men, and that the details of the scheme were presently discussed soberly and in all their bearings.

"I shall have the honour presently," said Fourier, "of coming back here to respond to M. le Comte's gracious invitation to dinner. Why shouldn't I bring the money with me then?"

"Indeed you must bring the money then," retorted the irascible old lady, "and let there be no shirking or delay. Promptitude is our great chance of success. I ought not to start later than Tuesday, and I could do so soon after the wedding ceremony. I could arrange to sleep at Lyons that night, at Dijon the next day, be in Paris by Thursday evening and in the King's presence on Friday."

"Provided you are not delayed," sighed the Comte.

"If I am delayed, my good André, then anyhow the game is up. But we are not going to anticipate misfortune and we are going to believe in our lucky star."

"Would to God I could bring myself to approve wholeheartedly of this expedition! The whole thing seems to me chivalrous and romantic rather than prudent, and Heaven knows how prudent we should be just now!"

"You look back on history, my dear brother," remarked Madame drily, "and you'll see that more great events have been brought about by chivalry and romance than by prudence and circumspection. The

---

[1] Déposition de Fourier. (Dossier de Marchant Arch. Guerre.)

romance of Joan of Arc delivered France from foreign yoke, the chivalry of François I. saved the honour of France after the disaster of Pavie, and it certainly was not prudence which set Henry of Navarre upon the throne of France and in the heart of his people. So for gracious' sake do not let us talk of prudence any more. Rather let us allow M. le préfet to return quietly to the Hôtel de Ville, so that he and Mme. Fourier may proceed to dress for to-night's ceremony, just as if nothing untoward had happened. In the meanwhile I will complete my preparations for Tuesday. There are one or two little details in connection with my journey—hostelries, servants, horses and so on—which you, my dear André, will kindly decide for me. And now, gentlemen," she added, rising from her chair, "I have the honour to wish you both a very good afternoon."

She did not wait long enough to allow M. le Comte time to ring for Hector, and she appeared so busy with her lace shawl that she was unable to do more than acknowledge with a slight inclination of the head M. le préfet's respectful salute. But then Mme. la Duchesse douairière d'Agen—though a fervent royalist herself—had a wholesome contempt for these opportunists. Fourier, celebrated mathematician, loaded with gifts and honours by Napoleon, who had made him a member of the Institute of Science and given him the prefecture of the Isère, had turned his coat very readily at the Restoration, and the oaths of loyalty which he had tendered to the Emperor seemed not to weigh overheavily upon his conscience when he reiterated them to the King.

Mme. la Duchesse d'Agen, therefore, did not willingly place her aristocratic fingers in the hand of a renegade, who she felt might turn renegade again if his personal interest so dictated it. Perhaps something of what lay behind Madame's curt nod to him, struck the préfet's sensibilities, for the high colour suddenly fled from his round face, and he did not attempt to approach her for the ceremonial hand-kissing. But he ran across the room as fast as his short legs would carry him, and he opened the door for her and bowed to her as she sailed past him with all the deference which in the olden days of the Empire he had accorded to the Empress Marie Louise.

"It is a mad scheme, my good M. Fourier," sighed the Comte when he found himself once more alone with the préfet, "but such as it is I can think of nothing better."

"M. le Comte," exclaimed the préfet with delight, "no one could think of anything better. Ah, the women of France!" he added ecstatically, "the women! how often have they saved France in moments of crises? France owes her grandeur to her women, M. le Comte!"

"And also her reverses, my dear M. Fourier," remarked the Comte drily.

When Bobby Clyffurde came back to Brestalou, after his long day's ride, he found the stately rooms of the old castle already prepared for the arrival of M. le Comte's guests. The large reception hall had been thrown open, as—after supper—M. le Comte would be receiving some of the notabilities of Grenoble in honour of a great occasion: the signature of the contrat de mariage between Mlle. Crystal de Cambray de Brestalou and M. Victor de Marmont. There was an array of liveried servants in the hall and along the corridor through which Bobby had to pass on the way to his own room: their liveries of purple with canary facings—the heraldic colours of the family of Cambray de Brestalou— hardly showed, in the flickering light of wax candles, the many ravages of moth and mildew which twenty years of neglect had wrought upon the once fine and brilliant cloth.

Downstairs the formal supper which was to precede the reception was laid for twenty guests. The table was resplendent with the silver so kindly lent by a benevolent and far-seeing king to those of his friends who had not the means of replacing the ancient family treasures filched from them by the revolutionary government.

There were no flowers upon the table, and only very few wax candles burned in the ormolu and crystal chandelier overhead. Flowers and wax candles were luxuries which must be paid for with ready money—a commodity which was exceedingly scarce in the grandiose Château de Brestalou—but they also were a luxury which could easily be dispensed with, for did not M. le Comte de Cambray set the fashions and give the tone to the whole département? and if he chose to have no flowers upon his supper table and but few candles in his silver sconces, why then society must take it for granted that such now was bon ton and the prevailing fashion at the Tuileries.

Bobby, knowing his host's fastidious tastes in such matters, had made a very careful toilet, all the while that his thoughts were busy with the wonderful news which Emery had brought this day, and which was all over Grenoble by now. He and his two companions had left Notre Dame de Vaulx soon after their déjeuner, and together had entered the city at five o'clock in the afternoon. On their way they had encountered the travelling-coach of Général Mouton-Duveret, who, accompanied by his aide-de-camp, was on his way to Gap, where he intended to organise strong resistance against Bonaparte.

He parleyed some time with Emery, whom he knew by sight and suspected of being an emissary of the Corsican. Emery, with true southern verve, gave the worthy general a highly-coloured account of the triumphal progress through Provence and the Dauphiné of

Napoleon, whom he boldly called "the Emperor." Mouton—in no way belying his name—was very upset not only by the news, but by his own helplessness with regard to Emery, who he knew would presently be in Grenoble distributing the usurper's proclamations all over the city, whilst he—Mouton—with his one aide-de-camp and a couple of loutish servants on the box of his coach, could do nothing to detain him.

As soon as the three men had ridden away, however, he sent his aide-de-camp back to Grenoble by a round-about way, ordering him to make as great speed as possible, and to see Général Marchand as soon as may be, so that immediate measures might be taken to prevent that emissary if not from entering the city, at least from posting up proclamations on public buildings.

But Mouton's aide-de-camp was no match against the enthusiasm and ingenuity of Emery and de Marmont, and when he—in his turn—entered Grenoble soon after five o'clock, he was confronted by the printed proclamations signed by the familiar and dreaded name "Napoleon" affixed to the gates of the city, to the Hôtel de Ville, the mairie, the prison, the barracks, and to every street corner in Grenoble.

The three friends had parted at the porte de Bonne, Emery to go to his friend Dumoulin, the glovemaker—de Marmont to his lodgings in the rue Montorge, whilst Bobby Clyffurde rode straight back to Brestalou.

A couple of hours later Victor de Marmont had also arrived at the castle. He too had made an elaborate toilet, and then had driven over in a hackney coach in advance of the other guests, seeing that he desired to have a final interview with M. le Comte before he affixed his name to his contrat de mariage with Mlle. de Cambray. An air of solemnity sat well upon his good-looking face, but it was obvious that he was trying—somewhat in vain—to keep an inward excitement in check.

M. le Comte de Cambray, believing that this excitement was entirely due to the solemnity of the occasion, had smiled indulgently—a trifle contemptuously too—at young de Marmont's very apparent eagerness. A vulgar display of feelings, an inability to control one's words and movements when under the stress of emotion was characteristic of the parvenus of to-day, and de Marmont's unfettered agitation when coming to sign his own marriage contract was only on a par with préfet Fourier's nervousness this afternoon.

The Comte received his future son-in-law with a gracious smile. The thought of an alliance between Mlle. de Cambray de Brestalou and a de Marmont of Nowhere had been a bitter pill to swallow, but M. le Comte was too proud to show how distasteful it had been. Chatting pleasantly the two men repaired together to the library.

III

Bobby Clyffurde—immaculately dressed in fine cloth coat and satin breeches, with fine Mechlin lace at throat and wrist, and his light brown hair tied at the nape of the neck with a big black bow—came down presently to the reception room. He found the place silent and deserted.

But the stately apartment looked more cosy and home-like than usual. A cheerful fire was burning in the monumental hearth and the soft light of the candles fixed in sconces round the walls tempered to a certain degree that bare and severe look of past grandeur which usually hung upon every corner of the old château.

Clyffurde went up to the tall hearth. He rested his hand on the ledge of the mantel and leaning his forehead against it he stared moodily into the fire.

Thoughts of all that he had learned in the past few hours, of the new chapter in the book of the destinies of France, begun a few days ago in the bay of Jouan, crowded in upon his mind. What difference would the unfolding of that new chapter make to the destinies of the Comte de Cambray and of Crystal? What had Fate in store for the bold adventurer who was marching across France with a handful of men to reconquer a throne and remake an empire? what had she in store for the stiff-necked aristocrat of the old regime who still believed that God himself had made special laws for the benefit of one class of humanity, and that He had even created them differently to the rest of mankind?

And what had Fate in store for the beautiful, delicate girl whose future had been so arbitrarily settled by two men—father and lover— one the buyer, the other the seller of her exquisite person, the shrine of her pure and idealistic soul—and bargained for by father and lover as the price of so many acres of land—a farm—a château—an ancestral estate?

Father and lover were sitting together even now discussing values—the purchase price—"You give me back my lands, I will give you my daughter!" Blood money! soul money! Clyffurde called it as he ground his teeth together in impotent rage.

What folly it was to care! what folly to have allowed the tendrils of his over-sensitive heart to twine themselves round this beautiful girl, who was as far removed from his destiny as were the ambitions of his boyhood, the hopes, the dreams which the hard circumstances of fate had forced him to bury beneath the grave-mound of rigid and unswerving duty.

But what a dream it had been, this love for Crystal de Cambray! It had filled his entire soul from the moment when first he saw her— down in the garden under an avenue of ilex trees which cast their mysterious shadows over her; her father had called to her and she had come across to where he—Clyffurde—stood silently watching this approaching vision of loveliness which never would vanish from his mental gaze again.

Even at that supreme moment, when her blue eyes, her sweet smile, the exquisite grace of her took possession of his soul, even then he knew already that his dream could have but one awakening. She was already plighted to another, a happier man, but even if she were free, Crystal would never have bestowed a thought upon the stranger—the commonplace tradesman, whose only merit in her sight lay in his friendship with another gallant English gentleman.

And knowing this—when he saw her after that, day after day, hour after hour—poor Bobby Clyffurde grew reconciled to the knowledge that the gates of his Paradise would for ever be locked against him: he grew contented just to peep through those gates; and the Angel who was on guard there, holding the flaming sword of caste prejudice against him, would relent at times and allow him to linger on the threshold and to gaze into a semblance of happiness.

Those thoughts, those dreams, those longings, he had been able to endure; to-day reality had suddenly become more insistent and more stern: the Angel's flaming sword would sear his soul after this, if he lingered any longer by the enchanted gates: and thus had the semblance of happiness yielded at last to dull regret.

He sank into a chair and buried his face in his hands.

IV

The sound of the opening and shutting of a door, the soft frou-frou of a woman's skirt roused him from his gloomy reverie, and caused him to jump to his feet.

Mlle. Crystal was coming across the long reception room, walking with a slow and weary step toward the hearth. She was obviously not yet aware of Clyffurde's presence, and he had full leisure to watch her as she approached, to note the pallor of her cheeks and lips and that pathetic look of childlike self-pity and almost of appeal which veiled the brilliance of her deep blue eyes.

A moment later she saw him and came more quickly across the room, with hand extended, and an air of gracious condescension in her whole attitude.

"Ah! M. Clyffurde," she said in perfect English, "I did not know you were here ... and all alone. My father," she added, "is occupied with serious matters downstairs, else he would have been here to receive you."

"I know, Mademoiselle," he said after he had kissed the tips of three cold little fingers which had been held out to him. "My friend de Marmont is with him just now: he desired to speak with M. le Comte in private ... on a matter which closely concerns his happiness."

"Ah! then you knew?" she asked coldly.

"Yes, Mademoiselle, I knew," he replied.

She had settled herself down in a high-backed chair close to the hearth, the ruddy light of the wood-fire played upon her white satin gown, upon her bare arms, and the ends of her lace scarf, upon her satin shoes and the bunch of snowdrops at her breast, but her face was in shadow and she did not look up at Clyffurde, whilst he—poor fool!—stood before her, absorbed in the contemplation of this dainty picture which mayhap after to-night would never gladden his eyes again.

"You are a great friend of M. de Marmont?" she asked after a while.

"Oh, Mademoiselle—a friend?" he replied with a self-deprecatory shrug of the shoulders, "friendship is too great a name to give to our chance acquaintanceship. I met Victor de Marmont less than a fortnight ago, in Grenoble...."

"Ah yes! I had forgotten—he told me that he had first met you at the house of a M. Dumoulin ..."

"In the shop of M. Dumoulin, Mademoiselle," broke in Clyffurde with his good-humoured smile. "M. Dumoulin, the glovemaker, with whom I was transacting business at the moment when M. de Marmont walked in, in order to buy himself a pair of gloves."

"Of course," she added coldly, "I had forgotten...."

"You were not likely to remember such a trivial circumstance, Mademoiselle. M. de Marmont saw me after that here as guest in your father's house. He was greatly surprised at finding me—a mere tradesman—in such an honoured position. Surprise laid the foundation of pleasing intercourse between us, but you see, Mademoiselle, that M. de Marmont has no cause to boast of his friendship with me."

"Oh! M. de Marmont is not so prejudiced...."

"As you are, Mademoiselle?" he asked quietly, for she had paused and he saw that she bit her lips with her tiny white teeth as if she meant to check the words that would come tumbling out.

Thus directly questioned she gave a little shrug of disdain.

"My opinions in the matter are not in question, Sir," she said coldly.

She smothered a little yawn which may have been due to ennui, but also to the tingling of her nerves. Clyffurde saw that her hands were never still for a moment; she was either fingering the snowdrops in her belt or smoothing out the creases in her lace scarf; from time to time she raised her head and a tense expression came into her face, as if she were trying to listen to what was going on elsewhere in the house—downstairs perhaps—in the library where she was being finally bargained for and sold.

Clyffurde felt an intense—an unreasoning pity for her, and because of that pity—the gentle kinsman of fierce love—he found it in his heart to forgive her all her prejudices, that almost arrogant pride of caste which was in her blood, for which she was no more responsible than she was for the colour of her hair or the vivid blue of her eyes; she seemed so forlorn—such a child, in the midst of all this decadent grandeur. She was being so ruthlessly sacrificed for ideals that were no longer tenable, that had ceased to be tenable five and twenty years ago when this château and these lands were overrun by a savage and vengeful mob, who were loudly demanding the right to live in happiness, in comfort, and in freedom. That right had been denied to them through the past centuries by those who were of her own kith and kin, and it was snatched with brutal force, with lust of hate and thirst for reprisals, by the revolutionary crowd when it came into its own at last.

Something of the pity which he felt for this beautiful and innocent victim of rancour, oppression and prejudice, must have been manifest in Clyffurde's earnest eyes, for when Crystal looked up to him and met his glance she drew herself up with an air of haughty detachment. And with that, she wished to convey still more tangibly to him the idea of that barrier of caste which must for ever divide her from him.

Obviously his look of pity had angered her, for now she said abruptly and with marked coldness:

"My father tells me, Sir, that you are thinking of leaving France shortly."

"Indeed, Mademoiselle," he replied, "I have trespassed too long as it is on M. le Comte's gracious hospitality. My visit originally was only for a fortnight. I thought of leaving for England to-morrow."

A little lift of the eyebrows, an unnecessary smoothing of an invisible crease in her gown and Crystal asked lightly:

"Before the ... my wedding, Sir?"

"Before your wedding, Mademoiselle."

She frowned—vaguely stirred to irritation by his ill-concealed indifference. "I trust," she rejoined pointedly, "that you are satisfied with your trade in Grenoble."

The little shaft was meant to sting, but if Bobby felt any pain he certainly appeared to bear it with perfect good-humour.

"I am quite satisfied," he said. "I thank you, Mademoiselle."

"It must be very pleasing to conclude such affairs satisfactorily," she continued.

"Very pleasing, Mademoiselle."

"Of course—given the right temperament for such a career—it must be so much more comfortable to spend one's life in making money—buying and selling things and so on—rather than to risk it every day for the barren honour of serving one's king and country."

66

"As you say, Mademoiselle," he said quite imperturbably, "given the right temperament, it certainly is much more comfortable."

"And you, Sir, I take it, are the happy possessor of such a temperament."

"I suppose so, Mademoiselle."

"You are content to buy and to sell and to make money? to rest at ease and let the men who love their country and their king fight for you and for their ideals?"

Her voice had suddenly become trenchant and hard, her manner contemptuous—at strange variance with the indifferent kindliness wherewith she had hitherto seemed to regard her father's English guest. Certainly her nerves—he thought—were very much on edge, and no doubt his own always unruffled calm—the combined product of temperament, nationality and education—had an irritating effect upon her. Had he not been so intensely sorry for her, he would have resented this final taunt of hers—an arrow shot this time with intent to wound.

But as it was he merely said with a smile:

"Surely, Mademoiselle, my contentment with my own lot, and any other feelings of which I may be possessed, are of such very little consequence—seeing that they are only the feelings of a very commonplace tradesman—that they are not worthy of being discussed."

Then as quickly her manner changed: the contemptuous look vanished from her eyes, the sarcastic curl from her lips, and with one of those quick transitions of mood which were perhaps the principal charm of Crystal de Cambray's personality, she looked up at Bobby with a winning smile and an appeal for forgiveness.

"Your pardon, Sir," she said softly. "I was shrewish and ill-tempered, and deserve a severe lesson in courtesy. I did not mean to be disagreeable," she added with a little sigh, "but my nerves are all a-quiver to-day and this awful news has weighed upon my spirit...."

"What awful news, Mademoiselle?" he asked.

"Surely you have heard?"

"You mean the news about Napoleon ... ?"

"I mean the awful certainty," she retorted with a sudden outburst of vehemence, "that that brigand, that usurper, that scourge of mankind has escaped from an all too lenient prison where he should never have been confined, seeing how easy was escape from it. I mean that all the horrors of the past twenty years will begin again now, misery, starvation, exile probably. Oh, surely," she added with ever-increasing passion, "surely God will not permit such an awful thing to happen; surely he will strike the ogre dead, ere he devastates France once again!"

"I am afraid that you must not reckon quite so much on divine interference, Mademoiselle. A nation—like every single individual—

must shape its own destiny, and must not look to God to help it in its political aims."

"And France must look once more to England, I suppose. It is humiliating to be always in need of help," she said with an impatient little sigh.

"Each nation in its turn has it in its power to help a sister. Sometimes help may come from the weaker vessel. Do you remember the philosopher's fable of the lion and the mouse? France may be the mouse just now—some day it may be in her power to requite the lion."

She shook her head reprovingly. "I don't know," she said, "that I approve of your calling France—the mouse."

"I only did so in order to drive my parable still further home."

Then as she looked a little puzzled, he continued—speaking very slowly this time and with an intensity of feeling which was quite different to his usual pleasant, good-tempered, oft-times flippant manner: "Mademoiselle Crystal—if you will allow me to speak of such an insignificant person as I am—I am at present in the position of the mouse with regard to your father and yourself—the lions of my parable. You might so easily have devoured me, you see," he added with a quaint touch of humour. "Well! the time may come when you may have need of a friend, just as I had need of one when I came here—a stranger in a strange land. Events will move with great rapidity in the next few days, Mademoiselle Crystal, and the mouse might at any time be in a position to render a service to the lion. Will you remember that?"

"I will try, Monsieur," she replied.

But already her pride was once more up in arms. She did not like his tone, that air of protection which his attitude suggested. And indeed she could not think of any eventuality which would place the Comte de Cambray de Brestalou in serious need of a tradesman for his friend.

Then as quickly again her mood softened and as she raised her eyes to his he saw that they were full of tears.

"Indeed! indeed!" she said gently, "I do deserve your contempt, Sir, for my shrewishness and vixenish ways. How can I—how can any of us—afford to turn our backs upon a loyal friend? To-day too, of all days, when that awful enemy is once more at our gates! Oh!" she added, clasping her hands together with a sudden gesture of passionate entreaty, "you are English, Sir—a friend of all those gallant gentlemen who saved my dear father and his family from those awful revolutionaries—you will be loyal to us, will you not? The English hate Bonaparte as much as we do! you hate him too, do you not? you will do all you can to help my poor father through this awful crisis? You will, won't you?" she pleaded.

"Have I not already offered you my humble services, Mademoiselle?" he rejoined earnestly.

Indeed this was a very serious ordeal for quiet, self-contained Bobby Clyffurde—an Englishman, remember—with all an Englishman's

68

shyness of emotion, all an Englishman's contempt of any display of sentiment. Here was this beautiful girl—whom he loved with all the passionate ardour of his virile, manly temperament—sitting almost at his feet, he looking down upon her fair head, with its wealth of golden curls, and into her blue eyes which were full of tears.

Who shall blame him if just then a desperate longing seized him to throw all prudence, all dignity and honour to the winds and to clasp this exquisite woman for one brief and happy moment in his arms—to forget the world, her position and his—to risk disgrace and betray hospitality, for the sake of one kiss upon her lips? The temptation was so fierce—indeed for one short second it was all but irresistible—that something of the battle which was raging within his soul became outwardly visible, and in the girl's tear-dimmed eyes there crept a quick look of alarm—so strange, so ununderstandable was his glance, the rigidity of his attitude—as if every muscle had become taut and every nerve strained to snapping point, while his face looked hard and lined, almost as if he were fighting physical pain.

V

Thus a few seconds went by in absolute silence—while the great gilt clock upon its carved bracket ticked on with stolid relentlessness, marking another minute—and yet another—of this hour which was so full of portent for the destinies of France. Clyffurde would gladly have bartered the future years of his life for the power to stay the hand of Time just now—for the power to remain just like this, standing before this beautiful woman whom he loved, feeling that at any moment he could take her in his arms and kiss her eyes and her lips, even if she were unwilling, even if she hated him for ever afterwards.

The sense of power to do that which he might regret to the end of his days was infinitely sweet, the power to fight against that all-compelling passion was perhaps sweeter still. Then came the pride of victory. The habits of a lifetime had come to his aid: self-respect and self-control, hard and wilful taskmasters, fought against passion, until it yielded inch by inch.

The battle was fought and won in those few moments of silence: the strain of the man's attitude relaxed, the set lines on his face vanished, leaving it serene and quietly humorous, calm and self-deprecatory. Only his voice was not quite so steady as usual, as he said softly:

"Mademoiselle Crystal, is there anything that I can do for you?—now at once, I mean? If there is, I do entreat you most earnestly to let me serve you."

69

Had the pure soul of the woman been touched by the fringe of that magnetic wave of passion even as it rose to its utmost height, nearly sweeping the man off his feet, and in its final retreat leaving him with quivering nerves and senses bruised and numb? Did something of the man's suffering, of his love and of his despair appear—despite his efforts—upon his face and in the depth of his glance?—and thus made visible did they—even through their compelling intensity—cause that invisible barrier of social prejudices to totter and to break? It were difficult to say. Certain it is that Crystal's whole heart warmed to the stranger as it had never warmed before. She felt that here was a man standing before her now, whose promises would never be mere idle words, whose deeds would speak more loudly than his tongue. She felt that in the midst of all the enmity which encompassed her and her father in their newly regained home and land, here at any rate was a friend on whom they could count to help, to counsel and to accomplish. And deep down in the very bottom of her soul there was a curious unexplainable longing that circumstances should compel her to ask one day for his help, and a sweet knowledge that that help would be ably rendered and pleasing to receive.

But for the moment, of course, there was nothing that she could ask: she would be married in a couple of days—alas! so soon!—and after that it would be to her husband that she must look for devotion, for guidance and for sympathy.

A little sigh of regret escaped her lips, and she said gently:

"I thank you, Sir, from the bottom of my heart, for the words of friendship which you have spoken. I shall never forget them, never! and if at any time in my life I am in trouble ..."

"Which God forbid!" he broke in fervently.

"If any time I have need of a friend," she resumed, "I feel that I should find one in you. Oh! if only I could think that you would extend your devotion to my poor country, and to our King ..." she exclaimed with passionate earnestness.

"You love your country very dearly, Mademoiselle," he rejoined.

"I think that I love France more than anything else in the world," she replied, "and I feel that there is no sacrifice which I would deem too great to offer up for her."

"And by France you mean the Bourbon dynasty," he said almost involuntarily, and with an impatient little sigh.

"I mean the King, by the grace of God!" she retorted proudly.

She had thrown back her head with an air of challenge as she said this, meeting his glance eye to eye: she looked strong and wilful all of a sudden, no longer girlish and submissive. And to the man who loved her, this trait of power and latent heroism added yet another to the many charms which he saw in her. Loyal to her country and to her king she would be loyal in all things—to husband, kindred and to friends.

70

But he realised at the same time how impossible it would be for any man to win her love if he were an enemy to her cause. St. Genis—royalist, émigré, retrograde like herself—had obviously won his way to her heart chiefly by the sympathy of his own convictions. But what of de Marmont, to whom she was on the eve of plighting her troth? de Marmont the hot-headed Bonapartist who owned but one god—Napoleon—and yet had deliberately, and with cynical opportunism hidden his fanatical aims and beliefs from the woman whom he had wooed and won?

The thought of that deception—and of the awakening which would await the girl-wife on the very morrow of her wedding-day mayhap, was terribly repellent to Clyffurde's straightforward, loyal nature, and bitter was the contention within his soul as he found himself at the cross-roads of a divided duty. Every instinct of chivalry towards the woman loudly demanded that he should warn her—now—at once—before it was too late—before she had actually pledged her life and future to a man whom her very soul—if she knew the truth—would proclaim a renegade and a traitor; and every instinct of loyalty to the man—that male solidarity of sex which will never permit one man—if he be a gentleman—to betray another—prompted him to hold his peace.

Crystal's gentle voice fell like dream-tones upon his ear. Vaguely only did he hear what she said. She was still speaking of France, of all that the country had suffered and all that was due to her from her sons and daughters: she spoke of the King, God's own anointed as she called him, endowed with rights divine, and all the while his thoughts were far away, flying on the wings of memory to the little hamlet among the mountains where two enthusiasts had exhausted every panegyric in praise of their own hero, whom this girl called a usurper and a brigand. He remembered every trait in de Marmont's face, every inflexion of his voice as he said with almost cruel cynicism: "She will learn to love me in time."

That, Clyffurde knew now, Crystal de Cambray would never do. Indifferent to de Marmont to-day, she would hate and loathe him the day that she discovered how infamously he had deceived her: and to Clyffurde's passionate temperament the thought of Crystal's future unhappiness was absolutely intolerable.

Here indeed was a battle far more strenuous and difficult of issue than that of a man's will against his passions: here was a problem far more difficult to solve than any that had assailed Bobby Clyffurde throughout his life.

His heart cried out "She must know the truth: she must. To-day! this minute, while there was yet time! Anon she will be pledged irrevocably to a man who has lied to her, whom she will curse as a renegade, a traitor, false to his country, false to his king!"

And the words hovered on his lips: "Mademoiselle Crystal! do

71

not plight your troth to de Marmont! he is no friend of yours, his people are not your people! his God is not your God! and there is neither blessing nor holiness in an union 'twixt you and him!"

But the words remained unspoken, because the unwritten code—the bond 'twixt man and man—tried to still this natural cry of his heart and reason argued that he must hold his peace. His heart rebelled, contending that to remain silent was cowardly—that his first duty was to the woman whom he loved better than his soul, whilst ingrained principles, born and bred in the bone of him, threw themselves into the conflict, warning him that if he spoke he would be no better than an informer, meriting the contempt alike of those whom he wished to help and of the man whom he would betray.

It was one sound coming from below which settled the dispute 'twixt heart and reason—the sound of de Marmont's voice which though he was apparently speaking of indifferent matters had that same triumphant ring in it which Clyffurde had heard at Notre Dame de Vaulx this morning.

The sound had caused Crystal to give a quick gasp and to clasp her hands against her breast, as she said with a nervous little laugh:

"Imagine how happy we are to have M. de Marmont's support in this terrible crisis! His influence in Grenoble and in the whole province is very great: his word in the town itself may incline the whole balance of public feeling on the side of the King, and who knows, it may even help to strengthen the loyalty of the troops. Oh! that Corsican brigand little guesses what kind of welcome we in the Dauphiné are preparing for him!"

Her enthusiasm, her trust, her loyalty ended the conflict in Clyffurde's mind far more effectually than any sober reasoning could have done. He realised in a moment that neither abstract principles, nor his own feelings in the matter, were of the slightest account at such a juncture.

What was obvious, certain, and not to be shirked, was duty to a woman who was on the point of being shamefully deceived, also duty to the man whose hospitality he had enjoyed. To remain silent would be cowardly—of that he became absolutely certain, and once Bobby had made up his mind what duty was no power on earth could make him swerve from its fulfilment.

"Mlle. Crystal," he began slowly and deliberately, "just now, when I was bold enough to offer you my friendship, you deigned to accept it, did you not?"

"Indeed I did, Sir," she replied, a little astonished. "Why should you ask?"

"Because the time has come sooner than I expected for me to prove the truth of that offer to you. There is something which I must say to you which no one but a friend ought to do. May I?"

But before she could frame the little "Yes!" which already

72

trembled on her lips, her father's voice and de Marmont's rang out from the further end of the room itself.

The folding doors had been thrown open: M. le Comte and his son-in-law elect were on the point of entering and had paused for a moment just under the lintel. De Marmont was talking in a loud voice and apparently in response to something which M. le Comte had just told him.

"Ah!" he said, "Mme. la Duchesse will be leaving Brestalou? I am sorry to hear that. Why should she go so soon?"

"An affair of business, my dear de Marmont," replied the Comte. "I will tell you about it at an early opportunity."

After which there was a hubbub of talk in the corridors outside, the sound of greetings, the pleasing confusion of questions and answers which marks the simultaneous arrival of several guests.

Crystal rose and turned to Bobby with a smile.

"You will have to tell me some other time," she said lightly. "Don't forget!"

The psychological moment had gone by and Clyffurde cursed himself for having fought too long against the promptings of his heart and lost the precious moments which might have changed the whole of Crystal's future. He cursed himself for not having spoken sooner, now that he saw de Marmont with glowing eyes and ill-concealed triumph approach his beautiful fiancée and with the air of a conqueror raise her hand to his lips.

She looked very pale, and to the man who loved her so ardently and so hopelessly it seemed as if she gave a curious little shiver and that for one brief second her blue eyes flashed a pathetic look of appeal up to his.

VI

M. le Comte's guests followed closely on the triumphant bridegroom's heels: M. le préfet, fussy and nervous, secretly delighted at the idea of affixing his official signature to such an aristocratic contrat de mariage as was this between Mlle. de Cambray de Brestalou and M. Victor de Marmont, own nephew to Marshal the duc de Raguse; Madame la préfète, resplendent in the latest fashion from Paris, the Duc and Duchesse d'Embrun, cousins of the bride, the Vicomte de Génevois and his mother, who was Abbess of Pont Haut and godmother by proxy to Crystal de Cambray; whilst Général Marchand, in command of the troops of the district, fresh from the Council of War which he had hastily convened, was trying to hide behind a débonnaire

73

manner all the anxiety which "the brigand's" march on Grenoble was causing him.

The chief notabilities of the province had assembled to do honour to the occasion, later on others would come, lesser lights by birth and position than this select crowd who would partake of the souper des fiançailles before the contrat was signed in their presence as witnesses to the transaction.

Everyone was talking volubly: the ogre's progress through France—no longer to be denied—was the chief subject of conversation. Some spoke of it with contempt, others with terror. The ex-Bonapartists Fourier and Marchand were loudest in their curses against "the usurper."

Clyffurde, silent and keeping somewhat aloof from the brilliant throng, saw that de Marmont did not enter into any of these conversations. He kept resolutely close to Crystal, and spoke to her from time to time in a whisper, and always with that assured air of the conqueror, which grated so unpleasantly on Clyffurde's irritable nerves.

The Comte, affable and gracious, spoke a few words to each of his guests in turn, whilst Mme. la Duchesse douairière d'Agen was talking openly of her forthcoming return journey to the North.

"I came in great haste," she said loudly to the circle of ladies gathered around her, "for my little Crystal's wedding. But I was in the middle of a Lenten retreat at the Sacred Heart, and I only received permission from my confessor to spend three days in all this gaiety."

"When do you leave us again, Mme. la Duchesse?" queried Mlle. Marchand, the General's daughter, in a honeyed voice.

"On Tuesday, directly after the religious ceremony, Mademoiselle," replied Madame, whilst M. le préfet tried to look unconcerned. He had brought the money over as Mme. la Duchesse had directed. Twenty-five millions of francs in notes and drafts had been transferred from the cellar of the Hôtel de Ville to his own pockets first and then into the keeping of Madame. He had driven over from the Hôtel de Ville in his private coach, he himself in an agony of fear every time the road looked lonely, or he heard the sound of horse's hoofs upon the road behind him—for there might be mounted highwaymen about. Now he felt infinitely relieved; he had shifted all responsibility of that vast sum of money on to more exalted shoulders than his own, and inwardly he was marvelling how coolly Mme. la Duchesse seemed to be taking such an awful responsibility.

Now Hector threw open the great doors and announced that M. le Comte was served. Through the vast corridor beyond appeared a vista of liveried servants in purple and canary, wearing powdered perruque, silk stockings and buckled shoes.

There was a general hubbub in the room, the men moved towards the ladies who had been assigned to them for partners. M. le Comte in his grandest manner approached Mme. la Duchesse d'Embrun in order to conduct her down to supper. An air of majestic grandeur, of solemnity and splendid decorum pervaded the fine apartment; it sought out every corner of the vast reception room, flickered round every wax candle; it spread itself over the monumental hearth, the stiff brocade-covered chairs, the gilt consoles and tall mirrors. It emanated alike from the graciousness of M. le Comte de Cambray and the pompousness of his majordomo. Hector in fact appeared at this moment as the high priest in a temple of good manners and bon ton: the muscles of his face were rigid, his mouth was set as if ready to pronounce sacrificial words; in his right hand he carried a gold-headed wand, emblem of his high office.

But suddenly there was a disturbance—an unseemly noise came from the further end of the corridor, where rose the magnificent staircase. Hector's face became a study in rapidly changing expressions: from pompousness, to astonishment, then horror, and finally wrath when he realised that an intruder in stained cloth clothes and booted and spurred was actually making his way through the ranks of liveried and gaping servants and loudly demanding to speak with M. le Comte.

Such an unseemly disturbance had not occurred at the Château de Brestalou since Hector had been installed there as majordomo nearly twelve months ago, and he was on the point of literally throwing himself upon the impious malapert who thus dared to thrust his ill-clad person upon the brilliant company, when he paused—more aghast than before. In this same impious malapert he had recognised M. le Marquis de St. Genis!

The young man looked to be labouring under terrible excitement: his face was flushed and he was panting as if he had been running hard:

"M. le Comte!" he cried breathlessly as soon as he caught sight of Hector, "tell M. le Comte that I must speak with him at once."

"But M. le Marquis ... M. le Marquis ..."

This was all that poor, bewildered Hector could stammer: his slowly-moving brain was torn between the duties of his position and his respect for M. le Marquis, and in the struggle the worthy man was enduring throes of anxiety.

Fortunately M. le Comte himself put an end to Hector's dilemma. He had recognised St. Genis' voice. Unlike his majordomo, he knew at once that something terribly grave must have happened, else the young man would never have committed such a serious breach of good manners. And M. le Comte himself was never at a loss how to turn any situation to a dignified and proper issue: he murmured a quick and courteous apology to Mme. la Duchesse d'Embrun and a comprehensive one to all his guests, then he hastened to meet St. Genis at the door.

Already St. Genis had entered. His rough clothes and muddy boots looked strangely in contrast to the immaculate get-up of the

Comte's guests, but of this he hardly seemed to be aware. His face was flushed; with his right hand he clutched a small riding cane, and his glowering dark eyes swept a rapid glance over every one in the room.

And to the Comte he said hoarsely: "I must offer you my humblest apologies, my dear Comte, for obtruding my very untidy person upon you at this hour. I have walked all the way from Grenoble, as I could not get a hackney-coach, else I had been here earlier and spared you this unpleasantness."

"You are always welcome in this house, my good Maurice," said the Comte in his loftiest manner, "and at any hour of the day."

And he added with a certain tone of dignified reproach: "I did ask you to be my guest to-night, if you remember."

"And I," said St. Genis, "was churlish enough to refuse. I would not have come now only that I felt I might be in time to avert the most awful catastrophe that has yet fallen upon your house."

Again his restless, dark eyes—sullen and wrathful and charged with a look of rage and of hate—wandered over the assembled company. The look frightened the ladies. They took to clinging to one another, standing in compact little groups together, like frightened birds, watchful and wide-eyed. They feared that the young man was mad. But the men exchanged significant glances and significant smiles. They merely thought that St. Genis had been drinking, or that jealousy had half-turned his brain.

Only Clyffurde, who stood somewhat apart from the others, knew—by some unexplainable intuition—what it was that had brought Maurice de St. Genis to this house in this excited state and at this hour. He felt excited too, and mightily thankful that the catastrophe would be brought about by others—not by himself.

But all his thoughts were for Crystal, and an instinctive desire to stand by her and to shield her if necessary from some unknown or unguessed evil, made him draw nearer to her. She stood on the fringe of the little crowd—as isolated as Bobby was himself.

De Marmont—whose face had become the colour of dead ashes— had left her side: one step at a time and very slowly he was getting nearer and nearer to St. Genis, as if the latter's wrath-filled eyes were drawing him against his will.

At the young man's ominous words, M. le Comte's sunken cheeks grew a shade more pale.

"What catastrophe, mon Dieu!" he exclaimed, "could fall on my house that would be worse than twenty years of exile?"

"An alliance with a traitor, M. le Comte," said St. Genis firmly.

A gasp went round the room, a sigh, a cry. The women looked in mute horror from one man to the other, the men already had their right hand on their swords. But Clyffurde's eyes were fixed upon Crystal, who pale, silent, rigid as a marble statue, with lips parted and nostrils quivering, stood not five paces away from him, her dilated eyes

76

wandering ceaselessly from the face of St. Genis to that of de Marmont and thence to that of her father. But beyond that look of tense excitement she revealed nothing of what she thought and felt.

Already de Marmont—his hand upon his sword—had advanced menacingly towards St. Genis.

"M. le Marquis," he said between set teeth, "you will, by God! eat those words, or——"

"Eat my words, man?" retorted St. Genis with a harsh laugh. "By Heaven! have I not come here on purpose to throw my words into your lying face?"

There was a brief but violent skirmish, for de Marmont had made a movement as if he meant to spring at his rival's throat, and Général Marchand and the Vicomte de Génevois, who happened to be near, had much ado to seize and hold him: even so they could not stop the hoarse cries which he uttered:

"Liar! Liar! Liar! Let me go! Let me get to him! I must kill him! I must kill him!"

The Comte interposed his dignified person between the two men.

"Maurice," he said, in tones of calm and dispassionate reproof, "your conduct is absolutely unjustifiable. You seem to forget that you are in the presence of ladies and of my guests. If you had a quarrel with M. de Marmont...."

"A quarrel, my dear Comte?" exclaimed St. Genis, "nay, 'tis no quarrel I have with him: and my conduct would have been a thousand times more vile if I had not come to-night and stopped his hand from touching that of Mlle. Crystal de Cambray—his hand which was engaged less than two hours ago in affixing to the public buildings of Grenoble the infamous message of the Corsican brigand to the army and the people of France."

A hoarse murmur—a sure sign that men or women are afraid—came from every corner of the room.

"The message?—What message?"

Some people turned instinctively to M. le préfet, others to Général Marchand. Every one knew that Bonaparte had landed on the Littoral, every one had heard the rumour that he was marching in triumph through Provence and the Dauphiné—but no one had altogether believed this—as for a message—a proclamation—a call to the army—and this in Grenoble itself. No one had heard of that—every one had been at home, getting dressed for this festive function, thinking of good suppers and of wedding bells. It was as if after a clap of thunder and a flash of lightning the house was found to be in flames. M. le préfet in answer to these mute queries had shrugged his shoulders, and Général Marchand looked grim and silent.

But St. Genis with arm uplifted and shaking hand pointed a finger at de Marmont.

"Ask him," he cried. "Ask him, my dear Comte, ask the miserable traitor who with lies and damnable treachery has stolen his way into your house, has stolen your regard, your hospitality, and was on the point of stealing your most precious treasure—your daughter! Ask him! He knows every word of that infamous message by heart! I doubt not but a copy of it is inside his coat now. Ask him! Général Mouton-Duveret met him outside Grenoble in company with that cur Emery and I saw him with mine own eyes distributing these hellish papers among our townspeople and pinning them up at the street-corners of our city."

While St. Genis was speaking—or rather screaming—for his voice, pitched high, seemed to fill the entire room—every glance was fixed upon de Marmont. Every one of course expected a contradiction as hot and intemperate as was the accusation. It was unthinkable, impossible that what St. Genis said could be true. They all knew de Marmont well. Nephew of the Duc de Raguse who had borne the lion's share in surrendering Paris to the allies and bringing about the downfall of the Corsican usurper, he was one of the most trusted members of the royalist set in Dauphiné. They had talked quite freely before him, consulted with him when local Bonapartism appeared uncomfortably rampant. De Marmont was one of themselves.

And yet he said nothing even now when St. Genis accused him and hurled insult upon insult at him:—he said nothing to refute the awful impeachment, to justify his conduct, to explain his companionship with Emery. His face was still livid, but it was with rage—not indignation. Marchand and Génevois still held him by the arms, else he and St. Genis would have been at one another's throat before now. But his gestures as he struggled to free himself, the imprecations which he uttered were those of a man who was baffled and found out—not of one who is innocent.

But as St. Genis continued to speak and worked himself up every moment into a still greater state of excitement, de Marmont gradually seemed to calm down. He ceased to curse: he ceased to struggle, and on his face—which still was livid—there gradually crept a look of determination and of defiance. He dug his teeth into his under lip until tiny drops of blood appeared at the corner of his mouth and trickled slowly down his chin.

Marchand and Génevois relaxed the grip upon his arms, since he no longer fought, and thus released he contrived to pull himself together. He tossed back his head and looked his infuriated accuser boldly in the face.

By the time St. Genis paused in his impassioned denunciation, he had himself completely under control: only his eyes appeared to glow with an unnatural fire, and little beads of moisture appeared upon his brow and matted the dark hair against his forehead. The Comte de Cambray at this juncture would certainly have interposed with one of those temperate speeches, full of dignity and brimming over with lofty sentiments, which he knew so well how to deliver, but de Marmont gave him no time to begin. When St. Genis paused for breath, he suddenly freed himself completely with a quick movement, from Marchand's and Génevois' hold; and then he turned to the Comte and to the rest of the company:

"And what if I did pin the Emperor's proclamation on the walls of Grenoble," he said proudly and with a tremor of enthusiasm in his voice, "the Emperor, whom treachery more vile than any since the days of the Iscariot sent into humiliation and exile! The Emperor has come back!" cried the young devotee with that extraordinary fervour which Napoleon alone—of all men that have ever walked upon this earth—was able to suscitate: "his Imperial eagles once more soar over France carrying on their wings her honour and glory to the outermost corners of Europe. His proclamation is to his people who have always loved him, to his soldiers who in their hearts have always been true to him. His proclamation?" he added as with a kind of exultant war-cry he drew a roll of paper from his pocket and held it out at arm's length above his head, "his proclamation? Here it is! Vive l'Empereur! by the grace of God!"

Who shall attempt to describe the feelings of all those who were assembled round this young enthusiast as he hurled his challenge right in the face of those who called him a liar and a traitor? Surely it were a hard task for the chronicler to search into the minds and hearts of this score of men and women—who worshipped one God and reverenced one King—at the moment when they saw that King threatened upon his throne, their faith mocked and their God blasphemed: that the young man spoke words of truth no one thought of denying. Napoleon's name had the power to strike terror in the heart of every citizen who desired peace above all things and of every royalist who wished to see King Louis in possession of the throne of his fathers. But the army which had fought under him, the army which he had led in triumph and to victory from one end of the Continent of Europe to the other, that army still loved him and had never been rightly loyal to King Louis. The horrors of war which had lain so heavily over France and over Europe for the past twenty years were painfully vivid still in everybody's mind, and all these horrors were intimately associated with the name which stood out now in bold characters on the paper which de Marmont was triumphantly waving.

M. le Comte had become a shade or two paler than he had been before: he looked very old, very careworn, all of a sudden, and his pale eyes had that look in them which comes into the eyes of the old after years of sorrow and of regret.

But never for a moment did he depart from his attitude of dignity. When de Marmont's exultant cry of "Vive l'Empereur!" had ceased to echo round the majestic walls of this stately château, he straightened out his spare figure and with one fine gesture begged for silence from his guests.

Then he said very quietly: "M. Marmont, this is neither the place nor the opportunity which I should have chosen for confronting you with all the lies which you have told in the past ten months ever since you entered my house as an honoured guest. But M. de St. Genis has left me no option. Burning with indignation at your treachery he came hot-foot to unmask you, before my daughter's fair hand had affixed her own honourable name beneath that of a cheat and a traitor.... Yes! M. de Marmont," he reiterated with virile force, breaking in on the hot protests which had risen to the young man's lips, "no one but a cheat and a traitor could thus have wormed himself into the confidence of an old man and of a young girl! No one but a villainous blackguard could have contemplated the abominable deceptions which you have planned against me and against my daughter."

For a moment or two after the old man had finished speaking Victor de Marmont remained silent. There were murmurs of indignation among the guests, also of approval of the Comte's energetic words. De Marmont was in the midst of a hostile crowd and he knew it. Here was no drawing-room quarrel which could be settled at the point of a sword. Though—as Fate and man so oft ordain it—a woman was the primary reason for the quarrel, she was not its cause; and the hostility expressed against him by every glance which de Marmont encountered was so general and so great, that it overawed him even in the midst of his enthusiasm.

"M. le Comte," he said at last, and he made a great effort to appear indifferent and unconcerned, "I wish for your daughter's sake that M. de St. Genis had chosen some other time to make this fracas. We who have learned chivalry at the Emperor's school would have hit our enemy when he was in a position to defend himself. This, obviously, I cannot do at this moment without trespassing still further upon your hospitality, and causing Mlle. Crystal still more pain. I might even make a direct appeal to her, since the decision in this matter rests, I imagine, primarily with her, but with the Emperor at our gates, with the influence of his power and of his pride dominating my every thought, I will with your gracious permission relieve you of my unwelcome presence without taking another leaf out of M. de St. Genis' book."

"As you will, Monsieur," said the Comte stiffly.

De Marmont bowed quite ceremoniously to him, and the Comte—courtly and correct to the last—returned his salute with equal ceremony. Then the young man turned to Crystal.

For the first time, perhaps, since the terrible fracas had begun, he realised what it all must mean to her. She did not try to evade his look, or to turn away from him. On the contrary she looked him straight in the face, and watched him while he approached her, without retreating one single step. But she watched him just as one would watch an abject and revolting cur, that was too vile and too mean even to merit a kick.

Crystal's blue eyes were always expressive, but they had never been so expressive as they were just then. De Marmont met her glance squarely, and he read in it everything that she meant to convey—her contempt, her loathing, her hatred—but above all her contempt. So overwhelming, so complete was this contempt that it made him wince, as if he had been struck in the face with a whip.

He stood still, for he knew that she would never allow him to kiss her hand in farewell, and he had had enough of insults—he knew that he could not bear that final one.

A red mist suddenly gathered before his eyes, a mad desire to strike, to wound or to kill, and with it a wave of passion—he called it Love—for this woman, such as he had never felt for her before. He gave her back with a glance, hatred for hatred, but whereas her hatred for him was smothered in contempt, his for her was leavened with a fierce and dominant passion.

All this had taken but a few seconds in accomplishment. M. le Comte had not done more than give a sign to Hector to see M. de Marmont safely out of the castle, and Maurice de St. Genis had only had time to think of interposing, if de Marmont tried to take Crystal's hand.

Only a few seconds, but a lifetime of emotion was crammed into them. Then de Marmont, with Crystal's look of loathing still eating into his soul, caught sight of Clyffurde who stood close by—Clyffurde whose one thought throughout all this unhappy scene had been of Crystal, who through it all had eyes and ears only for her.

Some kind of instinct made the young girl look up to him just then: probably only in response to a wave of memory which brought back to her at that very moment, the words of devotion and offer of service which he had spoken awhile ago; or it may have been that same sense which had told her at the time that here was a man whom she could always trust, that he would always prove a friend, as he had promised, and the look which she gave him was one of simple confidence.

But de Marmont just happened to intercept that look. He had never been jealous of Clyffurde of course. Clyffurde—the foreigner, the bourgeois tradesman—never could under any circumstances be a rival to reckon with. At any other time he would have laughed at the idea of Mlle. Crystal de Cambray bestowing the slightest favour upon the Englishman. But within the last few seconds everything had become different. Victor de Marmont, the triumphant and wealthy suitor of Mlle. de Cambray, had become a pariah among all these ladies and gentlemen, and he had become a man scorned by the woman whom he had wooed and thought to win so easily.

The fierce love engendered for Crystal in his turbulent heart by

81

all the hatred and all the scorn which she lavished upon him, brought an unreasoning jealousy into being. He felt suddenly that he detested Clyffurde. He remembered Clyffurde's nationality and its avowed hatred of the hero whom he—de Marmont—worshipped. And he realised also that that same hatred must of necessity be a bond between the Englishman and Crystal de Cambray.

Therefore—though this new untamed jealousy seized hold of him with extraordinary power, though it brought that ominous red film before his eyes, which makes a man strike out blindly and stupidly against his rival, it also suggested to de Marmont a far simpler and far more efficacious way of ridding himself once for all of any fear of rivalry from Clyffurde.

When he had bowed quite formally to Crystal he looked up at Bobby and gave him a pleasant and friendly nod.

"I suppose you will be coming with me, my good Clyffurde," he said lightly, "we are rowing in the same boat, you and I. We were a very happy party, were we not? you and Emery and I when Général Mouton met us outside Grenoble: for we had just heard the glorious news that the Emperor is marching triumphantly through France."

Then he turned once more to St. Genis: "Did not," he said, "the General's aide-de-camp tell you that, M. de St. Genis?"

St. Genis had—during these few seconds while de Marmont held the centre of the stage—succeeded in controlling his excitement, at any rate outwardly. He was so absolutely master of the situation and had put his successful rival so completely to rout, that the sense of satisfaction helped to soothe his nerves: and when de Marmont spoke directly to him, he was able to reply with comparative calm.

"Had you," he said to de Marmont, "attempted to deny the accusation which I have brought against you, I was ready to confront you with the report which Général Mouton's aide-de-camp brought into the town."

"I had no intention of denying my loyalty to the Emperor," rejoined de Marmont, "but I would like to know what report Général Mouton's aide-de-camp brought into Grenoble. The worthy General did not belie his name, I assure you, he looked mightily scared when he recognised Emery."

"He was alone with his aide-de-camp and in his coach," retorted St. Genis, "whilst that traitor Emery, you and your friend Mr. Clyffurde were on horseback—you gave him the slip easily enough."

"That's true, of course," said de Marmont simply. "Well, shall we go, my dear Clyffurde?"

He had accomplished the purpose of his jealousy even more effectually than he could have wished. He looked round and saw that everyone had thrown a casual glance of contempt upon Clyffurde and then turned away to murmur with scornful indifference: "I always mistrusted that man." Or: "The Comte ought never to have had the fellow in the house," while the words: "English spy!" and "Informer" were on every lip.

But Clyffurde had made no movement during this brief colloquy. He saw—just as de Marmont did—that everyone was listening more with indifference than with horror. He—the stranger—was of so little consequence after all!—a tradesman and an Englishman—what mattered what his political convictions were? De Marmont was an object of hatred, but he—Clyffurde—was only one of contempt.

He heard the muttered words: "English spy!" "Informer!" and others of still more overwhelming disdain. But he cared little what these people said. He knew that they would never trouble to hear any justification from himself—they would not worry their heads about him a moment longer once he had left the house in company with de Marmont.

He was not quite sure either whether de Marmont's spite had been directed against himself, personally, or that it was merely the outcome of his present humiliating position.

M. le Comte had not bestowed more than a glance upon him and that from under haughtily raised brows and across half the width of the room: but Crystal had looked up to him, and was still looking, and it was that look which had driven all the blood from Clyffurde's face and caused his lips to set closely as if with a sense of physical pain.

The insults which her father's guests were overtly murmuring, she had in her mind and her eyes were conveying them to him far more plainly than her lips could have done:

"English spy—traitor to friendship and to trust—liar, deceiver, hypocrite." That and more did her scornful glance imply. But she said nothing. He tried to plead with eyes as expressive as were her own, and she merely turned away from him, just as if he no longer existed. She drew her skirt closer round her and somehow with that gesture she seemed to sweep him entirely out of her existence.

Even Mme. la Duchesse had not one glance for him. To these passionate, hot-headed, impulsive royalists, an adherent of the Corsican ogre was lower than the scum of the earth. They loathed de Marmont because he had been one of themselves: he was a traitor, and not one man there but would have liked to see him put up against a wall and summarily shot. But the stranger they wiped out of their lives.

Was there any chance for Clyffurde, if he tried to defend himself? None of a certainty. He could not call the accusation a lie, since he had been in the company of Emery and of de Marmont most of the day, and mere explanations would have fallen on deaf and unwilling ears.

Clyffurde knew this, nor did he attempt any explanation. There is a certain pride in the heart of every English gentleman which in moments of acute crisis rises to its full power and height. That pride would not allow Clyffurde to utter a single word in his own defence. The futility of attempting it also influenced his decision. He scorned the idea of speaking on his own behalf, words which were doomed to be disbelieved.

In a moment he had found himself absolutely isolated in the centre of the room, not far from the hearth where he had stood a little while ago talking to Crystal, and close to the chair where she had sat with the light of the fire playing upon her satin gown. The cushions still bore the impress of her young figure as she had leaned up against them: the sight of it was an additional pain which almost made Clyffurde wince.

He bowed silently and very low to Crystal and to Mme. la Duchesse, and then to all the ladies and gentlemen who cold-shouldered him with such contemptuous ostentation. De Marmont with head erect and an air of swagger was already waiting for him at the door. Clyffurde in taking leave of M. le Comte made a violent effort to say at any rate the one word which weighed upon his heart.

"Will you at least permit me, M. le Comte," he said, "to thank you for ..."

But already the Comte had interrupted him, even before the words were clearly out of his mouth.

"I will not permit you, Sir," he broke in firmly, "to speak a single word other than a plain denial of M. de St. Genis' accusations against you."

Then as Clyffurde relapsed into silence, M. le Comte continued with haughty peremptoriness:

"A plain 'yes' or 'no' will suffice, Sir. Were you or were you not in the company of those traitors Emery and de Marmont when Général Mouton-Duvernet came upon them outside Grenoble?"

"I was," replied Clyffurde simply.

With a stiff nod of the head the Comte turned his back abruptly upon him; no one took any further notice of the "English spy." The accused had been condemned without enquiry and without trial. In times like these all one's friends must be above suspicion. Clyffurde knew that there was nothing to be said. With a quickly suppressed sigh, he too turned away and in his habitual, English, dogged way he resolutely set his teeth, and with a firm soldierly step walked quietly out of the room.

"Hector, see that M. de Marmont's coach is ready for him," said M. le Comte with well assumed indifference; "and that supper is no longer delayed."

He then once more offered his arm to Mme. la Duchesse d'Embrun. "Mme. la Duchesse," he said in his most courtly manner, "I beg that you will accept my apologies for this unforeseen interruption. May I have the honour of conducting you to supper?"

CHAPTER IV

THE EMPRESS' MILLIONS

I

De Marmont, having successfully shot his poisoned arrow and brought down his enemy, had no longer any ill-feeling against Clyffurde. His jealousy had been short-lived; it was set at rest by the brief episode which had culminated in the Englishman's final exit from the Castle of Brestalou.

Not a single detail of that moving little episode had escaped de Marmont's keen eyes: he had seen Crystal's look of positive abhorrence wherewith she had regarded Clyffurde, he had seen the gathering up of her skirts away—as it were—from the contaminating propinquity of the "English spy."

And de Marmont was satisfied.

He was perfectly ready to pick up the strained strands of friendship with the Englishman and affected not to notice the latter's absorption and moodiness.

"Can I drive you into Grenoble, my good Clyffurde?" he asked airily as he paused on the top of the perron steps, waiting for the hackney coach.

"I thank you," replied Clyffurde; "I prefer to walk."

"It is eight kilometres and a pitch-dark night."

"I know my way, I thank you."

"Just as you like."

He paused a moment, and began humming the "Marseillaise." Clyffurde started walking down the monumental steps.

"Well, I'll say 'good-night,' de Marmont," he said coldly. "And 'good-bye,' too."

"You are not going away?" queried the other.

"As soon as I can get the means of going."

"Troops will be on the move all over the country soon. Foreigners will be interned. You will have some difficulty in getting away."

"I know that. That's why I want to make arrangements as early as possible."

"Where will you stay in the meanwhile?"

"Possibly at the 'Trois-Dauphins' if I can get a room."

"I shall see you again then. The Emperor will stay there while he is in Grenoble. Well, good-night, my dear friend," said de Marmont, as he extended a cordial hand to Clyffurde, who, in the dark, evidently failed to see it. "And don't take the insults of all these fools too much to heart." And he gave an expressive nod in the direction of the stately castle behind him.

"They are dolts," he continued airily; "if they possessed a grain of sense they would have kept on friendly terms with me. As that old fool's son-in-law I could have saved him from all the reprisals which will inevitably fall on all these royalist traitors, now that the Emperor has come into his own again."

Clyffurde was half-way down the stone steps when these words of de Marmont struck upon his ear. Instinctively he retraced his steps. There was a suggestion of impending danger to Crystal in what the young man had said.

"What do you mean by talking about reprisals?" he asked.

"Oh! ... only the inevitable," replied de Marmont. "The people of the Dauphiné never cared for these royalists, you know ... and didn't learn to like them any better in these past eleven months since the Restoration. M. le Comte de Cambray has been very high and mighty since his return from exile. He may yet come to wish that he had never quitted the comfortable little provincial town in England where he gave drawing lessons and French lessons to some very bourgeois boys.... But here's that coach at last!" he continued with that jaunty air which he had assumed since turning his back upon the reception halls of Brestalou. "Are you sure that you would rather walk than drive with me?"

"No," replied Clyffurde abruptly, "I am not sure. Thank you very much. I think that if you don't object to my somewhat morose company I would like a lift as far as Grenoble."

He wanted to make de Marmont talk, to hear what the young man had to say. From it he thought that he could learn more accurately what danger would threaten Brestalou in the event of Napoleon's successful march to Paris.

That the great adventurer's triumph would be short-lived Clyffurde was perfectly sure. He knew the temper of England and believed in the military genius of Wellington. England would never tolerate for a moment longer than she could help that the firebrand of Europe should once more sit upon the throne of France, and unless the allies had greatly altered their policy in the past ten months and refused England the necessary support, Wellington would be more than a match for the decimated army of Bonaparte.

But a few weeks—months, perhaps, might elapse before Napoleon was once again put entirely out of action—and this time more completely and more effectually than with a small kingdom wherein to dream again of European conquests; during those weeks and months Brestalou and its inhabitants would be at the mercy of the man from Corsica—the island of unrest and of never sleeping vendetta.

De Marmont was ready enough to talk. He knew nothing, of course, of Napoleon's plans and ideas save what Emery had told him.

But what he lacked in knowledge he more than made up in imagination. Excitement too had made him voluble. He talked freely and incessantly: "The Emperor would do this.... The Emperor will never tolerate that ..." was all the time on his lips.

He bragged and he swaggered, launched into passionate eulogies of the Emperor, and fiery denunciations of his enemies. Berthier, Clark, Foucher, de Marmont, they all deserved death. Ney alone was to be pardoned, for Ney was a fine soldier—always supposing that Ney would repent. But men like the Comte de Cambray were a pest in any country—mischief-making and intriguing. Bah! the Emperor will never tolerate them.

Suddenly Clyffurde—who had become half-drowsy, lulled to somnolence by de Marmont's incessant chatter and the monotonous jog-trot of the horses—woke to complete consciousness. He pricked his ears and in a moment was all attention.

"They think that they can deceive me," de Marmont was saying airily. "They think that I am as great a fool as they are, with their talk of Mme. la Duchesse's journey north, directly after the wedding! Bah! any dolt can put two and two together: the Comte tells me in one breath that he had a visit from Fourier in the afternoon, and that the Duchesse—who only arrived in Brestalou yesterday—would leave again for Paris on the day after to-morrow, and he tells it me with a mysterious air, and adds a knowing wink, and a promise that he would explain himself more fully later on. I could have laughed—if it were not all so miserably stupid."

He paused for want of breath and tried to peer through the window of the coach.

"It is pitch-dark," he said, "but we can't be very far from the city now."

"I don't see," rejoined Clyffurde, ostentatiously smothering a yawn, "what M. le préfet's visit to Brestalou had to do with the Duchesse's journey to the north. You have got intrigues on the brain, my good de Marmont."

And with well-feigned indifference, he settled himself more cosily into the dark corner of the carriage.

De Marmont laughed. "What Fourier's afternoon visit has to do with Mme. d'Agen's journey?" he retorted, "I'll tell you, my good Clyffurde. Fourier went to see M. le Comte de Cambray this afternoon because he is a poltroon. He is terrified at the thought that the unfortunate Empress' money and treasure are still lying in the cellars of the Hôtel de Ville and he went out to Brestalou in order to consult with the Comte what had best be done with the money."

"I didn't know the ex-Empress' money was lying in the cellar of the Hôtel de Ville," remarked Clyffurde with well-assumed indifference.

"Nor did I until Emery told me," rejoined de Marmont. "The money is there though: stolen from the Empress Marie Louise by that

87

arch-intriguer Talleyrand. Twenty-five millions in notes and drafts! the Emperor reckons on it for current expenses until he has reached Paris and taken over the Treasury."

"Even then I don't see what Mme. la Duchesse d'Agen has to do with it."

"You don't," said de Marmont drily: "but I did in a moment. Fourier wouldn't keep the money at the Hôtel de Ville: the Comte de Cambray would not allow it to be deposited in his house. They both want the Bourbon to have it. So—in order to lull suspicion—they have decided that Madame la Duchesse shall take the money to Paris."

"Well!—perhaps!—" said Clyffurde with a yawn. "But are we not in Grenoble yet?"

Once more he lapsed into silence, closed his eyes and to all intents and purposes fell asleep, for never another word did de Marmont get out of him, until Grenoble was reached and the rue Montorge.

Here de Marmont had his lodgings, three doors from the "Hôtel des Trois-Dauphins," where fortunately Clyffurde managed to secure a comfortable room for himself.

He parted quite amicably from de Marmont, promising to call in upon him in the morning. It would be foolish to quarrel with that young wind-bag now. He knew some things, and talked of a great many more.

II

Preparations against the arrival of the Corsican ogre were proceeding apace. Général Marchand had been overconfident throughout the day—which was the 5th of March: "The troops," he said, "were loyal to a man. They were coming in fast from Chambéry and Vienne; the garrison would and could repulse that band of pirates, and take upon itself to fulfil the promise which Ney had made to the King— namely to bring the ogre to His Majesty bound and gagged in an iron cage."

But the following day, which was the 6th, many things occurred to shake the Commandant's confidence: Napoleon's proclamation was not only posted up all over the town, but the citizens were distributing the printed leaflets among themselves: one of the officers on the staff pointed out to Général Marchand that the 4th regiment of artillery quartered in Grenoble was the one in which Bonaparte had served as a lieutenant during the Revolution—the men, it was argued, would never turn their arms against one whom they had never ceased to idolize: it

88

would not be safe to march out into the open with men whose loyalty was so very doubtful.

There was a rumour current in the town that when the men of the 5th regiment of engineers and the 4th of artillery were told that Napoleon had only eleven hundred men with him, they all murmured with one accord: "And what about us?"

Therefore Général Marchand, taking all these facts into consideration, made up his mind to await the ogre inside the walls of Grenoble. Here at any rate defections and desertions would be less likely to occur than in the field. He set to work to organise the city into a state of defence; forty-seven guns were put in position upon the ramparts which dominate the road to the south, and he sent a company of engineers and a battalion of infantry to blow up the bridge of Ponthaut at La Mure.

The royalists in the city, who were beginning to feel very anxious, had assembled in force to cheer these troops as they marched out of the city. But the attitude of the sapeurs created a very unpleasant impression: they marched out in disorder, some of them tore the white cockade from their shakos, and one or two cries of "Vive l'Empereur!" were distinctly heard in their ranks.

At La Mure, M. le Maire argued very strongly against the destruction of the bridge of Ponthaut: "It would be absurd," he said, "to blow up a valuable bridge, since not one kilometre away there was an excellent ford across which Napoleon could march his troops with perfect ease." The sapeurs murmured an assent, and their officer, Colonel Delessart, feeling the temper of his men, did not dare insist.

He quartered them at La Mure to await the arrival of the infantry, and further orders from Général Marchand. When the 5th regiment of infantry was reported to have reached Laffray, Delessart had the sapeurs out and marched out to meet them, although it was then close upon midnight.

While Delessart and his troops encamped at Laffray, Cambronne—who was in command of Napoleon's vanguard—himself occupied La Mure. This was on the 7th. The Mayor—who had so strongly protested against the destruction of the bridge of Ponthaut—gathered the population around him, and in a body men, women and children marched out of the borough along the Corps-Sisteron road in order to give "the Emperor" a rousing welcome.

It was still early morning. Napoleon at the head of his Old Guard entered La Mure; a veritable ovation greeted him, everyone pressed round him to see him or touch his horse, his coat, his stirrups; he spoke to the people and held the Mayor and municipal officials in long conversation.

Just as practically everywhere else on his route, he had won over every heart; but his small column which had been eleven hundred strong when he landed at Jouan, was still only eleven hundred strong:

89

he had only rallied four recruits to his standard. True, he had met with no opposition, true that the peasantry of the Dauphiné had loudly acclaimed him, had listened to his harangues and presented him with flowers, but he had not had a single encounter with any garrison on his way, nor could he boast of any defections in his favour; now he was nearing Grenoble—Grenoble, which was strongly fortified and well garrisoned—and Grenoble would be the winning or losing cast of this great gamble for the sovereignty of France.

It was close on eleven when the great adventurer set out upon this momentous stage of his journey: the Polish Lancers leading, then the chasseurs of his Old Guard with their time-worn grey coats and heavy bear-skins; some of them were on foot, others packed closely together in wagons and carts which the enthusiastic agriculturists of La Mure had placed at the disposal of "the Emperor."

Napoleon himself followed in his coach, his horse being led along. Amidst thundering cries of "God speed" the small column started on its way.

As for the rest, 'tis in the domain of history; every phase of it has been put on record:—Delessart—worried in his mind that he had not been able to obey Général Marchand's orders and destroy the bridge of Ponthaut—his desire to communicate once more with the General; his decision to await further orders and in the meanwhile to occupy the narrow defile of Laffray as being an advantageous position wherein to oppose the advance of the ogre: all this on the one side.

On the other, the advance of the Polish Lancers, of the carts and wagons wherein are crowded the soldiers of the Old Guard, and Napoleon himself, the great gambler, sitting in his coach gazing out through the open windows at the fair land of France, the peaceful valley on his left, the chain of ice-covered lakes and the turbulent Drac; on his right beyond the hills frowning Taillefer, snow-capped and pine-clad, and far ahead Grenoble still hidden from his view as the future too was still hidden—the mysterious gate beyond which lay glory and an Empire or the ignominy of irretrievable failure.

History has made a record of it all, and it is not the purpose of this true chronicle to do more than recall with utmost brevity the chief incident of that memorable encounter, the Polish Lancers galloping back with the report that the narrow pass was held against them in strong force: the Old Guard climbing helter-skelter out of carts and wagons, examining their arms, making ready: Napoleon stepping quickly out of his coach and mounting his charger.

On the other side Delessart holding hurried consultation with the Vicomte de St. Genis whom Général Marchand has despatched to him with orders to shoot the brigand and his horde as he would a pack of wolves.

Napoleon is easily recognisable in the distance, with his grey overcoat, his white horse and his bicorne hat; presently he dismounts and walks up and down across the narrow road, evidently in a state of great mental agitation.

Delessart's men are sullen and silent; a crowd of men and women from Grenoble have followed them up thus far; they work their way in and out among the infantrymen: they have printed leaflets in their hands which they cram one by one into the hands or pockets of the soldiers—copies of Napoleon's proclamation.

Now an officer of the Old Guard is seen to ride up the pass. Delessart recognises him. They were brothers in arms two years ago and served together under the greatest military genius the world has ever known. Napoleon has sent the man on as an emissary, but Delessart will not allow him to speak.

"I mean to do my duty," he declares.

But in his voice too there has already crept that note of sullenness which characterised the sapeurs from the first.

Then Captain Raoul, own aide-de-camp to Napoleon, comes up at full gallop: nor does he draw rein till he is up with the entire front of Delessart's battalion.

"Your Emperor is coming," he shouts to the soldiers, "if you fire, the first shot will reach him: and France will make you answerable for this outrage!"

While he shouts and harangues the men are still sullen and silent. And in the distance the lances of the Polish cavalry gleam in the sun, and the shaggy bear-skins of the Old Guard are seen to move forward up the pass. Delessart casts a rapid piercing glance over his men. Sullenness had given place to obvious terror.

"Right about turn! ... Quick! ... March!" he commands.

Resistance obviously would be useless with these men, who are on the verge of laying down their arms. He forces on a quick march, but the Polish Lancers are already gaining ground: the sound of their horses' hoofs stamping the frozen ground, the snorting, the clanging of arms is distinctly heard. Delessart now has no option. He must make his men turn once more and face the ogre and his battalion before they are attacked in the rear.

As soon as the order is given and the two little armies stand face to face the Polish Lancers halt and the Old Guard stand still.

And it almost seems for the moment as if Nature herself stood still and listened, and looked on. The genial midday sun is slowly melting the snow on pine trees and rocks; one by one the glistening tiny crystals blink and vanish under the warmth of the kiss; the hard, white road darkens under the thaw and slowly a thin covering of water spreads over the icy crust of the lakes.

Napoleon tells Colonel Mallet to order the men to lower their arms. Mallet protests, but Napoleon reiterates the command, more peremptorily this time, and Mallet must obey. Then at the head of his old chasseurs, thus practically disarmed, the Emperor—and he is every

91

inch an Emperor now—walks straight up to Delessart's opposing troops.

Hot-headed St. Genis cries: "Here he is!—Fire, in Heaven's name!"

But the sapeurs—the old regiment in which Napoleon had served as a young lieutenant in those glorious olden days—are now as pale as death, their knees shake under them, their arms tremble in their hands.

At ten paces away from the foremost ranks Napoleon halts:

"Soldiers," he cries loudly. "Here I am! your Emperor, do you know me?"

Again he advances and with a calm gesture throws open his well-worn grey redingote.

"Fire!" cries St. Genis in mad exasperation.

"Fire!" commands Delessart in a voice rendered shaky with overmastering emotion.

Silence reigns supreme. Napoleon still advances, step by step, his redingote thrown open, his broad chest challenging the first bullet which would dare to end the bold, adventurous, daring life.

"Is there one of you soldiers here who wants to shoot his Emperor? If there is, here I am! Fire!"

Which of these soldiers who have served under him at Jena and Austerlitz could resist such a call. His voice has lost nothing yet of its charm, his personality nothing of its magic. Ambitious, ruthless, selfish he may be, but to the army, a friend, a comrade as well as a god.

Suddenly the silence is broken. Shouts of "Vive l'Empereur!" rend the air, they echo down the narrow valley, re-echo from hill to hill and reverberate upon the pine-clad heights of Taillefer. Broken are the ranks, white cockades fly in every direction, tricolours appear in their hundreds everywhere. Shakos are waved on the points of the bayonets, and always, always that cry: "Vive l'Empereur!"

Sapeurs and infantrymen crowd around the little man in the worn grey redingote, and he with that rough familiarity which bound all soldiers' hearts to him, seizes an old sergeant by the ends of his long moustache:

"So, you old dog," he says, "you were going to shoot your Emperor, were you?"

"Not me," replies the man with a growl. "Look at our guns. Not one of them was loaded."

Delessart, in despair yet shaken to the heart, his eyes swimming in tears, offers his sword to Napoleon, whereupon the Emperor grasps his hand in friendship and comforts him with a few inspiring words.

Only St. Genis has looked on all this scene with horror and contempt. His royalist opinions are well known, his urgent appeal to Delessart a while ago to "shoot the brigand and his hordes" still rings in every soldier's ear. He is half-crazy with rage and there is quite an element of terror in the confused thoughts which crowd in upon his brain.

Already the sapeurs and infantrymen have joined the ranks of the Old Guard, and Napoleon, with that inimitable verve and inspiring eloquence of which he was pastmaster, was haranguing his troops. Just then three horsemen, dressed in the uniform of officers of the National Guard and wearing enormous tricolour cockades as large as soup-plates on their shakos, are seen to arrive at a break-neck gallop down the pass from Grenoble.

St. Genis recognised them at a glance: they were Victor de Marmont, Surgeon-Captain Emery and their friend the glovemaker, Dumoulin. The next moment these three men were at the feet of their beloved hero.

"Sire," said Dumoulin the glovemaker, "in the name of the citizens of Grenoble we hereby offer you our services and one hundred thousand francs collected in the last twenty-four hours for your use."

"I accept both," replied the Emperor, while he grasped vigorously the hands of his three most devoted friends.

St. Genis uttered a loud and comprehensive curse: then he pulled his horse abruptly round and with such a jerk that it reared and plunged madly forward ere it started galloping away with its frantic rider in the direction of Grenoble.

III

And Grenoble itself was in a turmoil.

In the barracks the cries of "Vive l'Empereur!" were incessant; Général Marchand was indefatigable in his efforts to still that cry, to rouse in the hearts of the soldiers a sense of loyalty to the King.

"Your country and your King," he shouted from barrack-room to barrack-room.

"Our country and our Emperor!" responded the soldiers with ever-growing enthusiasm.

The spirit of the army and of the people were Bonapartist to the core. They had never trusted either Marchand or préfet Fourier, who had turned their coats so readily at the Restoration: they hated the émigrés—the Comte de Cambray, the Vicomte de St. Genis, the Duc d'Embrun—with their old-fashioned ideas of the semi-divine rights of the nobility second only to the godlike ones of the King. They thought them arrogant and untamed, over-ready to grab once more all the privileges which a bloody Revolution had swept away.

To them Napoleon, despite the brilliant days of the Empire, despite his autocracy, his militarism and his arrogance, represented

93

"the people," the advanced spirit of the Revolution; his downfall had meant a return to the old regime—the regime of feudal rights, of farmers general, of heavy taxation and dear bread.

"Vive l'Empereur!" was cried in the barracks and "Vive l'Empereur!" at the street corners.

A squadron of Hussars had marched into Grenoble from Vienne just before noon: the same squadron which a few months ago at a revue by the Comte d'Artois in the presence of the King had shouted "Vive l'Empereur!" What faith could be put in their loyalty now?

But two infantry regiments came in at the same time from Chambéry and on these Général Marchand hoped to be able to reckon. The Comte Charles de la Bédoyère was in command of the 7th regiment, and though he had served in Prussia under Napoleon he had tendered his oath loyally to Louis XVIII. at the Restoration. He was a tried and able soldier and Marchand believed in him. The General himself reviewed both infantry regiments on the Place d'Armes on their arrival, and then posted them upon the ramparts of the city, facing direct to the southeast and dominating the road to La Mure.

De la Bédoyère remained in command of the 7th.

For two hours he paced the ramparts in a state of the greatest possible agitation. The nearness of Napoleon, of the man who had been his comrade in arms first and his leader afterwards, had a terribly disturbing effect upon his spirit. From below in the city the people's mutterings, their grumbling, their sullen excitement seemed to rise upwards like an intoxicating incense. The attitude of the troops, of the gunners, as well as of the garrison and of his own regiment, worked more potently still upon the Colonel's already shaken loyalty.

Then suddenly his mind is made up. He draws his sword and shouts: "Vive l'Empereur!"

"Soldiers!" he calls. "Follow me! I will show you the way to duty! Follow me! Vive l'Empereur!"

"Vive l'Empereur!" vociferate the troops.

"After me, my men! to the Bonne Gate! After me!" cries De la Bédoyère.

And to the shouts of "Vive l'Empereur!" the 7th regiment of infantry passes through the gate and marches along the streets of the suburb on towards La Mure.

Général Marchand, hastily apprised of the wholesale defection, sends Colonel Villiers in hot haste in the wake of De la Bédoyère. Villiers comes up with the latter two kilomètres outside Grenoble. He talks, he persuades, he admonishes, he scolds, De la Bédoyère and his men are firm.

"Your country and your king!" shouts Villiers.

"Our country and our Emperor!" respond the men. And they go to join the Old Guard at Laffray while Villiers in despair rides back into Grenoble.

In the town the desertion of the 7th has had a very serious effect. The muttered cries of "Vive l'Empereur!" are open shouts now. Général Marchand is at his wits' ends. He has ordered the closing of every city gate, and still the soldiers in batches of tens and twenties at a time contrive to escape out of the town carrying their arms and in many cases baggage with them. The royalist faction—the women as well as the men—spend the whole day in and out of the barrack-rooms talking to the men, trying to infuse into them loyalty to the King, and to cheer them up by bringing them wine and provisions.

In the afternoon the Vicomte de St. Genis, sick, exhausted, his horse covered with lather, comes back with the story of the pass of Laffray, and Napoleon's triumphant march toward Grenoble. Marchand seriously contemplates evacuating the city in order to save the garrison and his stores.

Préfet Fourier congratulates himself on his foresight and on that he has transferred the twenty-five million francs from the cellars of the Hôtel de Ville into the safe keeping of M. le Comte de Cambray. He and Général Marchand both hope and think that "the brigand and his horde" cannot possibly be at the gates of Grenoble before the morrow, and that Mme. la Duchesse d'Agen would be well on her way to Paris with the money by that time.

Marchand in the meanwhile has made up his mind to retire from the city with his troops. It is only a strategical measure, he argues, to save bloodshed and to save his stores, pending the arrival of the Comte d'Artois at Lyons, with the army corps. He gives the order for the general retreat to commence at two o'clock in the morning.

Satisfied that he has done the right thing, he finally goes back to his quarters in the Hotel du Dauphiné close to the ramparts. The Comte de Cambray is his guest at dinner, and toward seven o'clock the two men at last sit down to a hurried meal, both their minds filled with apprehension and not a little fear as to what the next few days will bring.

"It is, of course, only a question of time," says the Comte de Cambray airily. "Monseigneur le Comte d'Artois will be at Lyons directly with forty thousand men, and he will easily crush that marauding band of pirates. But this time the Corsican after his defeat must be put more effectually out of harm's way. I, personally, was never much in favour of Elba."

"The English have some islands out in the Atlantic or the Pacific," responds Général Marchand with firm decision. "It would be safest to shoot the brigand, but failing that, let the English send him to one of those islands, and undertake to guard him well."

"Let us drink to that proposition, my dear Marchand," concludes M. le Comte with a smile.

Hardly had the two men concluded this toast, when a fearful din is heard, "regular howls" proceeding from the suburb of Bonne. The

95

windows of the hotel give on the ramparts and the house itself dominates the Bonne Gate and the military ground beyond it. Hastily Marchand jumps up from the table and throws open the window. He and the Comte step out upon the balcony.

The din has become deafening: with a hand that slightly trembles now Général Marchand points to the extensive grounds that lie beyond the city gate, and M. le Comte quickly smothers an exclamation of terror.

A huge crowd of peasants armed with scythes and carrying torches which flicker in the frosty air have invaded the slopes and flats of the military zone. They are yelling "Vive l'Empereur!" at the top of their voices, and from walls and bastions reverberates the answering cry "Vive l'Empereur!" vociferated by infantrymen and gunners and sapeurs, and echoed and re-echoed with passionate enthusiasm by the people of Grenoble assembled in their thousands in the narrow streets which abut upon the ramparts.

And in the midst of the peasantry, surrounded by them as by a cordon, Napoleon and his small army, just reinforced by the 7th regiment of infantry, have halted—expectant.

Napoleon's aide-de-camp, Capitaine Raoul, accompanied by half a dozen lancers, comes up to the palisade which bars the immediate approach to the city gates.

"Open!" he cries loudly, so loudly that his young, firm voice rises above the tumult around. "Open! in the name of the Emperor!"

Marchand sees it all, he hears the commanding summons, hears the thunderous and enthusiastic cheers which greet Captain Raoul's call to surrender. He and the Comte de Cambray are still standing upon the balcony of the hotel that faces the gate of Bonne and dominates from its high ground the ramparts opposite. White-cheeked and silent the two men have gazed before them and have understood. To attempt to stem this tide of popular enthusiasm would inevitably be fatal. The troops inside Grenoble were as ready to cross over to "the brigand's" standard as was Colonel de la Bédoyère's regiment of infantry.

The ramparts and the surrounding military zone were lit up by hundreds of torches; by their flickering light the two men on the balcony could see the faces of the people, and those of the soldiers who were even now being ordered to fire upon Raoul and the Lancers.

Colonel Roussille, who is in command of the troops at the gate, sends a hasty messenger to Général Marchand: "The brigand demands that we open the gate!" reports the messenger breathlessly.

"Tell the Colonel to give the order to fire," is Marchand's peremptory response.

"Are you coming with me, M. le Comte?" he asks hurriedly. But he does not wait for a reply. Wrapping his cloak around him, he goes in the wake of the messenger. M. le Comte de Cambray is close on his heels.

Five minutes later the General is up on the ramparts. He has thrown a quick, piercing glance round him. There are two thousand men up here, twenty guns, ammunition in plenty. Out there only peasants and a heterogeneous band of some fifteen hundred men. One shot from a gun perhaps would send all that crowd flying, the first fusillade might scatter "the band of brigands," but Marchand cannot, dare not give the positive order to fire; he knows that rank insubordination, positive refusal to obey would follow.

He talks to the men, he harangues, he begs them to defend their city against this "horde of Corsican pirates."

To every word he says, the men but oppose the one cry: "Vive l'Empereur!"

The Comte de Cambray turns in despair to M. de St. Genis, who is a captain of artillery and whose men had hitherto been supposed to be tried and loyal royalists.

"If the men won't fire, Maurice," asks the Comte in despair, "cannot the officers at least fire the first shot?"

"M. le Comte," replies St. Genis through set teeth, for his heart was filled with wrath and shame at the defection of his men, "the gunners have declared that if the officers shoot, the men will shatter them to pieces with their own batteries."

The crowds outside the gate itself are swelling visibly. They press in from every side toward the city loudly demanding the surrender of the town. "Open the gates! open!" they shout, and their clamour becomes more insistent every moment. Already they have broken down the palisades which surround the military zone, they pour down the slopes against the gate. But the latter is heavy, and massive, studded with iron, stoutly resisting axe or pick.

"Open!" they cry. "Open! in the Emperor's name!"

They are within hailing distance of the soldiers on the ramparts: "What price your plums?" they shout gaily to the gunners.

"Quite cheap," retort the latter with equal gaiety, "but there's no danger of the Emperor getting any."

The women sing the old couplet:

"Bon! Bon! Napoléon
Va rentrer dans sa maison!"

and the soldiers on the ramparts take up the refrain:

"Nous allons voir le grand Napoléon
Le vainqueur de toutes les nations!"

"What can we do, M. le Comte?" says Général Marchand at last. "We shall have to give in."

"I'll not stay and see it," replies the Comte. "I should die of shame."

Even while the two men are talking and discussing the possibilities of an early surrender, Napoleon himself has forced his way through the tumultuous throng of his supporters, and accompanied by Victor de Marmont and Colonel de la Bédoyère he advances as far as the gate which still stands barred defiantly against him.

"I command you to open this gate!" he cries aloud.

Colonel Roussille, who is in command, replies defiantly: "I only take orders from the General himself."

"He is relieved of his command," retorts Napoleon.

"I know my duty," insists Roussille. "I only take orders from the General."

Victor de Marmont, intoxicated with his own enthusiasm, maddened with rage at sight of St. Genis, whose face is just then thrown into vivid light by the glare of the torches, cries wildly: "Soldiers of the Emperor, who are being forced to resist him, turn on those treacherous officers of yours, tear off their epaulettes, I say!"

His shrill and frantic cries seem to precipitate the inevitable climax. The tumult has become absolutely delirious. The soldiers on the ramparts tumble over one another in a mad rush for the gate, which they try to break open with the butt-end of their rifles; but they dare not actually attack their own officers, and in any case they know that the keys of the city are still in the hands of Général Marchand, and Général Marchand has suddenly disappeared.

Feeling the hopelessness and futility of further resistance, he has gone back to his hotel, and is even now giving orders and making preparations for leaving Grenoble. Préfet Fourier, hastily summoned, is with him, and the Comte de Cambray is preparing to return immediately to Brestalou.

"We shall all leave for Paris to-morrow, as early as possible," he says, as he finally takes leave of the General and the préfet, "and take the money with us, of course. If the King—which God forbid!—is obliged to leave Paris, it will be most acceptable to him, until the day when the allies are once more in the field and ready to crush, irretrievably this time, this Corsican scourge of Europe."

One or two of the royalist officers have succeeded in massing together some two or three hundred men out of several regiments who appear to be determined to remain loyal.

St. Genis is not among these: his men had been among the first to cry "Vive l'Empereur!" when ordered to fire on the brigand and his hordes. They had even gone so far as to threaten their officers' lives.

Now, covered with shame, and boiling with wrath at the defection, St. Genis asks leave of the General to escort M. le Comte de Cambray and his party to Paris.

"We shall be better off for extra protection," urges M. le Comte de Cambray in support of St. Genis' plea for leave. "I shall only have the coachman and two postillions with me. M. de St. Genis would be of immense assistance in case of footpads."

"The road to Paris is quite safe, I believe," says Général Marchand, "and at Lyons you will meet the army of M. le Comte d'Artois. But perhaps M. de St. Genis had better accompany you as far as there, at any rate. He can then report himself at Lyons. Twenty-five millions is a large sum, of course, but the purpose of your journey has remained a secret, has it not?"

"Of course," says M. le Comte unhesitatingly, for he has completely erased Victor de Marmont from his mind.

"Well then, all you need fear is an attack from footpads—and even that is unlikely," concludes Général Marchand, who by now is in a great hurry to go. "But M. de St. Genis has my permission to escort you."

The General entrusts the keys of the Bonne Gate to Colonel Roussille. He has barely time to execute his hasty flight, having arranged to escape out of Grenoble by the St. Laurent Gate on the north of the town. In the meanwhile a carter from the suburb of St. Joseph outside the Bonne Gate has harnessed a team of horses to one of his wagons and brought along a huge joist: twenty pairs of willing and stout arms are already manipulating this powerful engine for the breaking open of the resisting gate. Already the doors are giving way, the hinges creak; and while Général Marchand and préfet Fourier with their small body of faithful soldiers rush precipitately across the deserted streets of the town, Colonel Roussille makes ready to open the Gate of Bonne to the Emperor and to his soldiers.

"My regiment was prepared to turn against me," he says to his men, "but I shall not turn against them."

Then he formally throws open the gate.

Ecstatic delight, joyful enthusiasm, succeeds the frantic cries of a while ago. Napoleon entering the city of Grenoble was nearly crushed to death by the frenzy of the crowd. Cheered to the echoes, surrounded by a delirious populace which hardly allowed him to move, it was hours before he succeeded in reaching the Hôtel des Trois-Dauphins, where he was resolved to spend the night, since it was kept by an ex-soldier, one of his own Old Guard of the Italian campaign.

The enthusiasm was kept up all night. The town was illuminated. Until dawn men and women paraded the streets singing the "Marseillaise" and shouting "Vive l'Empereur!"

In a small room, simply furnished but cosy and comfortable, the great adventurer, who had conquered half the world and lost it and had now set out to conquer it again, sat with half a dozen of his most faithful friends: Cambronne and Raoul, Victor de Marmont and Emery.

On the table spread out before him was an ordnance map of the province; his clenched hand rested upon it; his eyes, those eagle-like, piercing eyes which had so often called his soldiers to victory, gazed out straight before him, as if through the bare, white-washed walls of this humble hotel room he saw the vision of the brilliant halls of the Tuileries, the imperial throne, the Empress beside him, all her faithlessness and pusillanimity forgiven, his son whom he worshipped, his marshals grouped around him; and with a gesture of proud defiance he threw back his head and said loudly:

"Until to-day I was only an adventurer. To-night I am a prince once more."

IV

It was the next morning in that same sparsely-furnished and uncarpeted room of the Hôtel des Trois-Dauphins that Napoleon spoke to Victor de Marmont, to Emery and Dumoulin about the money which had been stolen last year from the Empress and which he understood had been deposited in the cellars of the Hôtel de Ville.

"I am not going," he said, "to levy a war tax on my good city of Grenoble, but my good and faithful soldiers must be paid, and I must provision my army in case I encounter stronger resistance at Lyons than I can cope with, and am forced to make a détour. I want the money—the Empress' money, which that infamous Talleyrand stole from her. So you, de Marmont, had best go straight away to the Hôtel de Ville and in my name summon the préfet to appear before me. You can tell him at once that it is on account of the money."

"I will go at once, Sire," replied de Marmont with a regretful sigh, "but I fear me that it is too late."

"Too late?" snapped out the Emperor with a frown, "what do you mean by too late?"

"I mean that Fourier has left Grenoble in the trail of Marchand, and that two days ago—unless I'm very much mistaken—he disposed of the money."

"Disposed of the money? You are mad, de Marmont."

"Not altogether, Sire. When I say that Fourier disposed of the Empress' money I only mean that he deposited it in what he would deem a safe place."

"The cur!" exclaimed Napoleon with a yet tighter clenching of his hand and mighty fist, "turning against the hand that fed him and made him what he is. Well!" he added impatiently, "where is the money now?"

"In the keeping of M. le Comte de Cambray at Brestalou," replied de Marmont without hesitation.

"Very well," said the Emperor, "take a company of the 7th regiment with you to Brestalou and requisition the money at once."

"If—as I believe—the Comte no longer has the money by him?—"

"Make him tell you where it is."

"I mean, Sire, that it is my belief that M. le Comte's sister and daughter will undertake to take the money to Paris, hoping by their sex and general air of innocence to escape suspicion in connection with the money."

"Don't worry me with all these details, de Marmont," broke in Napoleon with a frown of impatience. "I told you to take a company with you and to get me the Empress' money. See to it that this is done and leave me in peace."

He hated arguing, hated opposition, the very suggestion of any difficulty. His followers and intimates knew that; already de Marmont had repented that he had allowed his tongue to ramble on quite so much. Now he felt that silence must redeem his blunder—silence now and success in his undertaking.

He bent the knee, for this homage the great Corsican adventurer and one-time dictator of civilised Europe loved to receive: he kissed the hand which had once wielded the sceptre of a mighty Empire and was ready now to grasp it again. Then he rose and gave the military salute.

"It shall be done, Sire," was all that he said.

His heart was full of enthusiasm, and the task allotted to him was a congenial one: the baffling and discomfiture of those who had insulted him. If—as he believed—Crystal would be accompanying her aunt on the journey toward Paris, then indeed would his own longing for some sort of revenge for the humiliation which he had endured on that memorable Sunday evening be fully gratified.

It was with a light and swinging step that he ran down the narrow stairs of the hotel. In the little entrance hall below he met Clyffurde.

In his usual impulsive way, without thought of what had gone before or was likely to happen in the future, he went up to the Englishman with outstretched hand.

"My dear Clyffurde," he said with unaffected cordiality, "I am glad to see you! I have been wondering what had become of you since we parted on Sunday last. My dear friend," he added ecstatically, "what glorious events, eh?"

He did not wait for Clyffurde's reply, nor did he appear to notice the latter's obvious coldness of manner, but went prattling on with great volubility.

"What a man!" he exclaimed, nodding significantly in the direction whence he had just come. "A six days' march—mostly on foot and along steep mountain paths! and to-day as fresh and vigorous as if he had just had a month's holiday at some pleasant watering place! What luck to be serving such a man! And what luck to be able to render him really useful service! The tables will be turned, eh, my dear Clyffurde?" he added, giving his taciturn friend a jovial dig in the ribs, "and what lovely discomfiture for our proud aristocrats, eh? They will be sorry to have made an enemy of Victor de Marmont, what?"

Whereupon Clyffurde made a violent effort to appear friendly and jovial too.

"Why," he said with a pleasant laugh, "what madcap ideas are floating through your head now?"

"Madcap schemes?" ejaculated de Marmont. "Nothing more or less, my dear Clyffurde, than complete revenge for the humiliation those de Cambrays put upon me last Sunday."

"Revenge? That sounds exciting," said Clyffurde with a smile, even while his palm itched to slap the young braggart's face.

"Exciting, par Dieu! Of course it will be exciting. They have no idea that I guessed their little machinations. Mme. la Duchesse d'Agen travelling to Paris forsooth! Aye! but with five and twenty millions sewn somewhere inside her petticoats. Well! the Emperor happens to want his own five and twenty millions, if you please. So Mme. la Duchesse or M. le Comte will have to disgorge. And I shall have the pleasing task of making them disgorge. What say you to that, friend Clyffurde?"

"That I am sorry for you," replied the other drily.

"Sorry for me? Why?"

"Because it is never a pleasing task to bully a defenceless woman—and an old one at that."

De Marmont laughed aloud. "Bully Mme. la Duchesse d'Agen?" he exclaimed. "Sacré tonnerre! what do you take me for. I shall not bully her. Fifty soldiers don't bully a defenceless woman. We shall treat Mme. la Duchesse with every consideration: we shall only remove five and twenty millions of stolen money from her carriage, that is all."

"You may be mistaken about the money, de Marmont. It may be anywhere except in the keeping of Mme. la Duchesse."

"It may be at the Château de Brestalou in the keeping of M. le Comte de Cambray: and this I shall find out first of all. But I must not stand gossiping any longer. I must see Colonel de la Bédoyère and get the men I want. What are your plans, my dear Clyffurde?"

"The same as before," replied Bobby quietly. "I shall leave Grenoble as soon as I can."

"Let the Emperor send you on a special mission to Lord Grenville, in London, to urge England to remain neutral in the coming struggle."

"I think not," said Clyffurde enigmatically.

De Marmont did not wait to ask him to what this brief remark had applied; he bade his friend a hasty farewell, then he turned on his heel, and gaily whistling the refrain of the "Marseillaise," stalked out of the hotel.

Clyffurde remained standing in the narrow panelled hall, which just then reeked strongly of stewed onions and of hot coffee; he never moved a muscle, but remained absolutely quiet for the space of exactly two minutes; then he consulted his watch—it was then close on midday—and finally went back to his room.

V

An hour after dawn that self-same morning the travelling coach of M. le Comte de Cambray was at the perron of the Château de Brestalou.

At the last moment, when M. le Comte, hopelessly discouraged by the surrender of Grenoble to the usurper, came home at a late hour of the night, he decided that he too would journey to Paris with his sister and daughter, taking the money with him to His Majesty, who indeed would soon be in sore need of funds.

At that same late hour of the night M. le Comte discovered that with the exception of faithful Hector and one or two scullions in the kitchen his male servants both indoor and out had wandered in a body out to Grenoble to witness "the Emperor's" entry into the city. They had marched out of the château to the cry of "Vive l'Empereur!" and outside the gates had joined a number of villagers of Brestalou who were bent on the same errand.

Fortunately one of the coachmen and two of the older grooms from the stables returned in the early dawn after the street demonstrations outside the Emperor's windows had somewhat calmed down, and with the routine of many years of domestic service had promptly and without murmurings set to to obey the orders given to them the day before: to have the travelling berline ready with four horses by seven o'clock.

It was very cold: the coachman and postillions shivered under their threadbare liveries. The coachman had wrapped a woollen comforter round his neck and pulled his white beaver broad-brimmed hat well over his brows, as the northeast wind was keen and would blow into his face all the way to Lyons, where the party would halt for the night. He had thick woollen gloves on and of his entire burly person only the tip of his nose could be seen between his muffler and the brim of his hat. The postillions, whip in hand, could not wrap themselves up quite so snugly: they were trying to keep themselves warm by beating their arms against their chest.

M. le Comte, aided by Hector, was arranging for the disposal of leather wallets underneath the cushions of the carriage. The wallets contained the money—twenty-five millions in notes and drafts—a godsend to the King if the usurper did succeed in driving him out of the Tuileries.

Presently the ladies came down the perron steps with faithful

Jeanne in attendance, who carried small bags and dressing-cases. Both the ladies were wrapped in long fur-lined cloaks and Mme. la Duchesse d'Agen had drawn a hood closely round her face; but Crystal de Cambray stood bareheaded in the cold frosty air, the hood of her cloak thrown back, her own fair hair, dressed high, forming the only covering for her head.

Her face looked grave and even anxious, but wonderfully serene. This should have been her wedding morning, the bells of old Brestalou church should even now have been ringing out their first joyous peal to announce the great event. Often and often in the past few weeks, ever since her father had formally betrothed her to Victor de Marmont, she had thought of this coming morning, and steeled herself to be brave against the fateful day. She had been resigned to the decree of the father and to the necessities of family and name—resigned but terribly heartsore. She was obeying of her own free will but not blindly. She knew that her marriage to a man whom she did not love was a sacrifice on her part of every hope of future happiness. Her girlish love for St. Genis had opened her eyes to the possibilities of happiness; she knew that Life could hold out a veritable cornucopia of delight and joy in a union which was hallowed by Love, and her ready sacrifice was therefore all the greater, all the more sublime, because it was not offered up in ignorance.

But all that now was changed. She was once more free to indulge in those dreams which had gladdened the days and nights of her lonely girlhood out in far-off England: dreams which somehow had not even found their culmination when St. Genis first told her of his love for her. They had always been golden dreams which had haunted her in those distant days, dreams of future happiness and of love which are seldom absent from a young girl's mind, especially if she is a little lonely, has few pleasures and is surrounded with an atmosphere of sadness.

Crystal de Cambray, standing on the perron of her stately home, felt but little sorrow at leaving it to-day: she had hardly had the time in one brief year to get very much attached to it: the sense of unreality which had been born in her when her father led her through its vast halls and stately parks had never entirely left her. The little home in England, the tiny sitting-room with its bow window, and small front garden edged with dusty evergreens, was far more real to her even now. She felt as if the last year with its pomp and gloomy magnificence was all a dream and that she was once more on the threshold of reality now, on the point of waking, when she would find herself once more in her narrow iron bed and see the patched and darned muslin curtains gently waving in the draught.

But for the moment she was glad enough to give herself to the delight of this sudden consciousness of freedom. She sniffed the sharp, frosty air with dilated nostrils like a young Arab filly that scents the illimitable vastness of meadowland around her. The excitement of the coming adventure thrilled her: she watched with glowing eyes the preparations for the journey, the bestowal under the cushions of the carriage of the money which was to help King Louis to preserve his throne.

In a sense she was sorry that her father and her aunt were coming too. She would have loved to fly across country as a trusted servant of her King; but when the time came to make a start she took her place in the big travelling coach with a light heart and a merry face. She was so sure of the justice of the King's cause, so convinced of God's wrath against the usurper, that she had no room in her thoughts for apprehension or sadness.

The Comte de Cambray on the other hand was grave and taciturn. He had spent hours last evening on the ramparts of Grenoble. He had watched the dissatisfaction of the troops grow into open rebellion and from that to burning enthusiasm for the Corsican ogre. St. Genis had given him a vivid account of the encounter at Laffray, and his ears were still ringing with the cries of "Vive l'Empereur!" which had filled the streets and ramparts of Grenoble until he himself fled back to his own château, sickened at all that he had seen and heard.

He knew that the King's own brother, M. le Comte d'Artois, was at Lyons even now with forty thousand men who were reputed to be loyal, but were not the troops of Grenoble reputed to be loyal too? and was it likely that the regiments at Lyons would behave so very differently to those at Grenoble?

Thus the wearisome journey northwards in the lumbering carriage proceeded mostly in silence. None of the occupants seemed to have much to say. Mme. la Duchesse d'Agen and M. le Comte sat on the back seats leaning against the cushions; Crystal de Cambray and ever-faithful Jeanne sat in front, making themselves as comfortable as they could.

There was a halt for déjeuner and change of horses at Rives, and here Maurice de St. Genis overtook the party. He proposed to continue the journey as far as Lyons on horseback, riding close by the off side of the carriage. Here as well as at the next halt, at St. André-le-Gaz, Maurice tried to get speech with Crystal, but she seemed cold in manner and unresponsive to his whispered words. He tried to approach her, but she pleaded fatigue and anxiety, and he was glad then that he had made arrangements not to travel beside her in the lumbering coach. His position on horseback beside the carriage would, he felt, be a more romantic one, and he half-hoped that some enterprising footpad would give him a chance of displaying his pluck and his devotion.

A start was made from St. André-le-Gaz at six o'clock in the afternoon. Crystal was getting very cramped and tired, even the fine views over the range of the Grande Chartreuse and the long white plateau of the Dent de Crolles, with the wintry sunset behind it, failed to enchain her attention. Her father and her aunt slept most of the time each in a corner of the carriage, and after the start from St. André-le-Gaz, comforted with hot coffee and fresh bread and the prospect of Lyons now only some sixty kilomètres away, Crystal settled herself against the cushions and tried to get some sleep.

The incessant shaking of the carriage, the rattle of harness and wheels, the cracking of the postillions' whips, all contributed to making her head ache, and to chase slumber away. But gradually her thoughts became more confused, as the dim winter twilight gradually faded into night and a veil of impenetrable blackness spread itself outside the windows of the coach.

The northeasterly wind had not abated: it whistled mournfully through the cracks in the woodwork of the carriage and made the windows rattle in their framework. On the box the coachman had much ado to see well ahead of him, as the vapour which rose from the flanks and shoulders of his steaming horses effectually blurred every outline on the road. The carriage lanthorns threw a weird and feeble light upon the ever-growing darkness. To' right and left the bare and frozen common land stretched its lonely vastness to some distant horizon unseen.

VI

Suddenly the cumbrous vehicle gave a terrific lurch, which sent the unsuspecting Jeanne flying into Mme. la Duchesse's lap and threw Crystal with equal violence against her father's knees. There was much cracking of whips, loud calls and louder oaths from coachman and postillions, much creaking and groaning of wheels, another lurch—more feeble this time—more groaning, more creaking, more oaths and finally the coach with a final quivering as it were of all its parts settled down to an ominous standstill.

Whereafter the oaths sounded more muffled, while there was a scampering down from the high altitude of the coachman's box and a confused murmur of voices.

It was then close on eight o'clock: Lyons was distant still some dozen miles or so—and the night by now was darker than pitch.

M. le Comte, roused from fitful slumbers and trying to gather his wandering wits, put his head out of the window: "What is it, Pierre?" he called out loudly. "What has happened?"

"It's this confounded ditch, M. le Comte," came in a gruff voice from out the darkness. "I didn't know the bridge had entirely broken down. This sacré government will not look after the roads properly."

"Are you there, Maurice?" called the Comte.

But strangely enough there came no answer to his call. M. de St. Genis must have fallen back some little distance in the rear, else he surely would have heard something of the clatter, the shouts and the swearing which were attending the present unfortunate contretemps.

"Maurice! where are you?" called the Comte again. And still no answer.

Pierre was continuing his audible mutterings. "Darkness as black as——": then he shouted with a yet more forcible volley of oaths: "Jean! you oaf! get hold of the off mare, can't you? And you, what's your name, you fool? ease the near gelding. Heavens above, what dolts!"

"Stop a moment," cried M. le Comte, "wait till the ladies can get out. This pulling and lurching is unbearable."

"Ease a moment," commanded Pierre stolidly. "Go to the near door, Jean, and help the master out of the carriage."

"Hark! what was that?" It was M. le Comte who spoke. There had been a momentary lull in the creaking and groaning of the wheels, while the two young postillions obeyed the coachman's orders to "ease a moment," and one of them came round to help the ladies and his master out of the lurching vehicle; only the horses' snorting, the champing of their bits and pawing of the hard ground broke the silence of the night.

M. le Comte had opened the near door and was half out of the carriage when a sound caught his ear which was in no way connected with the stranded vehicle and its team of snorting horses. Yet the sound came from horses—horses which were on the move not very far away and which even now seemed to be coming nearer.

"Who goes there? Maurice, is that you?" called M. le Comte more loudly.

"Stand and deliver!" came the peremptory response.

"Stand yourself or I fire," retorted the Comte, who was already groping for the pistol which he kept inside the carriage.

"You murderous villain!" came with the inevitable string of oaths from Pierre the coachman. "You ..."

The rest of this forceful expletive was broken and muffled. Evidently Pierre had been summarily gagged. There was a short, sharp scuffle somewhere on ahead; cries for help from the two postillions which were equally sharply smothered. The horses began rearing and plunging.

"One of you at the leaders' heads," came in a clear voice which in this impenetrable darkness sounded weirdly familiar to the occupants of the carriage, who awed, terrified by this unforeseen attack sat motionless, clinging to one another inside the vehicle.

Alone the Comte had not lost his presence of mind. Already he had jumped out of the carriage, banging the door to behind him, despite feeble protests from his sister; pistol in hand he tried with anxious eyes to pierce the inky blackness around him.

A muffled groan on his right caused him to turn in that direction.

"Release my coachman," he called peremptorily, "or I fire."

"Easy, M. le Comte," came as a sharp warning out of the night, in those same weirdly familiar tones; "as like as not you would be shooting your own men in this infernal darkness."

"Who is it?" whispered Crystal hoarsely. "I seem to know that voice."

"God protect us," murmured Jeanne. "It's the devil's voice, Mademoiselle."

Mme. la Duchesse said nothing. No doubt she was too frightened to speak. Her thin, bony fingers were clasped tightly round her niece's hands.

Suddenly there was another scuffle by the door, the sharp report of a pistol and then that strangely familiar voice called out again:

"Merely as a matter of form, M. le Comte!"

"You will hang for this, you rogue," came in response from the Comte.

But already Crystal had torn her hands out of Mme. la Duchesse's grasp and now was struggling to free herself from Jeanne's terrified and clinging embrace.

"Father!" she cried wildly. "Maurice! Maurice! Help! Let me go, Jeanne! They are hurting him!"

She had succeeded in pushing Jeanne roughly away and already had her hand on the door, when it was opened from the outside, and the flickering light of a carriage lanthorn fell full on the interior of the vehicle. Neither Crystal nor Mme. la Duchesse could effectually suppress a sudden gasp of terror, whilst Jeanne threw her shawl right over her head, for of a truth she thought that here was the devil himself.

The light illumined the lanthorn-bearer only fitfully, but to the terror-stricken women he appeared to be preternaturally tall and broad, with wide caped coat pulled up to his ears and an old-fashioned tricorne hat on his head; his face was entirely hidden by a black mask, and his hands by black kid gloves.

"I pray you ladies," he said quietly, and this time the voice was obviously disguised and quite unrecognisable. "I pray you have no fear. Neither I nor my men will do you or yours the slightest harm, if you will allow me without any molestation on your part to make an examination of the interior of your carriage."

Mme. la Duchesse and Jeanne remained silent: the one from fear, the other from dignity. But it was not in Crystal's nature to submit quietly to any unlawful coercion.

"This is an infamy," she protested loudly, "and you, my man, will swing on the nearest gallows for it."

"No doubt I should if I were found out," said the man imperturbably, "but the military patrols of M. le Comte d'Artois don't come out as far as this: nevertheless I must ask you ladies not to detain me on my business any longer. My men are at the door and it is over a quarter of an hour ago since we placed M. de St. Genis temporarily yet effectually hors de combat. I pray you, therefore, step out without delay so that I may proceed to ascertain whether there is anything in this carriage likely to suit my requirements."

"You must be a madman as well as a thief," retorted Crystal loudly, "to imagine that we would submit to such an outrage."

"If you do not submit, Madame," said the man calmly, "I will order my man to shoot M. le Comte in the right leg."

"You would not dare...."

But the miscreant turned his head slowly round and called over his shoulder into the night:

"Attention, my men! M. le Comte de Cambray!—have you got him?"

"Aye! aye, sir!" came from out the darkness.

Crystal gave a wild scream, and with an agonised gesture of terror clutched the highway robber by the coat.

"No! no!" she cried. "Stop! stop! no! Father! Help!"

"Mademoiselle," said the man, quietly releasing his coat from her clinging hands, "remember that M. le Comte is perfectly safe if you will deign to step out of the carriage without further delay."

He held the lanthorn in one hand, the other was suddenly imprisoned by Crystal's trembling fingers.

"Sir," she pleaded in a voice broken by terror and anxiety, "we are helpless travellers on our way to Paris, driven out of our home by the advancing horde of Corsican brigands. Our little all we have with us. You cannot take that all from us. Let us give you some money of our own free will, then the shame of robbing women who have in the darkness of the night been rendered helpless will not rest upon you. Oh! have pity upon us. Your voice is so gentle you must be good and kind. You will let us proceed on our way, will you not? and we'll take a solemn oath that we'll not attempt to put any one on your track. You will, won't you? I swear to you that you will be doing a far finer deed thereby than you can possibly dream of."

"I have some jewelry about my person," here interposed Madame's sharp voice drily, "also some gold. I agree to what my niece says. We'll swear to do nothing against you when we reach Lyons, if you will be content with what we give you of our own free will and let us go in peace."

The man allowed both ladies to speak without any interruption on his part. He even allowed Crystal's dainty fingers to cling around his gloved hand for as long as she chose: no doubt he found some pleasure in this tearful appeal from such beautiful lips, for Crystal looked divinely pretty just then, with the flickering light of the lanthorn throwing her fair head into bold relief against the surrounding gloom. Her blue eyes were shining with unshed tears, her delicate mouth was quivering with the piteousness of her appeal.

But when Mme. la Duchesse had finished speaking and began to divest herself of her rings he released his hand very gently and said in his even, quiet voice:

"Your pardon, Madame; but as it happens I have no use for ladies' trinkets, while all that you have been good enough to tell me only makes me the more eager to examine the contents of this carriage."

"But there's nothing of value in it," asserted Madame unblushingly, "except what we are offering you now."

"That is as may be, Madame. I would wish to ascertain."

"You impious malapert!" she cried out wrathfully, "would you dare lay hands upon a woman?"

"No, Madame, certainly not," he replied. "I will merely, as I have had the honour to tell you, order my men to shoot M. le Comte de Cambray in the right leg."

"You vagabond! you thief! you wouldn't dare," expostulated Madame, who seemed now on the verge of hysteria.

"Attention, my men!" he called once more over his left shoulder.

"It is no use, ma tante," here interposed Crystal with sudden calm. "We must yield to brute force. Let us get out and allow this abominable thief to wreak his impious will with us, else we lay ourselves open to further outrage at his hands. Be sure that retribution, swift and certain, will overtake him in the end."

"Come! that's wisely spoken," said the man, who seemed in no way perturbed by the scornful glances which Crystal and Madame now freely darted upon him. He stood a little aside, holding the door open for them to step out of the carriage.

"Where is M. le Comte de Cambray?" queried Crystal as she brushed past him.

"Close by," he replied, "to your right now, Mademoiselle, and perfectly safe, and M. le Marquis de St. Genis is not two hundred mètres away, equally secure and equally safe. Here, le Bossu," he added, calling out into the night, "ease the gag round your prisoner's mouth a little so that he may speak to the ladies."

While Madame la Duchesse groped her way along in the direction whence came sounds of stirring, groaning and not a little cursing which proclaimed the presence of some men held captive by others, Crystal remained beside the carriage door as if rooted to the spot. The feeble light of the lanthorn had shown her at a glance that the masked miscreant had taken every precaution for the success of his nefarious purpose. How many men he had with him altogether, she

110

could not of course ascertain: half a dozen perhaps, seeing that her father, the coachman and two postillions had been overpowered and were being closely guarded, whilst she distinctly saw that two men at least were standing behind their chief at this moment in order to ward off any possible attack against him from the rear, while he himself was engaged in the infamous task of robbing the coach of its contents.

Crystal saw him start to work in a most methodical manner. He had stood the lanthorn on the floor of the carriage and was turning over every cushion and ransacking every pocket. The leather wallets which he found, he examined with utmost coolness, seeing indeed that they were stuffed full of banknotes and drafts. His huge caped coat appeared to have immense pockets, into which those precious wallets disappeared one by one.

She knew of course that resistance was useless: the occasional glint of the feeble lanthorn light upon the pistols held by the men close beside her taught her the salutary lesson of silence and dignity. She clenched her hands until her nails were almost driven into the flesh of her palms, and her face now glowed with a fierce and passionate resentment. This money which might have saved the King and France from the immediate effects of the usurper's invasion was now the booty of a common thief! Wild thoughts of vengeance coursed through her brain: she felt like a tiger-cat that was being robbed of its young. Once—unable to control herself—she made a wild dash forward, determined to fight for her treasure, to scratch or to bite—to do anything in fact rather than stand by and see this infamous spoliation. But immediately her hands were seized, and an ominous word of command rang out weirdly through the night.

"Resistance here! Attention over there!"

Her father's safety was a guarantee of her own acquiescence. Struggling, fighting was useless! the abominable thief must be left to do his work in peace.

It did not take long. A minute or two later he too had stepped out of the carriage. He ordered one of his followers to hold the lanthorn and then quietly took up his stand beside the open door.

"Now, ladies, an you desire it," he said calmly, "you may continue your journey. Your coachman and your men are close here, on the road, securely bound. M. de St. Genis is not far off—straight up the road—you cannot miss him. We leave you free to loosen their bonds. To horse, my men!" he added in a loud, commanding voice. "Le Bossu, hold my horse a moment! and you ladies, I pray you accept my humble apologies that I do not stop to see you safely installed."

As in a dream Crystal heard the bustle incident on a number of men getting to horse: in the gloom she saw vague forms moving about hurriedly, she heard the champing of bits, the clatter of stirrup and bridle. The masked man was the last to move. After he had given the order to mount he stood for nearly a minute by the carriage door, exactly facing Crystal, not five paces away.

His companion had put the lanthorn down on the step, and by its light she could see him distinctly: a mysterious, masked figure who, with wanton infamy, had placed the satisfaction of his dishonesty and of his greed athwart the destiny of the King of France.

Crystal knew that through the peep-holes of his mask, the man's eyes were fixed intently upon her and the knowledge caused a blush of mortification and of shame to flood her cheeks and throat. At that moment she would gladly have given her life for the power to turn the tables upon that abominable rogue, to filch from him that precious treasure which she had hoped to deposit at the feet of the King for the ultimate success of his cause: and she would have given much for the power to tear off that concealing mask, so that for the rest of her life she might be able to visualise that face which she would always execrate.

Something of what she felt and thought must have been apparent in her expressive eyes, for presently it seemed to her as if beneath the narrow curtain that concealed the lower part of the man's face there hovered the shadow of a smile.

The next moment he had the audacity slightly to raise his hat and to make her a bow before he finally turned to go. Crystal had taken one step backward just then, whether because she was afraid that the man would try and approach her, or because of a mere sense of dignity, she could not herself have said. Certain it is that she did move back and that in so doing her foot came in contact with an object lying on the ground. The shape and size of it were unmistakable, it was the pistol which the Comte must have dropped when first he stepped out of the carriage, and was seized upon by this band of thieves. Guided by that same strange and wonderful instinct which has so often caused women in times of war to turn against the assailants of their men or devastation of their homes, Crystal picked up the weapon without a moment's hesitation; she knew that it was loaded, and she knew how to use it. Even as the masked man moved away into the darkness, she fired in the direction whence his firm footsteps still sent their repeated echo.

The short, sharp report died out in the still, frosty air; Crystal vainly strained her ears to catch the sound of a fall or a groan. But in the confusion that ensued she could not distinguish any individual sound. She knew that Mme. la Duchesse and Jeanne had screamed, she heard a few loud curses, the clatter of bits and bridles, the snorting of horses and presently the noise of several horses galloping away, out in the direction of Chambéry.

Then nothing more.

M. le Comte as well as the coachman and postillions were lying helpless and bound somewhere in the darkness. It took the three women some time to find them first and then to release them.

Crystal with great presence of mind had run to the horses' heads, directly after she had fired that random shot. The poor, frightened animals had reared and plunged, and had thereby succeeded in dragging the heavy carriage out of the ditch. After which they had stopped, rigid for a moment and trembling as horses will sometimes when they are terrified, before they start running away for dear life. That moment was Crystal's opportunity and fortunately she took it at the right time and in the right way.

A hand on the leaders' bridles, a soothing voice, the absence of further alarming noises tended at once to quieten the team—a set of good steady Normandy draft-horses with none too much corn in their bellies to heat their sluggish blood.

While Crystal stood at her post, Mme. la Duchesse—cool and practical—found her way firstly to M. le Comte, then to the coachman and postillions, and ordering Jeanne to help her, she succeeded in freeing the men from their bonds.

Then calling to one of them to precede her with a lanthorn, she started on the quest for Maurice de St. Genis. He was found—as that abominable thief had said—some two hundred yards up the road, very securely bound and with his own handkerchief tied round his mouth, but otherwise comfortably laid on a dry bit of roadside grass.

Mme. la Duchesse would not reply to his questions, but after he was released and able to stand up she made him give her a brief account of his adventure. It had all been so sudden and so quick—he had fallen back a little behind the carriage as soon as the night had set in, as he thought it safer to keep along the edge of the road. He was feeling tired and drowsy, and allowing his horse to amble along in the slow jog-trot peculiar to its race. No doubt his attention had for some time been on the wander, when, all at once, in the darkness someone seized hold of his horse by the bridle and forced it back upon its haunches. The next moment Maurice felt himself grabbed by the leg, and dragged off his horse: he shouted for help, but the carriage was on ahead and its own rattle prevented the shouts from being heard. After which he was bound and gagged and summarily left to lie by the roadside. He had had no chance against the ruffians, as they were numerous, but they did not attempt to ill-use him in any way.

Slowly hobbling towards the carriage beside Mme. la Duchesse, for he was cramped and stiff, Maurice told her all there was to tell. He had heard the distant scuffle, the shouts and calls, also one pistol-shot at the end, but he had been rendered helpless even before the carriage had come to a halt in the ditch.

It was M. le Comte who in his accustomed measured tones now gave Maurice de St. Genis the details of this awful adventure: the ransacking of the carriage by the mysterious miscreant—the loss of the twenty-five millions, the complete shattering of all hope to help the King with this money in the hour of his need, and finally Crystal's desperate act of revenge, as she shot the pistol off into the darkness, hoping at least to disable the impudent rogue who had done them and the King such a fatal injury.

St. Genis listened to it all with lips held tightly pressed together, firm determination causing every muscle in his body to grow taut and firm with the earnestness of his resolve.

When M. le Comte had finished speaking, and with a sigh of discouragement had suggested an immediate continuation of his journey, Maurice said resolutely:

"Do you go on straightway to Lyons with the ladies, my dear Comte, but I shall not leave this neighbourhood till by some means or other I find those miscreants and lay their infamous leader by the heel."

"Well spoken, Maurice," said the Comte guardedly, "but how will you do it?—it is late and the night darker than ever."

"You must spare me one of your horses, my dear Comte," replied the young man, "as mine apparently has been stolen by those abominable thieves, and I'll ride back to the nearest village—you remember we passed it not half an hour ago. I'll get lodgings there and get some information. In the meanwhile perhaps you will see M. le Comte d'Artois immediately, tell him all that has happened and beg him to send me as early in the morning as possible a dozen cavalrymen or so, to help me scour the country. I'll be on the look-out for them on this road by six o'clock, and, please God! the day shall not go by before we have those infamous marauders by the heels. Twenty-five millions, remember, are not dragged about open country quite so easily as those thieves imagine. They are bound to leave some trace of their whereabouts sometimes."

He appeared so confident and so cheerful that some of his optimism infected M. le Comte too. The latter promised to get an audience of M. le Comte d'Artois that very evening, and of course the necessary cavalry patrol would at once be forthcoming.

"God grant you success, Maurice," he added fervently, and the young man's energy and enthusiasm were also rewarded by a warm, glowing look from Crystal.

A quarter of an hour afterwards, M. le Comte's travelling coach was once more ready for departure. Pierre had been given his orders to make due haste for Lyons, and to drive a unicorn team of three horses instead of a regulation four, whereupon he had muttered a string of oaths which would have caused a Paris wine-shop loafer to blush.

One of the horses thereupon was detached from the team for Maurice's use and made ready with one of the postillions' saddles; the other postillion had to climb up to the seat next to the coachman: all three men were feeling not a little shamed at the sorry rôle which they had just played, and they vowed revenge against the mysterious thieves who had sprung upon them unawares and in the dark, or Mordieu! they would have suffered severely for their impudence.

In silence M. le Comte, Mme. la Duchesse and Crystal, followed by faithful Jeanne, re-entered the carriage. No one had been hurt. M. le Comte's arms felt a little stiff from the cords which had bound them behind his back and Jeanne was inclined to be hysterical, but Crystal felt a fierce resentment burning in her heart. Somehow she had no hope that Maurice would succeed, even though she threw him at the last a kindly and encouraging smile. Her one hope was that she had inflicted a painful if not a deadly wound upon the shameless robber of the King's money.

Soon the party was once more comfortably settled and the cumbrous vehicle, after another violent lurch, was once more on its way.

"Farewell, Maurice! good luck!" called M. le Comte at the last.

The young man waited until the heavy carriage swung more easily upon its springs, then he mounted his horse, turned its head in the opposite direction and rode slowly back up the road.

Inside the vehicle all was silent for a while, then M. le Comte asked quietly:

"Did he find everything?"

"Everything," replied Crystal.

"I put in five wallets."

"Yes. He took them all."

"It is curious they should have fallen on us just by that broken bridge."

"They were lying in wait for us, of course."

"Knowing that we had the money, do you think?" asked the Comte.

"Of course," replied Crystal with still that note of bitter resentment in her voice.

"But who, besides ourselves and the préfet? ..." began the Comte, who clearly was very puzzled.

"Victor de Marmont for one ..." retorted the girl.

"Surely you don't suppose that he would play the rôle of a highwayman and ..."

"No, I don't," she broke in somewhat impatiently, "he wouldn't have the pluck for one thing, and moreover the masked man was considerably taller than Victor."

"Well, then?"

"It is only an idea, father, dear," she said more gently, "but somehow I cannot believe that this was just ordinary highway robbery. This road is supposed to be quite safe: travellers are not warned against armed highwaymen, and marauders wouldn't be so well horsed and clothed. My belief is that it was a paid gang stationed at the broken bridge on purpose to rob us and no one else."

"Maurice will soon be after them to-morrow, and I'll see M. le Comte d'Artois directly we get to Lyons," said the Comte after a slight pause, during which he was obviously pondering over his daughter's suggestion.

"It won't be any use, father," Crystal said with a sigh. "The whole thing has been organised, I feel sure, and the head that planned this abominable robbery will know how to place his booty in safety."

Whereupon the Comte sighed, for he was too well-bred to curse in the presence of his daughter and his sister, Mme. la Duchesse had said nothing all this while: nor did she offer any comment upon the mysterious occurrence all the time that the next stage of the wearisome journey proceeded.

VIII

Less than an hour later the coach came to a halt once more.

M. le Comte woke up with a start.

"My God!" he exclaimed, "what is it now?"

Crystal had not been asleep: her thoughts were too busy, her brain too much tormented with trying to find some plausible answer to the riddle which agitated her: "Who had planned this abominable robbery? Was it indeed Victor de Marmont himself? or had a greater, a mightier mind than his discovered the secret of this swift journey to Paris and ordered the clever raid upon the treasure?"

The rumble of the wheels had—though she was awake—prevented her from hearing the rapid approach of a number of horses in the wake of the coach, until a peremptory: "Halt! in the name of the Emperor!" suddenly chased every other thought away; like her father she murmured: "My God! what is it now?"

This time there was no mystery, there would be no puzzlement as to the meaning of this fresh attack. The air was full of those sounds that denote the presence of many horses and of many men; there was, too, the clinking of metal, the champing of steel bits, the brief words of command which proclaimed the men to be soldiers.

They appeared to be all round the coach, for the noise of their presence came from everywhere at once.

Already the Comte had put his head out of the window: "What is it now?" he asked again, more peremptorily this time.

"In the name of the Emperor!" was the loud reply.

"We do not halt in the name of an usurper," said the Comte. "En avant, Pierre!"

"You urge those horses on at your peril, coachman," was the defiant retort.

A quick word of command was given, there was more clanking of metal, snorting of horses, loud curses from Pierre on the box, and the commanding voice spoke again:

"M. le Comte de Cambray!"

"That is my name!" replied the Comte. "And who is it, pray, who dares impede peaceful travellers on their way?"

"By order of the Emperor," was the curt reply.

"I know of no such person in France!"

"Vive l'Empereur!" was shouted defiantly in response.

Whereupon M. le Comte de Cambray—proud, disdainful and determined to show no fear or concern, withdrew from the window and threw himself back against the cushions of the carriage.

"What in the Virgin's name is the meaning of this?" murmured Mme. la Duchesse.

"God in heaven only knows," sighed the Comte.

But obviously the coach had not been stopped by a troop of mounted soldiers for the mere purpose of proclaiming the Emperor's name on the high road in the dark. The same commanding voice which had answered the Comte's challenge was giving rapid orders to dismount and to bring along one of the carriage lanthorns.

The next moment the door of the coach was opened from without, and the light of the lanthorn held up by a man in uniform fell full on the figure and on the profile of Victor de Marmont.

"M. le Comte, I regret," he said coldly, "in the name of the Emperor I must demand from you the restitution of his property."

The Comte shrugged his shoulders and vouchsafed no reply.

"M. le Comte," said de Marmont, more peremptorily this time, "I have twenty-four men with me, who will seize by force if necessary that which I herewith command you to give up voluntarily."

Still no reply. M. le Comte de Cambray would think himself bemeaned were he to parley with a traitor.

"As you will, M. le Comte," was de Marmont's calm comment on the old man's attitude. "Sergeant!" he commanded, "seize the four persons in this coach. Three of them are women, so be as gentle as you can. Go round to the other door first."

"Father," now urged Crystal gently, "do you think that this is wise—or dignified?"

"Wisely spoken, Mlle. Crystal," rejoined de Marmont. "Have I not said that I have two dozen soldiers with me—all trained to do their

117

duty? Why should M. le Comte allow them to lay hands upon you and on Mme. la Duchesse?"

"It is an outrage," broke in the Comte savagely. "You and your soldiers are traitors, rebels and deserters."

"But we are in superior numbers, M. le Comte," said de Marmont with a sneer. "Would it not be wiser to yield with a good grace? Mme. la Duchesse," he added with an attempt at geniality, "yours was always the wise head, I am told, that guided the affairs of M. le Comte de Cambray in the past. Will you not advise him now?"

"I would, my good man," retorted the Duchesse, "but my wise counsels would benefit no one now, seeing that you have been sent on a fool's errand."

De Marmont laughed.

"Does Mme. la Duchesse mean to deny that twenty-five million francs belonging to the Emperor are hidden at this moment inside this coach?"

"I deny, Monsieur de Marmont, that any twenty-five million francs belong to the son of an impecunious Corsican attorney—and I also deny that any twenty-five million francs are in this coach at the present moment."

"That is exactly what I desire to ascertain, Madame."

"Ascertain by all means then," quoth Madame impatiently, "the other thief ascertained the same thing an hour ago, and I must confess that he did so more profitably than you are like to do."

"The other thief?" exclaimed de Marmont, greatly puzzled.

"It is as Mme. la Duchesse has deigned to tell you," here interposed the Comte coolly. "I have no objection to your knowing that I had intended to convey to His Majesty the King—its rightful owner—a sum of money—originally stolen by the Corsican usurper from France—but that an hour ago a party of armed thieves—just like yourself—attacked us, bound and gagged me and my men, ransacked my coach and made off with the booty."

"And I thank God now," murmured Crystal involuntarily, "that the money has fallen into the hands of a common highwayman rather than in those of the scourge of mankind."

"M. le Comte ..." stammered de Marmont, who, still incredulous, yet vaguely alarmed, was nevertheless determined not to accept this extraordinary narrative with blind confidence.

But M. le Comte de Cambray's dignity rose at last to the occasion: "You choose to disbelieve me, Monsieur?" he asked quietly.

De Marmont made no reply.

"Will my word of honour not suffice?"

"My orders, M. le Comte," said de Marmont gruffly, "are that I bring back to my Emperor the money that is his. I will not leave one stone unturned ..."

"Enough, Monsieur," broke in the Comte with calm dignity. "We will alight now, if your soldiers will stand aside."

And for the second time on this eventful night, Mme. la Duchesse d'Agen and Mlle. Crystal de Cambray, together with faithful Jeanne, were forced to alight from the coach and to stand by while the cushions of the carriage were being turned over by the light of a flickering lanthorn and every corner of the interior ransacked for the elusive treasure.

"There is nothing here, mon Colonel," said a gruff voice out of the darkness, after a while.

A loud curse broke from de Marmont's lips.

"You are satisfied?" asked the Comte coldly, "that I have told you the truth?"

"Search the luggage in the boot," cried de Marmont savagely, without heeding him, "search the men on the box! bring more light here! That money is somewhere in this coach, I'll swear. If I do not find it I'll take every one here back a prisoner to Grenoble ... or ..."

He paused, himself ashamed of what he had been about to say.

"Or you will order your soldiers to lay hands upon our persons, is that it, M. de Marmont?" broke in Crystal coldly.

He made no reply, for of a truth that had been his thought: foiled in his hope of rendering his beloved Emperor so signal a service, he had lost all sense of chivalry in this overwhelming feeling of baffled rage.

Crystal's cold challenge recalled him to himself, and now he felt ashamed of what he had just contemplated, ashamed, too, of what he had done. He hated the Comte ... he hated all royalists and all enemies of the Emperor ... but he hated the Comte doubly because of the insults which he (de Marmont) had had to endure that evening at Brestalou. He had looked upon this expedition as a means of vengeance for those insults, a means, too, of showing his power and his worth before Crystal and of winning her through that power which the Emperor had given him, and through that worth which the Emperor had recognised.

But, though he hated the Comte he knew him to be absolutely incapable of telling a deliberate lie, and absolutely incapable of bartering his word of honour for the sake of his own safety.

Crystal's words brought this knowledge back to his mind; and now the desire seized him to prove himself as chivalrous as he was powerful. He was one of those men who are so absolutely ignorant of a woman's nature that they believe that a woman's love can be won by deeds as apart from personality, and that a woman's dislike and contempt can be changed into love. He loved Crystal more absolutely now than he had ever done in the days when he was practically her accepted suitor: his unbridled and capricious nature clung desperately to that which he could not hold, and since he had felt—that evening at Brestalou—that his political convictions had placed an insuperable

119

barrier between himself and Crystal de Cambray, he felt that no woman on earth could ever be quite so desirable.

His mistake lay in this: that he believed that it was his political convictions alone which had turned Crystal away from him: he felt that he could have won her love through her submission once she was his wife, now he found that he would have to win her love first and her wifely submission would only follow afterwards.

Just now—though in the gloom he could only see the vague outline of her graceful form, and only heard her voice as through a veil of darkness—he had the longing to prove himself at once worthy of her regard and deserving of her gratitude.

Without replying to her direct challenge, he made a vigorous effort to curb his rage, and to master his disappointment. Then he gave a few brief commands to his sergeant, ordering him to repair the disorder inside the coach, and to stop all further searching both of the vehicle and of the men.

Finally he said with calm dignity: "M. le Comte, I must offer you my humble apologies for the inconvenience to which you have been subjected. I humbly beg Mme. la Duchesse and Mademoiselle Crystal to accept these expressions of my profound regret. A soldier's life and a soldier's duty must be my excuse for the part I was forced to take in this untoward happening. Mme. la Duchesse, I pray you deign to re-enter your carriage. M. le Comte, if there is aught I can do for you, I pray you command me...."

Neither the Duchesse nor the Comte, however, deigned to take the slightest notice of the abominable traitor and of his long tirade. Madame was shivering with cold and yawning with fatigue, and in her heart consigned the young brute to everlasting torments.

The Comte would have thought it beneath his dignity to accept any explanation from a follower of the Corsican usurper. Without a word he was now helping his sister into the carriage.

Jeanne, of course, hardly counted—she was dazed into semi-imbecility by the renewed terrors she had just gone through: so for the moment Victor felt that Crystal was isolated from the others. She stood a little to one side—he could only just see her, as the sergeant was holding up the lanthorn for Mme. la Duchesse to see her way into the coach. M. le Comte went on to give a few directions to the coachman.

"Mademoiselle Crystal!" murmured Victor softly.

And he made a step forward so that now she could not move toward the carriage without brushing against him. But she made no reply.

"Mademoiselle Crystal," he said again, "have you not one single kind word for me?"

"A kind word?" she retorted almost involuntarily, "after such an outrage?"

"I am a soldier," he urged, "and had to do my duty."

"You were a soldier once, M. de Marmont—a soldier of the King. Now you are only a deserter."

"A soldier of the Emperor, Mademoiselle, of the man who led France to victory and to glory, and will do so again, now that he has come back into his own once more."

"You and I, M. de Marmont," she said coldly, "look at France from different points of view. This is neither the hour nor the place to discuss our respective sentiments. I pray you, allow me to join my aunt in the carriage. I am cold and tired, and she will be anxious for me."

"Will you at least give me one word of encouragement, Mademoiselle?" he urged. "As you say, our points of view are very different. But I am on the high road to fortune. The Emperor is back in France, the army flocks to his eagles as one man. He trusts me and I shall rise to greatness under his wing. Mademoiselle Crystal, you promised me your hand, I have not released you from that promise yet. I will come and claim it soon."

"Excitement seems to have turned your brain, M. de Marmont," was all that Crystal said, and she walked straight past him to the carriage door.

Victor smothered a curse. These aristos were as arrogant as ever. What lesson had the revolution and the guillotine taught them? None. This girl who had spent her whole life in poverty and exile, and was like—after a brief interregnum—to return to exile and poverty again, was not a whit less proud than her kindred had been when they walked in their hundreds up the steps of the guillotine with a smile of lofty disdain upon their lips.

Victor de Marmont was a son of the people—of those who had made the revolution and had fought the whole of Europe in order to establish their right to govern themselves as they thought best, and he hated all these aristos—the men who had fled from their country and abandoned it when she needed her sons' help more than she had ever done before.

The aristocrat was for him synonymous with the émigré—with the man who had raised a foreign army to fight against France, who had brought the foreigner marching triumphantly into Paris. He hated the aristocrat, but he loved Crystal, the one desirable product of that old regime system which he abhorred.

But with him a woman's love meant a woman's submission. He was more determined than ever now to win her, but he wanted to win her through her humiliation and his triumph—excitement had turned his brain? Well! so be it, fear and oppression would turn her heart and crush her pride.

He made no further attempt to detain her: he had asked for a kind word and she had given him withering scorn. Excitement had turned his brain ... he was not even worthy of parley—not even worthy of a formal refusal!

To his credit be it said that the thought of immediate revenge did not enter his mind then. He might have subjected her then and there to deadly outrage—he might have had her personal effects searched, her person touched by the rough hands of his soldiers. But though his estimate of a woman's love was a low one, it was not so base as to imagine that Crystal de Cambray would ever forgive so dastardly an insult.

As she walked past him to the door, however, he said under his breath:

"Remember, Mademoiselle, that you and your family at this moment are absolutely in my power, and that it is only because of my regard for you that I let you all now depart from here in peace."

Whether she heard or not, he could not say; certain it is that she made no reply, nor did she turn toward him at all. The light of the lanthorn lit up her delicate profile, pale and drawn, her tightly pressed lips, the look of utter contempt in her eyes, which even the fitful shadow cast by her hair over her brows could not altogether conceal.

The Comte had given what instructions he wished to Pierre. He stood by the carriage door waiting for his daughter: no doubt he had heard what went on between her and de Marmont, and was content to leave her to deal what scorn was necessary for the humiliation of the traitor.

He helped Crystal into the carriage, and also the unfortunate Jeanne; finally he too followed, and pulled the door to behind him.

Victor did not wait to see the coach make a start. He gave the order to remount.

"How far are we from St. Priest?" he asked.

"Not eight kilomètres, mon Colonel," was the reply.

"En avant then, ventre-à-terre!" he commanded, as he swung himself into the saddle.

The great high road between Grenoble and Lyons is very wide, and Pierre had no need to draw his horses to one side, as de Marmont and his troop, after much scrambling, champing of bits and clanking of metal, rode at a sharp trot past the coach and him.

For some few moments the sound of the horses' hoofs on the hard road kept the echoes of the night busy with their resonance, but soon that sound grew fainter and fainter still—after five minutes it died away altogether.

M. de Comte put his head out of the window.

"Eh bien, Pierre," he called, "why don't we start?"

The postillion cracked his whip; Pierre shouted to his horses; the heavy coach groaned and creaked and was once more on its way.

In the interior no one spoke. Jeanne's terror had melted in a silent flow of tears.

Lyons was reached shortly before midnight. M. le Comte's carriage had some difficulty in entering the town, as by orders of M. le

Comte d'Artois it had already been placed in a state of defence against the possible advance of the "band of pirates from Corsica." The bridge of La Guillotière had been strongly barricaded and it took M. le Comte de Cambray some little time to establish his identity before the officer in command of the post allowed him to proceed on his way.

The town was fairly full owing to the presence of M. le Comte d'Artois, who had taken up his quarters at the archiepiscopal palace, and of his staff, who were scattered in various houses about the town. Nevertheless M. le Comte and his family were fortunate enough in obtaining comfortable accommodation at the Hotel Bourbon.

The party was very tired, and after a light supper retired to bed.

But not before M. le Comte de Cambray had sent a special autographed message to Monseigneur le Comte d'Artois explaining to him under what tragic circumstances the sum of twenty-five million francs destined to reach His Majesty the King had fallen into a common highwayman's hands and begging that a posse of cavalry be sent out on the road after the marauders and be placed under the orders of M. le Marquis de St. Genis, who would be on the look-out for their arrival. He begged that the posse should consist of not less than thirty men, seeing that some armed followers of the Corsican brigand were also somewhere on the way.

CHAPTER V

THE RIVALS

I

The weather did not improve as the night wore on: soon a thin, cold drizzle added to the dreariness and to Maurice de St. Genis' ever-growing discomfort.

He had started off gaily enough, cheered by Crystal's warm look of encouragement and comforted by the feeling of certainty that he would get even with that mysterious enemy who had so impudently thrown himself athwart a plan which had service of the King for its sole object.

Maurice had not exchanged confidences with Crystal since the adventure, but his ideas—without his knowing it—absolutely coincided with hers. He, too, was quite sure that no common footpad had engineered their daring attack. Positive knowledge of the money and its destination had been the fountain from which had sprung the comedy of the masked highwayman and his little band of robbers. Maurice mentally reckoned that there must have been at least half a dozen of these bravos—of the sort that in these times were easily enough hired in any big city to play any part, from that of armed escort to nervous travellers to that of seeker of secret information for the benefit of either political party—loafers that hung round the wine-shops in search of a means of earning a few days' rations, discharged soldiers of the Empire some of them, whose loyalty to the Restoration had been questioned from the first.

Maurice had no doubt that whatever motive had actuated the originator of the bold plan to possess himself of twenty-five million francs, he had deliberately set to work to employ men of that type to help him in his task.

It had all been very audacious and—Maurice was bound to admit—very well carried out. As for the motive, he was never for a moment in doubt. It was a Bonapartist plot, of that he felt sure, as well as of the fact that Victor de Marmont was the originator of it all. He probably had not taken any active part in the attack, but he had employed the men—Maurice would have taken an oath on that!

The Comte de Cambray must have let fall an unguarded hint in the course of his last interview with de Marmont at Brestalou, and when Victor went away disgraced and discomfited he, no doubt, thought to take his revenge in the way most calculated to injure both the Comte and the royalist cause.

Satisfied with this mental explanation of past events, St. Genis had ridden on in the darkness, his spirits kept up with hopes and thoughts of a glaring counter revenge. But his limbs were still stiff and bruised from the cramped position in which he had lain for so long, and presently, when the cold drizzle began to penetrate to his bones, his enthusiasm and confidence dwindled. The village seemed to recede further and further into the distance. He thought when he had ridden through it earlier in the evening that it was not very far from the scene of the attack—a dozen kilomètres perhaps—now it seemed more like thirty; he thought too that it was a village of some considerable size—five hundred souls or perhaps more—he had noticed as he rode through it a well-illuminated, one-storied house, and the words "Débit de vins" and "Chambres pour voyageurs" painted in bold characters above the front door. But now he had ridden on and on along the dark road for what seemed endless hours—unconscious of time save that it was dragging on leaden-footed and wearisome ... and still no light on ahead to betray the presence of human habitations, no distant church bells to mark the progress of the night.

At last, in desperation, Maurice de St. Genis had thought of wrapping himself in his cloak and getting what rest he could by the roadside, for he was getting very tired and saddle-sore, when on his left he perceived in the far distance, glimmering through the mist, two small lights like bright eyes shining in the darkness.

What kind of a way led up to those welcome lights, Maurice had, of course, no idea; but they proclaimed at any rate the presence of human beings, of a house, of the warmth of fire; and without hesitation the young man turned his horse's head at right angles from the road.

He had crossed a couple of ploughed fields and an intervening ditch, when in the distance to his right and behind him he heard the sound of horses at a brisk trot, going in the direction of Lyons.

Maurice drew rein for a moment and listened until the sound came nearer. There must have been at least a score of mounted men—a military patrol sent out by M. le Comte d'Artois, no doubt, and now on its way back to Lyons. Just for a second or two the young man had thoughts of joining up with the party and asking their help or their escort: he even gave a vigorous shout which, however, was lost in the clang and clatter of horses' hoofs and of the accompanying jingle of metal.

He turned his horse back the way he had come; but before he had recrossed one of the ploughed fields, the troop of mounted men—whatever they were—had passed by, and Maurice was left once more in solitude, shouting and calling in vain.

There was nothing for it then, but to turn back again, and to make his way as best he could toward those inviting lights. In any case nothing could have been done in this pitch-dark night against the highway thieves, and St. Genis had no fear that M. le Comte d'Artois would fail to send him help for his expedition against them on the morrow.

The lights on ahead were getting perceptibly nearer, soon they detached themselves still more clearly in the gloom—other lights appeared in the immediate neighbourhood—too few for a village—thought Maurice, and grouped closely together, suggesting a main building surrounded by other smaller ones close by.

Soon the whole outline of the house could be traced through the enveloping darkness: two of the windows were lighted from within, and an oil lamp, flickering feebly, was fixed in a recess just above the door. The welcome words: "Chambres pour voyageurs. Aristide Briot, propriétaire," greeted Maurice's wearied eyes as he drew rein. Good luck was apparently attending him for, thus picking his way across fields, he had evidently struck an out-of-the-way hostelry on some bridle path off the main road, which was probably a short cut between Chambéry and Vienne.

Be that as it may, he managed to dismount—stiff as he was—and having tried the door and found it fastened, he hammered against it with his boot.

A few moments later, the bolts were drawn and an elderly man in blue blouse and wide trousers, his sabots stuffed with straw, came shuffling out of the door.

"Who's there?" he called in a feeble, querulous voice.

"A traveller—on horseback," replied Maurice. "Come, petit père," he added more impatiently, "will you take my horse or call to one of your men?"

"It is too late to take in travellers," muttered the old man. "It is nearly midnight, and everyone is abed except me."

"Too late, morbleu?" exclaimed the young man peremptorily. "You surely are not thinking of refusing shelter to a traveller on a night like this. Why, how far is it to the nearest village?"

"It is very late," reiterated the old man plaintively, "and my house is quite full."

"There's a shake-down in the kitchen anyway, I'll warrant, and one for my horse somewhere in an outhouse," retorted Maurice as without more ado he suddenly threw the reins into the old man's hand and unceremoniously pushed him into the house.

The man appeared to hesitate for a moment or two. He grumbled and muttered something which Maurice did not hear, and his shrewd eyes—the knowing eyes of a peasant of the Dauphiné—took a rapid survey of the belated traveller's clothes, the expensive caped coat, the well-made boots, the fashionable hat, which showed up clearly now by the light from within.

Satisfied that there could be no risk in taking in so well-dressed a traveller, feeling moreover that a good horse was always a hostage for the payment of the bill in the morning, the man now, without another word or look at his guest, turned his back on the house and led the horse away—somewhere out into the darkness—Maurice did not take the trouble to ascertain where.

He was under shelter. There was the remnant of a wood-fire in the hearth at the corner, some benches along the walls. If he could not get a bed, he could certainly get rest and warmth for the night. He put down his hat, took off his coat, and kicked the smouldering log into a blaze; then he drew a chair close to the fire and held his numbed feet and hands to the pleasing warmth.

Thoughts of food and wine presented themselves too, now that he felt a little less cold and stiff, and he awaited the old man's return with eagerness and impatience.

The shuffling of wooden sabots outside the door was a pleasing sound: a moment or two later the old man had come back and was busying himself with once more bolting his front door.

"Well now, père Briot," said Maurice cheerily, "as I take it you are the proprietor of this abode of bliss, what about supper?"

"Bread and cheese if you like," muttered the man curtly.

"And a bottle of wine, of course."

"Yes. A bottle of wine."

"Well! be quick about it, petit père. I didn't know how hungry I was till you talked of bread and cheese."

"Would you like some cold meat?" queried the man indifferently.

"Of course I should! Have I not said that I was hungry?"

"You'll pay for it all right enough?"

"I'll pay for the supper before I stick a fork into it," rejoined Maurice impatiently, "but in Heaven's name hurry up, man! I am half dead with sleep as well as with hunger."

The old man—a real peasant of the Dauphiné in his deliberate manner and shrewd instincts of caution—once more shuffled out of the room, and St. Genis lapsed into a kind of pleasant torpor as the warmth of the fire gradually crept through his sinews and loosened all his limbs, while the anticipation of wine and food sent his wearied thoughts into a happy day-dream.

Ten minutes later he was installed before a substantial supper, and worthy Aristide Briot was equally satisfied with the two pieces of silver which St. Genis had readily tendered him.

"You said your house was full, petit père," said Maurice after a while, when the edge of his hunger had somewhat worn off. "I shouldn't have thought there were many travellers in this out-of-the-way place."

"The place is not out-of-the-way," retorted the old man gruffly. "The road is a good one, and a short cut between Vienne and Chambéry. We get plenty of travellers this way!"

"Well! I did not strike the road, unfortunately. I saw your lights in the distance and cut across some fields. It was pretty rough in the dark, I can tell you."

"That's just what those other cavaliers said, when they turned up here about an hour ago. A noisy crowd they were. I had no room for them in my house, so they had to go."

St. Genis at once put down his knife and fork.

"A noisy crowd of travellers," he exclaimed, "who arrived here an hour ago?"

"Parbleu!" rejoined the other, "and all wanting beds too. I had no room. I can only put up one or two travellers. I sent them on to Levasseur's, further along the road. Only the wounded man I could not turn away. He is up in our best bedroom."

"A wounded man? You have a wounded man here, petit père?"

"Oh! it's not much of a wound," explained the old man with unconscious irrelevance. "He himself calls it a mere scratch. But my old woman took a fancy to him: he is young and well-looking, you understand.... She is clever at bandages too, so she has looked after him as if he were her own son."

Mechanically, St. Genis had once more taken up his knife and fork, though of a truth the last of his hunger had vanished. But these Dauphiné peasants were suspicious and queer-tempered, and already

127

the young man's surprise had matured into a plan which he would not be able to carry through without the help of Aristide Briot. Noisy cavaliers—he mused to himself—a wounded man! ... wounded by the stray shot aimed at him by Crystal de Cambray! Indeed, St. Genis had much ado to keep his excitement in check, and to continue with a pretence at eating while Briot watched him with stolid indifference.

"Petit père," said the young man at last with as much unconcern as he could affect. "I have been thinking that you have—unwittingly—given me an excellent piece of news. I do believe that the man in your best bedroom upstairs is a friend of mine whom I was to have met at Lyons to-day and whose absence from our place of tryst had made me very anxious. I was imagining that all sorts of horrors had happened to him, for he is in the secret service of the King and exposed to every kind of danger. His being wounded in some skirmish either with highway robbers or with a band of the Corsican's pirates would not surprise me in the least, and the fact that he had some half-dozen mounted men with him confirms me in my belief that indeed it is my friend who is lying upstairs, as he often has to have an escort in the exercise of his duties. At any rate, petit père," he concluded as he rose from the table, "by your leave, I'll go up and ascertain."

While he rattled off these pretty proceeds of his own imagination, Maurice de St. Genis kept a sharp watch on Aristide Briot's face, ready to note the slightest sign of suspicion should it creep into the old man's shrewd eyes.

Briot, however, did not exhibit any violent interest in his guest's story, and when the latter had finished speaking he merely said, pointing to the remnants of food upon the table:

"I thought you said that you were hungry."

"So I was, petit père," rejoined Maurice impatiently, "so I was: but my hunger is not so great as it was, and before I eat another morsel I must satisfy myself that it is my friend who is safe and well in your old woman's care."

"Oh! he is well enough," grunted Briot, "and you can see him in the morning."

"That I cannot, for I shall have to leave here soon after dawn. And I could not get a wink of sleep whilst I am in such a state of uncertainty about my friend."

"But you can't go and wake him now. He is asleep for sure, and my old woman wouldn't like him to be disturbed, after all the care she has given him."

St. Genis, fretting with impatience, could have cursed aloud or shaken the obstinate old peasant roughly by the shoulders.

"I shouldn't wake him," he retorted, irritated beyond measure at the man's futile opposition. "I'll go up on tiptoe, candle in hand—you shall show me the way to his room—and I'll just ascertain whether the wounded man is my friend or not, then I'll come down again quietly and finish my supper.

"Come, petit père, I insist," he added more peremptorily, seeing that Briot—with the hesitancy peculiar to his kind—still made no movement to obey, but stood close by scratching his scanty locks and looking puzzled and anxious.

Fortunately for him Maurice understood the temperament of these peasants of the Dauphiné, he knew that with their curious hesitancy and inherent suspiciousness it was always the easiest to make up their minds for them.

So now—since he was absolutely determined to come to grips with that abominable thief upstairs, before the night was many minutes older—he ceased to parley with Briot.

A candle stood close to his hand on the table, a bit of kindling wood lay in a heap in one corner, with the help of the one he lighted the other, then candle in hand he walked up to the door.

"Show me the way, petit père," he said.

And Aristide Briot, with a shrug of the shoulders which implied that he there and then put away from him any responsibility for what might or might not occur after this, and without further comment, led the way upstairs.

II

On the upper landing at the top of the stairs Briot paused. He pointed to a door at the end of the narrow corridor, and said curtly:

"That's his room."

"I thank you, petit père," whispered St. Genis in response. "Don't wait for me, I'll be back directly."

"He is not yet in bed," was Briot's dry comment.

A thin streak of light showed underneath the door. As St. Genis walked rapidly toward it he wondered if the door would be locked. That certainly was a contingency which had not occurred to him. His design was to surprise a wounded and helpless thief in his sleep and to force him then and there to give up the stolen money, before he had time to call for help.

But the miscreant was evidently on the watch, Briot still lingered on the top of the stairs, there were other people sleeping in the house, and St. Genis suddenly realised that his purpose would not be quite so easy of execution as he had hot-headedly supposed.

But the end in view was great, and St. Genis was not a man easily deterred from a set purpose. There was the royalist cause to aid and Crystal to be won if he were successful.

He knocked resolutely at the door, then tried the latch. The door was locked: but even as the young man hesitated for a moment wondering what he would do next, a firm step resounded on the floor on the other side of the partition and the next moment the door was opened from within, and a peremptory voice issued the usual challenge:

"Who goes there?"

A tall figure appeared as a massive silhouette under the lintel. St. Genis had the candle in his hand. He dropped it in his astonishment.

"Mr. Clyffurde!" he exclaimed.

At sight of St. Genis the Englishman, whose right arm was in a sling, had made a quick instinctive movement back into the room, but equally quickly Maurice had forestalled him by placing his foot across the threshold.

Then he turned back to Aristide Briot.

"That's all right, petit père," he called out airily, "it is indeed my friend, just as I thought. I'm going to stay and have a little chat with him. Don't wait up for me. When he is tired of my company I'll go back to the parlour and make myself happy in front of the fire. Good-night!"

As Clyffurde no longer stood in the doorway, St. Genis walked straight into the room and closed the door behind him, leaving good old Aristide to draw what conclusions he chose from the eccentric behaviour of his nocturnal visitors.

With a rapid and wrathful gaze, St. Genis at once took stock of everything in the room. A sigh of satisfaction rose to his lips. At any rate the rogue could not deny his guilt. There, hanging on a peg, was the caped coat which he had worn, and there on the table were two damning proofs of his villainy—a pair of pistols and a black mask.

The whole situation puzzled him more than he could say. Certainly after the first shock of surprise he had felt his wrath growing hotter and hotter every moment, the other man's cool assurance helped further to irritate his nerves, and to make him lose that self-control which would have been of priceless value in this unlooked-for situation.

Seeing that Maurice de St. Genis was absolutely speechless with surprise as well as with anger, there crept into Clyffurde's deep-set grey eyes a strange look of amusement, as if the humour of his present position was more obvious than its shame.

"And what," he asked pleasantly, "has procured me the honour at this late hour of a visit from M. le Marquis de St. Genis?"

His words broke the spell. There was no longer any mystery in the situation. The condemnatory pieces of evidence were there, Clyffurde's connection with de Marmont was well known—the plot had become obvious. Here was an English adventurer—an alien spy—who had obviously been paid to do this dirty work for the usurper, and—as Maurice now concluded airily—he must be made to give up the money which he had stolen before he be handed over to the military authorities at Lyons and shot as a spy or a thief—Maurice didn't care which: the whole thing was turning out far simpler and easier than he had dared to hope.

"You know quite well why I am here," he now said, roughly. "Of a truth, for the moment I was taken by surprise, for I had not thought that a man who had been honoured by the friendship of M. le Comte de Cambray and of his family was a thief, as well as a spy."

"And now," said Clyffurde, still smiling and apparently quite unperturbed, "that you have been enlightened on this subject to your own satisfaction, may I ask what you intend to do?"

"Force you to give up what you have stolen, you impudent thief," retorted the other savagely.

"And how are you proposing to do that, M. de St. Genis?" asked the Englishman with perfect equanimity.

"Like this," cried Maurice, whose exasperation and fury had increased every moment, as the other man's assurance waxed more insolent and more cool.

"Like this!" he cried again, as he sprang at his enemy's throat.

A past master in the art of self-defence, Clyffurde—despite his wounded arm—was ready for the attack. With his left on guard he not only received the brunt of the onslaught, but parried it most effectually with a quick blow against his assailant's jaw.

St. Genis—stunned by this forcible contact with a set of exceedingly hard knuckles—fell back a step or two, his foot struck against some object on the floor, he lost his balance and measured his length backwards across the bed.

"You abominable thief ... you ..." he cried, choking with rage and with discomfiture as he tried to struggle to his feet.

But this he at once found that he could not do, seeing that a pair of firm and muscular knees were gripping and imprisoning his legs, even while that same all-powerful left hand with the hard knuckles had an unpleasant hold on his throat.

"I should have tried some other method, M. de St. Genis, had I been in your shoes," came in irritatingly sarcastic accents from his calm antagonist.

Indeed, the insolent rogue did not appear in the least overwhelmed by the enormity of his crime or by the disgrace of being so ignominiously found out. From his precarious position across the bed St. Genis had a good view of the rascal's finely knit figure, of his earnest face, now softened by a smile full of kindly humour and good-natured contempt.

An impartial observer viewing the situation would certainly have thought that here was an impudent villain vanquished and lying on his back, whilst being admonished for his crimes by a just man who had might as well as right on his side.

"Let me go, you confounded thief," St. Genis cried, as soon as the unpleasant grip on his throat had momentarily relaxed, "you accursed spy ... you ..."

"Easy, easy, my young friend," said the other calmly; "you have called me a thief quite often enough to satisfy your rage: and further epithets might upset my temper."

"Let go my throat!"

"I will in a moment or two, as soon as I have made up my mind what I am going to do with you, my impetuous young friend—whether I shall truss you like a fowl and put you in charge of our worthy host, as guilty of assaulting one of his guests, or whether I shall do you some trifling injury to punish you for trying to do me a grave one."

"Right is on my side," said St. Genis doggedly. "I do not care what you do to me."

"Right is apparently on your side, my friend. I'll not deny it. Therefore, I still hesitate."

"Like a rogue and a vagabond at dead of night you attacked and robbed those who have never shown you anything but kindness."

"Until the hour when they turned me out of their house like a dishonest lacquey, without allowing me a word of explanation."

"Then this is your idea of vengeance, is it, Mr. Clyffurde?"

"Yes, M. de St. Genis, it is. But not quite in the manner that you suppose. I am going to set you free now in order to set your mind at rest. But let me warn you that I shall be just as much on the alert against another attack from you as ever I was before, and that I could ward off two or even three assailants with my left arm and knee as easily as I warded off one. It is a way we have in England."

He relaxed his hold on Maurice's legs and throat, and the young man—fretting and fuming, wild with impotent wrath and with mortification—struggled to his feet.

"Are you proposing to give me some explanation to mitigate your crime?" he said roughly. "If so, let me tell you that I will accept none. Putting the question aside of your abominable theft, you have committed an outrage against people whom I honour, and against the woman whom I love."

"Nor do I propose to give you any explanation, M. de St. Genis," retorted Clyffurde, who still spoke quite quietly and evenly. "But for the sake of your own peace of mind, which you will I hope communicate to the people whom you honour, I will tell you a few simple facts."

Neither of the men sat down: they stood facing one another now across the table whereon stood a couple of tallow candles which threw fitful, yellow lights on their faces—so different, so strangely contrasted—young and well-looking both—both strongly moved by passion, yet one entirely self-controlled, while in the other's eyes that passion glowed fierce and resentful.

"I listen," said St. Genis curtly.

And Clyffurde began after a slight pause: "At the time that you

132

fell upon me with such ill-considered vigour, M. de St. Genis," he said, "did you know that but for my abominable outrage upon the persons whom you honour, the money which they would gladly have guarded with their life would have fallen into the hands of Bonaparte's agents?"

"In theirs or yours, what matters?" retorted St. Genis savagely, "since His Majesty is deprived of it now."

"That is where you are mistaken, my young friend," said the other quietly. "His Majesty is more sure of getting the money now than he was when M. le Comte de Cambray with his family and yourself started on that quixotic if ill-considered errand this morning."

St. Genis frowned in puzzlement:

"I don't understand you," he said curtly.

"Isn't it simple enough? You and your friends credited me with friendship for de Marmont: he is hot-headed and impetuous, and words rush out of his mouth that he should keep to himself. I knew from himself that Bonaparte had charged him to recover the twenty-five millions which M. le préfet Fourier had placed in the Comte de Cambray's charge."

"Why did you not warn the Comte then?" queried St. Genis, who, still mistrustful, glowered at his antagonist.

"Would he have listened to me, think you?" asked the other with a quiet smile. "Remember, he had turned me out of his house two nights before, without a word of courtesy or regret—on the mere suspicion of my intercourse with de Marmont. Were you too full with your own rage to notice what happened then? Mlle. Crystal drew away her skirts from me as if I were a leper. What credence would they have given my words? Would the Comte even have admitted me into his presence?"

"And so ... you planned this robbery ... you ..." stammered St. Genis, whose astonishment and puzzlement were rendering him as speechless as his rage had done. "I'll not believe it," he continued more firmly; "you are fooling me, now that I have found you out."

"Why should I do that? You are in my hands, and not I in yours. Bonaparte is victorious at Grenoble. I could take the money to him and earn his gratitude, or use the money for mine own ends. What have I to fear from you? What cause to fool you? Your opinion of me? M. le Comte's contempt or goodwill? Bah! after to-night are we likely to meet again?"

St. Genis said nothing in reply. Of a truth there was nothing that he could say. The Englishman's whole attitude bore the impress of truth. Even through that still seething wrath which refused to be appeased, St. Genis felt that the other was speaking the truth. His mind now was in turmoil of wonderment. This man who stood here before him had done something which he—St. Genis—could not comprehend. Vaguely he realised that beneath the man's actions there still lay a yet

133

deeper foundation of dignity and of heroism and one which perhaps would never be wholly fathomed.

It was Clyffurde who at last broke the silence between them:

"You, M. de St. Genis," he said lightly, "would under like circumstances have acted just as I did, I am sure. The whole idea was so easy of execution. Half a dozen loafers to aid me, the part of highwayman to play—an old man and two or three defenceless women—my part was not heroic, I admit," he added with a smile, "but it has served its purpose. The money is safe in my keeping now, within a few days His Majesty the King of France shall have it, and all those who strive to serve him loyally can rest satisfied."

"I confess I don't understand you," said St. Genis, as he seemed to shake himself free from some unexplainable spell that held him. "You have rendered us and the legitimate cause of France a signal service! Why did you do it?"

"You forget, M. de St. Genis, that the legitimate cause of France is England's cause as well."

"Are you a servant of your country then? I thought you were a tradesman engaged in buying gloves."

Clyffurde smiled. "So I am," he said, "but even a tradesman may serve his country, if he has the opportunity."

"I hope that your country will be duly grateful," said Maurice, with a sigh. "I know that every royalist in France would thank you if they knew."

"By your leave, M. de St. Genis, no one in France need know anything but what you choose to tell them...."

"You mean ..."

"That except for reassuring M. le Comte de Cambray and ... and Mlle. Crystal, there is no reason why they should ever know what passed between us in this room to-night."

"But if the King is to have the money, he ..."

"He will never know from me, from whence it comes."

"He will wish to know...."

"Come, M. de St. Genis," broke in Clyffurde, with a slight hint of impatience, "is it for me to tell you that Great Britain has more than one agent in France these days—that the money will reach His Majesty the King ultimately through the hands of his foreign minister M. le Comte de Jaucourt ... and that my name will never appear in connection with the matter? ... I am a mere servant of Great Britain—doing my duty where I can ... nothing more."

"You mean that you are in the British Secret Service? No?—Well! I don't profess to understand you English people, and you seem to me more incomprehensible than any I have known. Not that I ever believed that you were a mere tradesman. But what shall I say to M. le Comte de Cambray?" he added, after a slight pause, during which a new and strange train of thought altered the expression of wonderment on his face, to one that was undefinable, almost furtive, certainly undecided.

"All you need say to M. le Comte," replied Clyffurde, with a slight tone of impatience, "is that you are personally satisfied that the money will reach His Majesty's hand safely, and in due course. At least, I presume that you are satisfied, M. de St. Genis," he continued, vaguely wondering what was going on in the young Frenchman's brain.

"Yes, yes, of course I am satisfied," murmured the other, "but ..."

"But what?"

"Mlle. Crystal would want to know something more than that. She will ask me questions ... she ... she will insist ... I had promised her to get the money back myself ... she will expect an explanation ... she ..."

He continued to murmur these short, jerky sentences almost inaudibly, avoiding the while to meet the enquiring and puzzled gaze of the Englishman.

When he paused—still murmuring, but quite inaudibly now—Clyffurde made no comment, and once more there fell a silence over the narrow room. The candles flickered feebly, and Bobby picked up the metal snuffers from the table and with a steady and deliberate hand set to work to trim the wicks.

So absorbed did he seem in this occupation that he took no notice of St. Genis, who with arms crossed in front of him, was pacing up and down the narrow room, a heavy frown between his deep-set eyes.

III

Somewhere in the house down below, an old-fashioned clock had just struck two. Clyffurde looked up from his absorbing task.

"It is late," he remarked casually; "shall we say good-night, M. de St. Genis?"

The sound of the Englishman's voice seemed to startle Maurice out of his reverie. He pulled himself together, walked firmly up to the table and resting his hand upon it, he faced the other man with a sudden gaze made up partly of suddenly conceived resolve and partly of lingering shamefacedness.

"Mr. Clyffurde," he began abruptly.

"Yes?"

"Have you any cause to hate me?"

"Why no," replied Clyffurde with his habitual good-humoured smile. "Why should I have?"

"Have you any cause to hate Mlle. Crystal de Cambray?"

"Certainly not."

135

"You have no desire," insisted Maurice, "to be revenged on her for the slight which she put upon you the other night?"

His voice had grown more steady and his look more determined as he put these rapid questions to Clyffurde, whose expressive face showed no sign of any feeling in response save that of complete and indifferent puzzlement.

"I have no desire with regard to Mlle. de Cambray," replied Bobby quietly, "save that of serving her, if it be in my power."

"You can serve her, Sir," retorted Maurice firmly, "and that right nobly. You can render the whole of her future life happy beyond what she herself has ever dared to hope."

"How?"

Maurice paused: once more, with a gesture habitual to him, he crossed his arms over his chest and resumed his restless march up and down the narrow room.

Then again he stood still, and again faced the Englishman, his dark enquiring eyes seeming to probe the latter's deepest thoughts.

"Did you know, Mr. Clyffurde," he asked slowly, "that Mlle. Crystal de Cambray honours me with her love?"

"Yes. I knew that," replied the other quietly.

"And I love her with my heart and soul," continued Maurice impetuously. "Oh! I cannot tell you what we have suffered—she and I— when the exigencies of her position and the will of her father parted us—seemingly for ever. Her heart was broken and so was mine: and I endured the tortures of hell when I realised at last that she was lost to me for ever and that her exquisite person—her beautiful soul—were destined for the delight of that low-born traitor Victor de Marmont."

He drew breath, for he had half exhausted himself with the volubility and vehemence of his diction. Also he seemed to be waiting for some encouragement from Clyffurde, who, however, gave him none, but sat unmoved and apparently supremely indifferent, while a suffering heart was pouring out its wails of agony into his unresponsive ear.

"The reason," resumed St. Genis somewhat more calmly, "why M. le Comte de Cambray was opposed to our union, was purely a financial one. Our families are of equal distinction and antiquity, but alas! our fortunes are also of equal precariousness: we, Sir, of the old noblesse gave up our all, in order to follow our King into exile. Victor de Marmont was rich. His fortune could have repurchased the ancient Cambray estates and restored to that honoured name all the brilliance which it had sacrificed for its principles."

Still Clyffurde remained irritatingly silent, and St. Genis asked him somewhat tartly:

"I trust I am making myself clear, Sir?"

"Perfectly, so far," replied the other quietly, "but I am afraid I

136

don't quite see how you propose that I could serve Mlle. Crystal in all this."

"You can with one word, one generous action, Sir, put me in a position to claim Crystal as my wife, and give her that happiness which she craves for, and which is rightly her due."

A slight lifting of the eyebrows was Clyffurde's only comment.

"Mr. Clyffurde," now said Maurice, with the obvious firm resolve to end his own hesitancy at last, "you say yourself that by taking this money to His Majesty, or rather to his minister, you, individually, will get neither glory nor even gratitude—your name will not appear in the transaction at all. I am quoting your own words, remember. That is so, is it not?"

"It is so—certainly."

"But, Sir, if a Frenchman—a royalist—were able to render his King so signal a service, he would not only gain gratitude, but recognition and glory.... A man who was poor and obscure would at once become rich and distinguished...."

"And in a position to marry the woman he loved," concluded Bobby, smiling.

Then as Maurice said nothing, but continued to regard him with glowing, anxious eyes, he added, smiling not altogether kindly this time,

"I think I understand, M. de St. Genis."

"And ... what do you say?" queried the other excitedly.

"Let me make the situation clear first, as I understand it, Monsieur," continued Bobby drily. "You are—and I mistake not—suggesting at the present moment that I should hand over the twenty-five millions to you, in order that you should take them yourself to the King in Paris, and by this act obtain not only favours from him, but probably a goodly share of the money, which you—presumably—will have forced some unknown highwayman to give up to you. Is that it?"

"It was not money for myself I thought of, Sir," murmured St. Genis somewhat shamefacedly.

"No, no, of course not," rejoined Clyffurde with a tone of sarcasm quite foreign to his usual easy-going good-nature. "You were thinking of the King's favours, and of a future of distinction and glory."

"I was thinking chiefly of Crystal, Sir," said the other haughtily.

"Quite so. You were thinking of winning Mlle. Crystal by a ... a subterfuge."

"An innocent one, Sir, you will admit. I should not be robbing you in any way. And remember that it is only Crystal's hand that is denied me: her love I have already won."

A look of pain—quickly suppressed and easily hidden from the other's self-absorbed gaze—crossed the Englishman's earnest face.

"I do remember that, Monsieur," he said, "else I certainly would never lend a hand in the ... subterfuge."

137

"You will do it then?" queried the other eagerly.

"I have not said so."

"Ah! but you will," pleaded Maurice hotly. "Sir! the eternal gratitude of two faithful hearts would be yours always—for Crystal will know it all, once we are married, I promise you that she will. And in the midst of her happiness she will find time to bless your generosity and your selflessness ... whilst I ..."

"Enough, I beg of you, M. de St. Genis," broke in Clyffurde now, with angry impatience. "Believe me! I do not hug myself with any thought of my own virtues, nor do I desire any gratitude from you: if I hand over the money to you, it is sorely against my better judgment and distinctly against my duty: but since that duty chiefly lies in being assured that the King of France will receive the money safely, why then by handing it over to you I have that assurance, and my conscience will rest at comparative ease. You shall have the money, Sir, and you shall marry Mlle. Crystal on the strength of the King's gratitude towards you. And Mlle. Crystal will be happy—if you keep silence over this transaction. But for God's sake let's say no more about it: for of a truth you and I are playing but a sorry rôle this night."

"A sorry rôle?" protested the other.

"Yes, a sorry rôle. Are you not deceiving a woman? Am I not running counter to my duty?"

"I but deceive Crystal temporarily. I love her and only deceive in order to win her. The end justifies the means: Nor do you, in my opinion, run counter to your duty...."

But Clyffurde interrupted him roughly: "I pray you, Sir, make no comment on mine actions. My own silent comments on these are hard enough to bear: your eulogies would raise bounds to my patience."

Whereupon he walked quickly up to the bed and from under the mattress extricated five leather wallets which he threw one by one upon the table.

"Here is the King's money," he said curtly; "you could never have taken it from me by force, but I give it over to you willingly now. If within a week from now I hear that the King has not received it, I will proclaim you a liar and a thief."

"Sir ... you dare ..."

"Nay! we'll not quarrel. I don't want to do you any hurt. You know from experience that I could kill you or wring your neck as easily as you could kill a child; but Mlle. Crystal's love is like a protecting shield all round you, so I'll not touch you again. But don't ask me to measure my words, for that is beyond my power. Take the money, M. de St. Genis, and earn not only the King's gratitude but also Mlle. Crystal's, which is far better worth having. And now, I pray you, leave me to rest. You must be tired too. And our mutual company hath become irksome to us both."

He turned his back on St. Genis and sat down at the table,

138

drawing paper, pen and inkhorn toward him, and with clumsy, left hand began laboriously to form written characters, as if St. Genis' presence or departure no longer concerned him.

An importunate beggar could not have been more humiliatingly dismissed. St. Genis had flushed to the very roots of his hair. He would have given much to be able to chastise the insolent Englishman then and there. But the latter had not boasted when he said that he could wring Maurice's neck as easily with his left hand as with his right, and Maurice within his heart was bound to own that the boast was no idle one. He knew that in a hand-to-hand fight he was no match for that heavy-framed, hard-fisted product of a fog-ridden land.

He would not trust himself to speak any more, lest another word cause prudence to yield to exasperation. Another moment of hesitation, a shrug of the shoulders—perhaps a muttered curse or two—and St. Genis picked up one by one the wallets from the table.

Clyffurde never looked up while he did so: he continued to form awkward, illegible characters upon the paper before him, as if his very life depended on being able to write with his left hand.

The next moment St. Genis had walked rapidly out of the room. Bobby left off writing, threw down his pen, and resting his elbow upon the table and his head in his hand, he remained silent and motionless while St. Genis' quick and firm footsteps echoed first along the corridor, then down the creaking stairs and finally on the floor below. After which there came the sound of the opening and shutting of a door, the dragging of a chair across a wooden floor, and nothing more.

All was still in the house at last. The old-fashioned clock downstairs struck half-past two.

With a smothered cry of angry contempt Clyffurde seized on the papers that lay scattered on the table and crushed them up in his hand with a gesture of passionate wrath.

Then he strode up to the window, threw open the rickety casement and let the pure cold air of night pour into the room and dissipate the atmosphere of cowardice, of falsehood and of unworthy love that still seemed to hang there where M. le Marquis de St. Genis had basely bargained for his own ends, and outraged the very name of Love by planning base deeds in its name.

CHAPTER VI

THE CRIME

I

Victor de Marmont had spent that same night in wearisome agitation. His mortification and disappointment would not allow him to rest.

He had brought his squad of cavalry up as far as St. Priest, which lies a little off the main road, about half-way between Lyons and the scene of de Marmont's late discomfiture. Here he and his men had spent the night, only to make a fresh start early the next morning—back for Grenoble—seeing that M. le Comte d'Artois with thirty or forty thousand troops was even now at Lyons.

When, an hour after leaving St. Priest, the little troop came upon a solitary horseman, riding a heavy carriage horse with a postillion's bridle, de Marmont at first had no other thought save that of malicious pleasure at recognising the man, whom just now he hated more cordially than any other man in the world.

M. de St. Genis—for indeed it was he—was peremptorily challenged and questioned, and his wrath and impotent attempts at arrogance greatly delighted de Marmont.

To make oneself actively unpleasant to a rival is apt to be a very pleasurable sensation. Victor had an exceedingly disagreeable half-hour to avenge and to declare St. Genis a prisoner of war, to order his removal to Grenoble pending the Emperor's pleasure, to command him to be silent when he desired to speak was so much soothing balsam spread upon the wounds which his own pride had suffered at Brestalou last Sunday eve.

It was not until a casual remark from the sergeant under his command caused him to notice the bulging pockets of St. Genis' coat, that Victor thought to give the order to search the prisoner.

The latter entered a vigorous protest: he fought and he threatened: he promised de Marmont the hangman's rope and his men terrible reprisals, but of course he was fighting a losing battle. He was alone against five and twenty, his first attempt at getting hold of the pistols in his belt was met with a threat of summary execution: he was dragged out of the saddle, his arms were forced behind his back, while rough hands turned out the precious contents of his coat-pockets! All that he could do was to curse fate which had brought these pirates on his way, and his own short-sightedness and impatience in not waiting

140

for the armed patrol which undoubtedly would have been sent out to him from Lyons in response to M. le Comte de Cambray's request.

Now he had the deadly chagrin and bitter disappointment of seeing the money which he had wrested from Clyffurde last night at the price of so much humiliation, transferred to the pockets of a real thief and spoliator who would either keep it for himself or—what in the enthusiastic royalist's eyes would be even worse—place it at the service of the Corsican usurper. He could hardly believe in the reality of his ill luck, so appalling was it. In one moment he saw all the hopes of which he had dreamed last night fly beyond recall. He had lost Crystal more effectually, more completely than he ever had done before. If the Englishman ever spoke of what had occurred last night ... if Crystal ever knew that he had been fool enough to lose the treasure which had been in his possession for a few hours—her contempt would crush the love which she had for him: nor would the Comte de Cambray ever relent.

De Marmont's triumph too was hard to bear: his clumsy irony was terribly galling.

"Would M. le Marquis de St. Genis care to continue his journey to Lyons now? would he prefer not to go to Grenoble?"

St. Genis bit his tongue with the determination to remain silent.

"M. de St. Genis is free to go whither he chooses."

The permission was not even welcome. Maurice would as lief be taken prisoner and dragged back to Grenoble as face Crystal with the story of his failure.

Quite mechanically he remounted, and pulled his horse to one side while de Marmont ordered his little squad to form once more, and after the brief word of command and a final sarcastic farewell, galloped off up the road back toward Lyons at the head of his men, not waiting to see if St. Genis came his way too or not.

The latter with wearied, aching eyes gazed after the fast disappearing troop, until they became a mere speck on the long, straight road, and the distant morning mist finally swallowed them up.

Then he too turned his horse's head in the same direction back toward Lyons once more, and allowing the reins to hang loosely in his hand, and letting his horse pick its own slow way along the road, he gave himself over to the gloominess of his own thoughts.

II

He too had some difficulty in entering the town. M. le Duc d'Orléans, cousin of the King, had just arrived to support M. le Comte d'Artois, and together these two royal princes had framed and posted up a proclamation to the brave Lyonese of the National Guard.

The whole city was in a turmoil, for M. le Duc d'Orléans—who was nothing if not practical—had at once declared that there was not the slightest chance of a successful defence of Lyons, and that by far the best thing to do would be to withdraw the troops while they were still loyal.

M. le Comte d'Artois protested; at any rate he wouldn't do anything so drastic till after the arrival of Marshal Macdonald, to whom he had sent an urgent courier the day before, enjoining him to come to Lyons without delay. In the meanwhile he and his royal cousin did all they could to kindle or at any rate to keep up the loyalty of the troops, but defection was already in the air: here and there the men had been seen to throw their white cockades into the mud, and more than one cry of "Vive l'Empereur!" had risen even while Monsieur himself was reviewing the National Guard on the Place Bellecour.

The bridge of La Guillotière was stoutly barricaded, but as St. Genis waited out in the open road while his name was being taken to the officer in command he saw crowds of people standing or walking up and down on the opposite bank of the river.

They were waiting for the Emperor, the news of whose approach was filling the townspeople with glee.

Heartsick and wretched, St. Genis, after several hours of weary waiting, did ultimately obtain permission to enter the city by the ferry on the south side of the city. Once inside Lyons, he had no difficulty in ascertaining where such a distinguished gentleman as M. le Comte de Cambray had put up for the night, and he promptly made his way to the Hotel Bourbon, his mind, at this stage, still a complete blank as to how he would explain his discomfiture to the Comte and to Crystal.

In the present state of M. le Comte d'Artois' difficulties the money would have been thrice welcome, and St. Genis felt the load of failure weighing thrice as heavily on his soul, and dreaded the reproaches—mute or outspoken—which he knew awaited him. If only he could have thought of something! something plausible and not too inglorious! There was, of course, the possibility that he had failed to come upon the track of the thieves at all—but then he had no business to come back so soon—and he didn't want to come back, only that there was always the likelihood of the Englishman speaking of what had occurred—not necessarily with evil intent ... but ... some words of his: "If within a week I hear that the King of France has not received this money, I will proclaim you a liar and a thief!" rang unpleasantly in St. Genis' ears.

The young man's mind, I repeat, was at this point still a blank as to what explanation he would give to the Comte de Cambray of his own miserable failure.

He was returning—after an ardent promise to overtake the thief and to force him to give up the money—without apparently having made any effort in that direction—or having made the effort, failing signally and ignominiously—a foolish and unheroic position in either case.

To tell the whole unvarnished truth, his interview with Clyffurde and his thoughtlessness in wandering along the road all alone, laden with twenty-five million francs, not waiting for the arrival of M. le Comte d'Artois' patrol, was unthinkable.

Then what? St. Genis, determined not to tell the truth, found it a difficult task to concoct a story that would be plausible and at the same time redound to his credit. His disappointment was so bitter now, his hopes of winning Crystal and glory had been so bright, that he found it quite impossible to go back to the hard facts of life—to his own poverty and the unattainableness of Crystal de Cambray—without making a great effort to win back what Victor de Marmont had just wrested from him.

Through the whirl of his thoughts, too, there was a vague sense of resentment against Clyffurde—coupled with an equally vague sense of fear. He, Maurice, might easily keep silent over the transaction of last night, but Clyffurde might not feel inclined to do so. He would want to know sooner or later what had become of the money ... had he not uttered a threat which made Maurice's cheeks even now flush with wrath and shame?

Certain words and gestures of the Englishman had stood out before Maurice's mind in a way that had stirred up those latent jealousies which always lurk in the heart of an unsuccessful wooer. Clyffurde had been generous—blind to his own interests—ready to sacrifice what recognition he had earned: he had spared his assailant and agreed to an unworthy subterfuge, and St. Genis' tormented brain began to wonder why he had done all this.

Was it for love of Crystal de Cambray?

St. Genis would not allow himself to answer that question, for he felt that if he did he would hate that hard-fisted Englishman more thoroughly than he had ever hated any man before—not excepting de Marmont. De Marmont was an evil and vile traitor who never could cross Crystal's path of life again.... But not so the Englishman, who had planned to serve her and who would have succeeded so magnificently but for his—Maurice's—interference!

If this explanation of Clyffurde's strangely magnanimous conduct was the true one, then indeed St. Genis felt that he would have everything to fear from him. For indeed was it so very unlikely that the Englishman was throughout acting in collusion with Victor de Marmont, who was known to be his friend?

Was it so very unlikely that—seeing himself unmasked—he had found a sure and rapid way of allowing the money to pass through St. Genis' hands into those of de Marmont, and at the same time hopelessly humiliating and discrediting his rival in the affections of Mlle. de Cambray?

143

That the suggestion of handing the money over to him had come originally from Maurice de St. Genis himself, the young man did not trouble himself to remember. The more he thought this new explanation of past events over, the more plausible did it seem and the more likely of acceptance by M. le Comte de Cambray and by Crystal, and St. Genis at last saw his way to appearing before them not only zealous but heroic—even if unfortunate—and it was with a much lightened heart that he finally drew rein outside the Hotel Bourbon.

III

M. le Comte de Cambray, it seems, was staying at the Hotel for a few days, so the proprietor informed M. de St. Genis. M. le Comte had gone out, but Mme. la Duchesse d'Agen was upstairs with Mlle. de Cambray.

With somewhat uncertain step St. Genis followed the obsequious proprietor, who had insisted on conducting M. le Marquis to the ladies' apartments himself. They occupied a suite of rooms on the first floor, and after a timid knock at the door, it was opened by Jeanne from within, and Maurice found himself in the presence of Crystal and of the Duchesse and obliged at once to enter upon the explanation which, with their first cry of surprise, they already asked of him.

"Well!" exclaimed Crystal eagerly, "what news?"

"Of the money?" murmured Maurice vaguely, who above all things was anxious to gain time.

"Yes! the King's money!" rejoined the girl with slight impatience. "Have you tracked the thieves? Do you know where they are? Is there any hope of catching them?"

"None, I am afraid," he replied firmly.

Crystal gave a cry of bitter disappointment and reproach. "Then, Maurice," she exclaimed almost involuntarily, "why are you here?"

And Mme. la Duchesse, folding her mittened hands before her, seemed mutely to be asking the same question.

"But did you come upon the thieves at all?" continued Crystal with eager volubility. "Where did they go to for the night? You must have come on some traces of their passage. Oh!" she added vehemently, "you ought not to have deserted your post like this!"

"What could I do," he murmured. "I was all alone ... against so many...."

"You said that you would get on the track of the thieves," she urged, "and father told you that he would speak with M. le Comte d'Artois as soon as possible. Monsieur has promised that an armed

144

patrol would be sent out to you, and would be on the lookout for you on the road."

"An armed patrol would be no use. I came back on purpose to stop one being sent."

"But why, in Heaven's name?" exclaimed the Duchesse.

"Because a troop of deserters with that traitor Victor de Marmont is scouring the road, and ..."

"We know that," said Crystal, "we were stopped by them last night, after you left us. They were after the money for the usurper, who had sent them, and I thanked God that twenty-five millions had enriched a common thief rather than the Corsican brigand."

"Surely, Maurice," said the Duchesse with her usual tartness, "you were not fool enough to allow the King's money to fall into that abominable de Marmont's hands?"

"How could I help it?" now exclaimed the young man, as if driven to the extremity of despair. "The whole thing was a huge plot beyond one man's power to cope with. I tracked the thieves," he continued with vehemence as eager as Crystal's, "I tracked them to a lonely hostelry off the beaten track—at dead of night—a den of cutthroats and conspirators. I tracked the thief to his lair and forced him to give the money up to me."

"You forced him? ... Oh! how splendid!" cried Crystal. "But then..."

"Ah, then! there was the hideousness of the plot. The thief, feeling himself unmasked, gave up his stolen booty; I forced him to his knees, and five wallets containing twenty-five million francs were safely in my pockets at last."

"You forced him—how splendid!" reiterated Crystal, whose glowing eyes were fixed upon Maurice with all the admiration which she felt.

"Yes! that money was in my pocket for the rest of the happy night, but the abominable thief knew well that his friend Victor de Marmont was on the road with five and twenty armed deserters in the pay of the Corsican brigand. Hardly had I left the hostelry and found my way back to the main road when I was surrounded, assailed, searched and robbed. I repeat!" continued St. Genis, warming to his own narrative, "what could I do alone against so many?—the thief and his hirelings I managed successfully, but with the money once in my possession I could not risk staying an hour longer than I could help in that den of cutthroats. But they were in league with de Marmont, and, though I would have guarded the King's money with my life, it was filched from me ere I could draw a single weapon in its defence."

He had sunk in a chair, half exhausted with the effort of his own eloquence, and now, with elbows resting on his knees and head buried in his hands, he looked the picture of heroic misery.

Crystal said nothing for a while; there was a deep frown of puzzlement between her eyes.

"Maurice," she said resolutely at last, "you said just now that the thief was in collusion with his friend de Marmont. What did you mean by that?"

"I would rather that you guessed what I meant, Crystal," replied Maurice without looking up at her.

"You mean ... that ..." she began slowly.

"That it was Mr. Clyffurde, our English friend," broke in Madame tartly, "who robbed us on the broad highway. I suspected it all along."

"You suspected it, ma tante, and said nothing?" asked the girl, who obviously had not taken in the full significance of Maurice's statement.

"I said absolutely nothing," replied Madame decisively, "firstly, because I did not think that I would be doing any good by putting my own surmises into my brother's head, and, secondly, because I must confess that I thought that nice young Englishman had acted pour le bon motif."

"How could you think that, ma tante?" ejaculated Crystal hotly: "a good motive? to rob us at dead of night—he, a friend of Victor de Marmont—an adherent of the Corsican! ..."

"Englishmen are not adherents of the Corsican, my dear," retorted Madame drily, "and until Maurice's appearance this morning, I was satisfied that the money would ultimately reach His Majesty's own hands."

"But we were taking the money to His Majesty ourselves."

"And Victor de Marmont was after it. Mr. Clyffurde may have known that.... Remember, my dear," continued Madame, "that these were my impressions last night. Maurice's account of the den of cutthroats has modified these entirely."

Again Crystal was silent. The frown had darkened on her face: there was a line of bitter resentment round her lips—a look of contempt, of hate, of a desire to hurt, in her eyes.

"Maurice," she said abruptly at last.

"Yes?"

"I did wound that thief, did I not?"

"Yes. In the shoulder ... it gave me a slight advantage ..." he said with affected modesty.

"I am glad. And you ... you were able to punish him too, I hope."

"Yes. I punished him."

He was watching her very closely, for inwardly he had been wondering how she had taken his news. She was strangely agitated, so Maurice's troubled, jealous heart told him; her face was flushed, her eyes were wet and a tiny lace handkerchief which she twisted between her fingers was nothing but a damp rag.

"Oh! I hate him! I hate him!" she murmured as with an impatient

146

gesture she brushed the gathering tears from her eyes. "Father had been so kind to him—so were we all. How could he? how could he?"

"His duty, I suppose," said St. Genis magnanimously.

"His duty?" she retorted scornfully.

"To the cause which he served."

"Duty to a usurper, a brigand, the enemy of his country. Was he, then, paid to serve the Corsican?"

"Probably."

"His being in trade—buying gloves at Grenoble—was all a plant then?"

"I am afraid so," said St. Genis, who much against his will now was sinking ever deeper and deeper in the quagmire of lying and cowardice into which he had allowed himself to drift.

"And he was nothing better than a spy!"

No one, not even Crystal herself, could have defined with what feelings she said this. Was it solely contempt? or did a strange mixture of regret and sorrow mingle with the scorn which she felt? Swiftly her thoughts had flown back to that Sunday evening—a very few days ago—when the course of her destiny was so suddenly changed once more, when her marriage with a man whom she could never love was broken off, when the possibilities once more rose upon the horizon of her life, of a renewed existence of poverty and exile in the wake of a dispossessed king.

That same evening a man whom she had hardly noticed before—a man neither of her own nationality nor of her own caste—this same Englishman, Clyffurde, had entered into her life—not violently or aggressively, but just with a few words of intense sympathy and with a genuine offer of friendship; and she somehow, despite much kindness which encompassed her always, had felt cheered and warmed by his words, and a strange and sweet sense of security against hurt and sorrow had entered her heart as she listened to them.

And now she knew that all that was false—false his sympathy, false his offers of friendship—his words were false, his hand-grasp false. Treachery lurked behind that kindly look in his eyes, and falsehood beneath his smile.

"He was nothing better than a spy!" The sting of that thought hurt her more than she could have thought possible. She had so few real friends and this one had proved a sham. Had she been alone she would have given way to tears, but before Maurice or even her aunt she was ashamed of her grief, ashamed of her feelings and of her thoughts. There was a great deal yet that she wished to know, but somehow the words choked her when she wanted to ask further questions. Fortunately Mme. la Duchesse was taking Maurice thoroughly to task. She asked innumerable questions, and would not spare him the relation of a single detail.

"Tell us all about it from the beginning, Maurice," she said. "Where did you first meet the rogue?"

And Maurice—weary and ashamed—was forced to embark on a minute account of adventures that were lies from beginning to end: he had stumbled across the wayside hostelry on a lonely by-path: he had found it full of cut-throats: he had stalked and waylaid their chief in his own room, and forced him to give up the money by the weight of his fists.

It was paltry and pitiable: nevertheless, St. Genis, as he warmed to his tale, lost the shame of it; only wrath remained with him: anger that he should be forced into this despicable rôle through the intrigues of a rival.

In his heart he was already beginning to find innumerable excuses for his cowardice: and his rage and hatred grew against Clyffurde as Madame's more and more persistent questions taxed his imagination almost to exhaustion.

When, after half an hour of this wearying cross-examination, Madame at last granted him a respite, he made a pretext of urgent business at M. le Comte d'Artois' headquarters and took his leave of the ladies. He waited in vain hope that the Duchesse's tact would induce her to leave him alone for a moment with Crystal. Madame stuck obstinately to her chair and was blind and deaf to every hint of appeal from him, whilst Crystal, who was singularly absorbed and had lent but a very indifferent ear to his narrative, made no attempt to detain him.

She gave him her hand to kiss, just as Madame had done; it lay hot and moist in his grasp.

"Crystal," he continued to murmur as his lips touched her fingers, "I love you ... I worked for you ... it is not my fault that I failed."

She looked at him kindly and sympathetically through her tears, and gave his hand a gentle little pressure.

"I am sure it was not your fault," she replied gently, "poor Maurice...."

It was not more than any kind friend would say under like circumstances, but to a lover every little word from the beloved has a significance of its own, every look from her has its hidden meaning. Somewhat satisfied and cheered Maurice now took his final leave:

"Does M. le Comte propose to continue his journey to Paris?" he asked at the last.

"Oh, yes!" Crystal replied, "he could not stay away while he feels that His Majesty may have need of him. Oh, Maurice!" she added suddenly, forgetting her absorption, her wrath against Clyffurde, her own disappointment—everything—in face of the awful possible calamity, and turning anxious, appealing eyes upon the young man, "you don't think, do you, that that abominable usurper will succeed in ousting the King once more from his throne?"

148

And St. Genis—remembering Laffray and Grenoble, remembering what was going on in Lyons at this moment, the silent grumblings of the troops, the defaced white cockades, the cries of "Vive l'Empereur!" which he himself had heard as he rode through the town—St. Genis, remembering all this, could only shake his head and shrug his shoulders in miserable doubt.

When he had gone at last, Crystal's thoughts veered back once more to Clyffurde and to his treachery.

"What abominable deceit, ma tante!" she cried, and quite against her will tears of wrath and of disappointment rose to her eyes. "What villainy! what odious, execrable treachery!"

Madame shrugged her shoulders and took up her knitting.

"These days, my dear," she said with unwonted placidity, "the world is so full of treachery that men and women absorb it by every pore."

"But I shall not leave it at that," rejoined Crystal resolutely. "I'll find a means of punishing that vile traitor ... I'll make him feel the hatred which he has so richly deserved—I shall not rest till I have made him suffer as he makes me suffer now...."

"My dear—my dear—" protested Mme. la Duchesse, not a little shocked at the girl's vehemence.

Indeed, Crystal's otherwise sweet, gentle, yielding personality seemed completely transformed: for the moment she was just a sensitive woman who has been hit and hurt, and whose desire for retaliation is keener, more relentless than that of a man. All the soft look in her blue eyes had gone—they looked dark and hard—her fair curls were matted against her damp forehead; indeed, Madame thought that for the moment all Crystal's beauty had gone—the sweet, submissive beauty of the girl, the grace of movement, the shy, appealing gentleness of her ways. She now looked all determination, resentment, and, above all, revenge.

"The dear child," sighed the Duchesse over her knitting, "it is the English blood in her. Those people never know how to accept the inevitable: they are always wanting to fight someone for something and never know when they are beaten."

CHAPTER VII

THE ASCENT OF THE CAPITOL

I

And the triumphal march from the gulf of Jouan continued uninterrupted to Paris.

After Laffray and Grenoble, Lyons, where the silk-weavers of La Guillotière assembled in their thousands to demolish the barricades which had been built up on their bridge against the arrival of the Emperor, and watched his entry into their city waving kerchiefs and hats in his honour, and tricolour flags and cockades fished out of cupboards, where they had lain hidden but not forgotten for one whole year.

After Lyons, Villefranche, where sixty thousand peasants and workmen awaited his arrival at the foot of the tree of Liberty, on the top of which a brass eagle, the relic of some old standard, glistened like gold as it caught the rays of the setting sun.

And Nevers, where the townsfolk urged the regiments as they march through the city to tear the white cockades from their hats! And Chalon-sur-Saône, where the workpeople commandeer a convoy of artillery destined for the army of M. le Comte d'Artois!

The préfets of the various départements, the bureaucracy of provinces and cities, are not only amazed but struck with terror:

"This is a new Revolution!" they cry in dismay.

Yes! it is a new Revolution! the revolt of the peasantry of the poor, the humble, the oppressed! The hatred which they felt against that old regime which had come back to them with its old arrogance and its former tyrannies had joined issue with the cult of the army for the Emperor who had led it to glory, to fortune and to fame.

The people and the army were roused by the same enthusiasm, and marched shoulder to shoulder to join the standard of Napoleon— the little man in the shabby hat and the grey redingote, who for them personified the spirit of the great revolution, the great struggle for liberty and its final victory.

The army of the Comte d'Artois—that portion of it which remained loyal—was powerless against the overwhelming tide of popular enthusiasm, powerless against dissatisfaction, mutterings and constant defections in its ranks. The army would have done well in Provence—for Provence was loyal and royalist, man, woman and child: but Napoleon took the route of the Alps, and avoided Provence; by the time he reached Lyons he had an army of his own and M. le Comte d'Artois—fearing more defections and worse defeats—had thought it prudent to retire.

It has often been said that if a single shot had been fired against his original little band Napoleon's march on Paris would have been stopped. Who shall tell? There are such "ifs" in the world, which no human mind can challenge. Certain it is that that shot was not fired. At Laffray, Randon gave the order, but he did not raise his musket himself; on the walls of Grenoble St. Genis, in command of the artillery and urged by the Comte de Cambray, did not dare to give the order or to fire a gun himself. "The men declare," he had said gloomily, "that they would blow their officers from their own guns."

And at Lyons there was not militiaman, a royalist, volunteer or a pariah out of the streets who was willing to fire that first and "single shot": and though Marshal Macdonald swore ultimately that he would do it himself, his determination failed him at the last when surrounded by his wavering troops he found himself face to face with the conqueror of Austerlitz and Jena and Rivoli and a thousand other glorious fights, with the man in the grey redingote who had created him Marshal of France and Duke of Tarente on the battlefields of Lombardy, his comrade-in-arms who had shared his own scanty army rations with him, slept beside him round the bivouac fires, and round whom now there rose a cry from end to end of Lyons: "Vive l'Empereur!"

II

Victor de Marmont did not wait for the arrival of the Emperor at Lyons: nor did he attempt to enter the city. He knew that there was still some money in the imperial treasury brought over from Elba, and his mind—always in search of the dramatic—had dwelt with pleasure on thoughts of the day when the Emperor, having entered Fontainebleau, or perhaps even Paris and the Tuileries, would there be met by his faithful de Marmont, who on bended knees in the midst of a brilliant and admiring throng would present to him the twenty-five million francs originally the property of the Empress herself and now happily wrested from the cupidity of royalist traitors.

The picture pleased de Marmont's fancy: he dwelt on it with delight, he knew that no one requited a service more amply and more generously than Napoleon: he knew that after this service rendered there was nothing to which he—de Marmont—young as he was, could not aspire—title, riches, honours, anything he wanted would speedily become his, and with these to his credit he could claim Crystal de Cambray once more.

Oh! she would be humbled again by then, she and her father too, the proud aristocrats, doomed once more to penury and exile, unless he—de Marmont—came forth like the fairy prince to the beggarmaid with hands laden with riches, ready to lay these at the feet of the woman he loved.

Yes! Crystal de Cambray would be humbled! De Marmont, though he felt that he loved her more and better than any man had ever loved any woman before, nevertheless had a decided wish that she should be humbled and suffer bitterly thereby. He felt that her pride was his only enemy: her pride and royalist prejudices. Of the latter he thought but little: confident of his Emperor's success, he thought that all those hot-headed royalists would soon realise the hopelessness of their cause—rendered all the more hopeless through its short-lived triumph of the past year—and abandon it gradually and surely, accepting the inevitable and rejoicing over the renewed glory which would come over France.

As for her pride! well! that was going to be humbled, along with the pride of the Bourbon princes, of that fatuous old king, of all those arrogant aristocrats who had come back after years of exile, as arrogant, as tyrannical as ever before.

These were pleasing thoughts which kept Victor de Marmont company on his way between Lyons and Fontainebleau. Once past Villefranche he sent the bulk of his escort back to Lyons, where the Emperor should have arrived by this time: he had written out a superficial report of his expedition, which the sergeant in charge of the little troop was to convey to the Emperor's own hands. He only kept two men with him, put himself and them into plain, travelling clothes which he purchased at Villefranche, and continued his journey to the north without much haste; the roads were safe enough from footpads, he and his two men were well armed, and what stragglers from the main royalist army he came across would be far too busy with their own retreat and their own disappointment to pay much heed to a civilian and seemingly harmless traveller.

De Marmont loved to linger on the way in the towns and hamlets where the news of the Emperor's approach had already been wafted from Grenoble, or Lyons, or Villefranche on the wings of wind or birds, who shall say? Enough that it had come, that the peasants, assembled in masses in their villages, were whispering together that he was coming—the little man in the grey redingote—l'Empereur!

And de Marmont would halt in those villages and stop to whisper with the peasants too: Yes! he was coming! and the whole of France was giving him a rousing welcome! There was Laffray and Grenoble and Lyons! the army rallied to his standard as one man!

And de Marmont would then pass on to another village, to another town, no longer whispering after a while, but loudly proclaiming the arrival of the Emperor who had come into his own again.

152

After Nevers he was only twenty-four hours ahead of Napoleon and his progress became a triumphant one: newspapers, despatches had filtrated through from Paris—news became authentic, though some of it sounded a little wild. Wherever de Marmont arrived he was received with acclamations as the man who had seen the Emperor, who had assisted at the Emperor's magnificent entry into Grenoble, who could assure citizens and peasantry that it was all true, that the Emperor would be in Paris again very shortly and that once more there would be an end to tyranny and oppression, to the rule of the aristocrats and a number of incompetent and fatuous princes.

He did not halt at Fontainebleau, for now he knew that the Court of the Tuileries was in a panic, that neither the Comte d'Artois, nor the Duc de Berry, nor any of the royal princes had succeeded in keeping the army together: that defections had been rife for the past week, even before Napoleon had shown himself, and that Marshal Ney, the bravest soldier in France, had joined his Emperor at Auxerre.

No! de Marmont would not halt at Fontainebleau. It was Paris that he wanted to see! Paris, which to-day would witness the hasty flight of the gouty and unpopular King whom it had never learned to love! Paris decking herself out like a bride for the arrival of her bridegroom! Paris waiting and watching, while once again on the Tuileries and the Hôtel de Ville, on the Louvre and the Luxembourg, on church towers and government buildings the old tricolour flag waved gaily in the wind.

He slept that night at a small hotel in the Louvre quarter, but the whole evening he spent on the Place du Carrousel with the crowd outside the Tuileries, watching the departure from the palace of the infirm King of France and of his Court. The crowd was silent and obviously deeply moved. The spectacle before it of an old, ailing monarch, driven forth out of the home of his ancestors, and forced after an exile of three and twenty years and a brief reign of less than one, to go back once more to misery and exile, was pitiable in the extreme.

Many forgot all that the brief reign had meant in disappointments and bitter regrets, and only saw in the pathetic figure that waddled painfully from portico to carriage door a monarch who was unhappy, abandoned and defenceless: a monarch, too, who, in his unheroic, sometimes grotesque person, was nevertheless the representative of all the privileges and all the rights, of all the dignity and majesty pertaining to the most ancient ruling dynasty in Europe, as well as of all the humiliations and misfortunes which that same dynasty had endured.

III

It is late in the evening of March 20th. A thin mist is spreading from the river right over Paris, and from the Place du Carrousel the lighted windows of the Tuileries palace appear only like tiny, dimly-flickering stars.

Here an immense crowd is assembled. It has waited patiently hour after hour, ever since in the earlier part of the afternoon a courier has come over from Fontainebleau with the news that the Emperor is already there and would be in Paris this night.

It is the same crowd which twenty-four hours ago shed a tear or two in sympathy for the departing monarch: now it stands here—waiting, excited, ready to cheer the return of a popular hero—half-forgotten, wildly acclaimed, madly welcomed, to be cursed again, and again forgotten so soon. It was a heterogeneous crowd forsooth! made up in great part of the curious, the idle, the indifferent, and in great part, too, of the Bonapartist enthusiasts and malcontents who had groaned under the reactionary tyranny of the Restoration—of malcontents, too, of no enthusiasm, who were ready to welcome any change which might bring them to prominence or to fortune. With here and there a sprinkling of hot-headed revolutionaries, cursing the return of the Emperor as heartily as they had cursed that of the Bourbon king: and here and there a few heart-sick royalists, come to watch the final annihilation of their hopes.

Victor de Marmont, wrapped in a dark cloak, stood among the crowd for a while. He knew that the Emperor would probably not be in Paris before night, and he loved to be in the very midst of the wave of enthusiasm which was surging higher and ever higher in the crowd, and hear the excited whispers, and to feel all round him, wrapping him closely like a magic mantle of warmth and delight, the exaltation of this mass of men and women assembled here to acclaim the hero whom he himself adored. Closely buttoned inside his coat he had scraps of paper worth the ransom of any king.

Among the crowd, too, Bobby Clyffurde moved and stood. He was one of those who watched this enthusiasm with a heart filled with forebodings. He knew well how short this enthusiasm would be: he knew that within a few weeks—days perhaps—the bold and reckless adventurer who had so easily reconquered France would realise that the Imperial crown would never be allowed to sit firmly upon his head. None in this crowd knew better that the present pageant and glory would be short-lived, than did this tall, quiet Englishman who listened with half an ear and a smile of good-natured contempt to the loud cries of "Vive l'Empereur!" which rose spontaneously whenever the sound of horses' hoofs or rattles of wheels from the direction of Fontainebleau suggested the approach of the hero of the day. None knew better than

154

he that already in far-off England another great hero, named Wellington, was organising the forces which presently would crush—for ever this time—the might and ambitions of the man whom England had never acknowledged as anything but a usurper and a foe.

And closely buttoned inside his coat Clyffurde had a letter which he had received at his lodgings in the Alma quarter only a few moments before he sallied forth into the streets. That letter was an answer to a confidential enquiry of his own sent to the Chief of the British Secret Intelligence Department resident in Paris, desiring to know if the Department had any knowledge of a vast sum of money having come unexpectedly into the hands of His Majesty the King of France, before his flight from the capital.

The answer was an emphatic "No!" The Intelligence Department knew of no such windfall. But its secret agents reported that Victor de Marmont, captain of the usurper's body-guard, had waylaid M. le Marquis de St. Genis on the high road not far from Lyons. The escort which had accompanied Victor de Marmont on that occasion had been dismissed by him at Villefranche, and the information which the British Secret Intelligence Department had obtained came through the indiscretion of the sergeant in charge of the escort, who had boasted in a tavern at Lyons that he had actually searched M. de St. Genis and found a large sum of money upon him, of which M. de Marmont promptly took possession.

When Bobby Clyffurde received this letter and first mastered its contents, the language which he used would have done honour to a Toulon coal-heaver. He cursed St. Genis' stupidity in allowing himself to be caught; but above all he cursed himself for his soft-heartedness which had prompted him to part with the money.

The letter which brought him the bad news seemed to scorch his hand, and brand it with the mark of folly. He had thought to serve the woman he loved, first, by taking the money from her, since he knew that Victor de Marmont with an escort of cavalry was after it, and, secondly, by allowing the man whom she loved to have the honour and glory of laying the money at his sovereign's feet. The whole had ended in a miserable fiasco, and Clyffurde felt sore and wrathful against himself.

And also among the crowd—among those who came, heartsick, hopeless, forlorn, to watch the triumph of the enemy as they had watched the humiliation of their feeble King—was M. le Comte de Cambray with his daughter Crystal on his arm.

They had come, as so many royalists had done, with a vague hope that in the attitude of the crowd they would discern indifference rather than exultation, and that the active agents of their party, as well as those of England and of Prussia, would succeed presently in stirring up a counter demonstration, that a few cries of "Vive le roi!" would prove to the army at least and to the people of Paris that acclamations for the usurper were at any rate not unanimous.

But the crowd was not indifferent—it was excited: when first the Comte de Cambray and Crystal arrived on the Place du Carrousel, a number of white cockades could be picked out in the throng, either worn on a hat or fixed to a buttonhole, but as the afternoon wore on there were fewer and fewer of these small white stars to be seen: the temper of the crowd did not brook this mute reproach upon its enthusiasm. One or two cockades had been roughly torn and thrown into the mud, and the wearer unpleasantly ill-used if he persisted in any royalistic demonstration. Crystal, when she saw these incidents, was not the least frightened. She wore her white cockade openly pinned to her cloak; she was far too loyal, far too enthusiastic and fearless, far too much a woman to yield her convictions to the popular feeling of the moment; and she looked so young and so pretty, clinging to the arm of her father, who looked a picturesque and harmless representative of the fallen regime, that with the exception of a few rough words, a threat here and there, they had so far escaped active molestation.

And the crowd presently had so much to see that it ceased to look out for white cockades, or to bait the sad-eyed royalists. A procession of carriages, sparse at first and simple in appearance, had begun to make its way from different parts of the town across the Place du Carrousel toward the Tuileries. They arrived very quietly at first, with as little clatter as possible, and drew up before the gates of the Pavillon de Flore with as little show as may be: the carriage doors were opened unostentatiously, and dark, furtive figures stepped out from them and almost ran to the door of the palace, so eager were they to escape observation, their big cloaks wrapped closely round them to hide the court dress or uniform below.

Ministers, dignitaries of the Court, Councillors of State; majordomos, stewards, butlers, body-servants; they all came one by one or in groups of twos or threes. As the afternoon wore on these arrivals grew less and less furtive; the carriages arrived with greater clatter and to-do, with finer liveries and more gorgeous harness. Those who stepped out of the carriage doors were no longer quick and stealthy in their movements: they lingered near the step to give an order or to chat to a friend; the big cloak no longer concealed the gorgeous uniform below, it was allowed to fall away from the shoulder, so as to display the row of medals and stars, the gold embroidery, the magnificence of the Court attire.

The Emperor had left Fontainebleau! Within an hour he would be in Paris! Everyone knew it, and the excitement in the crowd that watched grew more and more intense. Last night these same men and women had looked with mute if superficial sympathy on the departure of Louis XVIII. through these same palace gates: many eyes then became moist at the sight, as memory flew back twenty years to the murdered king—his flight to Varennes, his ignominious return, his weary Calvary from prison to court house and thence to the scaffold. And here was his brother—come back after twenty-three years of exile, acclaimed by the populace, cheered by foreign soldiers—Russians, Austrians, English—anything but French—and driven forth once more to exile after the brief glory that lasted not quite a year.

But this the crowd of to-day has already forgotten with the completeness peculiar to crowds: men, women, and children too, they are no longer mute, they talk and they chatter; they scream with astonishment and delight whenever now from more and more carriages, more and more gorgeously dressed folk descend. The ladies are beginning to arrive: the wives of the great Court dignitaries, the ladies of the Court and household of the still-absent Empress: they do not attempt to hide their brilliant toilettes, their bare shoulders and arms gleam through the fastenings of their cloaks, and diamonds sparkle in their hair.

The crowd has recognised some of the great marshals, the men who in the Emperor's wake led the French troops to victory in Italy, in Prussia, in Austria: Maret Duc de Bassano is there and the crowd cheers him, the Duc de Rovigo, Marshal Davout, Prince d'Eckmühl, General Excelmans, one of Napoleon's oldest companions at arms, the Duke of Gaeta, the Duke of Padua, a crowd of generals and superior officers. It seems like the world of the Sleeping Beauty and of the Enchanted Castle—which a kiss has awakened from its eleven months' sleep. The Empire had only been asleep, it had dreamed a bad dream, wherein its hero was a prisoner and an exile: now it is slowly wakening back to life and to reality.

The night wears on: darkness and fog envelop Paris more and more. Excitement becomes akin to anxiety. If the Emperor did leave Fontainebleau when the last courier said that he did, he should certainly be here by now. There are strange whispers, strange waves of evil reports that spread through the waiting crowd: "A royalist fanatic had shot at the Emperor! the Emperor was wounded! he was dead!"

Oh! the excitement of that interminable wait!

At last, just as from every church tower the bells strike the hour of nine, there comes the muffled sound of a distant cavalcade: the sound of horses galloping and only half drowning that of the rumbling of coach wheels.

It comes from the direction of the embankment, and from far away now is heard the first cry of "Vive l'Empereur!" The noise gets louder and more clear, the cries are repeated again and again till they merge into one great, uproarious clamour. Like the ocean when lashed by the wind, the crowd surges, moves, rises on tiptoe, subsides, falls back to crush forward again and once more to retreat as a heavy coach, surrounded by a thousand or so of mounted men, dashes over the cobbles of the Place du Carrousel, whilst the clamour of the crowd becomes positively deafening.

"Vive l'Empereur!"

The officers in the courtyard of the palace rush to the coach as it draws up at the Pavillon de Flore: one of them succeeds in opening the carriage door. The Emperor is literally torn out of the carriage, carried to the vestibule, where more officers seize him, raise him from the crowd, bear him along, hoisted upon their shoulders, up the monumental staircase.

Their enthusiasm is akin to delirium: they nearly tear their hero to pieces in their wild, mad, frantic welcome.

"In Heaven's name, protect his person," exclaims the Duc de Vicence anxiously; and he and Lavalette manage to get hold of the banisters and by dint of fighting and pushing succeed in walking backwards step by step in front of the Emperor, thus making a way for him.

Lavalette can hardly believe his eyes, and the Duc de Vicence keeps murmuring: "It is the Emperor! It is the Emperor!"

And he—the little stout man in green cloth coat and white breeches—walks up the steps of his reconquered palace like a man in a dream: his eyes are fixed apparently on nothing, he makes no movement to keep his too enthusiastic friends away: the smile upon his lips is meaningless and fixed.

"Vive l'Empereur!" vociferates the crowd.

Vive l'Empereur for one hundred days: a few weeks of joy, a few weeks of anxiety, a few weeks of indecision, of wavering and of doubt. Then defeat more irrevocable than before! exile more distant! despair more complete.

Vive l'Empereur while we shout with excitement, while we remember the disappointments of the past year, while we hope for better things from a hand that has lost its cunning, a mind that has lost its power.

Vive l'Empereur! Let him live for an hundred days, while we forget our enthusiasm and Europe prepares its final crushing blow. Let him live until we remember once again the horrors of war, the misery, the famine, the devastated homes! until once more we see the maimed and crippled crawling back wearily from the fields of glory, until our ears ring with the wails of widows and the cries of the fatherless.

Then let him no longer live, for he it is who has brought this misery on us through his will and through his ambition, and France has suffered so much from the aftermath of glory, that all she wants now is rest.

IV

Gradually—but it took some hours—the tumult and excitement in and round the Tuileries subsided. The Emperor managed to shut himself up in his study and to eat some supper in peace, while gradually outside his windows the crowd—who had nothing more to see and was getting tired of staring up at glittering panes of glass—went back more or less quietly to their homes.

Only in the courtyard of the Tuileries, the troopers of the cavalry which had formed the Emperor's escort from Fontainebleau tethered their horses to the railings, rolled themselves in their mantles and slept on the pavements, giving to this portion of the palace the appearance of a bivouac in a place which has been taken by storm.

One of the last to leave the Place du Carrousel was Bobby Clyffurde. The crowd was thin by this time, but it was the tired and the indifferent—the merely curious—who had been the first to go. Those who remained to the last were either the very enthusiastic who wanted to set up a final shout of "Vive l'Empereur!" after their idol had entirely disappeared from their view, or the malcontents who would not lose a moment to discuss their grievances, to murmur covert threats, or suggest revolt in some shape or form or kind.

Bobby slipped quickly past several of these isolated groups, indifferent to the dark and glowering looks of suspicion that were cast at his tall, muscular figure with the firm step and the defiant walk that was vaguely reminiscent of the British troops that had been in Paris last year at the time of the foreign occupation. He had skirted the Tuileries gardens and was walking along the embankment which now was dark and solitary save for some rowdy enthusiasts on ahead who, arm in arm in two long rows that reached from the garden railings to the parapet, were obstructing the roadway and shouting themselves hoarse with "Vive l'Empereur!"

Clyffurde, who was walking faster than they did, was just deliberating in his mind whether he would turn back and go home some other way or charge this unpleasant obstruction from the rear and risk the consequences, when he noticed two figures still further on ahead walking in the same direction as he himself and the rowdy crowd.

One of these two figures—thus viewed in the distance, through the mist and from the back—looked nevertheless like that of a woman, which fact at once decided Bobby as to what he would do next. He sprinted toward the crowd as fast as he could, but unfortunately he did not come up with them in time to prevent the two unfortunate pedestrians being surrounded by the turbulent throng which, still arm in arm and to the accompaniment of wild shouts, had formed a ring around them and were now vociferating at the top of raucous voices:

"À bas la cocarde blanche! À bas! Vive l'Empereur!"

A flickering street lamp feebly lit up this unpleasant scene. Bobby saw the vague outline of a man and of a woman, standing boldly in the midst of the hostile crowd while two white cockades gleamed defiantly against the dark background of their cloaks. To an Englishman, who was a pastmaster in the noble art of using fists and knees to advantage, the situation was neither uncommon nor very perilous. The crowd was noisy it is true, and was no doubt ready enough for mischief, but Clyffurde's swift and scientific onslaught from the rear staggered and disconcerted the most bold. There was a good deal more shouting, plenty of cursing; the Englishman's arms and legs seemed to be flying in every direction like the arms of a windmill; a good many thuds and bumps, a few groans, a renewal of the attack, more thuds and groans, and the discomfited group of roisterers fled in every direction.

Bobby with a smile turned to the two motionless figures whom he had so opportunely rescued from an unpleasant plight.

"Just a few turbulent blackguards," he said lightly, as he made a quick attempt at readjusting the set of his coat and the position of his satin stock. "There was not much fight in them really, and ..."

He had, of course, lost his hat in the brief if somewhat stormy encounter and now—as he turned—the thin streak of light from the street-lamp fell full upon his face with its twinkling, deep-set eyes, and the half-humorous, self-deprecatory curl of the firm mouth.

A simultaneous exclamation came from his two protégés and stopped the easy flow of his light-hearted words. He peered closely into the gloom and it was his turn now to exclaim, half doubting, wholly astonished:

"Mademoiselle Crystal ... M. le Comte...."

"Indeed, Sir," broke in the Comte slowly, and with a voice that seemed to be trembling with emotion, "it is to my daughter and to myself that you have just rendered a signal and generous service. For this I tender you my thanks, yet believe me, I pray you when I say that both she and I would rather have suffered any humiliation or ill-usage from that rough crowd than owe our safety and comfort to you."

There was so much contempt, hatred even, in the tone of voice of this old man whose manner habitually was a pattern of moderation and of dignity that for the moment Clyffurde was completely taken aback. Puzzlement fought with resentment and with the maddening sense that he was anyhow impotent to avenge even so bitter an insult as had just been hurled upon him—against a man of the Comte's years and status.

"M. le Comte," he said at last, "will you let me remind you that the other day when you turned me out of your house like a dishonest servant, you would not allow me to say a single word in my own justification? The man on whose word you condemned me then without a hearing, is a scatter-brained braggart who you yourself must know is not a man to be trusted and ..."

"Pardon me, Monsieur," broke in the Comte with perfect sangfroid, "even if I acted on that evening with undue haste and ill-considered judgment, many things have happened since which you yourself surely would not wish to discuss with me, just when you have rendered me a signal service."

"Your pardon, M. le Comte," retorted Clyffurde with equal coolness, "I know of nothing which could possibly justify the charges which, not later than last Sunday, you laid at my door."

"The charge which I laid at your door then, Mr. Clyffurde, has not been lifted from its threshold yet. I charged you with deliberately conspiring against my King and my country all the while that you were eating bread and salt at my table. I charged you with striving to render assistance to that Corsican usurper whom may the great God punish, and you yourself practically owned to this before you left my house."

"This I did not, M. le Comte," broke in Clyffurde hotly. "As a man of honour I give you my word, that except for my being in de Marmont's company on the day that he posted up the Emperor's proclamation in Grenoble, I had no hand in any political scheme."

"And you would have me believe you," exclaimed the Comte, with ever-growing vehemence, "when you talk of that Corsican brigand as 'the Emperor.' Those words, Sir, are an insult, and had you not saved my daughter and me just now from violence I would—old as I am—strike you in the face for them."

With an impatient sigh at the old man's hot-headed obstinacy, Clyffurde turned with a look of appeal to Crystal, who up to now had taken no part in the discussion: "Mademoiselle," he said gently, "will you not at least do me justice? Cannot you see that I am clumsy at defending mine own honour, seeing that I have never had to do it before?"

"I only see, Monsieur," she retorted coldly, "that you are making vain and pitiable efforts to regain my father's regard—no doubt for purposes of your own. But why should you trouble? You have nothing more to gain from us. Your clever comedy of a highwayman on the road has succeeded beyond your expectations. The Corsican who now sits in the armchair lately vacated by an infirm monarch whom you and yours helped to dethrone, will no doubt reward you for your pains. As for me I can only echo my father's feelings: I would ten thousand times sooner have been torn to pieces by a rough crowd of ignorant folk than owe my safety to your interference."

She took her father's arm and made a movement to go: instinctively Clyffurde tried to stop her: at her words he had flushed

161

with anger to the very roots of his hair. The injustice of her accusation maddened him, but the bitter resentment in the tone of her voice, the look of passionate hatred with which she regarded him as she spoke, positively appalled him.

"M. le Comte," he said firmly, "I cannot let you go like this, whilst such horrible thoughts of me exist in your mind. England gave you shelter for three and twenty years; in the name of my country's kindness and hospitality toward you, I—as one of her sons—demand that you tell me frankly and clearly exactly what I am supposed to have done to justify this extraordinary hatred and contempt which you and Mademoiselle Crystal seem now to have for me."

"One of England's sons, Monsieur!" retorted the Comte equally firmly. "Nay! you are not even that. England stands for right and for justice, for our legitimate King and the punishment of the usurper."

"Great God!" he exclaimed, more and more bewildered now, "are you accusing me of treachery against mine own country? This will I allow no man to do, not even ..."

"Then, Sir, I pray you," rejoined Crystal proudly, "go and seek a quarrel with the man who has unmasked you; who caught you red-handed with the money in your possession which you had stolen from us, who forced you to give up what you had stolen, and whom then you and your friend Victor de Marmont waylaid and robbed once more. Go then, Mr. Clyffurde, and seek a quarrel with the Marquis de St. Genis, who has already struck you in the face once and no doubt will be ready to do so again."

And what of Clyffurde's thoughts while the woman whom he loved with all the strength of his lonely heart poured forth these hideous insults upon him? Amazement, then wrath, bewilderment, then final hopelessness, all these sensations ran riot through his brain.

St. Genis had behaved like an abominable blackguard! this he gathered from what she said: he had lied like a mean skunk and betrayed the man who had rendered him an infinitely great service. Of him Clyffurde wouldn't even think! Such despicable, crawling worms did exist on God's earth: he knew that! but he possessed the happy faculty, the sunny disposition that is able to pass a worm by and ignore its existence while keeping his eyes fixed upon all that is beautiful in earth and in the sky. Of St. Genis, therefore, he would not think; some day, perhaps, he might be able to punish him—but not now—not while this poor, forlorn, heartsick girl pinned her implicit faith upon that wretched worm and bestowed on him the priceless guerdon of her love. An infinity of pity rose in his kindly heart for her and obscured every other emotion. That same pity he had felt for her before, a sweet, protecting pity—gentle sister to fiercer, madder love which had perhaps never been so strong as it was at this hour when, for the second time, he was about to make a supreme sacrifice for her.

162

That the sacrifice must be made, he already knew: knew it even when first St. Genis' name escaped her lips. She loved St. Genis and she believed in him, and he, Clyffurde, who loved her with every fibre of his being, with all the passionate ardour of his lonely heart, could serve her no better than by accepting this awful humiliation which she put upon him. If he could have justified himself now, he would not have done it, not while she loved St. Genis, and he—Clyffurde—was less than nothing to her.

What did it matter after all what she thought of him? He would have given his life for her love, but short of that everything else was anyhow intolerable—her contempt, her hatred? what mattered? since to-night anyhow he would pass out of her life for ever.

He was ready for the sacrifice—sacrifice of pride, of honour, of peace of mind—but he did want to know that that sacrifice would be really needed and that when made it would not be in vain: and in order to gain this end he put a final question to her:

"One moment, Mademoiselle," he said, "before you go will you tell me one thing at least; was it M. de St. Genis himself who accused me of treachery?"

"There is no reason why I should deny it, Sir," she replied coldly. "It was M. de St. Genis himself who gave to my father and to me a full account of the interview which he had with you at a lonely inn, some few kilomètres from Lyons, and less than two hours after we had been shamefully robbed on the highroad of money that belonged to the King."

"And did M. de St. Genis tell you, Mademoiselle, that I purposed to use that money for mine own ends?"

"Or for those of the Corsican," she retorted impatiently. "I care not which. Yes! Sir, M. de St. Genis told me that with his own lips and when I had heard the whole miserable story of your duplicity and your treachery, I—a helpless, deceived and feeble woman—did then and there register a vow that I too would do you some grievous wrong one day—a wrong as great as you had done not only to the King of France but to me and to my father who trusted you as we would a friend. What you did to-night has of course altered the irrevocableness of my vow. I owe, perhaps, my father's life to your timely intervention and for this I must be grateful, but ..."

Her voice broke in a kind of passionate sob, and it took her a moment or two to recover herself, even while Clyffurde stood by, mute and with well-nigh broken heart, his very soul so filled with sorrow for her that there was no room in it even for resentment.

"Father let us go now," Crystal said after a while with brusque transition and in a steady voice; "no purpose can be served by further recriminations."

163

"None, my dear," said the Comte in his usual polished manner. "Personally I have felt all along that explanations could but aggravate the unpleasantness of the present position. Mr. Clyffurde understands perfectly, I am sure. He had his axe to grind—whether personal or political we really do not care to know—we are not likely ever to meet again. All we can do now is to thank him for his timely intervention on our behalf and ..."

"And brand him a liar," broke in Clyffurde almost involuntarily and with bitter vehemence.

"Your pardon, Monsieur," retorted the Comte coldly, "neither my daughter nor I have done that. It is your deeds that condemn you, your own admissions and the word of M. de St. Genis. Would you perchance suggest that he lied?"

"Oh, no," rejoined Clyffurde with perfect calm, "it is I who lied, of course."

He had said this very slowly and as if speaking with mature deliberation: not raising his voice, nor yet allowing it to quiver from any stress of latent emotion. And yet there was something in the tone of it, something in the man's attitude, that suggested such a depth of passion that, quite instinctively, the Comte remained silent and awed. For the moment, however, Clyffurde seemed to have forgotten the older man's presence; wounded in every fibre of his being by the woman whom he loved so tenderly and so devotedly, he had spoken only to her, compelling her attention and stirring—even by this simple admission of a despicable crime—an emotion in her which she could not—would not define.

She turned large inquiring eyes on him, into which she tried to throw all that she felt of hatred and contempt for him. She had meant to wound him and it seemed indeed as if she had succeeded beyond her dearest wish. By the dim, flickering light of the street-lamp his face looked haggard and old. The traitor was suffering almost as much as he deserved, almost as much—Crystal said obstinately to herself—as she had wished him to do. And yet, at sight of him now, Crystal felt a strong, unconquerable pity for him: the womanly instinct no doubt to heal rather than to hurt.

But this pity she was not prepared to show him: she wanted to pass right out of his life, to forget once and for all that sense of warmth of the soul, of comfort and of peace which she had felt in his presence on that memorable evening at Brestalou. Above all, she never wanted to touch his hand again, the hand which seemed to have such power to protect and to shield her, when on that same evening she had placed her own in it.

Therefore, now she took her father's arm once more: she turned resolutely to go. One more curt nod of the head, one last look of undying enmity, and then she would pass finally out of his life for ever.

164

V

How Clyffurde got back to his lodgings that night he never knew. Crystal, after his final admission, had turned without another word from him, and he had stood there in the lonely, silent street watching her retreating form—on her father's arm—until the mist and gloom swallowed her up as in an elvish grave. Then mechanically he hunted for his hat and he, too, walked away.

That was the end of his life's romance, of course. The woman whom he loved with his very soul, who held his heart, his mind, his imagination captive, whose every look on him was joy, whose every smile was a delight, had gone out of his life for ever! She had turned away from him as she would from a venomous snake! she hated him so cruelly that she would gladly hurt him—do him some grievous wrong if she could. And Clyffurde was left in utter loneliness with only a vague, foolish longing in his heart—the longing that one day she might have her wish, and might have the power to wound him to death—bodily just as she had wounded him to the depth of his soul to-night.

For the rest there was nothing more for him to do in France. King Louis was not like to remain at Lille very long: within twenty-four hours probably he would continue his journey—his flight—to Ghent—where once more he would hold his court in exile, with all the fugitive royalists rallied around his tottering throne.

Clyffurde had already received orders from his chief at the Intelligence Department to report himself first at Lille, then—if the King and court had already left—at Ghent. If, however, there were plenty of men to do the work of the Department it was his intention to give up his share in it and to cross over to England as soon as possible, so as to take up the first commission in the new army that he could get. England would be wanting soldiers more urgently than she had ever done before: mother and sisters would be well looked after: he—Bobby—had earned a fortune for them, and they no longer needed a bread-winner now: whilst England wanted all her sons, for she would surely fight.

Clyffurde, who had seen the English papers that morning—as they were brought over by an Intelligence courier—had realised that the debates in Parliament could only end one way.

England would not tolerate Bonaparte; she would not even tolerate his abdication in favour of his own son. Austria had already declared her intention of renewing the conflict and so had Prussia. England's decision would, of course, turn the scale, and Bobby in his own mind had no doubt which way that decision would go.

The man whom the people of France loved, and whom his army idolised, was the disturber of the peace of Europe. No one would believe his protestations of pacific intentions now: he had caused too much devastation, too much misery in the past—who would believe in him for the future?

For the sake of that past, and for dread of the future, he must go—go from whence he could not again return, and Bobby Clyffurde—remembering Grenoble, remembering Lyons, Villefranche and Nevers—could not altogether suppress a sigh of regret for the brave man, the fine genius, the reckless adventurer who had so boldly scaled for the second time the heights of the Capitol, oblivious of the fact that the Tarpeian Rock was so dangerously near.

VI

At this same hour when Bobby Clyffurde finally bade adieu to all the vague hopes of happiness which his love for Crystal de Cambray had engendered in his heart, his whilom companion in the long ago—rival and enemy now—Victor de Marmont, was laying a tribute of twenty-five million francs at the feet of his beloved Emperor, and receiving the thanks of the man to serve whom he would gladly have given his life.

"What reward shall we give you for this service?" the Emperor had deigned to ask.

"The means to subdue a woman's pride, Sire, and make her thankful to marry me," replied de Marmont promptly.

"A title, what?" queried the Emperor. "You have everything else, you rogue, to please a woman's fancy and make her thankful to marry you."

"A title, Sire, would be a welcome addition," said de Marmont lightly, "and the freedom to go and woo her, until France and my Emperor need me again."

"Then go and do your wooing, man, and come back here to me in three months, for I doubt not by then the flames of war will have been kindled against me again."

CHAPTER VIII

THE SOUND OF REVELRY BY NIGHT

I

But the hand had lost its cunning, the mighty brain its indomitable will-power. Genius was still there, but it was cramped now by indecision—the indecision born of a sense of enmity around, suspicion where there should have been nothing but enthusiasm, and the blind devotion of the past.

The man who, all alone, by the force of his personality and of his prestige had reconquered France, who had been acclaimed from the Gulf of Jouan to the gates of the Tuileries as the saviour of France, the people's Emperor, the beloved of the nation returned from exile, the man who on the 20th of March had said with his old vigour and his old pride: "Failure is the nightmare of the feeble! impotence, the refuge of the poltroon!" the man who had marched as in a dream from end to end of France to find himself face to face with the whole of Europe in league against him, with a million men being hastily armed to hurl him from his throne again, now found the south of France in open revolt, the west ready to rise against him, the north in accord with his enemies.

He has not enough men to oppose to those millions, his arsenals are depleted, his treasury empty. And after he has worked sixteen hours out of the twenty-four at reorganising his army, his finances, his machinery of war, he has to meet a set of apathetic or openly hostile ministers, constitutional representatives, men who are ready to thwart him at every turn, jealous only of curtailing his power, of obscuring his ascendency, of clipping the eagle's wings, ere it soars to giddy heights again. And to them he must give in, from them he must beg, entreat: give up, give up all the time one hoped-for privilege after another, one power after another.

He yields the military dictatorship to other—far less competent—hands; he grants liberty to the press, liberty of debate, liberty of election, liberty to all and sundry: but suspicion lurks around him; they suspect his sincerity, his goodwill, they doubt his promises, they mistrust that dormant Olympian ambition which has precipitated France into humiliation and brought the strangers' armies within her gates.

The same man was there—the same genius who even now could have mastered all the enemies of France and saved her from her

167

present subjection and European insignificance, but the men round him were not the same. He, the guiding hand, was still there, but the machinery no longer worked as it had done in the past before disaster had blunted and stiffened the temper of its steel.

The men around the Emperor were not now as they were in the days of Jena and Austerlitz and Wagram. Their characters and temperaments had undergone a change. Disaster had brought on slackness, the past year of constant failures had engendered a sense of discouragement and demoralisation, a desire to argue, to foresee difficulties, to foretell further disasters.

He saw it all well enough—he the man with the far-seeing mind and the eagle-eyes that missed nothing—neither a look of indecision, nor an indication of revolt. He saw it all but he could do nothing, for he too felt overwhelmed by that wave of indecision and of discouragement. Faith in himself, energy in action, had gone. He envisaged the possibility of a vanquished and dismembered France.

Above all he had lost belief in his Star: the star of his destiny which, rising over the small island of Corsica, shining above a humble middle-class home, had guided him step by step, from triumph to triumph, to the highest pinnacle of glory to which man's ambition has ever reached.

That star had been dimmed once, its radiance was no longer unquenchable: "Destiny has turned against me," he said, "and in her I have lost my most valuable helpmate."

And now the whole of Europe had declared war against him, and in a final impassioned speech he turns to his ministers and to the representatives of his people: "Help me to save France!" he begs, "afterwards we'll settle our quarrels."

One hundred days after he began his dream-march, from the gulf of Jouan in the wake of his eagle, he started from Paris with the Army which he loved and which alone he trusted, to meet Europe and his fate on the plains of Belgium.

II

And in Brussels they danced, danced late into the night. No one was to know that within the next three days the destinies of the whole world would be changed by the hand of God.

And how to hide from timid eyes the sense of this oncoming destiny? how to stop for a few brief hours the flow of women's tears?

The ball should have been postponed—Her Grace of Richmond was willing that it should be so. How could men and women dance, flirt and make merry while Death was already reckoning the heavy toll of brave young lives which she would demand on the morrow? But who knows England who has not seen her at the hour of danger?

Put off the ball? why! perish the thought! The timid townsfolk of Brussels or the ladies of the French royalist party who were in great numbers in the city might think there was something amiss. What was amiss? some gallant young men would go on the morrow and conquer or die for England's honour! there's nothing amiss in that! Why put off the ball? The girls would be disappointed—they who like to dance—why should they be deprived of partners, just because some of them would lie dead on the battlefield to-morrow?

Open your salons, Madame la Duchesse! The soldiers of Britain will come to your ball. They will laugh and dance and flirt to-night as bravely as they will die to-morrow.

The sands of life are running low for them: in a few hours perhaps a bullet, a bayonet, who knows? will cut short that merry laugh, still the gallant heart that even now takes a last and fond farewell from a blushing partner, after a waltz, in a sweet-scented alcove with sounds of soft and distinct music around that stills the coming cannon's roar.

Gordon and Lancey, Crawford and Ponsonby and Halkett, aye! and Wellington too! What immortal names are spoken by the flunkeys to-night as they usher in these brave men into the hostess' presence. The ballroom is brilliantly illuminated with hundreds of wax candles, the women have put on their pretty dresses, displaying bare arms and dazzling shoulders; the men are in showy uniforms, glittering with stars and decorations: Orange, Brunswick, Nassau, English, Belgian, Scottish, French, all are there gay with gold and silver braid.

The confusion of tongues is greater surely than round the tower of Babel. German and French and English, Scots accent and Irish brogue, pedantic Hanoverian and lusty Brunswick tones, all and more of these varied sounds mingle with one another, and half-drown by their clamour the sweet strains of the Viennese orchestra that discoursed dreamy waltzes from behind a bower of crimson roses; whilst ponderous Flemish wives of city burgomasters gaze open-mouthed at the elegant ladies of the old French noblesse, and shy Belgian misses peep enviously at their more self-reliant English friends.

And the hostess smiles equally graciously to all: she is ready with a bright word of welcome for everybody now, just as she will be anon with a mute look of farewell, when—at ten o'clock—by Wellington's commands, one by one, one officer after another will slip out of this hospitable house, out into the rainy night, for a hurried visit to lodgings or barracks to collect a few necessaries, and then to work—to horse or march—to form into the ranks of battle as they had formed for the quadrille—squares to face the enemy—advance, deploy as they had done in the mazes of the dance! to fight as they had danced! to give their life as they had given a kiss.

Bobby Clyffurde only saw Crystal de Cambray from afar. He had his commission in Colin Halkett's brigade; his orders were the same as those of many others to-night: to put in an appearance at Her Grace's ball, to dispel any fears that might be confided to him through a fair partner's lips: to show confidence, courage and gaiety, and at ten o'clock to report for duty.

But the crowd in the ball-room was great, and Crystal de Cambray was the centre of a very close and exclusive little crowd, as indeed were all the ladies of the old French noblesse, who were here in their numbers. They had left their country in the wake of their dethroned king and despite the anxieties and sorrows of the past three months, while the star of the Corsican adventurer seemed to shine with renewed splendour, and that of the unfortunate King of France to be more and more on the wane, they had somehow filled the sleepy towns of Belgium—Ghent, Brussels, Charleroi—with the atmosphere of their own elegance and their unimpeachable good taste.

Clyffurde knew that the Comte de Cambray had settled in Brussels with his daughter and sister, pending the new turn in the fortunes of his cause: the English colony there provided the royalist fugitives with many friends, and Ghent was already overfull with the immediate entourage of the King. But Bobby had never met either the Comte or Crystal again.

He had crossed over to England almost directly after that final and fateful interview with them: he had obtained his commission and was back again in Belgium—as a fighting man, ready for the work which was expected from Britain's sons by the whole of Europe now.

And to-night he saw her again. His instinct, intuition, prescience, what you will, had told him that he would meet her here—and to his weary eyes, when first he caught sight of her across the crowded room, she had never seemed more exquisite, nor more desirable. She was dressed all in white, with arms and shoulders bare, her fair hair dressed in the quaint mode of the moment with a high comb and a multiplicity of curls. She had a bunch of white roses in her belt and carried a shawl of gossamer lace that encircled her shoulders, like a diaphanous cobweb, through which gleamed the shimmering whiteness of her skin.

She did not see him of course: he was only one of so many in a crowd of English officers who were about to fight and to die for her country and her cause as much as for their own. But to him she was the only living, breathing person in the room—all the others were phantoms or puppets that had no tangible existence for him save as a setting, a background for her.

And poor Bobby would so gladly have thrown all pride to the winds for the right to run straight to her across the width of the room, to fall at her feet, to encircle her knees, and to wring from her a word of

170

comfort or of trust. So strong was this impulse, that for one moment it seemed absolutely irresistible; but the next she had turned to Maurice de St. Genis, who was never absent from her side, and who seemed to hover over her with an air of proprietorship and of triumphant mastery which caused poor Bobby to grind his heel into the oak floor, and to smother a bitter curse which had risen insistent to his lips.

III

Madame la Duchesse d'Agen spoke to him once, while he stood by watching Crystal's dainty form walking through the mazes of a quadrille with her hand in that of St. Genis.

"They look well matched, do they not, Mr. Clyffurde?" Madame said in broken English and with something of her usual tartness; "and you? are you not going to recognise old friends, may I ask?"

He turned abruptly, whilst the hot blood rushed up to his cheek, so sudden had been the wave of memory which flooded his brain, at the sound of Madame's sharp voice. Now he stooped and kissed the slender little hand which was being so cordially held out to him.

"Old friends, Madame la Duchesse?" he queried with a quick sigh of bitterness. "Nay! you forget that it was as a traitor and a liar that you knew me last."

"It was as a young fool that I knew you all the time," she retorted tartly, even though a kindly look and a kindly smile tempered the gruffness of her sally. "The male creature, my dear Mr. Clyffurde," she added, "was intended by God and by nature to be a selfish beast. When he ceases to think of himself, he loses his bearings, flounders in a quagmire of unprofitable heroism which benefits no one, and generally behaves like a fool."

"Did I do all that?" asked Clyffurde with a smile.

"All of it and more. And look at the muddle you have made of things. Crystal has never got over that miserably aborted engagement of hers to de Marmont, and is no happier now with Maurice de St. Genis than she would have been with ... well! with anybody else who had had the good sense to woo and win her in a straightforward, proper and selfish masculine way."

"Mademoiselle de Cambray, I understand," rejoined Clyffurde stiffly, "is formally affianced now to M. de St. Genis."

"She is not formally affianced, as you so pedantically and affectedly put it, my friend," replied Madame with her accustomed acerbity. "But she probably will marry him, if he comes out of this abominable war alive, and if the King of France ... whom may God protect—comes into his own again. For His Majesty has taken those

171

two young jackanapes under his most gracious protection, and has promised Maurice a lucrative appointment at his court—if he ever has a court again."

"Then Mademoiselle de Cambray must be very happy, for which—if I dare say so—I am heartily rejoiced."

"So am I," said the Duchesse drily, "but let me at the same time tell you this: I have always known that Englishmen were peculiarly idiotic in certain important matters of life, but I must say that I had no idea idiocy could reach the boundless proportions which it has done in your case. Well!" she added with sudden gentleness, "farewell for the present, mon preux chevalier: it is not too late, remember, to bear in mind certain old axioms both of chivalry and of commonsense—the most obvious of which is that nothing is gained by sitting open-mouthed, whilst some one else gets the largest helpings at supper. And if it is any comfort to you to know that I never believed St. Genis' story of lonely inns, of murderous banditti and whatnots, well then, I give you that information for what you may choose to make of it."

And with a final friendly nod and a gentle pressure of her aristocratic hand on his, which warmed and comforted Bobby's sore heart, she turned away from him and was quickly swallowed up by the crowd.

IV

In spite of rain and blustering wind outside the fine ballroom—as the evening progressed—became unpleasantly hot. Dancing was in full swing and the orchestra had just struck up the first strains of that inspiriting new dance—the latest importation from Vienna—a dreamy waltz of which dowagers strongly disapproved, deeming it licentious, indecent, and certainly ungraceful, but which the young folk delighted in, and persisted in dancing, defying the mammas and all the proprieties.

Maurice de St. Genis after the last quadrille had led Crystal away from the ballroom to a small boudoir adjoining it, where the cool air from outside fanned the curtains and hangings and stirred the leaves and petals of a bank of roses that formed a background to a couple of seats—obviously arranged for the convenience of two persons who desired quiet conversation well away from prying eyes and ears.

Here Crystal had been sitting with Maurice for the past quarter of an hour, while from the ballroom close by came as in a dream to her the gentle lilt of the waltz, and from behind her, a cluster of sweet-scented crimson roses filled the air with their fragrance. Crystal didn't feel that she wanted to talk, only to sit here quietly with the sound of the music in her ears and the scent of roses in her nostrils. Maurice sat beside her, but he did not hold her hand. He was leaning forward with his elbows on his knees and he talked much and earnestly, the while she listened half absently, like one in a dream.

She had often heard, in the olden days in England, her aunt speak of the strange doings of that Doctor Mesmer in Paris who had even involved proud Marie Antoinette in an unpleasant scandal with his weird incantations and wizard-like acts, whereby people—sensible women and men—were sent at his will into a curious torpor, which was neither sleep nor yet wakefulness, and which produced a yet more strange sense of unreality and dreaminess, and visions of things unsubstantial and unearthly.

And sitting here surrounded with roses and with that languorous lilt in her ear, Crystal felt as if she too were under the influence of some unseen Mesmer, who had lulled the activity of her brain into a kind of wakeful sleep even while her senses remained keenly, vitally on the alert. She knew, for instance, that Maurice spoke of the coming struggle, the final fight for King and country. He had been enrolled in a Nassau regiment, under the command of the Prince of Orange: he expected to be in the thick of a fight to-morrow. "Bonaparte never waits," Crystal heard him say quite distinctly, "he is always ready to attack. Audacity and a bold use of his artillery were always his most effectual weapons."

And he went on to tell her of his own plans, his future, his hopes: he spoke of the possibility of death and of this being a last farewell. Crystal tried to follow him, tried to respond when he spoke of his love for her—a love, the strength of which—he said—she would never be able to gauge.

"If it were not for the strength of my love for you, Crystal," he said almost fiercely, "I could not bear to face possible death to-morrow ... not without telling you ... not without making reparation for my sin."

And still in that curious trance-like sense of aloofness, Crystal murmured vaguely:

"Sin, Maurice? What sin do you mean?"

But he did not seem to give her a direct reply: he spoke once more only of his love. "Love atones for all sins!" he reiterated once or twice with passionate earnestness. "Even God puts Love above everything on earth. Love is an excuse for everything. Love justifies everything. Such love as I have for you, Crystal, makes everything else—even sin, even cowardice—seem insignificant and meaningless."

She agreed with what he said, for indeed she felt too tired to argue the point, or even to get his sophistry into her head. Strangely enough she felt out of tune with him to-night—with him—Maurice—the lover of her girlhood, the man from whom she had parted with such desperate heartache three months ago, in the avenue at Brestalou. Then it had seemed as if the world could never hold any happiness for

173

her again, once Maurice had gone out of her life. Now he had come back into it. Chance and the favour of the King had once more made a future happy union with him possible. She ought to have been supremely happy, yet she was out of tune. His passionate words of love found only a cold response in her heart.

For the past three months she had constantly been at war with her own self for this: she hated and despised herself for that numbness of the heart which had so unaccountably taken all the zest and the joy out of her life. Does one love one day and become indifferent the next? What had become of the girlish love that had invested Maurice de St. Genis with the attributes of a hero? What had he done that the pedestal on which her ideality had hoisted him should have proved of such brittle clay?

He was still the gallant, high-born, well-bred gentleman whom she had always known; he was on the eve of fighting for his King and country, ready to give his life for the same cause which she loved so ardently; he was even now speaking tender words of love and of farewell. Yet she was out of tune with him. His words of Love almost irritated her, for they dragged her out of that delicious dream-like torpor which momentarily peopled the world for her with gold-headed, white-winged mysterious angels, and filled the air with soft murmurings and sweet sounds, and a divine fragrance that was not of this earth.

It must have been that she grew very sleepy—probably the heat weighed her eyelids down—certainly she found it impossible to keep her eyes open, and Maurice apparently thought that she felt faint. Always in the same vague way she heard him making suggestions for her comfort: "Could he get her some wine?" or "Should he try and find Madame la Duchesse?"

Then she realised how she longed for a little rest, for perfect solitude, for perfect freedom to give herself over to the sweet torpor which paralysed her brain and limbs—tired, sleepy, or under the subtle influence of some mysterious agency—she did not know which she was; but she did know that she would have given everything she could at this moment for a few minutes' complete solitude.

So she contrived to smile and to look up almost gaily into Maurice's anxious face: "I think really, Maurice," she said, "I am just a little bit sleepy. If I could remain alone for five minutes, I would go honestly to sleep and not be ashamed of myself. Could you ... could you just leave me for five or ten minutes? ... and ... and, Maurice, will you draw that screen a little nearer? ..." she added, affecting a little yawn; "nobody can see me then ... and really, really I shall be all right ... if I could have a few minutes' quiet sleep."

"You shall, Crystal, of course you shall," said Maurice, eager and anxious to do all that she wanted. He arranged a cushion behind her head, put a footstool to her feet and pulled the screen forward so that now—where she sat—no one could see her from the ballroom, and as in response to repeated encores from the dancers, the orchestra had embarked upon a new waltz, she was not likely to be disturbed.

"I'll try and find Mme. la Duchesse," he said after he had assured himself that she was quite comfortable, "and tell her that you are quite well, but must not be disturbed."

She caught his hand and gave it a little squeeze.

"You are kind, Maurice," she murmured.

She felt exactly like a tired child, now that she had been made so comfortable, and she liked Maurice so much, oh! so much! no brother could have been dearer.

"You won't go way without waking me, Maurice," she said as he bent down to kiss her.

"No, no, of course not," he replied; "it still wants a quarter before ten."

The screen shut off all the glare from the candles. The sense of isolation was complete and delicious: the roses smelt very sweet, the soft strains of the waltz sounded like elfin music.

V

Like elfin music—tender, fitful, dreamy!—an exquisite languor stole into Crystal's limbs. She was not asleep, yet she was in dreamland—all alone in semi-darkness, that was restful and soothing, and with the fragrance of crimson roses in her nostrils and their velvety petals brushing against her cheek.

Like elfin music!—sweet strains of infinite sadness—the tune of the Infinite mingling with the semblance of reality!

Like elfin music—or like the voice of a human being in pain—the note of sadness became the only real note now!

What really happened after this Crystal never rightly knew. Whenever in the future her memory went back to this hour, she could not be sure whether in truth she had been waking or dreaming, or at what precise moment she became fully conscious of a presence close beside her—just behind the bank of roses—and of a voice—low, earnest, quivering with passionate emotion—that reached her ear as if through the tender melodies played by the orchestra.

It almost seemed to her—when she thought over all the circumstances in her mind—that she must have been subtly conscious of the presence all along—all the while that Maurice was still with her and she felt so curiously languid, longing only for darkness and solitude.

Something encompassed her now that she could not define: the warmth of Love, the sense of protection and security—almost as if unseen arms, that were strong and devoted and selfless, held her closely, shielding her from evil and from the taint of selfish human passions.

And presently she heard her name—whispered low and with a note of tender appeal.

Her eyes were closed and she paid no heed: but the appeal was once more whispered—this time more insistently, and almost against her will she murmured:

"Who calls?"

"An unfortunate whom you hate and despise, and who would have given his life to serve you."

"Who is it?" she reiterated.

"A poor heart-broken wretch who could not keep away from your side, and longed for one more sound of your voice even though it uttered words more cruel than man can stand."

"What would you like to hear?"

"One word of comfort to ease that terrible sting of hate which has burned into my very soul, till every minute of life has become unendurable agony."

"How could I know," she asked, and now her eyes were wide open, gazing out into nothingness, not turned yet in the direction whence that dream-voice came: "how could I know that my hatred made you suffer or that you cared for comfort from me?"

"How could you know, Crystal?" the voice replied. "You could know that, my dear, just as surely as you know that in a stormy night the sky is dark, just as you know that when heavy clouds obscure the blue ether above, no ray of sunshine warms the shivering earth. Just as you know that you are beautiful and exquisite, so you knew, Crystal, that I loved you from the deepest depths of my soul."

"How could I guess?"

"By that subtle sense which every human being has. And you did guess it, Crystal, else you would not have hated me as you did."

"I hated you because I thought you a traitor."

"Is it too late to swear to you that my only thought was to serve you? ..."

"By working against my King and country?" she retorted with just this one brief flash of her old vehemence.

"By working for my country and for yours. This I swear by your sweet eyes—by your dear mouth that hurt me so cruelly that evening—I swear it by the damnable agony which you made me endure ... by the abject cowardice which dragged me to your side now like a whining wretch that craves for a crumb of comfort ... by all that you have made me suffer.... Crystal, I swear to you that I was never false ... false, great

176

God! when with every drop of my blood, with every fibre of my heart, with every nerve, every sinew, every thought I love you."

The voice was so low, never above a whisper, and all around her Crystal felt again that delicious sense of warmth—the breath of Love that brings man's heart so near to God—the sense of security in a man's all-encompassing Love which women prize above everything else on earth.

The music was just an accompaniment to that low, earnest whispering; the soft strains of the violins made it still seem like a voice that comes through a veil of dreams. Instinctively Crystal began to hum the waltz-tune and her little head with its quaint coronet of fair curls beat time to the languid lilt.

"Will you dance with me, Crystal?"

"No! no!" she protested.

"Just once—to-night. To-morrow we fight—let us dance to-night."

And before she could protest further, her will seemed to fall away from her: she knew that her father, her aunt would be angry, that—as like as not—Maurice would make a scene. She knew that Maurice—to whom she had plighted her troth—had branded this man as a liar and a traitor: her father believed him to be a traitor, and she ... Well! what had he done to disprove Maurice's accusations? A few words of passionate protestations! ... Did they count? ... He wore his King's uniform—many careless adventurers did that these strenuous times! ...

And he wanted her to dance ... ! how could she—Crystal de Cambray, the future wife of the Marquis de St. Genis, the cynosure of a great many eyes to-night—how could she show herself in public on his arm, in a crowded ballroom?

Yet she could not refuse. She could not. Surely it was all a dream, and in a dream man is but the slave of circumstance and has no will of his own.

She was very young and loved to dance: and she had heard that Englishmen danced well. Besides, it was all a dream. She would wake in a moment or two and find herself sitting quietly among the roses with Maurice beside her, telling her of his love, and of their happy future together.

VI

But in the meanwhile the dream was lasting. Her partner was a perfect dancer, and this new, delicious waltz—inspiriting yet languorous, rhythmical and half barbaric—sent a keen feeling of joy and of zest into Crystal's whole being.

177

She was not conscious of the many stares that were levelled at her as she suddenly appeared among the crowd in the ballroom, her face flushed with excitement, her perfect figure moving with exquisite grace to the measure of the dance.

The last dance together!

A few moments before, Clyffurde had made his way to the small boudoir in search of fresh air, and had withdrawn to a window embrasure away from a throng that maddened him in his misery of loneliness: then he realised that Crystal was sitting quite close to him, that St. Genis, who had been in constant attendance on her, presently left her to herself and that without even moving from where he was he could whisper into her ear that which had lain so heavily on his heart that at times he had felt that it must break under the intolerable load.

Then as the soft strains of the music from the orchestra struck upon his ear, the insistent whim seized him to make her dance with him, just once—to-night. To-morrow the cannon would roar once more—to-morrow Europe would make yet another stand against the bold adventurer whom seemingly nothing could crush.

To-morrow a bullet—a bayonet—a sword-thrust—but to-night a last dance together.

Those whims come at times to those who are doomed to die. Clyffurde's one hope of peace lay in death upon the battlefield. Life was empty now. He had fought against the burden of loneliness left upon him when Crystal passed finally out of his life. But the burden had proved unconquerable. Only death could ease him of the load: for life like this was stupid and intolerable.

Men would die within the next few days in their hundreds and in their thousands: men who were happy, who had wives and children, men on whose lives Love shed its happy radiance. Then why not he? who was more lonely than any man on earth—left lonely because the one woman who filled all the world for him, hated him and was gone from him for ever.

But a last dance with her to-night! The right to hold her in his arms! this he had never done, though his muscles had often ached with the longing to hold her. But dancing with her he could feel her against him, clasp her closely, feel her breath against his cheek.

She was not very tall and her head—had she chosen—could just have rested in the hollow of his shoulder. The thought of it sent the blood rushing hotly to his head and with his two strong hands he would at that moment have bent a bar of iron, or smashed something to atoms, in order to crush that longing to curse against Fate, against his destiny that had so wantonly dangled happiness before him, only to thrust him into utter loneliness again.

Then he spoke to her—and finally asked for the dance.

And now he held her, and guided her through the throng, her tiny feet moving in unison with his. And all the world had vanished: he had her to himself, for these few happy moments he could hold her and refuse to let her go. He did not care—nor did she—that many curious and some angry glances followed their every movement. Till the last bar was played, till the final chord was struck she was absolutely his—for she had given up her will to him.

The last dance together! He sent his heart to her, all his heart—and the music helped him, and the rhythm; the very atmosphere of the room—rose-scented—helped him to make her understand. He could have kissed her hair, so close were the heaped-up fair curls to his mouth; he could have whispered to her, and nobody would hear: he could have told her something at any rate, of that love which had filled his heart since all time, not months or years since he had known her, but since all time filling every minute of his life. He could have taught her what love meant, thrilled her heart with thoughts of might-have-been; he could have roused sweet pity in her soul, love's gentle mother that has the power to give birth to Love.

But he did not kiss her, nor did he speak: because though he was quite sure that she would understand, he was equally sure that she could not respond. She was not his—not his in the world of realities, at any rate. Her heart belonged to the friend of her childhood, the only man whom she would ever love—the man by whom he—poor Bobby!—had been content to be defamed and vilified in order that she should remain happy in her ideals and in her choice. So he was content only to hold her, his arm round her waist, one hand holding hers imprisoned—she herself becoming more and more the creature of his dreams, the angel that haunted him in wakefulness and in sleep: immortally his bride, yet never to be wholly his again as she was now in this heavenly moment where they stood together within the pale of eternity.

In this, their last dance together!

VII

Far into the night, into the small hours of the morning, Crystal de Cambray sat by the open window of her tiny bedroom in the small apartment which her father had taken for himself and his family in the rue du Marais.

She sat, with one elbow resting on the window-sill, her right hand fingering, with nervy, febrile movements, a letter which she held. Jeanne had handed it to her when she came home from the ball: M. de St. Genis, Jeanne explained, had given it to her earlier in the evening ... soon after ten o'clock it must have been ... M. le Marquis seemed in a great hurry, but he made Jeanne swear most solemnly that Mademoiselle Crystal should have the letter as soon as she came home

... also M. le Marquis had insisted that the letter should be given to Mademoiselle when she was alone.

Not a little puzzled—for had she not taken fond leave of Maurice shortly before ten o'clock, when he had told her that his orders were to quit the ball then and report himself at once at headquarters. He had seemed very despondent, Crystal thought, and the words which he spoke when finally he kissed her, had in them all the sadness of a last farewell. Crystal even had felt a tinge of remorse—when she saw how sad he was—that she had not responded more warmly to his kiss. It almost seemed as if her heart rebelled against it, and when he pressed her with his accustomed passionate ardour to his breast, she had felt a curious shrinking within herself, a desire to push him away, even though her whole heart went out to him with pity and with sorrow.

And now here was this letter. Crystal was a long time before she made up her mind to open it: the paper—damp with the rain—seemed to hold a certain fatefulness within its folds. At last she read the letter, and long after she had read it she sat at the open window, listening to the dreary, monotonous patter of the rain, and to the distant sounds of moving horses and men, the rattle of wheels, the bugle calls, the departure of the allied troops to meet the armies of the great adventurer on the billowing plains of Belgium.

This is what Maurice had written to her a few moments before he left; and it must have taken him some time to pen the lengthy epistle.

"My beautiful Crystal,

"I may never come back. Something tells me that my life, such as it is—empty and worthless enough, God knows—has nearly run its full course. But if I do come back to claim the happiness which your love holds out for me,—I will not face you again with so deep a stain upon mine honour. I did not tell you before because I was too great a coward. I could not bear to think that you would despise me—I could not encounter the look of contempt in your eyes: so I remained silent to the call of honour. And now I speak because the next few hours will atone for everything. If I come back you will forgive. If I fall you will mourn. In either case I shall be happy that you know. Crystal! in all my life I spoke only one lie, and that was three months ago, when I set out to reclaim the King's money, which had been filched from you on the high road, and returned empty-handed. I found the money and I found the thief. No thief he, Crystal, but just a quixotic man, who desired to serve his country, our cause and you. That man was your friend Mr. Clyffurde. I don't think that I was ever jealous of him. I am not jealous of him now. Our love, Crystal, is too great and too strong to fear rivalry from anyone. He had taken the money from you because he knew that Victor de Marmont, with a strong body of men to help him, would have filched it from you for the benefit of the Corsican. He took the money from you because he knew that neither you nor the Comte would have listened to any warnings from him. He took the money from you with the sole purpose of conveying it to the King. Then I found him and taunted him, until the temptation came to me to act the part of a coward and a traitor. And this I did, Crystal, only because I loved you—because I knew that I could never win you while I was poor and in humble circumstances. I soon found out that Clyffurde was a friend. I begged him to let me have the money so that I might take it to the King and earn consideration and a reward thereby. That was my sin, Crystal, and also that I lied to you to disguise the sorry rôle which I had played. Clyffurde gave me the money because I told him how we loved one another—you and I—and that happiness could only come to you through our mutual love. He acted well, though in truth I meant to do him no wrong. Later Victor de Marmont came upon me, and wrested the money from me, and I was helpless to guard that for which I had played the part of a coward.

"I have eased my soul by telling you this, Crystal, and I know that no hard thoughts of me will dwell in your mind whilst I do all that a man can do for honour, King and country.

"Remember that the next few hours, perhaps, will atone for everything, and that Love excuses all things.

"Yours in love and sorrow,

"Maurice."

The letter, crumpled and damp, remained in Crystal's hand all the while that she sat by the open window, and the sound of moving horses and men in the distance conjured up before her eyes mental visions of all that to-morrow might mean. The letter was damp with her tears now, they had fallen incessantly on the paper while she re-read it a second time and then re-read it again.

A quixotic man! Maurice said airily. How little he understood! How well she—Crystal—knew what had been the motive of that quixotic action. She had learned so much to-night in the mazes of a waltz. Now, when she closed her eyes, she could still feel the dreamy motion with that strong arm round her, and she could hear the sweet, languid lilt of the music, and all the delicious elvish whisperings that reached her ear through the monotonous cadence of the dance. Of what her heart had felt then, she need now no longer be ashamed: all that should shame her now were her thoughts in the past, the belief that the hand which had held hers on that evening—long ago—in Brestalou could possibly have been the hand of a traitor: that the low-toned voice that spoke to her so earnestly of friendship then could ever be raised for the utterance of a lie.

Of such thoughts indeed she could be ashamed, and of her cruelty that other night in Paris, when she had made him suffer so abominably through her injustice and her contempt.

"The next few hours, perhaps, will atone for everything," Maurice had added. Ah, well! perhaps! But they could not erase the past; they could not control the more distant future. Maurice would come back—Crystal prayed earnestly that he should—but Clyffurde was gone out of her life for ever. God alone knew how this renewed war would end! How could she hope ever to meet a friend who had gone away determined never to see her again?

A last dance together! Well! they had had it! and that was the end. The end of a sweet romance that had had no beginning. He had gone now, as Maurice had gone, as all the men had gone who had listened to their country's call, and she, Crystal, could not convey to him even by a message, by a word, that she understood all that he had done for her, all that his actions had meant of devotion, of self-effacement, of pure and tender Love.

A last dance together, and that had been the end. Even thoughts of him would be forbidden her after this: for her thoughts were no longer free of him, her heart was no longer free; her promise belonged to Maurice, but her heart, her thoughts were no longer hers to give.

It was all too late! too late! the next few hours might atone for the past but they could not call it back.

Weary and heart-sick Crystal crawled into bed when the grey light of dawn peeped cold and shy into her room. She could not sleep, but she lay quite still while one by one those distant sounds died away in the misty morning. In this semi-dreamlike state it seemed to her as if she must be able to distinguish the sound of his horse's hoofs from among a thousand others: it seemed as if something in herself must tell her quite plainly where he was, what he did, when he got to horse, which way he went. And presently she closed her eyes against the grey, monotonous light, and during one brief moment she felt deliciously conscious of a sweet, protecting presence somewhere near her, of soft whisperings of fondness and of friendship: the sound of a dream-voice reached her ear and once again as in the sweet-scented alcove she felt herself murmuring: "Who calls?" and once more she heard the tender wailing as of a stricken soul in pain: "A poor heart-broken wretch who could not keep away from your side."

And memory-echoes lingered round her, bringing back every sound of his mellow voice, every look in his eyes, the touch of his hand—oh! that exquisite touch!—and his last words before he asked her to dance: "With every drop of my blood, with every nerve, every sinew, every thought I love you."

And her heart with a long-drawn-out moan of unconquerable sorrow sent out into the still morning air its agonised call in reply:

"Come back, my love, come back! I cannot live without you! You have taught me what Love is—pure, selfless and protecting—you cannot go from me now—you cannot. In the name of that Love which your tender voice has brought into being, come back to me. Do not leave me desolate!"

CHAPTER IX

THE TARPEIAN ROCK

I

Rain, rain! all the morning! God's little tool—innocent-looking little tool enough—for the remodelling of the destinies of this world.

God chose to soak the earth on that day—and the formidable artillery that had swept the plateau of Austerlitz, the vales of Marengo, the cemetery of Eylau, was rendered useless for the time being because up in the inscrutable kingdom of the sky a cloud had chosen to burst—or had burst by the will of God—and water soaked the soft, spongy soil of Belgium and the wheels of artillery wagons sank axle-deep in the mud.

If only the ground had been dry! if only the great gambler—the genius, the hero, call him what you will, but the gambler for all that—if only he had staked his crown, his honour and that of Imperial France on some other stake than his artillery! If only ... ! But who shall tell?

Is it indeed a cloud-burst that changed the whole destinies of Europe? Ye materialists, ye philosophers! answer that.

Is it to the rain that fell in such torrents until close on midday of that stupendous 18th of June, that must be ascribed this wonderful and all-embracing change that came over the destinies of myriads of people, of entire nations, kingdoms and empires? Rather is it not because God just on that day of all days chose to show this world of pigmies—great men, valiant heroes, controlling genius and all-powerful conquerors—the entire extent of His might—so far and no further—and in order to show it, He selected that simple, seemingly futile means ... just a heavy shower of rain.

At half-past eleven the cannon began to roar on the plains of

183

Mont Saint Jean,[2] but not before. Before that it had rained: rained heavily, and the ground was soaked through, and the all-powerful artillery of the most powerful military genius of all times was momentarily powerless.

Had it not rained so persistently and so long that same compelling artillery would have begun its devastating work earlier in the day—at six mayhap, or mayhap at dawn, another five, six, seven hours to add to the length of that awful day: another five, six, seven hours wherein to tax the tenacity, the heroic persistence of the British troops: another five, six, seven hours of dogged resistance on the one side, of impetuous charges on the other, before the arrival of Blücher and his Prussians and the turning of the scales of blind Justice against the daring gambler who had staked his all.

But it was only at half-past eleven that the cannon began to roar, and the undulating plain carried the echo like a thunder-roll from heaving billow to heaving billow till it broke against the silent majesty of the forest of Soigne.

Here with the forest as a background is the highest point of Mont Saint Jean: and here beneath an overhanging elm—all day on horseback—anxious, frigid and heroic, is Wellington—with a rain of bullets all round him, watching, ceaselessly watching that horizon far away, wrapped now in fog, anon in smoke and soon in gathering darkness: watching for the promised Prussian army that was to ease the terrible burden of that desperate stand which the British troops were bearing and had borne all day with such unflinching courage and dogged tenacity.

It is in vain that his aides-de-camp beg him to move away from that perilous position.

"My lord," cries Lord Hill at last in desperation, "if you are killed, what are we to do?"

"The same as I do now," replies Wellington unmoved, "hold this place to the last man."

Then with a sudden outburst of vehemence, that seems to pierce almost involuntarily the rigid armour of British phlegm and British self-control, he calls to his old comrades of Salamanca and Vittoria:

"Boys, which of us now can think of retreating? What would England think of us, if we do?"

Heroic, unflinching and cool the British army has held its ground against the overwhelming power of Napoleon's magnificent cavalry. Raw recruits some of them, against the veterans of Jena and of Wagram! But they have been ordered to hold the place to the last man, and in close and serried squares they have held their ground ever since half-past eleven this morning, while one after another the flower of Napoleon's world-famed cavalry had been hurled against them.

---

[2] i.e. Waterloo.

Cuirassiers, chasseurs, lancers, up they come to the charge, like whirlwinds up the declivities of the plateau. Like a whirlwind they rush upon those stolid, immovable, impenetrable squares, attacking from every side, making violent, obstinate, desperate onsets upon the stubborn angles, the straight, unshakable walls of red coats; slashing at the bayonets with their swords, at crimson breasts with their lances, firing their pistols right between those glowing eyes, right into those firm jaws and set teeth.

The sound of bullets on breastplates and helmets and epaulettes is like a shower of hailstones upon a sheet of metal.

Twice, thrice, nay more—a dozen times—they return to the charge, and the plateau gleams with brandished steel like a thousand flashes of simultaneous fork-lightning on the vast canopy of a stormy sky.

From midday till after four, a kind of mysterious haze covers this field of noble deeds. Fog after the rain wraps the gently-billowing Flemish ground in a white semi-transparent veil—covers with impartial coolness all the mighty actions, the heroic charges and still more heroic stands, all the silent uncomplaining sufferings, the glorious deaths, all the courage and all the endurance.

Through the grey mists we see a medley of moving colours—blue and grey and scarlet and black—of shakos and sabretaches, of English and French and Hanoverian and Scotch, of epaulettes and bare knees; we hear the sound of carbine and artillery fire, the clank of swords and bayonets, the call of bugle and trumpet and the wail of the melancholy pibroch: tunics and gold tassels and kilts—a medley of sounds and of visions!

We see the attack on Hougoumont—the appearance of Bülow on the heights of Saint Lambert—the charge of the Inniskillings and the Scots Greys—the death of valiant Ponsonby. We see Marshal Ney Prince of Moskowa—the bravest soldier in France—we see him everywhere where the mêlée is thickest, everywhere where danger is most nigh. His magnificent uniform torn to shreds, his gold lace tarnished, his hair and whiskers singed, his face blackened by powder, indomitable, unconquered, superb, we hear him cry: "Where are those British bullets? Is there not one left for me?"

He knows—none better!—that the plains of Mont Saint Jean are the great gambling tables on which the supreme gambler—Napoleon, once Emperor of the French and master of half the world—had staked his all. "If we come out of this alive and conquered," he cries to Heymès, his aide-de-camp, "there will only be the hangman's rope left for us all."

And we see the gambler himself—Napoleon, Emperor still and still certain of victory—on horseback all day, riding from end to end of his lines; he is gayer than he has ever been before. At Marengo he was

185

despondent, at Austerlitz he was troubled: but at Waterloo he has no doubts. The star of his destiny has risen more brilliant than ever before.

"The day of France's glory has only just dawned," he calls, and his mind is full of projects—the triumphant march back into Paris—the Germans driven back to the Rhine—the English to the sea.

His only anxiety—and it is a slight one still—is that Grouchy with his fresh troops is so late in arriving.

Still, the Prussians are late too, and the British cannot hold the place for ever.

II

At three o'clock the fog lifts—the veil that has wrapped so many sounds, such awful and wonderful visions, in a kind of mystery, is lifted now, and it reveals ... what? Hougoumont invested—Brave Baring there with a handful of men—English, German, Brunswickians—making a last stand with ten rounds of ammunition left to them per man, and the French engineers already battering in the gates of the enclosing wall that surrounds the château and chapel of Goumont: the farm of La Haye Sainte taken—Ney there with his regiment of cuirassiers and five battalions of the Old Guard: and the English lines on the heights of Mont Saint Jean apparently giving way.

We see too a vast hecatomb: glory and might must claim their many thousand victims: the dead and dying lie scattered like pawns upon an abandoned chessboard, the humble pawns in this huge and final gamble for supremacy and power, for national existence and for liberty. Hougoumont, La Haye Sainte, Papelotte are sown with illustrious dead—but on the plateau of Mont Saint Jean the British still hold their ground.

Wellington is still there on the heights, with the majestic trees of Soigne behind him, the stately canopy of the elm above his head—more frigid than before, more heroic, but also more desperately anxious.

"Blücher or nightfall," he sighs as a fresh cavalry charge is hurled against those indomitable British squares. The thirteenth assault, and still they stand or kneel on one knee, those gallant British boys; bayonet in hand or carbine, they fire, fall out and re-form again: shaken, hustled, encroached on they may be, but still they stand and fire with coolness and precision ... the ranks are not broken yet.

Officers ride up to the field-marshal to tell him that the situation has become desperate, their regiments decimated, their men exhausted. They ask for fresh orders: but he has only one answer for them:

186

"There are no fresh orders, save to hold out to the last man."

And down in the valley at La Belle Alliance is the great gambler—the man who to-day will either be Emperor again—a greater, mightier monarch than even he has ever been—or who will sink to a status which perhaps the meanest of his erstwhile subjects would never envy.

But just now—at four o'clock—when the fog has lifted—he is flushed with excitement, exultant in the belief in victory.

The English centre on Mont Saint Jean is giving way at last, he is told.

"The beginning of retreat!" he cries.

And he, who had been anxious at Austerlitz, despondent at Marengo, is gay and happy and brimming full of hope.

"De Marmont," he calls to his faithful friend, "De Marmont, go ride to Paris now; tell them that victory is ours! No, no," he adds excitedly, "don't go all the way—ride to Genappe and send a messenger to Paris from there—then come back to be with us in the hour of victory."

And Victor de Marmont rides off in order to proclaim to the world at large the great victory which the Emperor has won this day over all the armies of Europe banded and coalesced against him.

From far away on the road of Ohain has come the first rumour that Blücher and his body of Prussians are nigh—still several hours' march from Waterloo but advancing—advancing. For hours Wellington has been watching for them, until wearily he has sighed: "Blücher or nightfall alone can save us from annihilation now."

The rumour—oh! it was merely the whispering of the wind, but still a rumour nevertheless—means fresh courage to tired, half-spent troops. Even deeds of unparalleled heroism need the stimulus of renewed hope sometimes.

The rumour has also come to the ears of the Emperor, of Ney and of all the officers of the staff. They all know that those magnificent British troops whom they have fought all day must be nigh to their final desperate effort at last—with naught left to them but their stubborn courage and that tenacity which has been ever since the wonder of the world.

They know, these brave soldiers of Napoleon—who have fought and admired the brave foe—that the 1st and 2nd Life Guards are decimated by now; that entire British and German regiments are cut up; that Picton is dead, the Scots Greys almost annihilated. They know what havoc their huge cavalry charges have made in the magnificent squares of British infantry; they know that heroism and tenacity and determination must give way at last before superior numbers, before fresh troops, before persistent, ever-renewed attacks.

Only a few fresh troops and Ney declares that he can conquer the final dogged endurance of the British troops, before they in their turn receive the support of Blücher and his Prussians, or before nightfall gives them a chance of rest.

So he sends Colonel Heymès to his Emperor with the urgent message: "More troops, I entreat, more troops and I can break the English centre before the Prussians come!"

None knew better than he that this was the great hazard on which the life and honour of his Emperor had been staked, that Imperial France was fighting hand to hand with Great Britain, each for her national existence, each for supremacy and might and the honour of her flag.

Imperial France—bold, daring, impetuous!

Great Britain—tenacious, firm and impassive!

Wellington under the elm-tree, calmly scanning the horizon while bullets whiz past around his head, and ordering his troops to hold on to the last man!

The Emperor on horseback under a hailstorm of shot and shell and bullets riding from end to end of his lines!

Ney and his division of cuirassiers and grenadiers of the Old Guard had just obeyed the Emperor's last orders which had been to take La Haye Sainte at all costs: and the intrepid Maréchal now, flushed with victory, had sent his urgent message to Napoleon:

"More troops! and I can yet break through the English centre before the arrival of the Prussians."

"More troops?" cried the Emperor in despair, "where am I to get them from? Am I a creator of men?"

And from far away the rumour: "Blücher and the Prussians are nigh!"

"Stop that rumour from spreading to the ears of our men! In God's name don't let them know it," adjures Napoleon in a message to Ney.

And he himself sends his own staff officers to every point of the field of battle to shout and proclaim the news that it is Grouchy who is nigh, Grouchy with reinforcements, Grouchy with the victorious troops from Ligny, fresh from conquered laurels!

And the news gives fresh heart to the Imperial troops:

"Vive l'Empereur!" they shout, more certain than ever of victory.

III

The grey day has yielded at last to the kiss of the sun. Far away at Braine l'Alleud a vivid streak of gold has rent the bank of heavy clouds. It is now close on seven o'clock—there are two more hours to nightfall and Blücher is not yet here.

188

Some of the Prussians have certainly debouched on Plancenoit, but Napoleon's Old Guard have turned them out again, and from Limale now comes the sound of heavy cannonade as if Grouchy had come upon Blücher after all and all hopes of reinforcements for the British troops were finally at an end.

Napoleon—Emperor still and still flushed with victory—looks through his glasses on the British lines: to him it seems that these are shaken, that Wellington is fighting with the last of his men. This is the hour then when victory waits—attentive, ready to bestow her crown on him who can hold out and fight the longest—on him who at the last can deliver the irresistible attack.

And Napoleon gives the order for the final attack, which must be more formidable, more overpowering than any that have gone before. The plateau of Mont Saint Jean, he commands, must be carried at all costs!

Cuirassiers, lancers and grenadiers, then, once more to the charge! strew once more the plains of Waterloo with your dying and your dead! Up, Milhaud, with your guards! Poret with your grenadiers! Michel with your chasseurs! Up, ye heroes of a dozen campaigns, of a hundred victories! Up, ye old growlers with the fur bonnets—Napoleon's invincible Old Guard! With Ney himself to lead you! a hero among heroes! the bravest where all are brave!

Have you ever seen a tidal wave of steel rising and surging under the lash of the gale? So they come now, those cuirassiers and lancers and chasseurs, their helmets, their swords, their lances gleaming in the golden light of the sinking sun; in closed ranks, stirrup to stirrup they swoop down into the valley, and rise again scaling the muddy heights. Superb as on parade, with their finest generals at their head: Milhaud, Hanrion, Michel, Mallet! and Ney between them all.

Splendid they are and certain of victory: they gallop past as if at a revue on the Place du Carrousel opposite the windows of the Tuileries; all to the repeated cry of "Vive l'Empereur!"

And as they gallop past the wounded and the dying lift themselves up from the blood-stained earth, and raise their feeble voices to join in that triumphant call: "Vive l'Empereur!" There's an old veteran there, who fought at Austerlitz and at Jena; he has three stripes upon his sleeve, but both his legs are shattered and he lies on the roadside propped up against a hedge, and as the superb cavalry ride proudly by he shouts lustily: "Forward, comrades! a last victorious charge! Long live the Emperor!"

After that who was to blame? Was human agency to blame? Did Ney—the finest cavalry leader in Napoleon's magnificent army, the veteran of an hundred glorious victories—did he make the one blunder of his military career by dividing his troops into too many separate columns rather than concentrating them for the one all-powerful attack upon the British centres? Did he indeed mistake the way and lead his splendid cavalry by round-about crossways to the plateau instead of by the straight Brussels road?

Or did the obscure traitor—over whom history has thrown a veil of mystery—betray this fresh advance against the British centre to Wellington?

Was any man to blame? Was it not rather the hand of God that had already fallen with almighty and divine weight upon the ambitious and reckless adventurer?—was it not the voice of God that spoke to him through the cannon's roar of Waterloo: "So far but no farther shalt thou go! Enough of thy will and thy power and thy ambition!—Enough of this scourge of bloodshed and of misery which I have allowed thee to wield for so long!—Enough of devastated homes, of starvation and of poverty! enough of the fatherless and of the widow!"

And up above on the plateau the British troops hear the thunder of thousands of horses' hoofs, galloping—galloping to this last charge which must be irresistible. And sturdy, wearied hands, black with powder and stained with blood, grasp more firmly still the bayonet, the rifle or the carbine, and they wait—those exhausted, intrepid, valiant men! they wait for that thundering charge, with wide-open eyes fixed upon the crest of the hill—they wait for the charge—they are ready for death—but they are not prepared to yield.

Along the edge of the plateau in a huge semicircle that extends from Hougoumont to the Brussels road the British gunners wait for the order to fire.

Behind them Wellington—eagle-eyed and calm, warned by God—or by a traitor but still by God—of the coming assault on his positions—scours the British lines from end to end: valiant Maitland is there with his brigade of guards, and Adam with his artillery: there are Vandeleur's and Vivian's cavalry and Colin Halkett's guards! heroes all! ready to die and hearing the approach of Death in that distant roar of thunder—the onrush of Napoleon's invincible cavalry.

Here, too, further out toward the east and the west, extending the British lines as far as Nivelles on one side and Brussels on the other, are William Halkett's Hanoverians, Duplat's German brigade, the Dutch and the Belgians, the Brunswickers, and Ompteda's decimated corps. The French royalists are here too, scattered among the foreign troops—brother prepared to fight brother to the death! St. Genis is among the Brunswickers. But Bobby Clyffurde is with Maitland's guards.

And now the wave of steel is surging up the incline: the gleam of shining metal pierces the distant haze, casques and lances glitter in the slowly sinking sun, whilst from billow to billow the echo brings to straining ears the triumphant cry "Vive l'Empereur!"

Five minutes later the British artillery ranged along the crest has made a huge breach in that solid, moving mass of horses and of steel. Quickly the breach is repaired: the ranks close up again! This is a parade! a review! The eyes of France are upon her sons! and "Vive l'Empereur!"

Still they come!

Volley after volley from the British guns makes deadly havoc among those glistering ranks!

But nevertheless they come!

No halt save for the quick closing up into serried, orderly columns. And then on with the advance!—like the surging up of a tidal wave against the cliffs—on with the advance! up the slopes toward the crest where those who are in the front ranks are mowed down by the British guns—their places taken by others from the rear—those others mowed down again, and again replaced—falling in their hundreds as they reach the crest, like the surf that shivers and dies as it strikes against the cliffs.

Ney's horse is killed under him—the fifth to-day—but he quickly extricates himself from saddle and stirrups and continues on his way—on foot, sword in hand—the sword that conquered at Austerlitz, at Eylau and at Moskowa. Round him the grenadiers of the Old Guard—they with the fur bonnets and the grizzled moustaches—tighten up their ranks.

They advance behind the cavalry! and after every volley from the British guns they shout loudly: "Vive l'Empereur!"

And anon the tidal wave—despite the ebb, despite the constant breaking of its surf—has by sheer force of weight hurled itself upon the crest of the plateau.

The Brunswickers on the left are scattered. Cleeves and Lloyd have been forced to abandon their guns: the British artillery is silenced and the chasseurs of Michel hold the extreme edge of the upland, and turn a deadly fusillade upon Colin Halkett's brigade already attacked by Milhaud and his guards and now severely shaken.

"See the English General!" cries Duchaud to his cuirassiers, "he is between two fires. He cannot escape."

No! he cannot but he seizes the colours of the 33rd whose young lieutenant has just fallen, and who threaten to yield under the devastating cross-fire: he brandishes the tattered colours, high up above his head—as high as he can hold them—he calls to his men to rally, and then falls grievously wounded.

But his guards have rallied. They stand firm now, and Duchaud, chewing his grey moustache, murmurs his appreciation of so gallant a foe.

"That side will win," he mutters, "who can best keep on killing."

IV

"Up, guards, and at them!"

Maitland's brigade of guards had been crouching in the corn—crouching—waiting for the order to charge—red-coated lions in the ripening corn—ready to spring at the word.

And Death the harvester in chief stands by with his scythe ready for the mowing.

"Up, guards, and at them!"

It is Maitland and his gallant brigade of guards—out of the corn they rise and front the three battalions of Michel's chasseurs who were the first to reach the highest point of the hill. They fire and Death with his scythe has laid three hundred low. The tricolour flag is riddled with grapeshot and Général Michel has fallen.

Then indeed the mighty wave of steel can advance no longer: for it is confronted with an impenetrable wall—a wall of living, palpitating, heroic men—men who for hours have stood their ground and fought for the honour of Britain and of her flag—men who with set teeth and grim determination were ready to sell their lives dearly if lives were to be sold—men in fact who have had their orders to hold out to the last man and who are going to obey those orders now.

"Up, guards, and at them," and surprised, bewildered, staggered, the chasseurs pause: three hundred of their comrades lie dead or dying on the ground. They pause: their ranks are broken: with his last dying sigh brave Général Michel tries to rally them. But he breathes his last ere he succeeds: his second in command loses his head. He should have ordered a bayonet charge—sudden, swift and sure—against that red wall that rushes at them with such staggering power: but he too tries to rally his men, to re-form their ranks—how can they re-form as for parade under the deadly fire of the British guards?

Confusion begins its deathly sway: the chasseurs—under conflicting orders—stand for full ten minutes almost motionless under that devastating fire.

And far away on the heights of Frischemont the first line of Prussian bayonets are seen silhouetted against the sunset sky.

Wellington has seen it. Blücher has come at last! One final effort, one more mighty gigantic, superhuman struggle and the glorious end would be in sight. He gives the order for a general charge.

"Forward, boys," cries Colonel Saltoun to his brigade. "Now is the time!"

Heads down the British charge. The chasseurs are already scattered, but behind the chasseurs, fronting Maitland's brigade, fronting Adam and his artillery, fronting Saltoun and Colborne the Fire-Eater, the Old Guard is seen to advance, the Old Guard who through twelve campaigns and an hundred victories have shown the world how to conquer and how to die.

When Michel's chasseurs were scattered, when their General fell; when the English lines, exhausted and shaken for a moment, rallied at Wellington's call: "Up, guards, and at them!" when from far away on the heights of Frischemont the first line of Prussian bayonets were silhouetted against the sunset sky, then did Napoleon's old growlers with their fur bonnets and their grizzled moustaches enter the line of action to face the English guards. They were facing Death and knew it but still they cried: "Vive l'Empereur!"

Heads down the British charge, whilst from Ohain comes the roar of Blücher's guns, and up from the east, Zieten with the Prussians rushes up to join in the assault.

Then the carnage begins: for the Old Guard is still advancing—in solid squares—solemn, unmoved, magnificent: the bronze eagles on their bonnets catch the golden rays of the setting sun. Thus they advance in face of deadly fire: they fall like corn before the scythe. A sublime suicide to the cry of "Vive l'Empereur!" and not one of the brigade is missing except those who are dead.

They know—none better—that this is the beginning of the end. Perhaps they do not care to live if their Emperor is to be Emperor no longer, if he is to be sent back to exile—to the prison of Elba or worse: and so they advance in serried squares, while Maitland's artillery has attacked them in the rear. Great gaps are made in those ranks, but they are quickly filled up again: the squares become less solid, smaller, but they remain compact. Still they advance.

But now close behind them Blücher's guns begin to thunder and Zieten's columns are rapidly gaining ground: all round their fur bonnets a hailstorm of grape-shot is raging whilst Adam's artillery is in action within fifty paces at their flank. But the old growlers who had suffered death with silent fortitude in the snows of Russia, who had been as grand in their defeat at Moscow and at Leipzic as they had been in the triumphs of Auerstadt or of Friedland—they neither staggered nor paused in their advance. On they went—carrying their muskets on their shoulders—a cloud of tirailleurs in front of them, right into the cross-fire of the British guns: their loud cry of "Vive l'Empereur" drowning that other awesome, terrible cry which someone had raised a while ago and which now went from mouth to mouth: "We are betrayed! Sauve qui peut!"

The Prussians were in their rear; the British were charging their front, and panic had seized the most brilliant cavalry the world had ever seen.

"Sauve qui peut" is echoed now and re-echoed all along the crest of the plateau. And the echo rolls down the slope into the valley where Reille's infantry and a regiment of cuirassiers, and three more battalions of chasseurs, are making ready to second the assault on

Mont Saint Jean. Reille and his infantry pause and listen: the cuirassiers halt in their upward movement, whilst up on the ridge of the plateau where Donzelot's grenadiers have attacked the brigade of Kempt and Lambert and Pack, the whisper goes from mouth to mouth:

"We are betrayed! Sauve qui peut!"

Panic seizes the younger men: they turn their horses' heads back toward the slopes. The stampede has commenced: very soon it grows. The British in front, the Prussians in the rear: "Sauve qui peut!"

Ney amongst them is almost unrecognisable. His face is coal-black with powder: he has no hat, no epaulettes and only half a sword: rage, anguish, bitterness are in his husky voice as he adjures, entreats, calls to the demoralised army—and insults it, execrates it in turn. But nothing but Death will stop that army now in its headlong flight.

"At least stop and see how a Marshal of France dies on the field of honour," he calls.

But the voice which led these same men to victory at Moskowa has lost its potency and its magic. The men cry "Vive Ney!" but they do not stand. The stampede has become general. In the valley below the infantry has started to run up the slope of La Belle Alliance: after it the cavalry with reins hanging loose, stirrups lost, casques, sabretaches, muskets—anything that impedes—thrown into the fields to right and left. La Haye Sainte is evacuated, Hougoumont is abandoned; Papelotte, Plancenoit, the woods, the plains are only filled with running men and the thunder of galloping chargers.

Alone the Old Guard has remained unshaken. Whilst all around them what was once the Grand Army is shattered, destroyed, melted like ice before a devastating fire, they have continued to advance, sublime in their fortitude, in their endurance, their contempt for death. One by one their columns are shattered and there are none now to replace those that fall. And as the gloom of night settles on this vast hecatomb on the plateau of Mont Saint Jean the conquerors of Jena and Austerlitz and Friedland make their last stand round the bronze eagle—all that is left to them of the glories of the past.

And when from far away the cry of "Sauve qui peut" has become only an echo, and the bronze eagle shattered by a bullet lies prone upon the ground shielded against capture in its fall by a circling mountain of dead, when finally Night wraps all the heroism, the glory, the sorrow and the horrors of this awful day in the sable folds of her all-embracing mantle, Napoleon's Old Guard has ceased to be.

And out in the western sky a streak of vivid crimson like human blood has broken the bosom of the clouds: the glow of the sinking sun rests on this huge dissolution of what was once so glorious and unconquered and great. Then it is that Wellington rides to the very edge of the plateau and fronts the gallant British troops at this supreme hour of oncoming victory, and lifting his hat high above his head he waves it three times in the air.

And from right and left they come, British, Hanoverians, Belgians and Brunswickers to deliver the final blow to this retreating army, wounded already unto death.

They charge now: they charge all of them, cavalry, infantry, gunners, forty thousand men who have forgotten exhaustion, forgotten what they have suffered, forgotten what they had endured. On they come with a rush like a torrent let loose; the confusion of sounds and sights becomes a pandemonium of hideousness, bugles and drums and trumpets and bagpipes all mingle, merge and die away in the fast gathering twilight.

And the tidal wave of steel recedes down the slopes of Mont Saint Jean, into the valley and thence up again on Belle Alliance, with a mêlée of sounds like the breaking of a gigantic line of surf against the irresistible cliffs, or the last drawn-out sigh of agony of dying giants in primeval times.

V

On the road to Genappe in the mystery of the moonlit night a solitary rider turned into a field and dismounted.

Carried along for a time by the stream of the panic, he found himself for a moment comparatively alone—left as it were high and dry by the same stream which here had divided and flowed on to right and left of him. He wore a grey redingote and a shabby bicorne hat.

Having dismounted he slipped the bridle over his arm and started to walk beside his horse back toward Waterloo.

A sleep-walker in pursuit of his dream!

Heavy banks of grey clouds chased one another with mad fury across the midsummer sky, now obscuring the cold face of the moon, now allowing her pale, silvery rays to light up this gigantic panorama of desolation and terror and misery. To right and left along the roads and lanes, across grassland and cornfields, canals, ditches and fences the last of the Grand Army was flying headlong, closely pursued by the Prussians. And at the farm of La Belle Alliance Wellington and Blücher had met and shaken hands, and had thanked God for the great and glorious victory.

But the sleep-walker went on in pursuit of his dream—he walked with measured steps beside his weary horse, his eyes fixed on the horizon far away, where the dull crimson glow of smouldering fires threw its last weird light upon this vast abode of the dead and the dying. He walked on—slowly and mechanically back to the scene of the overwhelming cataclysm where all his hopes lay irretrievably buried. He walked on—majestic as he had never been before, in the brilliant

195

throne-room of the Tuileries or the mystic vastness of Notre Dame when the Imperial crown sat so ill upon his plebeian head.... He walked on—silent, exalted and great—great through the magnitude of his downfall.

And to right and left of him, like the surf that recedes on a pebbly beach, the last of his once invincible army was flying back to France—back in the wake of those who had been lucky enough to fly before—bodies of men who had been the last to realise that an heroic stand round a fallen eagle could no longer win back that which was lost, and that if life be precious it could only be had in flight—bits of human wreckage too, forgotten by the tide—they all rolled and rushed and swept past the silent wayfarer ... quite close at times: so close that every man could see him quite distinctly, could easily distinguish by the light of the moon the grey redingote and the battered hat which they all knew so well—which they had been wont to see in the forefront of an hundred victorious charges.

Now half-blinded by despair and by panic they gazed with uncomprehending eyes on the man and on the horse and merely shouted to him as they rushed galloping or running by, "The Prussians are on us! Sauve qui peut!"

And the dreamer still looked on that distant crimson glow and in the bosom of those wind-swept clouds he saw the pictures of Austerlitz and Jena and Wagram, pictures of glory and might and victory, and the shouts which he heard were the ringing cheers round the bivouac fires of long ago.

CHAPTER X

THE LAST THROW

I

It was close on half-past nine and the moon full up on the stormy sky when a couple of riders detached themselves out of the surging mass of horses and men that were flying pell-mell towards Genappe, and slightly checking their horses, put them to a slower gallop and finally to a trot.

On their right a small cottage gleamed snow-white in the cold, searching light of the moon. A low wall ran to right and left of it and enclosed a small yard at the back of the cottage; the wall had a gate in it which gave on the fields beyond. At the moment that the two riders trotting slowly down the road reached the first angle of the wall, the gate was open and a man leading a white horse and wearing a grey redingote turned into the yard.

"My God! the Emperor!" exclaimed one of the riders as he drew rein.

They both turned their horses into the field, skirting the low, enclosing wall until they reached the gate. The white horse was now tethered to a post and the man in the grey redingote was standing in the doorway at the rear of the cottage. The two men dismounted and in their turn led their horses into the yard: at sight of them the man in the grey redingote seemed to wake from his sleep.

"Berthier," he said slowly, "is that you?"

"Yes, Sire,—and Colonel Bertrand is here too."

"What do you want?"

"We earnestly beg you, Sire, to come with us to Genappe. There is not the slightest hope of rallying any portion of your army now. The Prussians are on us. You might fall into their hands."

Berthier—conqueror and Prince of Wagram—spoke very earnestly and with head uncovered, but more abruptly and harshly than he had been wont to do of yore in the salons of the Tuileries or on the glory-crowned battlefields at the close of a victorious day.

"I am coming! I am coming!" said the Emperor with a quick sigh of impatience. "I only wanted to be alone a moment—to think things out—to ..."

"There is nothing quite so urgent, Sire, as your safety," retorted the Prince of Wagram drily.

The Emperor did not—or did not choose to—heed his great Marshal's marked want of deference. Perhaps he was accustomed to the moods of these men whom his bounty had fed and loaded with wealth and dignities and titles in the days of his glory, and who had proved only too ready, alas!—even last year, even now—to desert him when disaster was in sight.

Without another word he turned on his heel and pushing open the cottage door he disappeared into the darkness of the tiny room beyond. With an impatient shrug of the shoulders Berthier prepared to follow him. Colonel Bertrand busied himself with tethering the horses, then he too followed Berthier into the building.

It was deserted, of course, as all isolated cottages and houses had been in the vicinity of Quatre Bras or Mont Saint Jean. Bertrand struck a tinder and lighted a tallow candle that stood forlorn on a deal table in the centre of the room. The flickering light revealed a tiny cottage kitchen—hastily abandoned but scrupulously clean—white-washed walls, a red-tiled floor, the iron hearth, the painted dresser decorated with white crockery, shiny tin pans hung in rows against the walls and two or three rush chairs. Napoleon sat down.

"I again entreat you, Sire—" began Berthier more earnestly than before.

But the Emperor was staring straight out before him, with eyes that apparently saw something beyond that rough white wall opposite, on which the flickering candle-light threw such weird gargantuan shadows. The precious minutes sped on: minutes wherein death or capture strode with giant steps across the fields of Flanders to this lonely cottage where the once mightiest ruler in Europe sat dreaming of what might have been. The silence of the night was broken by the thunder of flying horses' hoofs, by the cries of "Sauve qui peut!" and distant volleys of artillery proclaiming from far away that Death had not finished all his work yet.

Bertrand and Berthier stood by, with heads uncovered: silent, moody and anxious.

Suddenly the dreamer roused himself for a moment and spoke abruptly and with his usual peremptory impatience: "De Marmont," he said. "Has either of you seen him?"

"Not lately, Sire," replied Colonel Bertrand, "not since five o'clock at any rate."

"What was he doing then?"

"He was riding furiously in the direction of Nivelles. I shouted to him. He told me that he was making for Brussels by a circuitous way."

"Ah! that is right! Well done, my brave de Marmont! Braver than your treacherous kinsman ever was! So you saw him, did you, Bertrand? Did he tell you that he had just come from Genappe?"

"Yes, Sire, he did," replied Bertrand moodily. "He told me that by your orders he had sent a messenger from there to Paris with news of your victory: and that by to-morrow morning the capital would be ringing with enthusiasm and with cheers."

"And by the time de Marmont came back from Genappe," interposed the Prince of Wagram with a sneer, "the plains of Waterloo were ringing with the Grand Army's 'Sauve qui peut!'"

"An episode, Prince, only an episode!" said Napoleon with an angry frown of impatience. "To hear you now one would imagine that Essling had never been. We have been beaten back, of course, but for the moment the world does not know that. Paris to-morrow will be be-flagged and the bells of Notre Dame will send forth their joyous peals to cheer the hearts of my people. And in Brussels this afternoon thousands of our enemies—Belgians, Dutch, Hanoverians, Brunswickers—were rushing helter-skelter into the town—demoralised and disorganised after that brilliant charge of our cuirassiers against the Allied left."

"Would to God the British had been among them too," murmured old Colonel Bertrand. "But for their stand ..."

"And a splendid stand it was. Ah! but for that.... To think that if Grouchy had kept the Prussians away, in only another hour we ..."

The dreamer paused in his dream of the might have been: then he continued more calmly:

"But I was not thinking of that just now. I was thinking of those who fled to Brussels this afternoon with the news of our victory and of Wellington's defeat."

"Even then the truth is known in Brussels by now," protested Berthier.

"Yes! but not before de Marmont has had the time and the pluck to save us and our Empire! ... Berthier," he continued more vehemently, "don't stand there so gloomy, man ... and you, too, my old Bertrand.... Surely, surely you have realised that at this terrible juncture we must utilise every circumstance which is in our favour.... That early news of our victory ... we can make use of that.... A big throw in this mighty game, but we can do it ... Berthier, do you see how we can do it ... ?"

"No, Sire, I confess that I do not," replied the Marshal gloomily.

"You do not see?" retorted the Emperor with a frown of angry impatience. "De Marmont did—at once—but he is young—and enthusiastic, whereas you.... But don't you see that the news of Wellington's defeat must have enormous consequences on the money markets of the world—if only for a few hours? ... It must send the prices on the foreign Bourses tumbling about people's ears and create an absolute panic on the London Stock Exchange. Only for a few hours of course ... but do you not see that if any man is wise enough to buy stock in London during that panic he can make a fortune by re-selling the moment the truth is known?"

"Even then, Sire," stammered Berthier, a little confused by this avalanche of seemingly irrelevant facts hurled at him at a moment when the whole map of Europe was being changed by destiny and her future trembled in the hands of God.

"Ah, de Marmont saw it all ... at once ..." continued the Emperor earnestly, "he saw eye to eye with me. He knows that money—a great deal of money—is just what I want now ... money to reorganise my army, to re-equip and reform it. The Chamber and my Ministers will never give me what I want.... My God! they are such cowards! and some of them would rather see the foreign troops again in Paris than Napoleon Emperor at the Tuileries. You should know that, Maréchal, and you, too, my good Bertrand. De Marmont knows it ... that is why he rode to Brussels at the hour when I alone knew that all was lost at Waterloo, but when half Europe still thought that the Corsican ogre had conquered again.... De Marmont is in Brussels now ... to-night he crosses over to England—to-morrow morning he and his broker will be in the Stock Exchange in London—calm, silent, watchful. An operation on the Bourse, what? like hundreds that have been done before ... but

199

in this case the object will be to turn one million into fifty so that with it I might rebuild my Empire again."

He spoke with absolute conviction, and with indomitable fervour, sitting here quietly, he—the architect of the mightiest empire of modern days—just as he used to do in the camps at Austerlitz and Jena and Wagram and Friedland—with one clenched hand resting upon the rough deal table, the flickering light of the tallow candle illuminating the wide brow, the heavy jaw, those piercing eyes that still gazed—in this hour of supreme catastrophe—into a glorious future destined never to be—scheming, planning, scheming still, even while his Grand Army was melting into nothingness all around him, and distant volleys of musketry were busy consummating the final annihilation of the Empire which he had created and still hoped to rebuild.

Berthier gave a quick sign of impatience.

Rebuild an Empire, ye gods!—an Empire!—when the flower of its manhood lies pale and stark like the windrows of corn after the harvester has done his work. Thoughts of a dreamer! Schemes of a visionary! How will the quaking lips which throughout the length and breadth of this vast hecatomb now cry, "Sauve qui peut!" how will they ever intone again the old "Vive l'Empereur!"

The conqueror of Wagram gave a bitter sigh and faithful Bertrand hung his head gloomily; but de Marmont had neither sighed nor doubted: but then de Marmont was young—he too was a dreamer, and an enthusiast and a visionary. His idol in his eyes had never had feet of clay. For him the stricken man was his Emperor still—the architect, the creator, the invincible conqueror—checked for a moment in his glorious work, but able at his will to rebuild the Empire of France again on the very ruins that smouldered now on the fields of Waterloo.

"I can do it, Sire," he had cried exultantly, when his Emperor first expounded his great, new scheme to him. "I can be in Brussels in an hour, and catch the midnight packet for England at Ostend. At dawn I shall be in London, and by ten o'clock at my post. I know a financier—a Jew, and a mightily clever one—he will operate for me. I have a million or two francs invested in England, we'll use these for our operations! Money, Sire! You shall have millions! Our differences on the Stock Exchange will equip the finest army that even you have ever had! Fifty millions? I'll bring you a hundred! God has not yet decreed the downfall of the Empire of France!"

So de Marmont had spoken this afternoon in the enthusiasm of his youth and of his hero-worship: and since then the great dreamer had continued to weave his dreams! Nothing was lost, nothing could be lost whilst enthusiasm such as that survived in the hearts of the young.

And still wrapped in his dream he sat on, while danger and death and disgrace threatened him on every side. Berthier and Bertrand entreated in vain, in vain tried to drag him away from this solitary

200

place, where any moment a party of Prussians might find and capture him.

Unceremoniously the Prince of Wagram had blown out the flickering light that might have attracted the attention of the pursuers. It was a very elementary precaution, the only one he or Bertrand was able to take. The horses were out in the yard for anyone to see, and the greatest spoil of victory might at any moment fall into the hands of the meanest Prussian soldier out for loot.

But the dreamer still sat on in the gloom, with the pale light of the moon streaming in through the narrow casement window and illumining that marble-like face, rigid and set, that seemed only to live by the glowing eyes—the eyes that looked into the future and the past and heeded not the awful present.

Close on a quarter of an hour went by until at last he jumped to his feet, with the sudden cry of "To Genappe!"

Berthier heaved a sigh of relief and Bertrand hurried out to unfasten the horses.

"You are impatient, Prince," said the Emperor almost gaily, as he strode with a firm step to the door. "You are afraid those cursed Prussians will put the Corsican ogre into a cage and send him at once to His Victorious Bourbon Majesty King Louis XVIII. Not so, my good Berthier, not so. The Star of my Destiny has not yet declined. I've done all the thinking I wanted to do. Now we'll to Genappe, where we'll rally the remnants of our army and then quietly await de Marmont's return with the millions which we want. After that we'll boldly on to Paris and defy my enemies there ... En avant, Maréchal! the Corsican ogre is not in the iron cage yet!"

Outside Bertrand was holding his stirrup for him. He swung himself lightly in the saddle and turned out of the farmyard gate into the open, throwing back his head and sniffing the storm-laden air as if he was about to lead his army to one of his victorious charges. Not waiting to see how close the other two men followed him, he put his horse at once at a gallop.

He rode on—never pausing—never looking round even on that gigantic desolation which the cold light of the moon weirdly and fitfully revealed—his mind was fixed upon a fresh throw on the gaming table of the world.

Overhead the storm-driven clouds chased one another with unflagging fury across the moonlit sky, now obscuring, now revealing that gigantic dissolution of the Grand Army, so like the melting of ice and frost under the fierce kiss of the sun.

More than men in an attack, less than women in a retreat, the finest cavalry Europe had ever seen was flying like sand before the wind: but the somnambulist rode on in his sleep, forgetting that on these vast and billowing fields twenty-six thousand gallant French heroes had died for the sake of his dreams.

Bertrand and the Prince of Wagram followed—gloomy and silent—they knew that all suggestions would be useless, all saner advice remain unheeded. Besides, de Marmont had gone, and after all, what did it all matter? What did anything matter, now that Empire, glory, hope, everything were irretrievably lost?

And in faithful Bertrand's deep-set eyes there came a strange, far-off look, almost of premonition, as if in his mind he could already see that lonely island rock in the Atlantic, and the great gambler there, eating out his heart with vain and bitter regrets.

II

But de Marmont had never had any doubts, never any forebodings: he only had boundless faith in his hero and boundless enthusiasm for his cause. Accustomed to handle money since early manhood, owner of a vast fortune which he had administered himself with no mean skill, he had no doubt that the Emperor's scheme for manufacturing a few millions in a wild gamble on the Stock Exchange was not only feasible but certain of success.

Undoubtedly the false news of Wellington's defeat would reach London to-morrow, as it had already reached Paris and Brussels. The panic in the money market was a foregone conclusion: the quick rise in prices when the truth became known was equally certain. It only meant forestalling the arrival of Wellington's despatches in London by four and twenty hours, and one million would make fifty during that time.

As de Marmont had told his Emperor, he had several hundred thousand pounds invested in England, on which he could lay his hands: operations on the Bourse were nothing new to him: and already while he was still listening with respect and enthusiasm to his Emperor's instructions, he was longing to get away. He knew the country well between here and Brussels, and he was wildly longing to be at work, to be flying across the low-lying land, on to Brussels and then across to England in the wake of the awful news of complete disaster.

He would steal the uniform of some poor dead wretch—a Belgium or a Hanoverian or a black Brunswicker, he didn't care which—it wouldn't take long to strip the dead, and the greatness of the work at stake would justify the sacrilege. In the uniform of one of the Allied army he could safely continue his journey to Brussels, and with luck could reach the city long before sunset.

In Brussels he would at once obtain civilian clothes and then catch the evening packet for England at Ostend. Oh, no! it was not likely that Wellington could send a messenger over to London quite so soon!

At this hour—it was just past five—he was still on Mont Saint Jean making another desperate stand against the Imperial cavalry with troops half worn out with discouragement and whose endurance must even now be giving way.

At this hour the Prussians had appeared at Braine L'Alleud, they had engaged Reille at Plancenoit, but Wellington and the British had still to hold their ground or the news which de Marmont intended to accompany to London might prove true after all.

Ye gods, if only that were possible! How gladly would Victor then have lost the hundred thousands which he meant to risk to-morrow! Wellington really vanquished before Blücher could come to his rescue! Napoleon once more victorious, as he had always been, and a mightier monarch than before! Then he, Victor de Marmont, the faithful young enthusiast who had never ceased to believe when others wavered, who at this last hour—when the whole world seemed to crumble away from under the feet of the man who had once been its master—was still ready to serve his Emperor, never doubting, always hoping, he would reap such a reward as must at last dazzle the one woman who could make that reward for him doubly precious.

Victor de Marmont had effected the gruesome exchange. He was now dressed in the black uniform of a Brunswick regiment wherein so many French royalists were serving. By a wide détour he had reached the approach to Brussels. Indeed it seemed as if the news which he had sent flying to Paris was true after all. Behind the forest of Soigne where he now was, the fields and roads were full of running men and galloping horses. The dull green of Belgian uniforms, the yellow facings of the Dutch, the black of Brunswickers, all mingled together in a moving kaleidoscopic mass of colour: men were flying unpursued yet panic-stricken towards Brussels, carrying tidings of an awful disaster to the allied armies in their haggard faces, their quivering lips, their blood-stained tunics.

De Marmont joined in with them: though his heart was full of hope, he too contrived to look pale and spent and panic-stricken at will—he heard the shouts of terror, the hastily murmured "All is lost! even the British can no longer stand!" as horses maddened with fright bore their half-senseless riders by. He set his teeth and rode on. His dark eyes glowed with satisfaction; there was no fear that the great gambler would stake his last in vain: the news would travel quick enough—as news of disaster always will. Brussels even now must be full of weeping women and children, as it soon would be of terror-driven men, of wounded and of maimed crawling into the shelter of the town to die in peace.

And as he rode, de Marmont thought more and more of Crystal. The last three months had only enhanced his passionate love for her and his maddening desire to win her yet at all costs. St. Genis would of course be fighting to-day. Perchance a convenient shot would put him

203

effectively out of the way. De Marmont had vainly tried in this wild gallopade to distinguish his rival's face among this mass of foreigners.

As for the Englishman! Well! no doubt he had disappeared long ago out of Crystal de Cambray's life. De Marmont had never feared him greatly. That one look of understanding between Crystal and Clyffurde, and the latter's strange conduct about the money at the inn, were alone responsible for the few twinges of jealousy which de Marmont had experienced in that quarter.

Indeed, the Englishman was a negligible quantity. De Marmont did not fear him. There was only St. Genis, and with the royalist cause rendered absolutely hopeless—as it would be, as it must be—St. Genis and the Comte de Cambray and all those stiff-necked aristocrats of the old regime who had thought fit to turn their proud backs on him at Brestalou three months ago, would be irretrievably ruined and discredited and would have to fly the country once more ... and Crystal, faced with the alternative of penury in England or a brilliant existence at the Tuileries as the wife of the Emperor's most faithful friend, would make her choice as he—de Marmont—never doubted that any woman would.

Hope for him had already become reality. Brussels was the half-way halt to the uttermost heights of his ambition. Fortune, the Emperor's gratitude, the woman he loved, all waited for him there. He reached the city just as that distant horizon in the west was lit up by a streak of brilliant crimson from the fast sinking sun: just when—had he but known it!—on the crest of Mont Saint Jean, Wellington had waved his hat over his head and given the heroic British army—exhausted, but undaunted—the order for a general charge; just when the Grand Army, finally checked in its advance, had first set up the ominous call that was like the passing-bell of its dying glory: "Sauve qui peut!"

III

"Sauve qui peut!"

Bobby Clyffurde heard the cry too through the fast gathering shadows of unconsciousness that closed in round his wearied senses, and, as a film that was so like the kindly veil of approaching Death spread over his eyes, he raised them up just once to that vivid crimson glow far out in the west, and on the winged chariot of the setting sun he sent up his last sigh of gratitude to God. All day he had called for Death—all day he had wooed her there where bullets and grape-shot were thickest—where her huge scythe had been most busily at work.

Sons of fond mothers, husbands, sweethearts that were dearly loved, brothers that would be endlessly mourned, lives that were more precious than any earthly treasures—the ghostly harvester claimed them all with impartial cruelty. And he—desolate and lonely—with no one greatly to care if he came back or no—with not a single golden thread of hope to which he might cling, without a dream to brighten the coming days of dreariness—with a life in the future that could hold nothing but vain regrets, Bobby had sought Death twenty times to-day and Death had resolutely passed him by.

But now he was grateful for that: he was thankful that he had lived just long enough to see the sunset, just long enough to take part in that last glorious charge in obedience to Wellington's inspiring command: "Up, guards, and at them!" he was glad to have lived just long enough to hear the "Sauve qui peut!" to know that the Grand Army was in full retreat, that Blücher had come up in time, that British pluck and British endurance had won the greatest victory of all times for Britain's flag and her national existence.

Now with a rough bandage hastily tied round his head where grape-shot had lacerated cheek and ear, with a bayonet thrust in the thigh and another in the arm, Bobby had remained lying there with many thousands round him as silent, as uncomplaining, as he—in the down-trodden corn—and with the tramp of thousands of galloping, fleeing horses, the clash of steel and fusillade of tirailleurs and artillery reaching his dimmed senses like a distant echo from the land of ghosts. And before his eyes—half veiled in unconsciousness, there flitted the tender, delicate vision of Crystal de Cambray: of her blue eyes and soft fair hair, done up in a quaint mass of tiny curls; of the scarf of filmy lace which she always liked to wrap round her shoulders, and through the lace the pearly sheen of her skin, of her arms, and of her throat. The air around him had become pure and rarified: that horrible stench of powder and smoke and blood no longer struck his nostrils—it was roses, roses all around him—crimson roses—sweet and caressing and fragrant—with soft, velvety petals that brushed against his cheek—and from somewhere close by came a dreamy melody, the half-sad, half-gay lilt of an intoxicating dance.

It was delicious! and Bobby, wearied, sore and aching in body, felt his soul lifted to some exquisite heights which were not yet heaven, of course, but which must of a truth form the very threshold of Paradise.

He saw Crystal more and more clearly every moment: now he was looking straight into her blue eyes, and her little hand, cool and white as snow, rested upon his burning forehead. She smiled on him—as on a friend—there was no contempt, no harshness in her look—only a great, consoling pity and something that seemed like an appeal!

Yes! the longer he himself looked into those blue eyes of hers, the more sure he was that there was an appeal in them. It almost seemed as if she needed him, in a way that she had never needed him before. Apparently she could not speak: she could not tell him what it was she wanted: but her little hands seemed to draw him up, out of the trodden, trampled corn, and having soothed his aches and pains they seemed to impel him to do something—that was important ... and imperative ... something that she wanted done.

He begged her to let him lie here in peace, for he was now comforted and happy. He was quite sure now that he was dead, that her sweet face had been the last tangible vision which he had seen on earth, ere he closed his eyes in the last long sleep.

He had seen her and she had gone. All of a sudden she had vanished, and darkness was closing in around him: the scent of roses faded into the air, which was now filled again with horrid sounds—the deafening roar of cannon, the sharp and incessant retort of rifle-fire, the awesome mêlée of cries and groans and bugle-calls and sighs of agony, and one deafening cry—so like the last wail of departing souls—which came from somewhere—not very far away: "Vive l'Empereur!"

Bobby raised himself to a sitting posture. His head ached terribly—he was stiff in every limb: a burning, almost intolerable pain gnawed at his thigh and at his left arm. But consciousness had returned and with it all the knowledge of what this day had meant: all round him there was the broken corn, stained with blood and mud, all round him lay the dead and the dying in their thousands. Far away in the west a crimson glow like fire lit up this vast hecatomb of brave lives sacrificed, this final agony of the vast Empire, the might and grandeur of one man laid low this day by the mightier hand of God.

It lit up with the weird light of the dying day the pallid, clean-shaven faces of gallant British boys, the rugged faces of the Scot, the olive skin of the child of Provence, the bronzed cheeks of old veterans: it threw its lurid glow on red coats and black coats, white facings and gilt epaulettes; it drew sparks as of still-living fire from breastplates and broken swords, discarded casques and bayonets, sabretaches and kilts and bugles and drums, and dead horses and arms and accoutrements and dead and dying men, all lying pell-mell in a huge litter with the glow of midsummer sunset upon them—poor little chessmen—pawns and knights—castles of strength and kings of some lonely mourning hearts—all swept together by the Almighty hand of the Great Master of this terrestrial game.

But with returning consciousness Bobby's gaze took in a wider range of vision. He visualised exactly where he was—on the south slope of Mont Saint Jean with La Haye Sainte on ahead a little to his left, and the whitewashed walls of La Belle Alliance still further away gleaming golden in the light of the setting sun.

He saw that on the wide road which leads to Genappe and Charleroi the once invincible cavalry of the mighty Emperor was fleeing helter-skelter from the scene of its disaster: he saw that the British—what was left of them—were in hot pursuit! He saw from far Plancenoit the scintillating casques of Blücher's Prussians.

And on the left a detachment of allied troops—Dutch, Belgian, Brunswickers—had just started down the slope of the plateau to join in this death-dealing pell-mell, where amongst the litter of dead and dying, in the confusion of pursuer and pursued, comrade fought at times against comrade, brother fired on brother—Prussian against British.

Down below behind the farm buildings of La Haye Sainte two battalions of chasseurs of the Old Guard had made a stand around a tattered bit of tricolour and the bronze eagle—symbol of so much decadent grandeur and of such undying glory. "A moi chasseurs," brave Général Pelet had cried. "Let us save the eagle or die beneath its wing."

And those who heard this last call of despair stopped in their headlong flight; they forged a way for themselves through the mass of running horses and men, they rallied to their flag, and with their tirailleurs—kneeling on one knee—ranged in a circle round them, they now formed a living bulwark for their eagle, of dauntless breasts and bristling bayonets.

And upon this mass of desperate men, the small body of raw Dutch and Belgian and German troops now hurled themselves with wild huzzas and blind impetuousness. Against this mass of heroes and of conquerors in a dozen victorious campaigns—men who had no longer anything to lose but life, and to whom life meant less than nothing now—against them a handful of half-trained recruits, drunk with the cry of "Victory" which drowned the roar of the cannon and the clash of sabres, drunk with the vision of glory which awaited them if that defiant eagle were brought to earth by them!

And as Bobby staggered to his feet he already saw the impending catastrophe—one of the many on this day of cumulative disasters. He saw the Dutch and the Belgians and the Brunswickers rush wildly to the charge—young men—enthusiasts—brave—but men whose ranks had twice been broken to-day—who twice had rallied to their colours and then had broken again—men who were exhausted—men who were none too ably led—men in fact—and there were many French royalists among their officers—who had not the physical power of endurance which had enabled the British to astonish the world to-day.

Bobby could see amongst them the Brunswickers and their black coats—he would have known them amongst millions of men. The full brilliance of the evening glow was upon them—on their black coats and the silver galoons and tassels; two of their officers had made a brave show in Brussels three days—or was it a hundred years?—ago at the Duchess of Richmond's ball. Bobby remembered them so well, for one of these two officers was Maurice de St. Genis.

Oh! how Crystal would love to see him now—even though her dear heart would be torn with anxiety for him—for he was fighting bravely, bravely and desperately as every one had fought to-day, as these chasseurs of the Old Guard—just the few of them that remained—

were fighting still even at this hour round that tattered flag and that bronze eagle, and with the cry of "Vive l'Empereur!" dying upon their lips.

Despair indeed on both sides—even at this hour when the merest incident might yet turn the issue of this world-conflict one way or the other. Bobby, as he steadied himself on his feet, had seen that the attack was already turning into a rout. Not only had Pelet's chasseurs held the Dutch and Brunswickers at bay, not only had their tirailleurs made deadly havoc among their assailants, but the latter now were threatened with absolute annihilation even whilst all around them their allies—British and Prussian—were crying "Victory!"

Bobby could see them quite clearly—for he saw with that subtle and delicate sense which only a great and pure passion can give!—he saw the danger at the very moment when it was born—at the precise instant when it threatened that handful of black-coated men, one of whose officers was named St. Genis. He saw the first sign of wavering, of stupefaction, that followed the impetuous charge: he saw the gaps in the ranks after that initial deadly volley from the tirailleurs. It almost seemed as if he could hear those shouts of "Vive l'Empereur!" and the rallying cry of commanding officers—it was all so near—not more than three hundred yards away, and the clear, stormy atmosphere carried sights and sounds upon its wing.

Another volley from the tirailleurs and the Dutch and Brunswickers turned to fly: in vain did their officers call, they wanted to get away! They tried to fly—to run, for now the chasseurs were at them with bayonets—they tried to run, but the ground was littered with their own wounded and dead—with the wounded and the dead of a long day of carnage: they stumbled at every step—fell over the dying and the wounded—over dead and wounded horses—over piles of guns and swords and bayonets, and sabretaches, over forsaken guns and broken carriages, litter that impeded them in front even as they were driven with the bayonet from the rear.

Bobby saw it all, for they were coming now—pursued and pursuers—as fast as ever they could; they were coming, these flying, black-coated men, casting away their gay trappings as well as their arms, trying to run—to get away—but stumbling, falling all the time—picking themselves up, falling and running again.

And in that one short moment while the whole brief tragedy was enacted before his eyes, Bobby also saw, in a vision that was equally swift and fleeting, the blue eyes of Crystal drowned in tears. He saw her with fair head drooping like a lily, he saw the quiver of her lips, heard the moan of pain that would come to her lips when the man she loved was brought home to her—dead. And in that same second—so full of portent—Bobby understood why it was that her sweet image had called to him for help just now. Again she called, again she beckoned—her blue eyes looked on him with an appeal that was all-compelling: her

208

two dear hands were clasped and she begged of him that he should be her friend.

Such visions come from God! no man sees them save he whose soul is great and whose heart is pure. Poor Bobby Clyffurde—lonely, heart-broken, desolate—saw the exquisite face that he would have loved to kiss—he saw it with the golden glow of evening upon the delicate cheeks, and with the lurid light of fire and battle upon the soft, fair hair.

And the greatness of his love helped him to understand what life still held for him—the happiness of supreme sacrifice.

All around him was death, but there was some life too: one or two poor, abandoned riderless horses were quietly picking bits of corn from between the piles of dead and dying men, or were standing, sniffing the air with dilated nostrils, and snorting with terror at the deafening noise. Bobby had steadied himself, neither his head nor his limbs were aching now—at any rate he had forgotten them—all that he remembered was what he saw, those black-coated Brunswickers who longed to fly and could not and who were being slaughtered like insects even as they stumbled and fled.

And Bobby caught the bridle of one of these poor, terror-stricken beasts that stood snorting and sniffing not far away: he crawled up into the saddle, for his thigh was numb and one of his arms helpless. But once on horseback he could get along—over trampled corn and over the dead—on toward that hideous corner behind the farm of La Haye Sainte where desperate men were butchering others that were more desperate than they—in among that seething crowd of black coats and fur bonnets, of silver tassels and of brass eagles, into a whirlpool of swords and bayonets and gun-fire from the tirailleurs—for there he had seen the man whom Crystal loved—for whose sake she would eat out her heart with mourning and regret.

In the deafening noise of shrieking and sighs and whizzing bullets and cries of agony he heard Crystal's voice telling him what to do. Already he had seen St. Genis struggling on his knees not fifty mètres away from the first line of tirailleurs, not a hundred from the advancing steel wall of fixed bayonets. Maurice had thrown back his head, in the hopelessness of his despair; the evening sun fell full upon his haggard, blood-stained face, upon his wide-open eyes filled with the terror of death. The next moment Bobby Clyffurde was by his side; all around him bullets were whizzing—all around him men sighed their last sigh of agony. He stooped over his saddle: "Can you pull yourself up?" he called. And with his one sound arm he caught Maurice by the elbow and helped him to struggle to his feet. The horse, dazed with terror, snorted at the smell of blood, but he did not move. Maurice, equally dazed, scrambled into the saddle—almost inert—a dead weight—a thing that impeded progress and movement; but the thing that Crystal loved above all things on earth and which Bobby knew he must wrest out of these devouring jaws of Death and lay—safe and sound—within the shelter of her arms.

IV

After that it meant a struggle—not for his own life, for indeed he cared little enough for that—but for the sake of the burden which he was carrying—a burden of infinite preciousness since Crystal's heart and happiness were bound up with it.

Maurice de St. Genis clung half inert to him with one hand gripping the saddle-bow, the other clutching Bobby's belt with convulsive tenacity. Bobby himself was only half conscious, dazed with the pain of wounds, the exertion of hoisting that dead weight across his saddle, the deafening noise of whizzing bullets round him, the boring of the frightened horse against its bridle, as it tried to pick its way through the tangled heaps upon the ground.

But every moment lessened the danger from stray bullets, and the chance of the bayonet charge from behind. The cries of "Vive l'Empereur!" round that still standing eagle were drowned in the medley and confusion of hundreds of other sounds. Bobby was just able to guide his horse away from the spots where the fighting was most hot and fierce, where Vivian's hussars attacked those two battalions of cuirassiers, where Adam's brigade of artillery turned the flank of the chasseurs and laid the proud bronze eagle low, where Ney and the Old Guard were showing to the rest of the Grand Army how grizzled veterans fought and died.

He rode straight up the plateau, however, but well to the right now, picking his way carefully with that blind instinct which the tracked beast possesses and which the hunted man sometimes receives from God.

The dead and the dying were less thick here upon the ground. It was here that earlier in the day the Dutch and the Belgians and the Brunswickers had supported the British left, during those terrific cavalry charges which British endurance and tenacity had alone been able to withstand. It was here that Hacke's Cumberland Hussars had broken their ranks and fled, taking to Brussels and thence to Ghent the news of terrific disaster. Bobby's lips were tight set and he snorted like a war-horse when he thought of that—when he thought of the misery and sorrow that must be reigning in Brussels now—and of the consternation at Ghent where the poor old Bourbon King was probably mourning his dead hopes and his vanished throne.

In Brussels women would be weeping; and Crystal—forlorn and desolate—would perhaps be sitting at her window watching the stream of fugitives that came in—wounded and exhausted—from the field of battle, recounting tales of a catastrophe which had no parallel in modern times: and Crystal, seeing and hearing this, would think of the man she loved, and believing him to be dead would break her heart with sorrow.

And when Bobby thought of that he was spurred to fresh effort, and he pulled himself together with a desperate tension of every nerve and sinew, fighting exhaustion, ignoring pain, conjuring up the vision of Crystal's blue eyes and her pleading look as she begged him to save her from lifelong sorrow and the anguish of future loneliness. Then he no longer heard the weird and incessant cannonade, he no longer saw the desolation of this utter confusion around him, he no longer felt exhausted, or the weight of that lifeless, impeding burden upon his saddle-bow.

Stray bands of fugitives with pursuers hot on their heels passed him by, stray bullets flew to right and left of him, whizzing by with their eerie, whistling sound; he was now on the outskirts of the great pursuit—anon he reached the crest of Mont Saint Jean at last, and almost blindly struck back eastward in the direction of the forest of Soigne.

It was blind instinct—and nothing more—that kept him on his horse: he clung to his saddle with half-paralysed knees, just as a drowning man will clutch a floating bit of wreckage that helps him to keep his head above the water. The stately trees of Soigne were not far ahead now: through the forest any track that bore to the left would strike the Brussels road; only a little more strength—another effort or two—the cool solitude of the wood would ease the weight of the burden and the throbbing of nerves and brain. The setting sun shone full upon the leafy edge of the wood; hazelnut and beech and oak and clumps of briar rose quivered under the rough kiss of the wind that blew straight across the lowland from the southwest, bringing with it still the confusion of sounds—the weird cannonades and dismal bugle-calls—in such strange contrast to the rustle of the leaves and the crackling of tiny twigs in the tangled coppice.

How cool and delicious it must be under those trees—and there was a narrow track which must lead straight to the Brussels road—the ground looked soft and mossy and damp after the rain—oh! for the strength to reach those leafy shadows, to plunge under that thicket and brush with burning forehead against those soft green leaves heavy with moisture! Oh! for the power to annihilate this distance of a few hundred yards that lie between this immense graveyard open to wind and scorching sun, and the green, cool moss and carpet of twigs and leaves and soft, sweet-smelling earth, on which a weary body and desolate soul might find eternal rest! . . .

V

On! on! through the forest of Soigne! There was no question as yet of rest.

Maurice had not yet wakened from his trance. Bobby vaguely wondered if he were not already dead. There was no stain of blood upon his fine uniform, but it was just possible that in stumbling, running and falling he had hit his head or received a blow which had deprived him of consciousness directly after he had scrambled into the saddle.

Bobby remembered how pale and haggard he had looked and how his hand had by the merest instinct clutched at the saddle-bow, and then had dropped away from it—helpless and inert. Now he lay quite still with his head resting against Bobby's shoulder.

Under the trees it was cool and the air was sweet and soothing: Bobby with his left hand contrived to tear a handful of leaves from the coppice as he passed: they were full of moisture and he pressed them against Maurice's lips and against his own.

The forest was full of sounds: of running men and horses, the rattle of wheels, and the calls of terror and of pain, with still and always that awesome background of persistent cannonade. But Bobby heard nothing, saw nothing save the narrow track in front of him, along which the horse now ambled leisurely, and from time to time—when he looked down—the pale, haggard face of the man whom Crystal loved.

At one moment Maurice opened his eyes and murmured feebly: "Where am I?"

"On the way to Brussels," Bobby contrived to reply.

A little later on horse and rider emerged out of the wood and the Brussels road stretched out its long straight ribbon before Bobby Clyffurde's dull, uncomprehending gaze.

Close by at his feet the milestone marked the last six kilomètres to Brussels. Only another half-dozen kilomètres—only another hour's ride at most! ... Only!!! ... when even now he felt that the next few minutes must see him tumbling head-foremost from the saddle.

Far away beyond the milestone on his right—in a meadow, the boundary of which touched the edge of the wood—women were busy tossing hay after the rain, all unconscious of the simple little tragedy that was being enacted so close to them: their cotton dresses and the kerchiefs round their heads stood out as trenchant, vivid notes of colour against the dull grey landscape beyond. A couple of haycarts were standing by: beside them two men were lighting their pipes. The wind was playing with the hay as the women tossed it, and their shrill laughter came echoing across the meadow.

And even now the ground was shaken with the repercussion of distant volleys of artillery, and along the road a stream of men were

212

running toward Brussels, horses galloped by frightened and riderless, or dragging broken gun-carriages behind them in the mud. The whole of that stream was carrying the news of Wellington's disaster to Brussels and to Ghent: not knowing that behind them had already sounded the passing bell for the Empire of France.

Bobby had drawn rein on the edge of the wood to give his horse a rest, and for a while he watched that running stream, longing to shout to them to turn back—there was no occasion to run—to see what had been done, to take a share in that glorious, final charge for victory. But his throat was too parched for a shout, and as he watched, he saw in among a knot of mounted men—fugitives like the others, pale of face, anxious of mien and with that intent look which men have when life is precious and has got to be saved—he saw a man in the same uniform that St. Genis wore—a Brunswicker in black coat and silver galoons—who stared at him, persistently and strangely, as he rode by.

The face though much altered by three days' growth of beard, and by the set of the shako worn right down to the brows, was nevertheless a familiar one. Bobby—stupefied, deprived for the moment of thinking powers, through sheer exhaustion and burning pain—taxed his weary brain in vain to understand the look of recognition which the man in the black uniform cast upon him as he passed.

Until a lightly spoken: "Hullo, my dear Clyffurde!" uttered gaily as the rider drew near to the edge of the road, brought the name of "Victor de Marmont!" to Bobby's quivering lips.

And just for the space of sixty seconds Fate rubbed her gaunt hands complacently together, seeing that she had brought these three men together—here on this spot—three men who loved the same woman, each with the utmost ardour and passion at his command—each even at this very moment striving to win her and to work for her happiness.

Behind them in the plains of Waterloo the cannon still was roaring: de Marmont was on his way to redeem the fallen fortunes of the hero whom he worshipped and to win imperial regard, imperial favours, fortune and glory wherewith to conquer a girl's obstinacy. St. Genis—pale and unconscious—seemed even in his unconsciousness to defy the power of any rival by the might of early love, of old associations, of similarity of caste and of political ideals. He had fought for the cause which she and he had both equally at heart and by his very helplessness now he seemed to prove that he could do no more than he had done and that he had the right to claim the solace and comfort which her girlish lips and her girlish love had promised him long ago.

Whilst Bobby had nothing to promise and nothing to give save devotion—his hope, his desire and his love were bounded by her happiness. And since her happiness lay in the life of the man whom he

213

had dragged out of the jaws of Death, what greater proof could he give of his love than to lay down his life for him and for her?

De Marmont's keen eyes took in the situation at a glance: he threw a quick look of savage hatred on St. Genis and cast one of contemptuous pity on Clyffurde. Then with a shrug of the shoulders and a light, triumphant laugh, he set spurs to his horse and rode swiftly away.

Bobby's lack-lustre eyes followed horse and rider down the road till they grew smaller and smaller still and finally disappeared in the distance. For a moment he felt puzzled. What was de Marmont doing in this stream of senseless, panic-stricken men? What was he doing in the uniform of one of the Allied nations? Why had he laughed so gaily and appeared so triumphant in his mien?

Did he not know then that his hero had fallen along with his mighty eagle? that the brief adventure begun in the gulf of Jouan had ended in a hopeless tragedy on the field of Waterloo? But why that uniform? Poor Bobby's head ached too much to allow him to think, and time was getting on.

The road now was deserted. The last of the fugitives formed but a cloud of black specks on the line of the horizon far off toward Brussels. From the hayfield there came the merry sound of women's laughter, while far away cannon and musketry still roared. And over the long, straight road—bordered with straight poplar trees—the setting sun threw ever-lengthening shadows.

Maurice opened his eyes.

"Where am I?" he asked again.

"Close to Brussels now," replied Bobby.

"To Brussels?" murmured St. Genis feebly. "Crystal!"

"Yes," assented Bobby. "Crystal! God bless her!" Then as St. Genis was trying to move, he added: "Can you shift a little?"

"I think so," replied the other.

"If you could ease the pressure on my leg ... steady, now! steady! ... Can you sit up in the saddle? ... Are you hurt? ..."

"Not much. My head aches terribly. I must have hit it against something. But that is all. I am only dizzy and sick."

"Could you ride on to Brussels alone, think you?"

"Perhaps."

"It is not far. The horse is very quiet. He will amble along if you give him his head."

"But you?"

"I'd like to rest. I'll find shelter in a cottage perhaps ... or in the wood."

St. Genis said nothing more for the moment. He was intent on sliding down from the saddle without too much assistance from Bobby. When he had reached the ground, it took him a little while to collect

214

himself, for his head was swimming: he closed his eyes and put out a hand to steady himself against a tree.

When Maurice opened his eyes again, Bobby was sitting on the ground by the roadside: the horse was nibbling a clump of fresh, green grass.

For the first time since that awful moment when stumbling and falling against a pile of dead, with Death behind and all around him, he had heard the welcome call: "Can you pull yourself up?" and felt the steadying grip upon his elbow—Maurice de St. Genis looked upon the man to whom he owed his life.

With that stained bandage round his head, dulled and bloodshot eyes, face blackened with powder and smoke and features drawn and haggard, Bobby Clyffurde was indeed almost unrecognisable. But Maurice knew him on the instant. Hitherto, he had not thought of how he had come out of that terrible hell-fire behind La Haye Sainte—indeed, he had quickly lost consciousness and never regained it till now: and now he knew that the same man who in the narrow hotel room near Lyons had ungrudgingly rendered him a signal service—had risked his life to-day for his—Maurice's sake.

No one could have entered that awful mêlée and faced the bayonet charge of Pelet's cuirassiers and the hail of bullets from their tirailleurs without taking imminent risk of death. Yet Clyffurde had done it. Why? Maurice—wide-eyed and sullen—could only find one answer to that insistent question.

That same deadly pang of jealousy which had assailed his heart after the midnight interview at the inn now held him in its cruel grip again. He felt that he hated the man to whom he owed his life, and that he hated himself for this mean and base ingratitude. He would not trust himself to speak or to look on Bobby at all, lest the ugly thoughts which were floating through his mind set their stamp upon his face.

"Will you ride on to Brussels?" he said at last. "I can wait here ... and perhaps you could send a conveyance for me later on. M. le Comte de Cambray would ..."

"M. le Comte de Cambray and Mademoiselle Crystal are even now devoured with anxiety about you," broke in Clyffurde as firmly as he could. "And I could not ride to Brussels—even though some one were waiting for me there—I really am not able to ride further. I would prefer to sit here and rest."

"I don't like to leave you ... after ... after what you have done for me ... I would like to ..."

"I would like you to scramble into that saddle and go," retorted Bobby with a momentary return to his usual good-natured irony, "and to leave me in peace."

"I'll send out a conveyance for you," rejoined St. Genis. "I know M. le Comte de Cambray would wish ..."

215

"Mention my name to M. le Comte at your peril ..." began Clyffurde.

"But ..."

"By the Lord, man," now exclaimed Bobby with a sudden burst of energy, "if you do not go, I vow that sick as I am, and sick though you may be, I'll yet manage to punch your aching head."

Then as the other—still reluctantly—turned to take hold of the horse's bridle, he added more gently: "Can you mount?"

"Oh, yes! I am better now."

"You won't turn giddy, and fall off your horse?"

"I don't think so."

"Talk about the halt leading the blind!" murmured Clyffurde as he stretched himself out once more upon the soft ground, whilst Maurice contrived to hoist himself up into the saddle. "Are you safe now?" he added as the young man collected the reins in his hand, and planted his feet firmly into the stirrups.

"Yes! I am safe enough," replied St. Genis. "It is only my head that aches: and Brussels is not far."

Then he paused a moment ere he started to go—with lips set tight and looking down on Bobby, whose pale face had taken on an ashen hue:

"How you must despise me," he said bitterly.

But Bobby made no reply: he was just longing to be left alone, whilst the other still seemed inclined to linger.

"Would to God," Maurice said with a sigh, "that M. le Comte heard the evil news from other lips than mine."

"Evil news?" And Bobby, whom semi-consciousness was already taking off once more to the land of visions and of dreams—was brought back to reality—as if with a sudden jerk—with those two preposterous little words.

"What evil news?" he asked.

"The allied armies have retreated all along the line ... the Corsican adventurer is victorious ... our poor King ..."

"Hold your tongue, you young fool," cried Bobby hoarsely. "The Lord help you but I do believe you are about to blaspheme ..."

"But ..."

"The Allied Armies—the British Army, God bless it!—have covered themselves with glory—Napoleon and his Empire have ceased to be. The Grand Army is in full retreat ... the Prussians are in pursuit.... The British have won the day by their pluck and their endurance.... Thank God I lived just long enough to see it all, ere I fell..."

"But when we charged the cuirassiers ..." began St. Genis, not knowing really if Bobby was raving in delirium, or speaking of what he

216

knew. He wanted to ask further questions, to hear something more before he started for Brussels ... the only thing which he remembered with absolute certainty was that awful charge of his regiment against the cuirassiers, then the panic and the rout: and he judged the whole issue of the battle by what had happened to a detachment of Brunswickers.

And yet, of course—before the charge—he had seen and known all that Bobby told him now. That rush of the Brunswickers and the Dutch down the hillside was only a part of the huge and glorious charge of the whole of the Allied troops against the routed Grand Army of Napoleon. He had neither the physical strength nor the desire to think out all that it would mean to him personally if what Bobby now told him was indeed absolutely true.

He was longing to make the wounded man rouse himself just once more and reiterate the glad news which meant so much to him—Maurice—and to Crystal. But it was useless to think of that now. Bobby was either unconscious or asleep. For a moment a twinge of real pity made St. Genis' heart ache for the man who seemed to be left so lonely and so desolate: jealousy itself gave way before that more gentle feeling. After all, Crystal could only be true to the love of her childhood; her heart belonged to the companion, the lover, the ideal of her girlish dreams. This stranger here loved her—that was obvious—but Crystal had never looked on him with anything but indifference. Even that dance last night ... but of this Maurice would not think lest pity die out of his heart again ... and jealousy and hate walk hand in hand with base ingratitude.

He turned his horse's head round to the road, pressed his knees into its sides, and then as the poor, weary beast started to amble leisurely down the road, Maurice looked back for the last time on the prostrate, pathetic figure of the lonely man who had given his all for him: he looked at every landmark which would enable him to find that man again—the angle of the forest where it touched the meadow,—the milestone, the trees by the roadside—oh! he meant to do his duty, to do it well and quickly, to send the conveyance, to neglect nothing; then, with a sigh—half of bitterness, yet full of satisfaction—he finally turned away and looked straight out before him into the distance where Brussels lay, and where the happiness of Crystal's love called to him, and he would find rest and peace in the warm affection of her faithful heart.

CHAPTER XI

THE LOSING HANDS

I

An hour later Maurice de St. Genis was in Brussels. Though his head still ached his mind was clear, and thoughts of Crystal—of happiness with her now at last within sight—had chased every other thought away.

His home had been with the de Cambrays ever since those old, sad days in England; he had a home to go to now:—a home where the kindly friendship of the Comte as well as the love of Crystal was ready to welcome him. The warmth of anticipated happiness and well-being warmed his heart and gave strength to his body. The horrors of the past few hours seemed all to have melted away behind him on the Brussels road as did the remembrance of a man—wounded himself and spent—risking his life for the sake of a friend. Not that St. Genis meant to be ungrateful—nor did he forget that wounded man—lying alone and sick on the fringe of the wood by the roadside.

As soon as he had taken his horse round to the barracks in the rue des Comédiens, and before even he had a wash or had his uniform cleaned of stains and mud, he rushed to the headquarters of the Army Service to see how soon a conveyance could be sent out to his friend—and when he was unable to obtain what he wanted there, he rushed from hospital to hospital, thence to two or three doctors whom he knew of to see what could be done. But the hospitals were already over-full and over-busy: their ambulances were all already on the way: as for the doctors, they were all from home—all at work where their skill was most needed—an army of doctors, of ambulances and drivers would not suffice at this hour to bring all the wounded in from the spot where that awful battle was raging.

And Maurice saw time slipping by: he had already spent an hour in a fruitless quest. He longed to see Crystal and waxed impatient at the delay. Anon at the English hospital a kindly person—who listened sympathetically to his tale—promised him that the ambulance which was just setting out in the direction of Mont Saint Jean would be on the look-out for his wounded friend by the roadside; and Maurice with a sigh of relief felt that he had indeed done his duty and done his best.

At the English hospital Clyffurde would be splendidly looked after—nowhere else could he find such sympathetic treatment! And Maurice with a light heart went back to the barracks in the rue des Comédiens, where he had a wash and had his uniform cleaned.

Somewhat refreshed, though still very tired, he hurried round to the rue du Marais, where the Comte de Cambray had his lodgings. The first sight of Brussels had already told him the whole pitiable tale of panic and of desolation which had filled the city in the wake of the fugitive troops. The streets were encumbered with vehicles of every kind—carts, barouches, barrows—with horses loosely tethered, with the wounded who lay about on litters of straw along the edges of the pavement, in doorways, under archways in the centre of open places, with crowds of weeping women and crying children wandering aimlessly from place to place trying to find the loved one who might be lying here, hurt or mayhap dying.

And everywhere men in tattered uniforms, with grimy hands and faces, and boots knee-deep in stains of mud, stood about or sat in the empty carts, talking, gesticulating, giving sundry, confused and contradictory accounts of the great battle—describing Napoleon's decisive victory—Wellington's rout—the prolonged absence of Blücher and the Prussians, cause of the terrible disaster.

M. le Comte d'Artois had rushed precipitately from Brussels up to Ghent to warn His Majesty the King of France that all hope of saving his throne was now at an end, and that the wisest course to pursue was to return to England and resign himself once more to obscurity and exile.

M. le Prince de Condé too had gone off to Antwerp in a huge barouche, having under his care the treasure and jewels of the crown hastily collected three months ago at the Tuileries.

In every open space a number of prisoners were being guarded by mixed patrols of Dutch, Belgian or German soldiers, and their cry of "Vive l'Empereur!" which they reiterated with unshakable obstinacy roused the ire of their captors, and provoked many a savage blow, and many a broken head.

But St. Genis did not pause to look on these sights: he had not the strength to stand up in the midst of these confused masses of terror-driven men and women, and to shout to them that they were fools—that all their panic must be turned to joy, their lamentations to shouts of jubilation. News of victory was bound to spread through the city within the next hour, and he himself longed only to see Crystal, to reassure her as to his own safety, to see the light of happiness kindled in her eyes by the news which he brought. He had not the strength for more.

It was old Jeanne who opened the door at the lodgings in the rue du Marais when Maurice finally rang the bell there.

"M. le Marquis!" she exclaimed. "Oh! but you are ill."

"Only very tired and weak, Jeanne," he said. "It has been an awful day."

"Ah! but M. le Comte will be pleased!"

"And Mademoiselle Crystal?" asked Maurice with a smile which had in it all the self-confidence of the accepted lover.

"Mademoiselle Crystal will be happy too," said Jeanne. "She has been so unhappy, so desperately anxious all day."

"Can I see her?"

"Mademoiselle is out for the moment, M. le Marquis. And M. le Comte has gone to the Cercle des Légitimistes in the rue des Cendres—perhaps M. le Marquis knows—it is not far."

"I would like to see Mademoiselle Crystal first. You understand, don't you, Jeanne?"

"Yes, I do, M. le Marquis," sighed faithful Jeanne, who was always inclined to be sentimental.

"How long will she be, do you think?"

"Oh! another half hour. Perhaps more. Mademoiselle has gone to the cathedral. If M. le Marquis will give himself the trouble to walk so far, he cannot fail to see Mademoiselle when she comes out of church."

But already—before Jeanne had finished speaking—Maurice had turned on his heel and was speeding back down the narrow street. Tired and weak as he was, his one idea was to see Crystal, to hear her voice, to see the love-light in her eyes. He felt that at sight of her all fatigue would be gone, all recollections of the horrors of this day wiped out with the first look of joy and relief with which she would greet him.

II

The service was over, and the congregation had filed out of the cathedral. Crystal was one of the last to go. She stood for a long while in the porch looking down with unseeing eyes on the bustle and excitement which went on in the Place down below. Her mind was not here. It was far indeed from the crowd of terror-stricken or gossiping men and women, of wounded soldiers, terrified peasantry and anxious townsfolk that encumbered the precincts of the stately edifice.

From the remote distance—out toward the south—came the boom and roar of cannon and musket fire—almost incessant still. There was her heart! there her thoughts! with the brave men who were fighting for their national existence—with the British troops and with their sufferings—and she stood here, staring straight out before her—dry-eyed and pale and small white hands clasped tightly together.

The greater part of to-day she had sat by the open window in the shabby drawing-room in the rue du Marais, listening to that awful fusillade, wondering with mind well-nigh bursting with horror and with misery which of those cruel shots which she heard in the dim

220

distance would still for ever the brave and loyal heart that had made so many silent sacrifices for her.

And her father, vaguely thinking that she was anxious about Maurice—vaguely wondering that she cared so much—had done his best to try and comfort her: "She need not fear much for Maurice," he had told her as reassuringly as he could—"the Brunswickers were not likely to suffer much. The brunt of the conflict would fall upon the British. Ah! but they would lose very heavily. Wellington had not more than seventy thousand men to put up against the Corsican's troops; and only a hundred and fifty cannon against two hundred and eighty. Yes, the British would probably be annihilated by superior forces: but no doubt the other allies—and the Brunswickers—would come off a great deal better."

But Mme. la Duchesse douairière d'Agen offered no such consolation. She contented herself with saying that she was sure in her mind that Maurice would come through quite safely, and that she prayed to God with all her heart and soul that the gallant British troops would not suffer too heavily. Then with her fine, gentle hand she patted Crystal's fair curls which were clinging matted and damp against the young girl's burning forehead. And she stooped and kissed those aching dry blue eyes and whispered quite under her breath so that Crystal could not be sure if she heard correctly: "May God protect him too! He is a brave and a good man!"

And then Crystal had gone out to seek peace and rest in beautiful old Ste. Gudule, so full of memories of other conflicts, other prayers, other deeds of heroism of long ago. Here in the dim light and the silence and the peace, her quivering nerves had become somewhat stilled: and when she came out she was able just for the moment neither to see or hear the terror-mongers down below and only to think of the heroes out there on the field of battle for whom she had just prayed with such passionate earnestness.

Suddenly in the crowd she recognised Maurice. He was coming up the cathedral steps, looking for her, no doubt—Jeanne must have directed him. When he drew near to her, he saw that a look of happy surprise and of true joy lit up the delicate pathos of her face. He ran quickly to her now. He would have taken her in his arms—here in face of the crowd—but there was something in her manner which instinctively sobered him and he had to be content with the little cold hands which she held out to him and with imprinting a kiss upon her finger tips.

Already in his eyes she had read that the news which he brought was not so bad as rumour had foretold.

"Maurice," she cried excitedly, with a little catch in her throat, "you are well and safe, thank God! And what news? ..."

"The news is good," Maurice replied. "Victory is assured by now. It has been a hard day, but we have won."

She said nothing for a moment. But the tears gathered in her eyes, her lips quivered and Maurice knew that she was thanking God. Then she turned back to him and he could see her face glowing with excitement.

"And our allies," she asked, and now that little catch in her throat was more marked, "the British troops? ... We heard that they behaved like heroes, and bore the brunt of this awful battle."

"I don't know much about the British troops, my sweet," he replied lightly, "but what news I have I will have to impart to your father as well as to you. So it will have to keep until I see him ... but just now, Crystal, while we are alone ... I have other things to say to you."

But it is doubtful if Crystal heard more than just the first words which he had spoken, for she broke in quite irrelevantly:

"You don't know about the British troops, Maurice? Oh! but you must know! ... Don't you know what British regiments were engaged?..."

"I know that none of our own people were in British regiments, Crystal," he retorted somewhat drily, "whereas the Brunswickers and Nassauers were as much French as German ... they fought gallantly all day ... you do not ask so much about them."

"But ..." she stammered while a hot flush spread over her cheeks, "I thought ... you said ..."

"Are you not content for the moment, Crystal," he called out with tender reproach, "to know that victory has crowned our King and his allies and that I have come back to you safely out of that raging hell at Waterloo? Are you not glad that I am here?"

He spoke more vehemently now, for there was something in Crystal's calm attitude which had begun to chill him. Had he not been in deadly danger all the day? Had she not heard that distant cannon's roar which had threatened his life throughout all these hours? Had he not come back out of the very jaws of Death?

And yet here she stood white as a lily and as unruffled; except for that one first exclamation of joy not a single cry from the heart had forced itself through her pale, slightly trembling lips: yet she was sweet and girlish and tender as of old and even now at the implied reproach her eyes had quickly filled with tears.

"How can you ask, Maurice?" she protested gently. "I have thought of you and prayed for you all day."

It was her quiet serenity that disconcerted him—the kindly tone of her voice—her calm, unembarrassed manner checked his passionate impulse and caused him to bite his underlip with vexation until it bled.

The shadows of evening were closing in around them: from the windows of the houses close by dim, yellow lights began to blink like eyes. Overhead, the exquisite towers of Ste. Gudule stood out against the stormy sky like perfect, delicate lace-work turned to stone, whilst the glass of the west window glittered like a sheet of sapphires and emeralds and rubies, as it caught the last rays of the sinking sun. Crystal's graceful figure stood out in its white, summer draperies, clear and crystalline as herself against the sombre background of the cathedral porch.

And Maurice watched her through the dim shadows of gathering twilight: he watched her as a fowler watches the bird which he has captured and never wholly tamed. Somehow he felt that her love for him was not quite what it had been until now: that she was no longer the same girlish, submissive creature on whose soft cheeks a word or look from him had the power to raise a flush of joy.

She was different now—in a curious, intangible way which he could not define.

And jealousy reared up its threatening head more insistently:— bitter jealousy which embraced de Marmont, Clyffurde, Fate and Circumstance—but Clyffurde above all—the stranger hitherto deemed of no account, but who now—wounded, abandoned, dying, perhaps— seemed a more formidable rival than Maurice awhile ago had deemed possible.

He cursed himself for that touch of sentiment—he called it cowardice—which the other night, after the ball, had prompted him to write to Crystal. But for that voluntary confession—he thought—she could never have despised him. And following up the train of his own thoughts, and realising that these had not been spoken aloud, he suddenly called out abruptly:

"Is it because of my letter, Crystal?"

She gave a start, and turned even paler than she had been before. Obviously she had been brought roughly back from the land of dreams.

"Your letter, Maurice?" she asked vaguely, "what do you mean?"

"I wrote you a letter the other night," he continued, speaking quickly and harshly, "after the ball. Did you receive it?"

"Yes."

"And read it?"

"Of course."

"And is it because of it that your love for me has gone?"

He had not meant to put his horrible suspicions into words. The very fact—now that he had spoken—appeared more tangible, even irremediable. She did not reply to his taunt, and he came a little closer to her and took her hand, and when she tried to withdraw it from his grasp he held it tightly and bent down his head so that in the gathering gloom he could read every line of her face.

"Because of what I told you in my letter you despised me, did you not?" he asked.

Again she made no reply. What could she say that would not hurt him far more than did her silence? The next moment he had drawn her back right into the shadow of the cathedral walls, into a dark angle,

223

where no one could see either her or him. He placed his hands upon her shoulders and compelled her to look him straight in the face.

"Listen, Crystal," he said slowly and with desperate earnestness. "Once, long ago, I gave you up to de Marmont, to affluence and to considerations of your name and of our caste. It all but broke my heart, but I did it because your father demanded that sacrifice from you and from me. I was ready then to stand aside and to give up all the dreams of my youth.... But now everything is different. For one thing, the events of the past hundred days have made every man many years older: the hell I went through to-day has helped to make a more sober, more determined man of me. Now I will not give you up. I will not. My way is clear: I can win you with your father's consent and give him and you all that de Marmont had promised. The King trusts me and will give me what I ask. I am no longer a wastrel, no longer poor and obscure. And I will not give you up—I swear it by all that I have gone through to-day. I will not! if I have to kill with my own hand every one who stands in my way."

And Crystal, smiling, quite kindly and a little abstractedly at his impulsive earnestness, gently removed his hands from her shoulders and said calmly:

"You are tired, Maurice, and overwrought. Shall we go in and wait for father? He will be getting anxious about me." And without waiting to see if he followed her, she turned to walk toward the steps.

St. Genis smothered a violent oath, but he said nothing more. He was satisfied with what he had done. He knew that women liked a masterful man and he meant every word which he said. He would not give her up ... not now ... and not to ... Ye gods! he would not think of that;—he would not think of the lonely roadside nor of the wounded man who had robbed him of Crystal's love. He had done his duty by Clyffurde—what more could he have done at this hour?—and he meant to do far more than that—he meant to go back to the English hospital as soon as possible, to see that Clyffurde had every attention, every care, every comfort that human sympathy can bestow. What more could he do? He would have done no good by going out with the ambulance himself—surely not—he would have missed seeing Crystal— and she would have fretted and been still more anxious ... his first duty was to Crystal ... and ... and ... St. Genis only thought of Crystal and of himself and the voice of Conscience was compulsorily stilled.

III

Having lulled his conscience to sleep and satisfied his self-love by a passionate tirade, Maurice followed Crystal down the steps at the west front of Ste. Gudule.

Immediately opposite them at the corner of the narrow rue de Ligne was the old Auberge des Trois Rois, from whence the diligence started twice a day in time to catch the tide and the English packet at Ostend. Maurice and Crystal stood for a moment together on the steps watching the bustle and excitement, the comings and goings of the crowd, which always attend such departures. All day there had been a steady stream of fugitives out of the town, taking their belongings with them: the diligence was for the well-to-do and the indifferent who hurried away to England to await the advent of more settled times.

Victor de Marmont had secured his place inside the coach. He had exchanged his borrowed uniform for civilian clothes, he had bestowed his belongings in the vehicle and he was standing about desultorily waiting for the hour of departure. The diligence would not arrive at Ostend till five o'clock in the morning: then with the tide the packet would go out, getting into London well after midday. Chance, as represented by the tide, had seriously handicapped de Marmont's plans. But enthusiasm and doggedness of purpose whispered to him that he still held the winning card. The English packet was timed to arrive in London by two o'clock in the afternoon, he would still have two hours to his credit before closing time on 'Change and another hour in the street. Time to find his broker and half an hour to spare: that would still leave him an hour wherein to make a fortune for his Emperor.

At one time he was afraid that he would not be able to secure a seat in the diligence, so numerous were the travellers who wished to leave Brussels behind them. But in this, Chance and the length of his purse favoured him: he bought his seat for an exorbitant price, but he bought it; and at nine o'clock the diligence was timed to start.

It was now half-past eight. And just then de Marmont caught sight of Crystal and St. Genis coming down the cathedral steps.

He had half an hour to spare and he followed them. He wanted to speak to Crystal—he had wanted it all day—but the difficulty of getting what clothes he required and the trouble and time spent in bargaining for a seat in the diligence had stood in his way. M. le Comte de Cambray would never, of course, admit him inside his doors, and it would have meant hanging about in the rue du Marais and trusting to a chance meeting with Crystal when she went out, and for this he had not the time.

And the chance meeting had come about in spite of all adverse circumstances: and de Marmont followed Crystal through the crowded streets, hoping that St. Genis would take leave of her before she went indoors. But even if he did not, de Marmont meant to have a few words with Crystal. He was going to win a gigantic fortune for the Emperor—one wherewith that greatest of all adventurers could once again

225

recreate the Empire of France: he himself—rich already—would become richer still and also—if his coup succeeded—one of the most trusted, most influential men in the recreated Empire. He felt that with the offer of his name he could pour out a veritable cornucopia of abundant glory, honours, wealth at a woman's feet. And his ambition had always been bound up in a great measure with Crystal de Cambray. He certainly loved her in his way, for her beauty and her charm; but, above all, he looked on her as the very personification of the old and proud regime which had thought fit to scorn the parvenu noblesse of the Empire, and for a powerful adherent of Napoleon to be possessed of a wife out of that exclusive milieu was like a fresh and glorious trophy of war on a conqueror's chariot-wheel.

De Marmont had the supreme faith of an ambitious man in the power of wealth and of court favour. He knew that Napoleon was not a man who ever forgot a service efficiently rendered, and would repay this one—rendered at the supreme hour of disaster—with a surfeit of gratitude and of gifts which must perforce dazzle any woman's eyes and conquer her imagination.

Besides his schemes, his ambitions, the future which awaited him, what had an impecunious wastrel like St. Genis to offer to a woman like Crystal de Cambray?

Outside the house in the rue du Marais where the Comte de Cambray lodged, St. Genis and Crystal paused, and de Marmont, who still kept within the shadows, waited for a favourable opportunity to make his presence known.

"I'll find M. le Comte and bring him back with me," he heard St. Genis saying. "You are sure I shall find him at the Légitimiste?"

"Quite sure," Crystal replied. "He did not mean to leave the Cercle till about nine. He is sure to wait for every bit of news that comes in."

"It will be a great moment for me, if I am the first to bring in authentic good news."

"You will be quite the first, I should say," she assented, "but don't let father stay too long talking. Bring him back quickly. Remember I haven't heard all the news yet myself."

St. Genis went up to the front door and rang the bell, then he took leave of Crystal. De Marmont waited his opportunity. Anon, Jeanne opened the door, and St. Genis walked quickly back down the street.

Crystal paused a moment by the open door in order to talk to Jeanne, and while she did so de Marmont slipped quickly past her into the house and was some way down the corridor before the two women had recovered from their surprise. Jeanne, as was her wont, was ready to scream, but despite the fast gathering gloom Crystal had at once recognised de Marmont. She turned a cold look upon him.

"An intrusion, Monsieur?" she asked quietly.

226

"We'll call it that, Mademoiselle, an you will," he replied imperturbably, "and if you will kindly order your servant to go, it shall be a very brief one."

"My father is from home," she said.

De Marmont smiled and shrugged his shoulders.

"I know that," he said, "or I would not be here."

"Then your intrusion is that of a coward, if you knew that I was unprotected."

"Are you afraid of me, Crystal?" he asked with a sneer.

"I am afraid of no one," she replied. "But since you and I have nothing to say to one another, I beg that you will no longer force your company upon me."

"Your pardon, but there is something very important which I must say to you. I have news of to-day's doings out there at Waterloo, which bear upon the whole of your future and upon your happiness. I myself leave for England in less than half an hour. I was taking my place in the diligence outside the Trois Rois when I saw you coming down the cathedral steps. Fate has given me an opportunity for which I sought vainly all day. You will never regret it, Crystal, if you listen to me now."

"I listen," she broke in coolly. "I pray you be as brief as you can."

"Will you order the servant to go?"

For a moment longer she hesitated. Commonsense told her that it was neither prudent nor expedient to hold converse with this man, who was an avowed and bitter enemy of her cause. But he had spoken of the doings at Waterloo and spoken of them in connection with her own future and her happiness, and—prudent or not—she wanted to hear what he had to say, in the vague hope that from a chance word carelessly dropped by Victor de Marmont she would glean, if only a scrap, some news of that on which St. Genis would not dwell but on which hung her heart and her very life—the fate of the British troops.

After all he might know something, he might say something which would help her to bear this intolerable misery of uncertainty: and on the merest chance of that she threw prudence to the winds.

"You may go, Jeanne," she said. "But remain within call. Leave the front door open," she added. "M. le Comte and M. le Marquis will be here directly."

"Oh! you are well protected," said Victor de Marmont with a careless shrug of the shoulders, as Jeanne's heavy, shuffling footsteps died away down the corridor.

"Now, M. de Marmont," said Crystal coolly. "I listen."

She was leaning back against the wall—her hands behind her, her pale face and large blue eyes with their black dilated pupils turned questioningly upon him. The walls of the corridor were painted white, after the manner of Flemish houses, the tiled floor was white too, and Crystal herself was dressed all in white, so that the whole scene made up of pale, soft tints looked weird and ghostly in the twilight and Crystal like an ethereal creature come down from the land of nymphs and of elves.

And de Marmont, too—like St. Genis a while ago—felt that never had this beautiful woman—she was no longer a girl now—looked more exquisite and more desirable, and he—conscious of the power which fortune and success can give, thought that he could woo and win her once again in spite of caste-prejudice and of political hatred. St. Genis had felt his position unassailable by virtue of old associations, common sympathies and youthful vows: de Marmont relied on feminine ambition, love of power, of wealth and of station, and at this moment in Crystal's shining eyes he only read excitement and the unspoken desire for all that he was prepared to offer.

"I have only a few moments to spare, Crystal," he said slowly, and with earnest emphasis, "so I will be very brief. For the moment the Emperor has suffered a defeat—as he did at Eylau or at Leipzic—his defeats are always momentary, his victories alone are decisive and abiding. The whole world knows that. It needs no proclaiming from me. But in order to retrieve that momentary defeat of to-day he has deigned to ask my help. The gods are good to me! they have put it within my power to help my Emperor in his need. I am going to England to-night in order to carry out his instructions. By to-morrow afternoon I shall have finished my work. The Empire of France will once more rise triumphant and glorious out of the ashes of a brief defeat; the Emperor once more, Phœbus-like, will drive the chariot of the Sun, Lord and Master of Europe, greater since his downfall, more powerful, more majestic than ever before. And I, who will have been the humble instrument of his reconquered glory, will deserve to the full his bounty and his gratitude."

He paused for lack of breath, for indeed he had talked fast and volubly: Crystal's voice, cold and measured, broke in on the silence that ensued.

"And in what way does all this concern me, M. de Marmont?" she asked.

"It concerns your whole future, Crystal," he replied with ever-growing solemnity and conviction. "You must have known all along that I have never ceased to love you: you have always been the only possible woman for me—my ideal, in fact. Your father's injustice I am willing to forget. Your troth was plighted to me and I have done nothing to deserve all the insults which he thought fit to heap upon me. I wanted you to know, Crystal, that my love is still yours, and that the fortune and glory which I now go forth to win I will place with inexpressible joy at your feet."

She shrugged her shoulders and an air of supreme indifference spread over her face. "Is that all?" she asked coldly.

"All? What do you mean? I don't understand."

"I mean that you persuaded me to listen to you on the pretence that you had news to tell me of the doings at Waterloo—news on which my happiness depended. You have not told me a single fact that concerns me in the least."

"It concerns you as it concerns me, Crystal. Your happiness is bound up with mine. You are still my promised wife. I go to win glory for my name which will soon be yours. You and I, Crystal, hand in hand! think of it! our love has survived the political turmoils—united in love, united in glory, you and I will be the most brilliant stars that will shine at the Imperial Court of France."

She did not try to interrupt his tirade, but looked on him with cool wonderment, as one gazes on some curious animal that is raving and raging behind iron bars. When he had finished she said quietly:

"You are mad, I think, M. de Marmont. At any rate, you had better go now: time is getting on, and you will lose your place in the diligence."

He was less to her than the dust under her feet, and his protestations had not even the power to rouse her wrath. Indeed, all that worried her at this moment was vexation with herself for having troubled to listen to him at all: it had been worse than foolish to suppose that he had any news to impart which did not directly concern himself. So now, while he, utterly taken aback, was staring at her open-mouthed and bewildered, she turned away, cold and full of disdain, gathering her draperies round her, and started to walk slowly toward the stairs. Her clinging white skirt made a soft, swishing sound as it brushed the tiled floor, and she herself—with her slender figure, graceful neck and crown of golden curls, looked, as the gloom of evening wrapped her in, more like an intangible elf—an apparition—gliding through space, than just a scornful woman who had thought fit to reject the importunate addresses of an unwelcome suitor.

She left de Marmont standing there in the corridor—like some presumptuous beggar—burning with rage and humiliation, too insignificant even to be feared. But he was not the man to accept such a situation calmly: his love for Crystal had never been anything but a selfish one—born of the desire to possess a high-born, elegant wife, taken out of the very caste which had scorned him and his kind: her acquiescence he had always taken for granted: her love he meant to win after his wooing of her hand had been successful—until then he could wait. So certain too was he of his own power to win her, in virtue of all that he had to offer, that he would not take her scorn for real or her refusal to listen to him as final.

IV

Before she had reached the foot of the stairs, he was already by her side, and with a masterful hand upon her arm had compelled her, by physical strength, to turn and to face him once more.

"Crystal," he said, forcing himself to speak quietly, even though his voice quivered with excitement and passionate wrath, "as you say, I have only a few moments to spare, but they are just long enough for me to tell you that it is you who are mad. I daresay that it is difficult to believe in the immensity of a disaster. M. de St. Genis no doubt has been filling your ears with tales of the allied armies' victories. But look at me, Crystal—look at me and tell me if you have ever seen a man more in deadly earnest. I tell you that I am on my way to aid the Emperor in reforming his Empire on a more solid basis than it has ever stood before. Have you ever known Napoleon to fail in what he set himself to do? I tell you that he is not crushed—that he is not even defeated. Within a month the allies will be on their knees begging for peace. The era of your Bourbon kings is more absolutely dead to-day than it has ever been. And after to-day there will be nothing for a royalist like your father or like Maurice de St. Genis but exile and humiliation more dire than before. Your father's fate rests entirely in your hands. I can direct his destiny, his life or his death, just as I please. When you are my wife, I will forgive him the insults which he heaped on me at Brestalou ... but not before.... As for Maurice de St. Genis ..."

"And what of him, you abominable cur?"

The shout which came from behind him checked the words on de Marmont's lips. He let go his hold of Crystal's arm as he felt two sinewy hands gripping him by the throat. The attack was so swift and so unexpected that he was entirely off his guard: he lost his footing upon the slippery floor, and before he could recover himself he was being forced back and back until his spine was bent nearly double and his head pressed down backward almost to the level of his knees.

"Let him go, Maurice! you might kill him. Throw him out of the door."

It was M. le Comte de Cambray who spoke. He and St. Genis had arrived just in time to save Crystal from a further unpleasant scene. She, however, had not lost her presence of mind. She had certainly listened to de Marmont's final tirade, because she knew that she was helpless in his hands, but she had never been frightened for a moment. Jeanne was within call, and she herself had never been timorous: at the same time she was thankful enough that her father and St. Genis were here.

Maurice was almost blind with rage: he would have killed de Marmont but for the Comte's timely words, which luckily had the effect of sobering him at this critical moment. He relaxed his convulsive grip on de Marmont's throat, but the latter had already lost his balance; he fell heavily, his body sliding along the slippery floor, while his head struck against the projecting woodwork of the door.

He uttered a loud cry of pain as he fell, then remained lying inert on the ground, and in the dim light his face took on an ashen hue.

In an instant Crystal was by his side.

"You have killed him, Maurice," she cried, as woman-like—tender and full of compassion now—she ran to the stricken man.

"I hope I have," said St. Genis sullenly. "He deserved the death of a cur."

"Father, dear," said Crystal authoritatively, "will you call to Jeanne to bring water, a sponge, towels—quickly: also some brandy."

She paid no heed to St. Genis: and she had already forgotten de Marmont's dastardly attitude toward herself. She only saw that he was helpless and in pain: she knelt by his side, pillowed his head on her lap, and with soothing, gentle fingers felt his shoulders, his arms, to see where he was hurt. He opened his eyes very soon and encountered those tender blue eyes so full of sweet pity now: "It is only my head, I think," he said.

Then he tried to move, but fell back again with a groan of pain: "My leg is broken, I am afraid," he murmured feebly.

"I had best fetch a doctor," rejoined M. le Comte.

"If you can find one, father, dear," said Crystal. "M. de Marmont ought to be moved at once to his home."

"No! no!" protested Victor feebly, "not home! to the Trois Rois ... the diligence.... I must go to England to-night ... the Emperor's orders."

"The doctor will decide," said Crystal gently. "Father, dear, will you go?"

Jeanne came with water and brandy. De Marmont drank eagerly of the one, and then sipped the other.

"I must go," he said more firmly, "the diligence starts at nine o'clock."

Again he tried to move, and a great cry of agony rose to his throat—not of physical pain, though that was great too, but the wild, agonising shriek of mental torment, of disappointment and wrath and misery, greater than human heart could bear.

"The Emperor's orders!" he cried. "I must go!"

Crystal was silent. There was something great and majestic, something that compelled admiration and respect in this tragic impotence, this failure brought about by uncontrolled passion at the very hour when success—perhaps—might yet have changed the whole destinies of the world. De Marmont lying here, helpless to aid his Emperor—through the furious and jealous attack of a rival—was at this moment more worthy of a good woman's regard than he had been in the flush of his success and of his arrogance, for his one thought was of

231

the Emperor and what he could no longer do for him. He tried to move and could not: "The Emperor's orders!" came at times with pathetic persistence from his lips, and Crystal—woman-like—tried to soothe and comfort him in his failure, even though his triumph would only have aroused her scorn.

And time sped on. From the towers of the cathedral came booming the hour of nine. The shadows in the narrow street were long and dark, only a pale thin reflex of the cold light of the moon struck into the open doorway and the white corridor, and detached de Marmont's pale face from the surrounding gloom.

The Emperor's orders and because of a woman these could now no longer be obeyed. If de Marmont had not seen Crystal on the cathedral steps, if he had not followed her—if he had not allowed his passion and arrogant self-will to blind him to time and to surroundings—who knows? but the whole map of Europe might yet have been changed.

A fortune in London was awaiting a gambler who chose to stake everything on a last throw—a fortune wherewith the greatest adventurer the world has ever known might yet have reconstituted an army and reconquered an Empire—and he who might have won that fortune was lying in the narrow corridor of an humble lodging house—with a broken leg—helpless and eating out his heart now with vain regret. Why? Because of a girl with fair curls and blue eyes—just a woman—young and desirable—another tiny pawn in the hands of the Great Master of this world's game.

The rain in the morning at Waterloo—Blücher's arrival or Grouchy's—a man's selfish passion for a woman who cared nothing for him—who shall dare to say that these tiny, trivial incidents changed the destinies of the world?

Think on it, O ye materialists! ye worshippers of Chance! Is it indeed the infinitesimal doings of pigmies that bring about the great upheavals of the earth? Do ye not rather see God's will in that fall of rain? God's breath in those dying heroes who fell on Mont Saint Jean? do ye not recognise that it was God's finger that pointed the way to Blücher and stretched de Marmont down helpless on the ground?

V

The arrival of M. le Comte de Cambray, accompanied by a doctor and two men carrying an improvised stretcher, broke the spell of silence that had fallen on this strange scene of pathetic failure which seemed but an humble counterpart of that great and irretrievable one which was being enacted at this same hour far away on the road to Genappe.

After the booming of the cathedral clock, de Marmont had ceased to struggle: he accepted defeat probably because he, too—in spite of himself—saw that the day of his idol's destiny was over, and that the brilliant Star which had glittered on the firmament of Europe for a quarter of a century had by the will of God now irretrievably declined. He had accepted Crystal's ministrations for his comfort with a look of gratitude. Jeanne had put a pillow to his head, and he lay now outwardly placid and quiescent.

Even, perhaps—for such is human nature and such the heart of youth—as he saw Crystal's sweet face bent with so much pity toward him a sense of hope, of happiness yet to be, chased the more melancholy thoughts away. Crystal was kind—he argued to himself— she has already forgiven—women are so ready to forgive faults and errors that spring from an intensity of love.

He sought her hand and she gave it—just as a sweet Sister of Mercy and Gentleness would do, for whom the individual man—even the enemy—does not exist—only the suffering human creature whom her touch can soothe. He persuaded himself easily enough that when he pressed her hand she returned the pressure, and renewed hope went forth once more soaring upon the wings of fancy.

Then the doctor came. M. le Comte had been fortunate in securing him—had with impulsive generosity promised him ample payment—and then brought him along without delay. He praised Mlle. de Cambray for her kindness to the patient, asked a few questions as to how the accident had occurred, and was satisfied that M. de Marmont had slipped on the tiled floor and then struck his head against the door. He was not likely to examine the purple bruises on the patient's throat: his business began and ended with a broken leg to mend. As M. le Comte de Cambray assured him that M. de Marmont was very wealthy, the worthy doctor most readily offered his patient the hospitality of his own house until complete recovery.

He then superintended the lifting of the sick man on to the stretcher, and having taken final leave of M. le Comte, Mademoiselle and all those concerned and given his instructions to the bearers, he was the first to leave the house.

M. le Comte, pleasantly conscious of Christian duty toward an enemy nobly fulfilled, nodded curtly to de Marmont, whom he hated with all his heart, and then turned his back on an exceedingly unpleasant scene, fervently wishing that it had never occurred in his house, and equally fervently thankful that the accident had not more fateful consequences. He retired to his smoking-room, calling to St. Genis and to Crystal to follow him.

But Crystal did not go at once. She stood in the dark corridor— quite still—watching the stretcher bearers in their careful, silent work,

233

little guessing on what a filmy thread her whole destiny was hanging at this moment. The Fates were spinning, spinning, spinning and she did not know it. Had the solemn silence which hung so ominously in the twilight not been broken till after the sick man had been borne away, the whole of Crystal's future would have been shaped differently.

But as with the rain at Waterloo, God had need of a tool for the furtherance of His will and it was Maurice de St. Genis whom He chose—Maurice who with his own words set the final seal to his destiny.

De Marmont's eyes as he was being carried over the threshold dwelt upon the graceful form of Crystal—clad all in white—all womanliness and gentleness now—her sweet face only faintly distinguishable in the gloom. St. Genis, whose nerves were still jarred with all that he had gone through to-day and irritated by Crystal's assiduity beside the sick man, resented that last look of farewell which de Marmont dared to throw upon the woman whom he loved. An ungenerous impulse caused him to try and aim a last moral blow at his enemy:

"Come, Crystal," he said coldly, "the man has been better looked after than he deserves. But for your father's interference I should have wrung his neck like the cowardly brute that he was."

And with the masterful air of a man who has both right and privilege on his side, he put his arm round Crystal's waist and tried to draw her away, and as he did so he whispered a tender: "Come, Crystal!" in her ear.

De Marmont—who at this moment was taking a last fond look at the girl he loved, and was busy the while making plans for a happy future wherein Crystal would play the chief rôle and would console him for all disappointments by the magnitude of her love—de Marmont was brought back from the land of dreams by the tender whisperings of his rival. His own helplessness sent a flood of jealous wrath surging up to his brain. The wild hatred which he had always felt for St. Genis ever since that awful humiliation which he had suffered at Brestalou, now blinded him to everything save to the fact that here was a rival who was gloating over his helplessness—a man who twice already had humiliated him before Crystal de Cambray—a man who had every advantage of caste and of community of sympathy! a man therefore who must be in his turn irretrievably crushed in the sight of the woman whom he still hoped to win!

De Marmont had no definite idea as to what he meant to do. Perhaps, just at this moment, the pale, intangible shadow of Reason had lifted up one corner of the veil that hid the truth from before his eyes—the absolute and naked fact that Crystal de Cambray was not destined for him. She would never marry him—never. The Empire of France was no more—the Emperor was a fugitive. To St. Genis and his caste belonged the future—and the turn had come for the adherents of the fallen Emperor to sink into obscurity or to go into exile.

Be that as it may, it is certain that in this fateful moment de Marmont was only conscious of an all-powerful overwhelming feeling of hatred and the determination that whatever happened to himself he must and would prevent St. Genis from ever approaching Crystal de Cambray with words of love again. That he had the power to do this he was fully conscious.

"Crystal!" he called, and at the same time ordered the bearers to halt on the doorstep for a moment. "Crystal, will you give me your hand in farewell?"

The young girl would probably have complied with his wish, but St. Genis interposed.

"Crystal," he said authoritatively, "your father has already called you. You have done everything that Christian charity demands...." And once more he tried to draw the young girl away.

"Do not touch her, man," called de Marmont in a loud voice, "a coward like you has no right to touch the hand of a good woman."

"M. de Marmont," broke in Crystal hotly, "you presume on your helplessness...."

"Pay no heed to the ravings of a maniac, Crystal," interposed St. Genis calmly, "he has fallen so low now, that contemptuous pity is all that he deserves."

"And contempt without pity is all that you deserve, M. le Marquis de St. Genis," cried de Marmont excitedly. "Ask him, Mademoiselle Crystal, ask him where is the man who to-day saved his life? whom I myself saw to-day on the roadside, wounded and half dead with fatigue, on horseback, with the inert body of M. de St. Genis lying across his saddle-bow. Ask him how he came to lie across that saddle-bow? and whether his English friend and mine, Bobby Clyffurde, did not—as any who passed by could guess—drag him out of that hell at Waterloo and bring him into safety, whilst risking his own life. Ask him," he continued, working himself up into a veritable fever of vengeful hatred, as he saw that St. Genis—sullen and glowering—was doing his best to drag Crystal away, to prevent her from listening further to this awful indictment, these ravings of a lunatic half-distraught with hate. "Ask him where is Clyffurde now? to what lonely spot he has crawled in order to die while M. le Marquis de St. Genis came back in gay apparel to court Mlle. Crystal de Cambray? Ah! M. de St. Genis, you tried to heap opprobrium upon me—you talked glibly of contempt and of pity. Of a truth 'tis I do pity you now, for Mademoiselle Crystal will surely ask you all those questions, and by the Lord I marvel how you will answer them."

He fell back exhausted, in a dead faint no doubt, and St. Genis with a wild cry like that of a beast in fury seized the nearest weapon that came to his hand—a heavy oak chair which stood against the wall

235

in the corridor—and brandished it over his head. He would—had not Crystal at once interposed—have killed de Marmont with one blow: even so he tried to avoid Crystal in order to forge for himself a clear passage, to free himself from all trammels so that he might indulge his lust to kill.

"Take the sick man away! quickly!" cried Crystal to the stretcher bearers. And they—realising the danger—the awfulness of the tragedy which, with that clumsy weapon wielded by a man who was maddened with rage, was hovering in the air, hurried over the threshold with their burden as fast as they could: then out into the street: and Crystal seizing hold of the front door shut it to with a loud bang after them.

<h1 style="text-align:center">VI</h1>

Then with a cry that was just primitive in its passion—savage almost like that of a lioness in the desert who has been robbed of her young—she turned upon St. Genis:

"Where is he now?" she called, and her voice was quite unrecognisable, harsh and hoarse and peremptory.

"Crystal, let me assure you," protested Maurice, "that I have already done all that lay in my power...."

"Where is he now?" she broke in with the same fierce intensity.

She stood there before him—wild, haggard, palpitating—a passionate creature passionately demanding to know where the loved one was. It seemed as if she would have torn the words out of St. Genis' throat, so bitter and intense was the look of contempt and of hatred wherewith she looked on him.

M. le Comte—very much upset and ruffled by all that he had heard—came out of his room just in time to see the stretcher-bearers disappearing with their burden through the front door, and the door itself closed to with a bang by Crystal. Truly his sense of decorum and of the fitness of things had received a severe shock and now he had the additional mortification of seeing his beautiful daughter—his dainty and aristocratic Crystal—in a state bordering on frenzy.

"My darling Crystal," he exclaimed, as he made his way quickly to her side and put a restraining hand upon her arm.

But Crystal now was far beyond his control: she shook off his hand—she paid no heed to him, she went closer up to St. Genis and once more repeated her ardent, passionate query:

"Where is he now?"

"At the English hospital, I hope," said St. Genis with as much cool dignity as he could command. "Have I not assured you, Crystal, that I've done all I could? ..."

"At the English hospital? ... you hope? ..." she retorted in a voice that sounded trenchant and shrill through the overwhelming passion which shook and choked it in her throat. "But the roadside—where you left him ... to die in a ditch perhaps ... like a dog that has no home? ... where was that?"

"I gave full directions at the English hospital," he replied. "I arranged for an ambulance to go and find him ... for a bed for him ... I...."

"Give me those directions," she commanded.

"On the way to Waterloo ... on the left side of the road ... close by the six kilomètre milestone ... the angle of the forest of Soigne is just there ... and there is a meadow which joins the edge of the wood where they were making hay to-day.... No driver can fail to find the place, Crystal ... the ambulance...."

But now she was no longer listening to him. She had abruptly turned her back on him and made for the door. Her father interposed.

"What do you want to do, Crystal?" he said peremptorily.

"Go to him, of course," she said quietly—for she was quite calm now—at any rate outwardly—strong and of set purpose.

"But you do not know where he is."

"I'll go to the English hospital first ... father, dear, will you let me pass?"

"Crystal," said M. le Comte firmly, as he stood his ground between his daughter and the door, "you cannot go rushing through the streets of Brussels alone—at this hour of the night—through all the soldiery and all the drunken rabble."

"He is dying," she retorted, "and I am going to find him...."

"You have taken leave of your senses, Crystal," said the Comte sternly. "You seem to have forgotten your own personal dignity...."

"Father! let me go!" she demanded—for she had tried to measure her physical strength against his, and he was holding her wrists now whilst a look of great anger was on his face.

"I tell you, Crystal," he said, "that you cannot go. I will do all that lies in my power in the matter: I promise you: and Maurice," he added harshly, "if he has a spark of manhood left in him will do his best to second me ... but I cannot allow my daughter to go into the streets at this hour of the night."

"But you cannot prevent your sister from doing as she likes," here broke in a tart voice from the back of the corridor. "Crystal, child! try and bear up while I run to the English hospital first and, if necessary, to the English doctor afterwards. And you, Monsieur my brother, be good enough to allow Jeanne to open the door for me."

And Madame la Duchesse d'Agen in bonnet and shawl, helpful and practical, made her way quietly to the door, preceded by faithful Jeanne. With a cry of infinite relief—almost of happiness—Crystal at last managed to disengage herself from her father's grasp and ran to the old woman: "Ma tante," she said imploringly, "take me with you ... if I do not go to find him now ... at once ... my heart will break."

M. le Comte shrugged his shoulders and stood aside. He knew that in an argument with his sister, he would surely be worsted: and there was a look in Madame's face which, even in this dim twilight, he knew how to interpret. It meant that Madame would carry out her programme just as she had stated it, and that she would take Crystal with her—with or without the father's consent. So, realising this, M. le Comte had but one course left open to him and that was to safeguard his own dignity by making the best of this situation—of which he still highly disapproved.

"Well, my dear Sophie," he said, "I suppose if you insist on having your way, you must have it: though what the women of our rank are coming to nowadays I cannot imagine. At the same time I for my part must insist that Crystal at least puts on a bonnet and shawl and does not career about the streets dressed like a kitchen wench."

"Crystal," whispered Madame, who was nothing if not practical, "do as your father wishes—it will save a lot of argument and save time as well."

But even before the words were out of Madame's mouth, Crystal was running along the corridor—ready to obey. At the foot of the stairs St. Genis intercepted her.

"Let me pass!" she cried wildly.

"Not before you have said that you have forgiven me!" he entreated as he clung to her white draperies with a passionate gesture of appeal.

An exclamation which was almost one of loathing escaped her lips and with a jerk she freed her skirt from his clutch. Then she ran quickly up the stairs. Outside the door of her own room on the first landing she paused for one minute, and from out of the gloom her voice came to him like the knell of passing hope.

"If he comes back alive out of the hell to which you condemned him," she said, "I may in the future endure the sight of you again.... If he dies ... may God forgive you!"

The opening and shutting of a door told him that she was gone, and he was left in company with his shame.

CHAPTER XII

THE WINNING HAND

Until far into the night the air reverberated with incessant cannonade—from the direction of Genappe and from that of Wavre—but just before dawn all was still. The stream of convoys which bore the wounded along the road to Brussels from Mont Saint Jean and Hougoumont and La Haye Sainte had momentarily ceased its endless course. The sky had that perfect serenity of a midsummer's night, starlit and azure with the honey-coloured moon sinking slowly down towards the west. Here at the edge of the wood the air had a sweet smell of wet earth and damp moss and freshly cut hay: it had all the delicious softness of a loved one's embrace.

Through the roar of distant cannonade, Bobby had slept. For a time after St. Genis left him he had watched the long straight road with dull, unseeing eyes—he had seen the first convoy, overfilled with wounded men lying huddled on heaped-up straw, and had thanked God that he was lying on this exquisitely soft carpet made of thousands of tiny green plants—moss, grass, weeds, young tendrils and growing buds and opening leaves that were delicious to the touch. He had quite forgotten that he was wounded—neither his head nor his leg nor his arm seemed to hurt him now: and he was able to think in peace of Crystal and of her happiness.

St. Genis would have come to her by then: she would be happy to see him safe and well, and perhaps—in the midst of her joy—she would think of the friend who so gladly offered up his life for her.

When the air around was no longer shaken by constant repercussion, Bobby fell asleep. It was not yet dawn, even though far away in the east there was a luminous veil that made the sky look like living silver. Behind him among the trees there was a moving and a fluttering—the birds were no longer asleep—they had not begun to sing but they were shaking out their feathers and opening tiny, round eyes in farewell to departing night.

That gentle fluttering was a sweet lullaby, and Bobby slept and dreamed—he dreamed that the fluttering became louder and louder, and that, instead of birds, it was a group of angels that shook their wings and stood around him as he slept.

One of the angels came nearer and laid a hand upon his head—and Bobby dreamed that the angel spoke and the words that it said filled Bobby's heart with unearthly happiness.

"My love! my love!" the angel said, "will you try and live for my sake?"

And Bobby would not open his eyes, for fear the angel should go away. And though he knew exactly where he was, and could feel the soft carpet of leaves, and smell the sweet moisture in the air, he knew that he must still be dreaming, for angels are not of this earth.

Then a strong kind hand touched his wrist, and felt the beating of his heart, and a rough, pleasant voice said in English: "He is exhausted and very weak, but the fever is not high: he will soon be all right." And to add to the wonderful strangeness of his dream, the angel's voice near him murmured: "Thank God! thank God!"

Why should an angel thank God that he—Bobby Clyffurde—was not likely to die?

He opened his eyes to see what it all meant, and he saw—bending over him—a face that was more exquisitely fair than any that man had ever seen: eyes that were more blue than the sky above, lips that trembled like rose-leaves in the breeze. He was still dreaming and there was a haze between him and that perfect vision of loveliness. And the kind, rough voice somewhere close by said: "Have you got that stretcher ready?" and two other voices replied, "Yes, Sir."

But the lips close above him said nothing, and it was Bobby now who murmured: "My love, is it you?"

"Your love for always," the dear lips replied, "nothing shall part us now. Yours for always to bring you back to life. Yours when you will claim me—yours for life."

They lifted him onto a stretcher, and then into a carriage and a very kind face which he quickly enough recognised as Mme. la Duchesse d'Agen's smiled very encouragingly upon him, whereupon he could not help but ask a very pertinent question:

"Mme. la Duchesse, is all this really happening?"

"Why, yes, my good man," Madame replied; and indeed there was nothing dreamlike in her tart, dry voice: "Crystal and I really have dragged Dr. Scott away from the bedside of innumerable other sick and wounded men, and also from any hope of well-earned rest to-night: we have also really brought him to a spot very accurately described by our worthy friend, St. Genis, but where, unfortunately, you had not chosen to remain, else we had found you an hour sooner. Is there anything else you want to know?"

"Oh, yes! Madame la Duchesse, many things," murmured Bobby. "Please go on telling me."

Madame laughed: "Well!" she said, "perhaps you would like to know that some kind of instinct, or perhaps the hand of God guided one of our party to the place where you had gone to sleep. You may also wish to know, that though you seem in a bad way for the present, you are going to be nursed back to life under Dr. Scott's own most hospitable roof: but since Crystal has undertaken to do the nursing, I imagine that my time for the next six weeks will be taken up in arguing with my dear and pompous brother that he will now have to give his consent to his daughter becoming the wife of a vendor of gloves."

240

Bobby contrived to smile: "Do you think that if I promised never to buy or sell gloves again, but in future to try and live like a gentleman—do you think then that he will consent?"

"I think, my dear boy," said Madame, subduing her harsh voice to tones of gentleness, "that after my brother knows all that I know and all that his daughter desires, he will be proud to welcome you as his son."

The doctor's wide barouche lumbered slowly along the wide, straight road. In the east the luminous veil that still hid the rising sun had taken on a hue of rosy gold: the birds, now fully awake, sang their morning hymn. From the direction of Wavre came once more the cannon's roar.

Inside the carriage Dr. Scott, sitting at the feet of his patient, gave a peremptory order for silence. But Bobby—immeasurably happy and contented—looked up and saw Crystal de Cambray—no longer a girl now, but a fair and beautiful woman who had learned to the last letter the fulsome lesson of Love. She sat close beside him, and her arm was round his reclining head, and, looking at her, he saw the lovelight in her dear eyes whenever she turned them on him. And anon, when Mme. la Duchesse engaged Dr. Scott in a close and heated argument, Bobby felt sweet-scented lips pressed against his own.

THE END

www.ingramcontent.com/pod-product-compliance
Lightning Source LLC
Chambersburg PA
CBHW011521240626
47154CB00009B/2911